OUT THERE

ABOUT A DONUT

George Opacic

Out There

Author: George Opacic

Publisher: Rutherford Press

For information, contact:

Rutherford Press,
PO Box 648
Qualicum Beach, BC, Canada V9K 1A0
info@rutherfordpress.ca

https://rutherfordpress.ca

ISBN # 978-1-988739-50-2

CONTENTS

Prologue

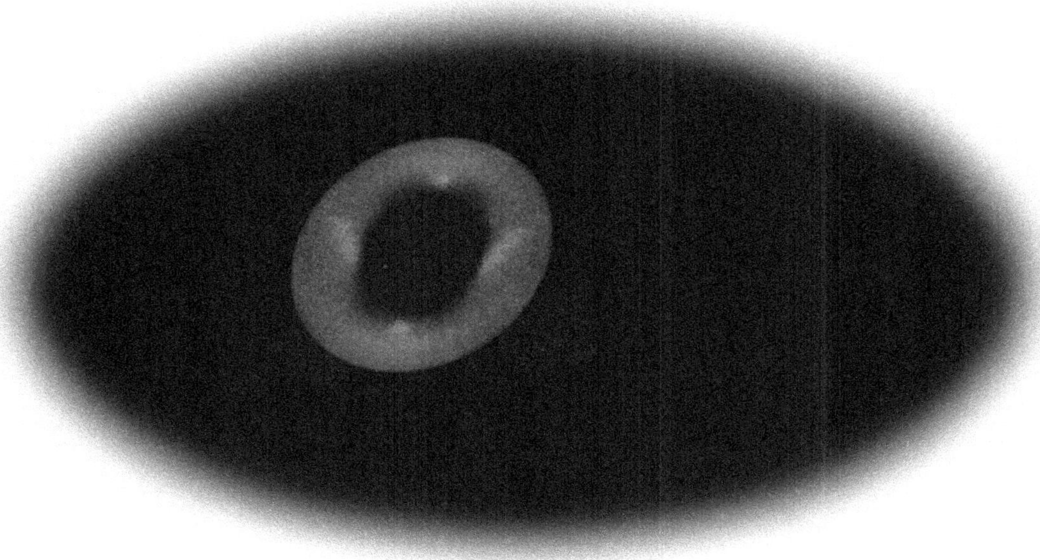

At the end of a long, white, hard-walled room, a man of extra girth, sporting a light beard and terror across his face, is wielding a fire extinguisher. He is desperately trying to reach an older man who is being engulfed in a fireball. The larger person is being impeded by someone in a spacesuit who is backing into him, stepping away from the fire.

The larger person finally manages to shove the spacesuited man roughly away against the wall while directing the fire extinguisher's spray on the victim. The person on fire is screaming in agony.

They are in front of an entrance to a two-metre-high oval airlock. The face of the man in the spacesuit can be seen flashing an enigmatic smile as the fire extinguisher is emptied over the burning man.

The spacesuited man slips away as two emergency responders come running.

A high-pitched wail is echoing across the long enclosure. A heavy fountain of sprinkler water finally comes on to flush away the remaining sources of fire on the older man. Water sizzles against clumps of red-hot magnesium that is spread randomly across the metal floor. The ceiling comes into view through thinning grey smoke. Lenses of cameras appear in the smoke in four places in the ceiling.

Friggen Puddles

L5 – SECTION P06K – 1791-23-04

It is dark. Silhouettes of wispy buildings are outlined by lights coming from behind them on what appears to be a slope a half kilometre away.

A First Responder is listening to music quietly coming from her hand-sized Pad attached to her shoulder strap: Bruce Cockburn's _Ting-the-Cauldron_ can barely be heard. Over her long, loose, white outfit's back hangs a vest with her Responder's red X and its 1st in a large silvery circle overlapping the intersection of the reflective X.

While it is pitch-black around the First Responder, very odd lights are shining up high, overhead and sloping away to both sides. They look like a carnival mirror reflection of lights from a town.

A strobe flash briefly illuminates a row of dwarf fruit trees next to a path. It becomes instantly dark again.

Another flash catches small pools of water formed in smooth brown dirt.

Another flash silhouettes a head and shoulders before it is zipped into a body bag. The body's arms are tightly folded, elbows sticking out, even while contained in the body bag, and the hands are at his throat. His mouth is frozen in desperation for air.

Coming steadily closer, a harsh beam of light from another First Responder captures the body bag being loaded onto an open aluminum trailer. The two women doing the loading are talking quietly.

"Shouldn't we let our *Security boss* do this?" There is the hint of a sneer.

The other First Responder does not want to play. "Marta's gonna be a while with the file prep for the crime scene…"

The second woman is dejected. "Shit. *Crime scene.* Like I didn't get enough of that back home in Tulsa." She attaches her light to her loose outfit then suggests, "Wanlee, why don't you get the tug backed in here while I strap him down? It. Whatever…"

Wanlee nods. "For all the commotion he caused, it doesn't take long to leave the human race, does it? Oh, Choi, can you co-log the bag before I leave?"

She shakes her head sadly at the body bag. Choi reaches over with her Pad, touches the Evidence Log button to take a picture, then Wanlee disappears into the night.

At the Morgue, next day

The body from the night before lies on a sterile table. It has had its autopsy and is partially covered by a lightly blood-splattered sheet.

A man with a prominent belly and a short, brown beard – Charon ["*Karon*"] whose name is actually Carmon Amleto – stops before walking in to the room as the distracted doctor inside is pulling the original sheet off.

Doc replaces it with a fresh sheet as he sees Charon hesitating at the doorway. The doctor waves him in. Doc is a fortyish man in excellent physical shape. The short lab-coat does little to hide well-developed thighs and calves shorn of hair.

He tightens one of his blue gloves as he gives Charon a pixie grin. "Hey, Charon. Pull the short straw?"

Still staring at anything but the body, "Hi, Doc. Yeah. Don't mind doing the duty. As long as you keep him covered up."

Doc loosely folds up the used sheet then dumps it into a yellow plastic container marked *BIOHAZARD*.

"Nothing happening at the Gates of Hades, then?" he grins wryly.

"*Sked* figured I didn't have much to do today… What'd he tell you?" Charon nods sideways at the body, without looking at it.

In his youth, Charon had always seen events through a negative prism. He grew up in a series of foster care homes and, at that time was justified in his negative assessment of life. His private mantra was, *Life is the shits and it ain't getting any better*. His lucky break came in meeting two of the prominent founders of the L5 Project, Larry Lachappel and Jim Dragosavljevic. These two took a liking to Carmon Amleto – his birth name – then when he took over the important role of designing, installing and operating L5's Ports, Dragosavljevic thought it funny to call the ports the "*Gates of Hades*". Therefore Carmon became *Charon*, the guardian of the Gates.

As compensation for the hard work in L5 during the early stages of the project, many colonists were offered "time off". They could take leave back on Earth. It was expected that they would act as ambassadors and visit various places to promote recruits for the colony.

The torus was designed for a comfortable capacity of 10,000 residents and at that time they had about a quarter-filled that number.

Charon took advantage of the leave soon after completing the design of L5's new Ports. He elected to take a tour of Malaysia. After his short tour, Charon returned in a worse mood than when he left. He did not confide to anyone why, other than to complain about what he saw of the severe deterioration of the planet's ecosystem.

Charon's negative mindset was largely suppressed in the endless work of building the L5 torus. He was active in stocking its enormous volume with life-sustaining materials and supplies. He took over the project to place Moon rock material around their torus.

Charon coordinated with the colony's new Moon base to supply the endless tonnes of material. It was shot over to the L5 location, captured by crews wearing "rainsuits" (hardened EVA outfits made for agile work in space), then placed under a webbing against the aluminum skin of the torus. This was essential to protect the colony from extended exposure to harmful cosmic rays. With hard work keeping him fully occupied, Charon's difficult youth seemed to be put behind him.

His mindset turned negative again when an explosion happened under his watch. A mysterious explosion occurred inside the L5 ports.

His mentor, Larry, was badly burned. Being in the early stages of the Project, their medical facilities were not yet sufficient to deal with that severity of burns, so Larry was immediately taken downside for extensive treatment in L5's alternative Earth-side city, Melbourne, Australia.

All this took a toll on Charon's mind. His mental state began again to decline steadily over the year or so after the explosion.

For this reason, Jim Dragosaveljvic made sure Charon was given the special task of finding out what happened in L5's orchard. He hoped that the unusual work will shake Charon out of his depression.

At the morgue, the doctor grabs the edge of the sheet and smiles slightly, but decides against pulling up the covering.

Charon goes through instant-panic-then-relief.

Dropping the corner of the sheet, "Anyway, it's Juergen Mittelsohn."

The "of course" is in his tone. "Guess we'll never know if he was a mole. Or maybe it'll all come out now. *Humph.*"

Doc turns to face Charon, pointedly saying, "He died from lack of breath."

"Doc, if you'd care to scrutinize my facial features, you should receive the distinct impression that I haven't broken into any version of a smile."

They stare at each other with blank expressions, daring the other to blink first. Doc loses.

"Of course, I had to say that. This is the only time that a practicing physician could say that and be totally accurate."

"I wait with my own breath duly bated." Charon leans against the nearby table, trying unsuccessfully to look nonchalant in this, to his delicate sensibilities, hostile environment.

Doc shows his exasperation with this situation. "Look. I've done every test I can – with my somewhat limited resources. Cut into and thoroughly dissected every possible cause of death under these circumstances, and there is absolutely no other statement that will cover it. If Juergen had been with you on one of your rock collecting expeditions outside, then I could say his suit ran out of air. And you know that there's never been an EVA accident – on the outside."

With a grimace, Charon receives the unintentional but painful verbal stab.

> FLASHBACK: *Charon is behind an older person, Larry, who is being engulfed in a fireball; a spacesuited person, Demyadin, is backing away from the fire in front of him at the entrance to a three-metre high oval airlock; a single view of Demyadin's enigmatic goateed face in the helmet; Charon uses a fire extinguisher…*

Smarting, "Please, Doc…" Charon tenses, willing the awful image out of his head. *Everybody thinks I should have done something more to save him from that screaming pain. I know they all still blame me.*

"Oh! I, I'm sorry, Charon. I didn't mean… Anyway. He didn't have air to breath, in the middle of an orchard, inside our highly secure torus of life-off-Earth. It's as simple as that. He died from lack of air."

Charon gives his head a shake. *Task at hand. Don't care what he thinks of me.*

"Ok ok. Let's press reset." He leans against a gurney, thinking, *Have to do well in this. But where the hell do I start?*

He brings his ample hands together in front, fingers touching and playing a random tune, quietly mumbling, "Offender, victim, location… The victim is Juergen. The location is the orchard, section P 6 k. The offender is…"

"What're you mumbling on about, Charon?"

"Crime triangle…" *No good. Smarten up, idiot!*

He reconsiders, "Actually, only works well if there's more than one incident. And nothing like this has ever happened before…" He stares up at another wall to try again. "Motive. Juergen's a probable mole… There've been a number of angry comments about the possibility…"

> FLASHBACK: *Juergen is eating at an L5 cafeteria; two young women seated at the next table keep glancing at him; they start talking at Juergen with anger in their eyes; one gets up and dumps her drink on him…*

He thinks, *So everybody's mad at him. That gives me, what? Eight thousand suspects, now?*

Shifting his feet and folding his muscular arms over his broad chest, Charon tries to find something to start with.

"Motive, opportunity… Nothing fits." Charon is frustrated.

In order to survive in difficult situations he has always been able to think himself out of trouble. "Doc, what, in your professional assessment, ah, is different about the way, the way, this, ah, body presented? What was distinct?" *Need facts.*

Throwing a hand into the air, the doctor spins around to stare at Juergen's covered remains. Charon places his Pad on the table, pressing Record.

"Here's what I saw. Juergen was in rigor mortis. Expired yesterday evening at 1791-22-47 according to the infrared evidence and confirmed by body temperature reading taken at 1791-23-04. I'll be more specific in the report."

Good. Facts. I can handle facts.

He waits for more from Doc. In rapid sentences, Doc adds:

"He was wearing standard clothing – his regular kurta, minimally decorated – nothing at all unusual in either the material, his choice of colors, or the way it was sitting on him. The material on his back, in all the right places, showed clear signs of having been sitting in the right kind of dirt for the right amount of time. The same dirt was on his shoe soles." He consults notes on his own Pad. "There was no tear visible in the clothing. His body showed no signs of trauma, external or internal, micro or macro – like, I mean intra-cellular or, ah, in general." He nods at Charon to confirm that he understands. "This was in comparison to his last physical about two weeks ago. His facial expression was consistent with desperation to get air. Lips were blue, eyes bulged, petechiae as expected. His hands were stiffened at his throat, but it was consistent with his trying to get air."

Charon chances a glance at the covered body. *What's going on here?*

Doc shakes his head in exasperation. "He died from lack of breath. The time of somatic death is confirmed by the digital infrared evidence. I can't add anything more substantial than that, damnit." Doc is pissed off.

They stand still, staring at the cloth-covered body.

"All that blood on the previous linen was just the autopsy. He was completely clean, like he just jumped out of a hot shower. No unexplained DNA, RNA or any movie Magicum." Doc is about to smile then thinks better of it. Then something occurs to him. *The test for hematoporphyrin. Have to find time to redo it with acetic acid instead of heating.*

Further distracting the doctor, Charon shakes his head sharply – *death* – and looks away from the sheet. Doc shakes his head to clear away the annoyances.

Charon grabs his Pad, touches the screen a couple times then holds it to show the doctor. It is Charon's first time seeing the images.

"And the camera's in infrared, they don't have anything more than his shadow in the orchard, until he drops and becomes still… Some kind of blur there." They both stare at the screen but cannot make out the cause of the blur. "Anyway, the time from his lack of movement to, ah, somatic death?…"

"Give it a generous three minutes."

Still showing the pictures on his Pad, "Doc, these digitals, here, that they took last night. Do you have a monitor I can use?"

Nodding toward the next room, "Yeah, sure. First, we can clean up over there and then let's see what he looked like last night."

Soon in the adjoining room, they scroll through the images taken the night before.

The monitor shows infrared images of the ground around the body. In other shots, in the light of the strobes, the body lies frozen in an agony of last empty breath. All around the body are small pockets of water.

Charon points to the water and starts scrolling faster, pointing out the puddles in every picture. They are both puzzled. *What the…*

"Don't get it. Shouldn't be water lying around. Rain is on Tuesdays. This is Friday."

The doctor shrugs, "Don't look at me! I don't do rain. Find out from Plumbing if they dropped any specials that night. Did Security mention it?"

"Haven't talked with anybody yet. Just got the note this morning. It had the digitals and just the outline. Report to follow…"

They contemplate the images for a while.

His Pad beeps. He reads from it.

Doc adds, "Oh. Wait a minute… Here's my update from the Security files… Yeah, this is from Marta, in Security." He finishes lamely. Of course Doc knows Marta is in Security, Doc used to follow her around like a puppy.

While Charon squints at the note, Doc melts into a smile, "Yeah. Marta..." He reminisces dreamily, *She carried by baby, but now she has another guy on her leash. Oh well...*

Charon bulls forward. "Just describes what her two First Responders saw. No hot tracks visible... only Juergen's cold footprints. Nothing suspicious around him. Nothing..."

He scrolls down the images, reading the comments. "Here. They saw the water, too, and took samples... It tests out as... clinically pure, other than for where it was."

Charon is puzzled. "Clinically pure? Rain is recycled, right?"

"Ah, yeah. Potable, but hardly clinically pure. Let me go through that report, will you? Wait a minute." Grateful for the distraction, Doc squints at one of the images from a distant infra-red camera. "Is that a shadow of something?"

Shaking his head, Charon touches his Pad a few times. "Don't think so. Probably an artifact."

The office's monitor now shows the new message. Doc opens it and starts reading. He is confused.

"Can't be. I don't know if anybody KEEPS clinically pure water inside the whole of L5. I mean, we make it and use it every once in a while, but nobody KEEPS it, and not THAT much!... What the hell!?"

Charon sits down in a chair, eyes on the ceiling, summarizing.

"Juergen's dead. He dies from lack of air. No visible trauma. No other tracks. There's little friggen puddles of clinically pure water all around him..." Charon shakes his head slowly, "I don't know, Doc. Either the Martians have beamed in, or something really serious is going on."

His face contorts, "Oh shit. This is an Air Issue, isn't it? Have to contact Structure to do a survey of the skin. Where's my checklist… contacts…"

Charon mumbles to himself as he scrolls through a list on his Pad. His groupings of names in the contact list reflect his odd mix of no-nonesenseness plus occasional word play: *Bosses; Structure; Rain Suitors; Nerds; Food; Moon proj, Outer Tech; Inner Tech; Docs; Limburgers*, etc. He selects Structure.

Marta

A *ding-ding* sounds.

Marta's apartment is at level 25. That means it is at 75% gravity of the donut-shaped artificial habitat sitting in Lagrange point 5 in the Earth and Moon gravitational system. The time is officially in the morning. For the eight thousand or so people living in L5, time is merely a convenient way of relating to when things happen.

Marta easily uses her arms with the low gravity to bounce out of a chair, do a high backflip that sends ripples along the cloth ceiling, then land at the front door. She adjusts her very light almost thigh-length kurti, then opens the door with a preliminary smile.

Then Marta beams, "Charon! So very glad to see you! Come on in, *please!*"

She grabs him and, despite his having twice as much mass as she has, Marta pulls him off his feet to place him inside like a big furry doll.

Charon rolls his eyes and stays limp like a good stuffed toy. *I was afraid of this. Don't want to get into any emotional thing just now, damnit!*

The low gravity allows his large body to be turned easily – but, there is his inertia. The latter causes Marta's body and face to become pressed around Charon's big belly as she frog-marches him backwards toward the couch.

Marta tosses her compliant rag doll onto the couch. To her annoyance, Charon bounces back to his feet and, unperturbed, and pulls out his Pad.

Marta tries to paw him as he holds the Pad out firmly like a shield.

Charon shakes his head. "Marta, this is business. Keep your clothes on. I wish you women would get off this Mother Artemis kick! We're only in L5, not some wild frontier. I'm here about Juergen, so settle down!"

Marta continues to paw him, but with less vigour. "Juergen's dead. You're alive. Let's live in the present, Charon, dear." She grabs for his shield. "Let me see your Pad."

Charon evades her, almost smiling at the game. Then her hand reaches down too low. Exasperated, he turns his back on her. This causes Marta's grip on that which is behind the lower part of his kurta to slip.

"Marta! I haven't got time for this! Sit down for chrissake!" He stiffly stares at her over his shoulder.

Reluctantly, Marta settles down, making sure her own kurta stays very loose.

"Listen, we have an Air Issue with Juergen's death. He was asphyxiated and there was no known cause. Just settle down and tell me what happened when you got the notice about a body in the orchard."

"Air Issue? Oh… Let me get my Pad,"

Marta reaches over to the low table between them. A breast dangles as she does so.

Oblivious, she touches the Pad a few times as she leans back. Her breast sort of slips under cover again.

"Here, let's see…It was… 1791-23-06 when Central's AI messaged me. Gail was with me and then a few minutes later, at 23-18, after I contacted them, Choi and Wanlee showed up at the orchard with a tug-'n-trailer. I told them to process the scene then take the deceased to the morgue when they finished their forensics and I'd arrive at the place later to finish up." She glances up coyly but finds that Charon is merely listening.

"As soon as I established where the body had been, I sent up a class 3 cam-drone to record everything in and near the perimeter. The locator was right on the money." She glances up. "It's too bad Juergen wasn't live with his Pad before his, ah, event. We might've been able to get to him in time." Marta sinks back into her couch.

"I kept about 50 metres away initially. Those puddles mostly extended to just over four metres from where his body was. Here, let me show you…"

Charon continues typing highlights on his Pad without looking up.

She sighs. Marta carries on. "I suppose you want me to meet you down at the orchard? The crime scene?"

Charon grins, "Glad to see you've taken an interest in your assigned role…" *There's so little for Security to do that it's usually just handed to anyone on the list with qualifications and the time to spare.*

Before he can say any more she is on him, planting a long, wet kiss.

The ground in the orchard is highly cultivated. It is fluffy and without a hint of grass or weeds. If one took some of the soil in hand, its tiny grains would make it feel more like course-ground flour. The artificial rain, agriculturalists found after experimenting, needed to be little more than a steady mist or the soil would compact back to the rock-hard material it originally was.

Widely spaced rows of dwarf apple and pear trees are growing between other cultivated rows that are presently sprouting little green shoots. In the distance is a collection of sheds and a maintenance yard for the agricultural equipment.

With the last of a submarine sandwich still stuck in his mouth, Charon is walking outside the perimeter that Marta's crew had set up the night before. He is holding his Pad in one hand and a metal-detecting device in the other. He wipes the last of his hasty breakfast from his lips then bends as low as he can to get under the perimeter tape.

Finished with his detector and his sub, he puts the device into a belt-holder. "Nothing there." Bending with a grunt under the perimeter tape, Charon walks past two rows of miniature fruit trees toward stakes that mark the spot where Juergen's body had been found. There are no water puddles left by now.

A flitter glides by overhead. Marta waves from it at Charon, then lands it further away between decorative (and oxygen-producing) perimeter shrubs.

Charon carries on inspecting the ground closer to where the body had been. In his mind, he reviews procedures. *The manual said to establish the **four corners** of the scene, but that was for an air vehicle… Same thing applies, I guess.*

He circles Juergen's final resting place at a distance then closes in, tightening the spiral, taking in what evidence he can find. *Which is, essentially, zippo.*

Marta, in proper Security attire, strides up to the marked perimeter.

"Have you finished around here, Charon? Can I come in?"

With a sigh, Charon turns toward her. "Yeah, just follow my tracks in, Marta."

Obeying, she sidles up beside him. "What'd you think? See any more in the light than we saw last night? Oh. The water's gone. Damnedest thing, eh? Did you see that hump way over there? What's that? And here, at the place where his feet…"

"Marta, I'm in the middle of things. Have you got somebody's community time to audit or something?"

She pretends to be hurt. "Ahh, Charon! Come on, I'm just trying to help… Oh wait a minute! No kidding. That hump really shouldn't be there."

They both stare at a low, discolored mound of dirt that is about ten metres beyond the perimeter tape, in a line leading from where Juergen's feet had been. It is beyond where Charon had recorded outside the perimeter.

Sweeping his detector en route, Charon leads Marta to the mound. As he walks near it, the footing becomes soggy. Tentatively shoving a shoe into the soil next to the mound, Charon's shoe comes out covered in sticky mud.

Marta holds onto Charon's arm as she peers around him to see better. "Don't dig too deep, Charon. Don't know what's in there."

They both stare at the mud, then look up instinctively to see if there could be a cause for the water to have been coming from the other side of the torus.

As they look straight up, the far side of L5 can be seen about one and a half kilometres away. There is the disconcerting view of a horizon that curves up over your head and comes back at you from behind.

Next day, in an L5 administrative meeting room

Five members of the L5 Executive Council, generally known as the Directors, are meeting with Charon in a clean but sparse boardroom.

As with all L5 buildings, the walls and ceiling started as a pale off-white and as thin as possible. Decorative colours are added later. The idea is to save mass, every gram of which must be flung up from the Moon station. Dwellings are often decorated wildly by residents but most official places are kept neutral-coloured.

The room's oval table can accommodate three times the six people present. Most are dressed in the comfortable, loose clothing they call kurtas (kurtis, for women, but nobody uses that term), each decorated according to their own whims.

This quarter, Jim Dragosavljevic (known as "Dragonslayer") is Chair. He is wearing a bright lime green/yellow turtle-necky-kurta. He made it himself. It looks it.

He is talking quietly to Jasmine Ramawikrama, whose pastel flower print kurta is lost next to his flaming turtle-neck thing.

Billy Cleghorn, in his usual black Morris designs on white kurta (which is intended to offset his very red face) is showing something on his Pad to Shawna McGiff and Monique. Although Monique's hair is legitimately silver, Billy plainly finds her smiling banter to be more pleasant than the abrasively serious tone of the much younger and hyper-focused Shawna.

Monique asks Billy, "Do you still want to go down to their PxT conference, Billy?"

He shrugs. "My schedule, here, is chock full. I'd rather not…"

Monique touches his arm gently. "You really should consider it, Billy. There's already a great deal of anticipation — excitement, really — with the crowds coming out to each of the *L5 Way* meetings. Those backroom shenanigans are ramping up again in so many of the governments — we need all the good publicity we can get."

Charon is tapping his Pad to connect up to the room's two-metre wall-screen, which seems to be much larger than its thin black support tube should be able to carry.

Dragonslayer continues speaking quietly to Jasmine as Charon turns on the screen.

"…If the Germans openly admit to placing Juergen as a mole, we may have a problem with their EU and NATO obligations. They and particularly the US will want to leverage this incident as a way of officially getting a delegation into L5."

Jasmine nods. "Yes, I've covered that earlier with Larry. That's why he's so keen to have Billy…" she glances at him, "…attend the Pax exTerra Conference. And on another front, he advises that we need to watch out for the Russian and German oligarchs. With that shit-kicking Russia got by China in their eastern territories, former territories, last year, they're looking to take it out on somebody. Larry's already got our Beltway Bandits on that one – they better come up with something acceptable this time, for all the retainer money we give them. Jim, have you heard of any possibilities about Juergen's death?"

She looks like she has a bad taste in her mouth as she adds, "Demyadin?"

With a pained expression, Dragonslayer leans in close. "You've been talking to Larry about his Lucifer-theory? Jasmine, we can't blame **everything** on Demyadin. No, I haven't heard anything else in particular. It's got everyone stumped." He scans the room. "Charon's a good person to have on the case, so let's see if he comes up with further ideas."

Dragonslayer smiles wryly as he turns to Charon, sitting two seats away.

Charon returns the smile, thinking, *Jim's the only guy I'd trust, fully. The rest are all ok, but he understands me.*

Seeing that Charon is ready, Dragonslayer raises his voice to be heard over the others chatting about downside and Demyadin. "Ok, Directors. Let's get to the reason you're all paid the big bucks."

"If you double my salary it'd still be zero." "Come on people – we all have real work to do, so lets get this over with."

Dragonslayer nods as he passes the meeting to his friend. "Charon, do you have your presentation ready? We might as well get going, here."

"Yes, thanks, Jim. I'll just…" Charon taps his Pad and the screen lights up with his link. It begins with a slowly moving collage of the orchard scene. "There. Everybody's probably poured over these pictures. I think there isn't anything more they can tell us, as they are. Juergen was asphyxiated. No other cause of death was found. No marks on his body that shouldn't be there. No tracks but his. No explanation for those friggen puddles of friggen clinically pure water."

Dragonslayer smiles at Charon's exasperation.

"Juergen's whereabouts have been tracked to within fifteen minutes of his probable time of death. He was in the fungus shed, doing time for that incident with the flitter. The time frame is all filled in, as you can see…"

The screen shows a table that lists times and corroborating evidence. Shawna asks, "I know we haven't devoted much in the way of resources to Doc's forensics lab. Like, is he satisfied that he, well, should we give him more resources?"

Glancing at Dragonslayer before answering, Charon gets a nod to answer Shawna. "Doc hasn't asked for anything more so I can only assume he did the best he could." He shrugs. "That's his field."

Charon opens a palm in a question. "So, how did Juergen die? We've brainstormed it at Security. Occam's Razor says the simplest solution that fits all the facts is the likely answer. The brainstorming session narrowed all the initial ideas down to three." He notices a few light snickers. "There were **four** of us in that meeting." He sends a glare at the snickerers.

He moves the cursor on his Pad to show his suggestions in order on the wall screen.

"Juergen choked himself. Well, his profile doesn't fit that option, and there aren't any deep marks on his neck and his hyoid is intact, so I think we have to cross that one out."

The cursor zips across the screen; then the next view comes up.

"He was captured, put in a suit or sealed room, deprived of air, killed, and dumped into the orchard." Several chuckles are heard around the room.

"In fact, Security did a full system search, using Pad activity, and for the last fifteen minutes of his life, we have no evidence that Juergen talked to or interacted in any way with anybody else on L5 during that time, nor can we find evidence that he spoke directly with anyone for the hour before his death. Secondly, there is no digital evidence of anybody else having been in that part of the orchard since the droid cultivator last went by about six days ago. A few of the autonomous vehicles and heli-flitters were in operation, it seems, all according to standard operations. Now, as we all know,

Structure needs to know everybody's location for rotational balance. Neither they nor Security show anybody else in that area with Juergen.

"Lastly, there aren't any corresponding marks on his body, and that explanation doesn't account for the water puddles or the mound. Leaving our third possibility."

Charon stares at the table before proceeding. *Here we go. They're going to think I'm crazy.* At that point, Marta enters. She apologetically gives Charon a half-wave, then slinks to an open chair and sits down quietly.

Charon waits until Marta is settled in. She sends him a sorry-shrug then turns dreamily to gaze with blank eyes at a side monitor that is scrolling through random pictures from around L5.

Puzzled and briefly distracted by her behaviour, Charon carries on. "Option three is that Juergen was subjected to something that extracted the oxygen in the air around him, which was then converted to pure H2O, forming puddles within four metres of his body."

He holds up his hands at the protests. Shawna lets out an exasperated, "Oh pleesse!"

"Ok, ok, I know. We don't have any way of doing that. But *nothing*… nothing else fits the facts… Now, we went back and *3D*ed the digitals that show the puddles. I want you to look at the pattern that emerges."

Despite their outright skepticism, the Directors stare at the screen. It shows one of the pictures with dotted circles around the body, connecting the puddles. The cursor follows each circle as Charon talks about it.

"As you can see, the largest puddles all form a tight and regular circle around his body, centring on his body. As he fell, the marks on the soft ground indicate that Juergen fell backward, with his feet staying in about the same place. So, where his head was, as he was standing, is the centre of the circle with the largest puddles."

He clears his throat. "The next largest puddles all make an even circle around the first one. And then the smaller puddles overlap a bit with two circles – one that's outside of the first two, and another one that's centred on where his head ends up."

The Directors follow Charon's cursor attentively, like a cat following a laser dot.

"Now, the fact that the circles seemed to stay centred on where Juergen's head was for at least the three minutes necessary for him to die, means that it is highly unlikely that this was not some sort of a phenomenon without a sole purpose." Charon leans back into his seat. *So there. Make of that what you will.*

"And then there's the mound."

The next view comes on.

"If we average the circles out, they're actually a bit elongated." He takes the cursor around the view in a circle then changes views.

"If we use the assumption that whatever did this was a device that originated above and to the front of Juergen, and if we draw a line perpendicular to the mound, then we connect the circles at an angle that makes them produced from a height, where the perpendicular line meets the circle origin, it's about ten metres above the orchard, right here. Right under THAT point is where we found the mound of water-soaked soil. To make matters worse — to pile on more of a mystery — the soil of that mound has been crystallized. Its mass is what the soil should be if undisturbed, but the soil was crystallized in an elliptical formation, being the most crystallized in the centre of the mound and becoming less as you get to the outside. I've asked our labs to report on the type of crystallization." He finishes in a rush. "Or whatever the hell they can come up with."

After a pause, he points with the cursor to a spot above the orchard. The next view superimposes a "ray-gun" aimed from that spot at Juergen.

Dragonslayer grins. "Cute device. Find that in Hades, Charon?"

Somewhat testily, "Listen, I'm just presenting the evidence and what comes out of it. Somebody else is going to have to make the story fit a hypothesis. So… allow me to add, since this was an Air Issue, I followed procedure and got the skin tested at that location, inside and out." He clicks on a file that opens on-screen.

"This report shows that there has been no disturbance of any of the layers, right down to the main hull, and that's from both sides. The mound was slowly layered away — Mbindu was on that team and most of you know he used to be an archaeologist."

Dragonslayer grins, "This must have been the fastest and weirdest bit of digging he ever did."

Charon looks around to see some blank faces. He stands up for emphasis. "It was an **emergency** and we all worked our butts off… Anyway, other than the mound, the soil and substrate were soaked, but apparently undisturbed. Other than the mound soil being crystallized. Now…" He sits down. "If anybody can add something more reasonable, I, for one, would be overjoyed to hear it."

Wilber White shakes his head, hard, under very wrinkled brows.

Shawna lets out the first part of a retort, "Oh pl…" But she peters out in the middle of her exclamation, mouth open.

Billy Cleghorn looks around. "I got a bad feelin' about this. Charon, I take it you've gone through a formal problem solving process?"

Charon nods, pointing to the screen which now shows a scrolling ladder-logic chain.

Silence, then quiet discussions with neighbours.

Dragonslayer clears his throat. "Hhmm. As this is the first time any of us Directors have seen this conclusion, I propose we slink off into our respective burrows to think about it… There being no objections I will adjourn the meeting. A wiki has been set up with all the evidence. I'm sure Charon would appreciate some cogent commentary. Yes?" He looks to Charon then around the room.

Marta rises slowly from her chair. With a confused frown, she turns as Billy draws up behind her. He reflexively avoids bumping into her.

Awkwardly, "Sorry, Marta. I guess we're all mystified…"

Marta half-nods, "Um."

Billy is about to say something else then notices Marta's blank look. He moves around her, catching Shawna's eye from across the desk. With a roll of his eyes he sends Shawna a smile-nod then heads for the now open door. On his way out he looks back to see Marta dropping into a chair, still out of it. Billy shrugs.

Marta is increasingly slipping into an amorphous inner world borne of over-activated synapses. Her mental world is becoming insusceptible to her senses. She is high.

On his way down the hall, Billy taps a note to Sked. He is one of the mentors to the crew that schedules peoples' communal activities.

> Billy Cleghorn: *It would be prudent to take Marta off active Security duties for the next 24 hours*

A low ding sounds a second later. He sees a thumbs-up on his Pad. Billy mumbles, "Huh. Must've integrated Carrot into Sked's decisions… Have to consider the consequences."

Behind him, Jasmine Ramawikrama has been silently gliding a step away. "Carrot?"

Billy contritely looks over his shoulder. "Hello lovely lady. You were listening to my random rambles?"

Jasmine steps up beside him as they stride down the long white hallway.

"Carrot?" She looks up at the older man with her assertive brown eyes.

His shoulders sag slightly as he continues along the hall. "Ok. The announcement to the Directors is coming real soon, so allow me to enlighten you, my dear." He takes her arm in his, then, leaning over slightly, Billy quietly tells her about Carrot.

Back in the meeting room, Marta is alone. She has slumped onto her arms at the table, appearing to be asleep in her chair.

Her inner world melds cloudy colours across a landscape of animated sounds

Poking up jauntily into pastel hills and falling into sticky dells

All around she hears the whooshing sizzle and pops of cheeky smells

Her legs caught in the stickiness of dells, she ripples to a field of bubbly mounds

Hard hands hold her.

Flying a flitter for fanciful flight.

Securely sheltered by a chic checkered sheet.

She, herself and everybody in creation opens their eyes

Their multitude of hands fling away the sheet of pixel squares which flutter in all directions

Gentler hands soothe her brows with cool cloths.

The unnoticed waterfall of sound falls away.

Marta struggles to wake up in her bed. Her two First Responders sit patiently on either side.

Having trouble forcing her eyes to focus, Marta rubs them. She moves clumsily.

"What?…"

Choi rubs Marta's arm. "Coming back to us?"

With a concerned look, Wanlee shakes her head at Marta. "You had us worried, Marta. Do you know how long you've been out?"

"Out?"

Choi nods. "Its been half a day since the Directors meeting."

"Huh? What… what meeting?"

Choi carries on, "Traced it back. You were handling a file that came from Juergen's place. Turns out he – or somebody – booby-trapped it."

Commiserative, Wanlee leans in closer to Marta. "Couldn't have been more than a grain. Lab is looking into it. Some kind of carfentanil derivative."

Having added her factual piece, Choi leans back and folds her arms over her chest, "Procedures, Marta. You need to wear gloves when handling evidence."

Wanlee comes to Marta's defence. "Geez, Choi. She nearly died. Give her a break."

Marta starts to drift back into the coloured hills. As she closes her eyes, Choi notices.

"Oh no you don't! Back to reality, Marta! Wake up!"

Casablanca

Dragonslayer and Jasmine are seated in L5's *Casablanca Café*. This food service location concentrates on south Mediterranean foods. Being quite early in the morning, very few people are present.

The two L5 Directors are seated in front of a huge, ground level, display of a Moroccan bazaar, whose digital inhabitants are very realistically going about their loud and colorful business.

Dragonslayer and Jasmine have a small table between them. It has a backgammon board built in. He puts a tiny cup of highly concentrated coffee to his lips between moves of the intricately made backgammon pieces. Enjoying their conversation, they shake the dice and move their pieces around the board.

Dragonslayer holds up his demi-cup of thick coffee. "This strong, it's actually not bad! I think it must be like what grandmother used to make. I'm glad we allocated a bit of room for the coffee plantings after all."

Jasmine grimaces. "Achh! You gotta be kidding, Jim! That stuff's just terrible! Well, ok, so you might claim that coffee's in your ancestral blood. Me, I don't mind a whack of caffeine as long as the flavor approximates what I'm used to."

He takes another light sip. Pensively looking into her eyes, "Jasmine, we've got a major problem brewing with the Juergen incident."

He passes his Pad across the table to her.

She nods as she reads from the white-on-black screen. "I know. Larry's getting constant heat from the Germans, down there. Now, we took your suggestion and we found that what you feared seems to be coming about. Larry received a request from the Peruvian ambassador on behalf of the EU, 49 and a half hours after Juergen died."

"They had no way of knowing about his death, of course." Dragonslayer makes another board move.

"Right. Just to be sure, all communication downside has been rechecked over this time period. AI *and* human eyes. No unauthorized chatter has occurred — well, there's that digital chess match that Fabrício has going on with whats-his-name, the chess master..."

"Kaminski is playing our man Fabrício," he adds.

"Kaminski, from what's left of Russia, yeah. So we're pretty sure that nobody from L5 has talked with anybody downside about it — shit! It's got our whole downside crew all worked up! A damn *mole*! And then there's that thing that happened to Marta!" He takes a few deep breaths. "Anyway, she's recovering, poor thing... Larry says the timeline shows that Juergen was supposed to call in every two days. As soon as he doesn't, Germany wants to see him."

He nods. "And it's certain that Juergen was the one using that anonymous FTP?"

Fiddling with a backgammon chip, she confirms, "You know that nobody here does that after they've acclimatized. At two months, Juergen had the record, by far, for length of use and for number of times. The average ends up at just over 46 hours between uses. All encrypted, of course."

"So other than seeing him press SEND, the lights are flashing over his name?" They both lower their voice.

Jasmine adds, "Right. And the anonymous FTP hasn't been used since his death." She thinks, *Probably have to tell Jim about our galloping AI, Carrot.*

Dragonslayer purses his lips. "Has it been deciphered? I mean, any of his messages?"

She glances around. "Confidential, ok?" The background noise from the Casablanca feed next to them comfortably masks their conversation.

He nods firmly.

"Carrot's just found the key this morning. I've got some of the messages here…"

"Carrot?"

Jasmine grins, "Oh, yeah, sorry. The other day they decided to rename it. 'Cyborganic' was too silly. Even the IT folks finally agreed. Now they're all over it. You were going to be informed later today." She smiles and pats his hand. "Honest, Jim. IT's been holding off because, well, have you notice the extraordinary, astounding pace that IT - in fact, *Carrot* - has been developing new projects over these past weeks?" She beams and arches her fingers together excitedly.

Dragonslayer enjoys her child-like display. "That's ok. I'm just the current Chief Executive. Why would anyone tell me anything important?"

They both chuckle.

Dragonslayer shakes his head. "So the fastest computer this side of Alpha Centauri, the only computer of any size that primarily has organic circuitry mated to our quantum computer technology – which is something they don't even know about anywhere downside – we're calling it 'Carrot'?!"

She looks around as she grins sheepishly. "Jim, what can I say? It certainly hides the facts. If anybody talks outside or goes downside and says that Carrot did this or that, it's not gonna get a second look. Is it? Besides, why would a guy with the nickname 'Dragonslayer' worry about a nickname like Carrot? Eh?"

Smiling, Jasmine touches Dragonslayer's Pad a few times to bring up a file. She passes the Pad back to him.

He starts reading but gets puzzled. "Not much here, is there? … Juergen seems to have been more interested in the upcoming PaxT than what we're doing in here."

"Yeah, 38 percent of his FTP time was about PaxT. About us, Juergen was just noting touristy stuff. This many dwellings, that many places to eat… He doesn't seem to've captured what we're actually doing, here."

She raises an eyebrow. "No. Thankfully nothing about Carrot, at least. It may be that he was asked to do the demographics thing at first. I guess they probably don't believe what they can see on any video feed. That we're doing very well, thank you, and that we're more than self-sufficient."

"Thanks in no small measure to the water and minerals we're shooting up from the moon, with the rocks." He rolls the dice and makes another move.

"Right. Nothing about Carrot. And…" She points to a file showing on his Pad, "…one reference to 'Prancing Tiger', whatever the hell that is. Larry's gonna work on it with our office in Lyon. Probably some Black Project mumblygook."

Jasmine smiles and waves to a person passing on the sidewalk. "Nothing there so far, Jim. Carrot's doing all the heuristic analysis – making sure there's no code embedded, etcetera."

A foursome takes a table not far away. Both table's occupants do the polite short wave and smile to each other. She tosses the dice and, still thinking, makes a routine backgammon move.

The twitch of a grin passes over Dragonslayer's face.

Quietly, Jasmine carries on, "The Germans want in. As soon as we gave their embassy the news, they officially asked for permission to send their own investigation team. They don't seem to believe Charon's analysis of the puddle circles."

He adds, "I have to say that there are responses coming from more than one direction, from downside. For instance, the amateurish behaviour of Juergen, but then there's Prancing Tiger, whatever that is. And there's this one paragraph that had me stumped."

"Which one?" Jasmine flicks through her Pad.

Dragonslayer finds a highlighted paragraph on his Pad and reads it out quietly. "It comes after Juergen's dissing the fabric material of our buildings."

He reads, "'*They said they will arrive at a propitious time...*' He must have used the spell-checker for that one. '*...and clean out the mutated genome. The life that Sol intended to inhabit the planets shall be rebooted. Gaia shall return anew to join with Europa.*' Whew! What a mash-job of cult-crazy shit!"

Jasmin's forehead wrinkles, seriously. "Where was *that*? I must have speed-read right past it!"

"Saw it early this morning. Like, five a.m. early. Thought the AI, ah, Carrot, was feeling a tweak of emotion. My Pad is normally off then, except for emergencies. It actually vibrated off the night-table. The fall is what woke me. As soon as I touched the Pad to pick it up, the AI was dictating that paragraph to me. You didn't get it?"

Confused, "No... Maybe it wanted to wait for us to talk first... Yes, here it is." She scrolls through the paragraph. "Well, I probably *would* have just scrolled past this bullshit. Humh! You think it's worth highlighting?"

He nods, "Like I said, there's more than one person, entity, group, involved here. All is not what it seems."

After Dragonslayer's next backgammon move she pauses to analyze her options with the next roll.

Watching her face for tells, Dragonslayer carries on. "On the face of what Juergen presents us, I'd have to say that I can't blame the Germans and Russians, really. But of course, that puts us in an awkward spot. We give them a fantastic-sounding situation and they use it to demand an investigation of their own. But the real reason they want in is the same reason they sent Juergen here in the first place. They want to spy on how we're doing so much more than anybody figured we could. With only three-quarters of the ten thousand people we're working toward, L5 is making products that are in demand downside and doing things that they just can't do in their orbital labs. Mating that manufacturing torus was a tough sell two years ago, Jasmine - thank you again for backing me."

She waves off his thanks as something on the backgammon board doesn't look right.

He notices her attention and hurries to add, "Now, with that manufacturing capability, the AI's running rings around every one of the so-called advanced economies on poor old Earth, including their orbiting labs." He sighs. "Our nuclear option might be forced on us much sooner than we wanted."

She sucks in and stiffens. "*Outright independence?* But it's too soon! Can we just put them off by letting in an investigative team?"

"Jasmine, that would be the thin edge of a very long and sharp wedge. Downsiders don't know how to get out of military mode. I'm not sure how long we can stay in Peru with our new launch facility. It was bad enough when we had to slink out of the Australian outback. Thank heavens for the New Zealand and Canadian support!"

Dragonslayer waves to a passing person. Smiling but speaking sideways to Jasmine, "As you well know, I've argued for a more proactive role in finally adopting the Pax exTerra protocol. Despite the Chinese."

Jasmine nods, "Of course, Jim. They can go pound salt, in the most polite terms." She sighs. "You may be right. Now might be the time to take another look at that option. Our official *strong* support numbers in OECD countries is climbing past eighteen percent – which also means that our opposition is beginning to solidify."

She tosses the dice again and absently moves a piece to become a blot (unprotected piece) in her Home table. "Larry says that one of his recruits from last year has really begun to shine when it comes to slicing through diplomatic bafflegab. He's going to take the lead working from our Lima office. I understand that he has a severe allergy to too many things up here, though. Knows he'll probably never live in L5. But Larry says he's the most committed person to the Four Guides he's ever seen – outside of the Original Founders."

Dragonslayer nods, absently. "If he's got Larry's support… What's his name?"

"Jimmy… Jimmy George! He's from a place called Haida Gwaii, originally, but his parents moved to the high Andes of Peru when he was a kid because of his severe allergies. They've gotten better, but, apparently, Jimmy's super shy about what used to be his major health issues. Hah! Larry said it's disconcerting seeing a Canadian Native speaking with a Peruvian accent!"

He corrects her with a smile, "Indigenous."

She returns the smile until she sees Dragonslayer move a backgammon piece onto the blot, then dumping her piece to the middle bar. Her smile turns into a grimace.

Dragonslayer is talking as he makes his moves. "Not as unusual as you might think. I'd like to meet him. But not this time. I think we're gonna have to send Charon to Germany."

He frames his proposal with his hands. "We want to speak to Juergen's family, personally, to express our sincere condolences. He's the eighteenth death we've had of L5ers outside of natural causes - well, including that horrible three-person crash of our moon lander. All the others were from dangerous situations..." He shakes his head sharply, thinking of the construction deaths early on.

Clearing away those memories, "And we have to see if Juergen's medical records in Germany could shed any light on this mystery. Genetic history that we don't have and so forth. What do you think?"

"Sounds like a plan. Let's conference the Directors and see if they like it." Jasmine thinks some more. "Yeah. Puts the ball back in their court." She adds with a sly twist of her mouth, "And Charon can take that contaminated file back down to see who doesn't want to touch it, eh?"

Another passing acquaintance greets her and they briefly exchange pleasantries.

Leaning back to Dragonslayer, "Do you think Charon's ok to go down? He'll have to talk to his old boss, and Larry's still pissed off he can't come back up until all the skin grafts are done."

Nodding, "Might be just as well, for both their sakes. Charon's still got that thorn in his brainstem. Not really sure, but maybe he thinks he shouldn't've taken part of the blame for the explosion."

"Is he still on about that? What he needs is some tender, loving…"

"God, not you too!"

"Ha, ha, ha! What me too?"

Dismissively, "Forget it, Jasmine. I don't want to discuss L5 womanhood right now, thanks."

She reaches for his arm but he leans back playfully, just out of reach.

Jasmine grins, "Is that why you're wearing that disgusting turtle-neck thing? To scare off the gentler sex? I'm going to make you a proper kurta."

Dragonslayer gives her his *withering stare* from under his eyebrows, but, unable to keep it up, he breaks into a grin. Then he gets serious.

"Jasmine."

"What?"

"We can't give Juergen a formal space burial! I mean, shit! Juergen's name with those who gave their lives to build L5?"

"Listen to what you're saying, Jim. Say after me:

"Love yourself."

Dragonslayer joins in.

"Love your family.

"Love your community.

"Love life."

Her face softens; she takes his hand. "L5 is an environment that **gives** life, but it's not on the same level as life itself… Jim?"

Pensively, "Yeah, I know… Juergen's treachery was merely in words. Forgiveness, and all that. Hell, I **wrote** half the L5 Manual." He lifts his head to look around slowly. "Still. It's hard…Gonna go talk with Tolstoy."

Jasmine tenderly strokes his hand. "Jim, dear, let's do the call first. Ok?"

He nods. Rolling a double five, he pulls all his pieces into the home table. Jasmine finally notices and expresses considerable displeasure in words and gestures.

Rather than relishing the win, Dragonslayer stays pensive, "So, who else was controlling Juergen? What's with that Gaia Europa bullshit?"

Night is defined in L5 simply by the dimmed lights.

A rendition of Bach's fugues played by a competent jazz pianist wafts from several coordinated speakers around a porch located down at the residence Level with the least gravity.

Dragonslayer is lounging on the porch. *My legs feel like they could almost float up from the chair.*

The sun mirrors have just faded away. A breathtaking view of low-power dwelling lights extends most of the way around the girth of the main residential area. The dark louvers, where mirror-assisted sunlight had been pouring across the interior, show a few very tiny and not too inspiring sparks of starlight poking their photons in.

Dragonslayer is quietly sitting with a very old, fragile, patrician-looking gentleman. Tolstoy.

Tolstoy groans and moves in his chair a little.

Dragonslayer speaks gently, "Old friend, you should come to the heavier levels and move your bones a little. As delightful as near-weightlessness is, you know that you're losing bone mass."

Tolstoy replies quietly in his Montreal accent, "Fuck off, Jim…Let me die in peace." He turns to his acolyte. "What the hell d'you want, anyway?"

The swearing brings a quick smile to Dragonslayer's weary face.

The music is now from Bruce Cockburn's _You Point To The Sky_.

"Good to see you're still kicking, Tolstoy."

Still quietly, as if reciting from memory, "And who the hell started calling me Tolstoy, anyway? My name's Benoit, not bloody Tolstoy..." He takes a serviette that lays ready on his thigh and wipes his mouth.

He softens. "Jim, my son..." He squints at Dragonslayer. "Jim. Remember. After the Transition. Take a flitter and spread me over the soil of L5. Jim..."

They sit in male blankness until the music becomes Bruce Cockburn's _High Winds, White Sky_.

Just quietly enough for Tolstoy to hear, Dragonslayer purrs, "Your Canadian roots are showing, my friend."

In an old man's voice, made as lyrical as he can, Tolstoy recites from something he'd written decades ago.

"Bruce Cockburn, exquisitely delighting the mind while ripping into our distracted consciousness... Neil Young artistically terraforming the harmonies of our brain... Gordon Lightfoot, troubadour par excellence, opening up a delightful world to our clouded eyes...Stan... Stan Rogers, the angry young poet, so evocative, creating instant classics... Lhasa..." he turns to Dragonslayer, "If there is still enough civilization left to scatter my ashes, I want her _Soon This Place Will Be Too Small_ to be played."

The plea brings a tear to Dragonslayer's eyes. Raising his eyes to distant lights on the other side of the torus, he croons, "At the end of time, only the music of our souls will remain."

Tolstoy considers that. "What's that from?"

Dragonslayer shrugs. "Don't know. Maybe I made it up. Might've dredged it up from some distant memory…"

A scrape of slippers is heard behind them. Anna, Tolstoy's nurse and long-time companion shuffles in the dark.

Dragonslayer faces her. "Anna, I'll just be a minute or two. Ok?"

"That's fine, Jim. Stay as long as you like." With affection, "He wakes up when you're here."

Flaring with more enthusiasm in his voice, Tolstoy points a wavering finger at Dragonslayer. "It was YOU, wasn't it! YOU named me Tolstoy, you son-of-a-bitch! Made me spend my last days away from…… I remember fall in my beautiful *Laurentides*…" Then he calms down; his brief tempest passes by. "Are we in L5, Jim?" His clouded eyes search around.

Dragonslayer nods. "Yes. See the lights from the other side." He slowly lifts his hand to guide Tolstoy's eyes. "The remarkable view that you made possible."

"Ha! Me. I just put a few words together. It was you, and all those brave people, and so many who died on Earth…" Tolstoy slowly bows his head. "Why do they keep *doing that* to themselves? Don't they see the beautiful majesty of the four simple Guides?"

Dragonslayer takes Tolstoy's withered arm as it waves shakily. He fingers the thin, fragile old hand. Another tear rolls down his cheek.

The old man mumbles, "Eunomos."

Dragonslayer nods. "Good order. They're not going to get there in **our** lifetime, old friend."

Lead Boots

IN AUSTRALIA

In the airport baggage claims area, crowds moving quickly this way and that, waiting or searching for their bags.

A huge sign over the carousel scrolls:

Welcome to Australia---

All Non-Residents must register HERE ☛

A group of seven people comes down two of the central glass elevators, with Charon in the middle of the main group. As soon as he is seen, reporters mob him. All but one of the people accompanying Charon are plain-clothes security – the other person is Jimmy George.

George is dressed in an eccentric mixture of Haida and Peruvian. He is young but in confident control of himself. Long black hair is tied loosely over his back. George's face and neck are reddened from a number of sensitivities to many things made by factories. He wears thin skin-coloured cotton gloves and pulls them up habitually when standing still - which isn't often.

The handlers expertly steer Charon through the mob to a door that says:

NO UNAUTHORIZED ENTRY

AIRPORT SECURITY

Standing for a minute at the door, Charon half-turns to survey the crowd.

Reporters and a large flock of groupies are yelling out, each trying to outdo each other.

Reporter 1: "Charon, is it true that nobody wears clothes on L5?"

Reporter 2: "What do you do with the dead bodies?"

Reporter 1: "Is it true that you're developing a super ray gun?"

Reporter 3: "When are you going to open up L5 to the rest of us?"

Before proceeding through the door, Charon smiles at Reporter 3, and waves to the rest of the reporters for the Photo Op. He ignores yelled questions, still smiling, then they carry on through the door.

As it closes on the mob, he whispers through smiling teeth to George beside him, "That long enough for pictures?"

George nods. "I'm sure our people got some good shots."

The handlers who've been surrounding Charon and George firmly encourage them into a half trot down a long corridor to a Security office. One of them stays outside the door while four guards precede George and Charon. Inside, the group does a perimeter search of the room with electronic bug detectors as well as pushing at the walls, then the four position themselves around the room, anticipating anything.

An oversized white couch with an uncomfortably low back is in the middle. Charon sits into it with relief. Still standing, Jimmy George taps at his Pad. His gloves get a work-out. He has a colourful hanky in continual use on his nose and forehead.

Satisfied, George raises a hand for attention. "Gentlemen, thank you for your help. I'd like to have a private word with Charon, now."

The four suited guards, one female, do not move from their positions around the room.

George smiles at the big guard who was leading the way.

George tries again. "Who's in charge?"

Nobody speaks.

Charon shifts around on the couch; a slight smile is directed at George, who takes another tack.

"You've been told not to talk to us. Fine. But I want to speak with your boss, so one of you scurry out and contact him or bring him in here. Right?"

The big guard finally decides to go to the door. He knocks.

"Messenhoef. Open door."

Messenhoef slips through the opening. It closes right after his heel leaves the doorway.

Charon stretches out on the couch. "Earth-normal gravity's a bitch. Like I'm wearing lead boots. Anyway, we're going to have to see about getting you to L5, Jimmy."

George takes a seat next to Charon. "My fondest dream. But not for a while. That special neoprene that's used on airlock seals and in EVA suits - what do you call them, Rainsuits?"

"No neoprene these days. And rainsuits are the hardened shells that my crew wears when they harvest moon rocks. Got their name from the construction crews who had to wear them during the periodic meteor showers."

"Oh! Got it. *Showers.* At thirty thousand klicks per hour. Well, Charon, they'd likely be my death, and I don't know what else'd do it for me, up there. It isn't like I could take a timer and get out of the place, eh? Just flying here from Lima was a major chore." He shakes his head and rubs his gloved hands absently.

"Well, thank you, again, for arranging things, Jimmy… Heh heh!"

George smiles back, quizzically. "What'r you laughin' at?"

"Sorry, Jimmy. Hearing that Peruvian accent coming from a Haida is, well, incongruous. Sorry. Oh, and by the way, I do appreciate how much you've extended yourself on this one. Really."

George rubs his exposed neck. "No problem. For the good of the cause."

Charon glances at the guards. "I understand this is your first trip since you moved to Peru?"

George shakes his head deliberately, then gives Charon a semi-fake punch in the shoulder. "Pushed me over the parapet, this did." He shrugs. "Probably good for me in the long run."

They both grin freely, ignoring the solemn guards standing over them. "Oh. And by the way, I'm positive I met long-lost cousins in Peru. But that's another story entirely."

The room's vents go into another period of louder noise. Under his breath and without moving his lips, George whispers, "Nearly got waylaid by these Germans in Lima." He shakes his head and gives a slight shake to indicate silence. "Then saw them on the plane. Oh well." He wipes his forehead.

The door opens. Messenhoef follows a dark-blue-suited man in. The dark-suit, Henry, smiles obsequiously at George and Charon.

"**Hello**, Jimmy! So very good to see you again! I am so pleased to see you out of Peru! And this must be the famous Mr. Charon! World famous! And *beyond* the world! Welcome back to Earth, Mr. Charon! My name is Heinrik Schumacher, but please call me Henry. I have been given the honour to accompany you to Frankfurt — to talk with the family of the late Juergen Mittelsohn. So we will be seeing a lot of each other for the next week or so." He half-bows to Charon as he extends his hand.

Henry adds, "Please to excuse my assistants' rigorous adherence to duty. They have orders to protect you at all costs…" he looks at George, "…from, from the public and any terrorists who may, so wrong-headedly display violent jealousy towards a representative of the great L5 community. Heh-heh."

Charon half rises to shake his hand but receives only a few limp fingers. "Charmed, I'm sure."

"A distinct honour, sir." Henry carries on, "Gentlemen, we have a brief meeting arranged in half an hour with experts in homicide investigation. The American FBI has very kindly offered their considerable assistance in apprehending the murderer of poor Juergen…"

Charon shakes his head, smiling. "We do not need the assistance of the FBI. The facts are clear, as far as the facts can take us."

Henry nods to himself, having expected push-back. "Please, Mr., ah, Charon, if I may call you that? Please be so kind as to not bring into this unfortunate tragedy the regrettable L5 disapproval of things American."

Maintaining a polite smile, Charon is firm. "Henry, I have no idea what you're referring to. People from the L5 community do not 'disapprove' of Americans. Perhaps the blind lust for money that half their population display, but that is another discussion altogether. A large percentage of our little band of pioneers, along with a goodly number of our supporters, *were* originally from the northern part of the Americas." Grinning, he steps closer to Henry's face, eliciting the very slightest twitch from Henry.

"What I am quite simply telling you is that we have put together the evidence in a very comprehensive, scientific way, and there is no need for further 'investigation' of that evidence." His eyes drill into Henry's, causing the German to glance away briefly.

He continues with a closer step to Henry. Charon's ample belly almost touches Henry's slim frame. "What I am here to do is to visit the family of Juergen, offer them our sincere condolences, deliver his body and possessions to them, and look into any possible family medical history that may have been a contributing factor to Juergen's death."

He holds up a hand as Henry tries to interrupt. "That's all that I am prepared to do. I have urgent work back in L5, and I am anxious to complete this mission as expeditiously as possible."

Henry is not used to receiving such absolute terms. He is, after all, a lifetime European diplomat.

"Of course, of course. And I am here to offer whatever assistance I can in your endeavours. It is only that since we have very kindly been given the offer of help from the world's most preeminent crime investigators…"

"No."

The finality of Charon's statement throws Henry off balance.

"…But but but, my dear Charon! Can you, can you not understand that, that the family is totally, ah, in *shock*! They just cannot, well, quite frankly, they cannot believe the wild story of a magical ray gun blasting the very water out of the air! Surely you must agree that a, an unbiased, ah, neutral party, looking at the scene and viewing the evidence from their professional perspective would provide the grieving family with real closure and the assurance that every possible stone has been turned…"

Charon puts up a stop hand. His belly does touch Henry's, causing the German to jerk back involuntarily.

George suppresses a grin as Charon's taller, larger body stands over Henry.

Enunciating with exaggerated precision, Charon says, "Look, I **am** prepared to share our evidence and detailed conclusions with you and the family. And **only** with you and the family. We have nothing to hide. But I will not allow this death, as tragic as it is for Juergen's family, to be used as a transparent pretense for FBI agents to extend their jurisdiction into L5. Is that clear?"

Henry becomes obsequious again. "My dear Charon! You have me all wrong! There was no intention whatsoever..."

"Enough." He puts his nose right to Henry's. "You and I both know what the agenda is." After a very uncomfortable moment, Henry turns away, shrugging helplessly at the guard, Messenhoef.

To the room in general, Charon says, "Let the recording show that you tried your damnedest."

Henry automatically looks down at his chest.

Smiling at Henry's involuntary glance, "Now, let's move on." Charon turns to wink at George.

"Oh. I have a file that Juergen had in his quarters. Our Security personnel placed it in a thick, sealed plastic envelope." He reaches into his briefcase, pulls out a blue medical glove, slips it on, then uses that hand to carefully extract the red plastic envelope. Holding it gingerly between thumb and finger, he turns suddenly to offer the envelope to Henry.

Eyes wide, Henry jumps back in alarm. "No-no! I don't... ah... please to save it for, for Juergen's lawyer!"

Charon grins, then slips the envelope back into his briefcase. "I understand, Jimmy, that my old friend Larry is waiting for us downtown?"

Blithely enjoying the exchange, George nods.

"Right as rain, friend. He's told me a thing or two about you, and I'm pleased to see that he was accurate as ever." He gets up to speak to the guards. "Gentlemen, lady. Shall we be off?"

Henry is nonplussed. "Ah, but…"

George takes on Charon's presumptive tone. "Are we using your limo, or shall we call a taxi, Henry?"

Charon slings his light cloth bag over his shoulder. "Time to shake my lead boots." He and George stand over Henry, waiting for him to make a move.

On Becoming Starstuff

A SYDNEY AFTERNOON

The e-limo is driving from Sydney's airport along O'Riordan Street to a building in the suburb of Beaconsfield. The hazy air is tinged in burnt orange. As a news reporter said, 'Even the ashes of the Outback are burning again."

In the cool of the limo, George is explaining, "We are in the rear of the Red Cross building. They had a convenient section on their second floor. Then we were able to expand from there. We don't mind helping them out with a significant lease payment."

The driver, Messenhoef, is the only guard still with them. Charon, George and Henry converse in the back of the e-limo. Low buildings zip past. It is mostly residential on the right-hand side. With the left-hand drive on Australian streets, the low office buildings pass by on the left side.

George, when at ease, speaks with pointed emphasis using his gloved hands. He speaks to Henry in a friendly and open manner, which takes the topic away from the darker undertext of their relationship.

"Larry tells me that a few years ago there were a number of, let's be kind and call them, incursions, into our old facilities in Lima. So, as a nod to L5's original help from

Canberra, I acquired this facility as a co-headquarters in a country more secure than Peru currently is." He smiles at Henry, as a lithe puma would smile at a scrawny coyote. "Peru has been subverted yet again by foreign oligarchs. This time, I strongly suspect, in order to put pressure on L5. Here, we constructed a large conference hall on the ground floor. It's become quite popular with the locals and tourists. Whenever we have meditations, hundreds sit in. And the display rooms are quite popular as well. The Australian Red Cross has donation boxes at the entrance. They are emptied often."

Henry feels he must insert his flea-in-the-ear. "I understand that L5 has plans to add a new tower on the lot behind the building? Six floors with options for another tower?"

George nods, "Yeah, well, we have a lot to do. Our main work here deals with commercial transactions with businesses across the planet – our spongemetals, crysaloys, ultra-pure chemicals, biostuff…"

"That is one thing I very much admire about your work, Jimmy. Biostuff. The spin value is beautiful. It de-toxifies an otherwise highly charged issue. You will, of course, know, and it is perhaps regrettable, that we still, in Germany, have many committed citizens who absolutely refuse to use products which contain your, ah, biostuff."

Dropping some pretense, "Yeah, yeah. Like Charon said, we know your agenda, so do us a favour, Henry." He waves a dismissive hand.

"Jimmy! Surely you're not accusing the German government of that old charge of deliberately fomenting misinformation among our own populus!"

"Henry. Please. We're all grownups in here. Even your news media admits that you're funding the anti-L5 groups in the US, while *they're* funding the German operation. Cute arrangement. Neither government can be accused of illegal activity in their own country. Take a timer, my friend." He finishes roughly.

The e-limo drives into a secured parking garage at the Red Cross building. With George's instructions and his key-card, they drive through the gate and up a ramp to the second floor. George notices that Messenhoef is adding whispered commentary to whatever cameras are recording their passage. Consulting his Pad, George directs the driver to stop in a designated visitor parking stall. After they all exit the limo and remove their few bags, the vehicle gets pulled through a whole-car detection unit, like it was going through a car-wash. Henry and Messenhoef stare quietly and impotently while their vehicle elicits numerous bleats from the detection equipment.

Henry shrugs and whispers to Messenhoef. As their vehicle disappears into the detection room, they turn more timidly to join Larry and George at the entrance to L5's offices. It is time for their bags to be moved through screening.

In a cubicle, the two Germans individually get electronically frisked.

Finished, Henry looks around, very perplexed. He scratches an itch on his chest. As Henry is being processed, the attendant shows Henry's read-out to George. They nod to each other knowingly.

Then the group takes a slidewalk to the building's second floor lobby. As they start on the slidewalk, George whispers to Charon and nods at Henry, who is in front with Messenhoef.

On the way, Henry looks around in admiration, whispering to the guard. He half-turns to speak over his shoulder.

"I must admit that your security arrangements are certainly setting the pace. Of course, we do not have the need, in our offices, to go to such extremes." He smiles to himself, pleased with his dig.

George leans closer to Charon, whispering, "And they'd love to know how we do it as they rebuild from that riot damage last month."

He speaks up to Henry, "Yeah, well, friend, the three bugs that you have on you've been fried, so you don't have to speak as loudly anymore to show off to your bosses."

Alarmed, Henry turns around. "**What**!! You have no right! One of them is implanted! You're going to give me cancer! You…"

"Take a timer, friend. Nobody gets cancer from what Security did."

Calmly, Charon raises a hand, "Henry, sit back and enjoy your time off line. You might actually learn something."

Carried along, Henry's concern is focused on his chest. He scratches aggressively at one spot and tries to feel the small lump. They get to the lobby in silence.

Messenhoef is politely but firmly taken by L5 Security away from the group.

George leads Charon and Henry into a meeting room whose far side of a glassy-smooth floor curves up for the last metre to seamlessly meet curving glass that bellies out. It rises over the rear of the building and comes back to join the roof line about a metre above the ceiling. The view is breath-taking, even from the second floor.

Henry sharply sucks in a lungful of air and puts his back to the near wall. He is most reluctant to get any closer to the view of Sydney's hazy, orange skyline.

George is delighted with his reaction. "Imagine what this would look like from twenty stories up."

From the main hall, a man strides with a slight limp toward them. His older face and arms display bandages and burn scars. His thigh-length kurta and pants are an off-white-green with a faint medium green design of leaves. He comes directly to Charon with both hands outstretched.

"Charon!" His scarred face allows only the hint of a smile.

"Larry! My dear friend. How are you doing?"

With sincerity, they embrace.

"You sonofabitch, Charon. I'm doing better every day. How've you been?"

"I'm…" His mouth still smiles while his eyes well up. "Larry…" He shakes his head hard.

> :FLASHBACK: *Larry is on his stomach writhing on the floor with his clothes burning as Charon desperately sprays him with a small fire extinguisher. A spacesuited figure is backing away from them but can be seen smiling…:*

Charon looks at Larry, reliving the flashback. "Larry. We, we have to talk privately."

With a distracted hand-wave at Larry, Henry turns his attention to George.

Glancing at Larry and Charon, George nods wisely, "Henry, please take a seat, here. I have Charon's report set up for you to view on the screen. You can use this remote to scroll through it at your leisure."

Using the controller before handing it over, George presses a few buttons causing curtains to draw together against the curved window, shutting off most of the light. A flexible, wide screen drops down in front of the curtains. George shows delight in being able to use the products of his previously long-distance management of L5's facilities.

Larry directs Charon out of the room with his hand on Charon's shoulder while Henry settles into a chair at the large oak table.

Fifteen minutes later, as the screen goes up and the curtains withdraw, Henry sits pensively at the table.

Larry leads Charon back into the room. They both look relaxed.

George is seated close to Henry. "Well Henry. That's every bit of it. At the request of your government, we've taken the extraordinary measure of bringing Juergen's body back to Earth. As you know, it is being shipped directly to them. We were going to give him our full ceremonial burial…"

"Thank you Jimmy. His family will be relieved to hear that they will be able to bury him in Frankfurt." He faces George. "Ah, just to satisfy my morbid curiosity, and in full confidence, of course, please to tell just **what is** a space burial?"

George looks at Charon for the answer. "No secret, Henry. We hold life sacred, as you know. The ceremony isn't complicated. The body is placed in the focused light of the sun, in a special vessel that sits outside of the main windows. The body turns back completely into starstuff and then that dust is spread by a flitter over the growing soil of L5."

Henry takes a moment to understand.

Charon carries on after a pause. "The memories that people wish to preserve of the departed are put into the permanent record of L5 for all to see forever after. For this reason, such memories are recorded only after a period of meditation about the Four Guides. Even though there was only an abbreviated ceremony for Juergen, because his stardust was not mingled with the soil of L5, he received some very touching comments. We've brought a copy of those for his family."

Henry shifts uncomfortably in his seat. "I wish…"

George waits while Henry struggles to bring his thoughts forth.

"Yes?"

Henry cocks his head and blinks rapidly struggling to find words. He wants to express a deep feeling but cannot force it out of his mouth.

Charon is about to speak but Larry quickly raises a finger to quiet him.

They wait for Henry to sort out his thoughts.

Henry finally lets out a stream of consciousness, talking to the walls. "I just wish I could *go* there! It must be so beautiful! The green fields and orchards circling around overhead and everyone playing in the grass, running around like carefree children and designing and building so many creative things…" His resolve to express diplomatic statements dissolves. "Down here, this is hell. We have no religion anymore. No moral compass. It is every dog for himself. And what have we truly invented that is new over the past fifty years? Nothing but new methods of sucking money from the people as they suffer under greater heat and floods and and…" Henry looks up from his lap and turns to Charon. "I so much want to be part of what you have in, in **heaven**! BUT YOU WON'T LET ME! You exclude everybody! You must open up the gates to let us good people in! We just want to be part of that new life!…" His head dances from side to side.

Emotion fizzles into a slow brood.

Henry continues to mope, staring at the window.

Larry motions to George and Charon for silence…

Henry looks over his shoulder at Larry, eyes pleading for an answer.

In smooth tones, Larry nods. "Thank you, Henry, for sharing that with us. I, myself, will say from my heart that I sympathize, sincerely, with your feelings, and with your wish to join us."

Henry shakes his head slowly, then turns to stare blankly at the window. Larry waits for Henry's attention to return to him.

"Henry, we are building a refuge, yes. But I have to say this, in fullest honesty – our refuge is no more than a way of preserving what is best about the human race, until we can ALL come to our senses. **Earth** is humanity's best refuge! It is the billions-year-old heaven that stands against the darkness of **not-life** in our known universe. Until the people of Earth wake up to see that ultimate reality, we, in L5, have pledged to keep the spark of **life** alive in that little refuge of our colony!"

Taking a seat carefully so that his tightened skin grafts will not overstretch, Larry glances at Charon.

The larger man takes the cue and plops down heavily next to him, still not adjusted to Earth-normal gravity. He has always been impressed with Larry's oratorical prowess. Charon listens attentively.

Larry carries on, "We truly welcome you and others like you to our simple, honest beliefs. As the schedule permits, more and more people can be supported in L5, and then other colonies will be built, as the need arises. But we must spread the message **here**! On our own once green Earth! Do you not agree that we absolutely must spare no expense to clear our air and oceans?… Henry? If you would like to learn more of our true and simple message, please feel free to join us later for meditations. I will not twist your arm, Henry. You may leave now and go to your hotel room outside. Or, you are welcome to stay the night here, with us."

Henry melts into his chair. George puts a hand on his shoulder. "Perhaps, Henry, you'd like to wash your face. The bathroom is right next to the elevator."

Henry is drained. He nods slightly as he wipes tears away then tries to push his chair back. It takes another try for him to rouse enough strength to get up.

He shuffles to the door. As it closes behind him, Charon gives Larry a puzzled look.

Larry shrugs. "I know. But I am sincere when I say that the fate of humanity depends on converts down here. The more people who truly sympathize with our aims, the sooner will the people of this benighted world lift up their eyes and see that they are wasting their lives being led around by the nose by a small bunch of entirely self-serving money-grubbing silver-back punks whose only goal is to acquire more wealth and power!"

He sighs, giving a wry smile to Charon.

"Sorry, Charon. You may see that I've changed a bit while back on Mother Earth." He clenches his fists. "I want L5 to work… **but I want Earth to work, too**! Millions have died over the past year alone. Gaia, the climate, has clamped down on us, **hard**!"

Hearing the word "*Gaia*", Charon begins to worry that Larry has perhaps changed a lot. He thinks, *The Gaia belief has been, not taboo in L5, but some consider it a competitor to the L5 Way philosophy.*

Larry slants his head wryly. "Help me down from my pulpit, will you? Jimmy is already immune to my rants." He drops into a chair. "If nothing else, we've sown the seed of doubt in Henry's mind." He gives a sideways glance in Charon's direction.

Minutes pass. Larry stares out the window. In a quieter voice, "Demyadin does worry me."

That catches Charon off guard, "Demyadin?" He thinks back. "Are you still thinking about… Demyadin was coming out of the airlock when that fire started."

Larry shakes off the image. "Do you know what happened to him after he left L5?… Some day…" he clenches his fists, "I want us to review that incident more fully."

Charon gives an involuntary shiver. "I don't really know… He left L5 under a dark cloud." Charon tries to clear away the mists of horrible memories of what he still believes, deep down, must have been his personal failure.

Larry has moved well beyond the hot searing pain of that day, and the ongoing pains of operations, one after the other. In his mind, it is a long-past incident better left to the mind's storage lockers. "He may not be talked about much by the Directors. I've raised my concerns with them. But he's a real pain in the proverbial, now – down here."

Larry turns to George, his burn-scarred face made as serious as the tight skin can be. "I don't say that lightly, Jimmy. Demyadin's been giving speeches of the most virulent sort against L5 and all we stand for. From the moment he landed back on Earth, he's been a growing thorn in our side – and making a swelling fortune for himself, doing it… Don't really know what to do with him. Worried about the Streisand Effect. I've been quietly following his rantings but I've been thinking recently that it's time to place the matter before the Executive for an action plan. Jim's with me in that."

Charon and George both sit up straight during Larry's explanation.

"Demyadin's been talking to new groups. Russian and German oligarchs, religious-right fundamentalists, billionaire self-serving shitheads, some of whom pretend to espouse parts of the Gaia philosophy. Not only pulling a Trump, but doing it with something that has attracted ignorant millennials to unabashedly raise a fortune. And I believe there are indications he's been getting ready for more dramatic steps. I just fear he's somehow involved in this Juergen situation."

"Gaia?" Charon shows innocent concern. He forces himself to put his hand on one of Larry's arm bandages, even as his gut shrivels tightly with animal fear of the pain he feels he had caused.

On the other side of Larry, George cringes involuntarily at the touch.

Taking the tone of a lecturer, Larry raises a finger. "Ah, yes. Gaia. The supposed precursor to our own philosophy. If you haven't already done so, Charon, you must speak with Jim and Tolstoy about how they put together our own *L5 Way* of thinking. I will take nothing at all away from what they have stitched together, because it works. It really does. But it owes its lifeforce to the Gaia principle that was the favourite of Lynn Margulis from fifty years ago."

Charon smiles with a pleasant memory. "Thank you for reminding me, Larry. Yes, late one evening on Tolstoy's patio, Jim, Marta, Jasmine and I were accosted by Tolstoy for what he thought was a blasphemous thing! I thought Anna was going to kick us out right then. He said we wanted to encode the *L5 Way* into some book of rules. '*An abominable straightjacket!*' he called that. Ha! He accused us of the crime of *Gatekeeping*! if you please. Haha! It took us the rest of the evening to calm him and Anna down."

Larry sinks into his seat. "Gatekeepers. We must not become damned gatekeepers, Charon." He spits out, "Not now. Humanity needs *creative* action, not going back to some old fucken rules of life as it once was in somebody's cloudy old mind!"

Origin

From **"The Official History of the L5 Space Colony"**

Mirroring the 1967 awakening of what became referred to as *the consciousness of human-scale culture* – in both Haight-Ashbury and Cambridge – meetings were called in two places after the Pandemic petered out in 2023. In a Western Australian town called Meekatharra, on a desolate plain east of abandoned gold mines which are east of the town, and also in Mica Creek, northeast of Osoyoos, Canada, close to the Washington state border.

The Australian *Meeka Outing* was organized by a small group of geologists, professional and amateur, who had met serendipitously while exploring the abandoned gold mines beyond Meekatharra.

It was not a geological meeting. The re-awakening at certain academic campuses was the primary topic of discussion by these earnest young scholars. In the Outback, free of controlling authorities, each spoke passionately, wanting to contribute, to participate in the global dialog. There was only one occasionally dissenting voice, M. Demyadin, who spoke freely at first, but expressed concern about the reliance by the others on technical solutions to a human problem. He went silent as the others jokingly called him a Luddite. Nevertheless, with the exciting evening discussion that had erupted amongst themselves about the future prospects for humanity and its technologies, the group decided that their ideas should be shared online. The response to that was surprising and overwhelming. It came from academics around the world, including from the person who was to become the L5 Project's principle founder Christoff Benoit, later lovingly known as Tolstoy.

A separate meeting that occurred the same year was at Mica Creek. This was off-handedly called the *Jim-Jam-Whoopla*. That evening's discussion around a campfire resulted from the day's impromptu shindig on a lenient farmer's field. While the intent had been to have a free and easy party in that remote location, conversation turned from the deplorable state of *special-interest-run governments* - *"SIRGs"*, as ranted on passionately by a graduate student - to the fanciful possibility of a utopia where a society's interests can be directed more particularly to respectfully advancing humanity. This led to participant J. Dragosavljevic to suggest a way for interested people's natural tendency toward overwhelming self-interest to be channeled into what he called a *pan-human sphere* via the basic principles of distributed blockchain technology. He went on to put a few attendees to sleep by explaining the principles of disintermediation, zero trust, immutable and universally accessible records of material goods' ownership, as well as the self-sovereign ownership of one's created data-of-living. He was later to enhance these principles into his *"infosouls"* concept.

Through the serendipitous bouncing of electrons on non-corporate, fediverse social media, a small contingent from each group found kindred spirits. They decided to meet in Perth during ANZAC celebrations two months later.

That meeting considered the possibility of finding a suitable place for their conceptual "utopia" but nothing could be agreed on until someone suggested a space colony. Those meeting participants gradually lost their abilities to concentrate after the evening meal and drinks, etc.

Next day, within a flurry of ensuing messages, the Lagrange (pronounced *lah grahnj*) proposal from the 1970s by Gerard K. O'Neill was placed on the table. It became the focus for everyone's attention, in each of their specialties, to help create their utopia. They called themselves *L5ers*. Funding was raised via cryptocurrency crowdfunding for a headquarters and launch pad facility in Western Australia. This was to be disguised as another medium-rocket launch enterprise for private corporations. The subterfuge was necessary because of the enmity that was evident in the first excited conversations which some new L5ers had when they returned to their respective homes (see the historical article, among others, archived at https://aeon.co/essays/the-dropout-a-history-from-postwar-paranoia-to-a-summer-of-love). It was considered prudent that the whole enterprise must go undercover until they were able to achieve a significant socially and scientifically acceptable milestone.

The group was able to get a major leg-up in the project with their recruitment of two current, promising but struggling, space industry startups. One, a severely underfunded but creative group calling themselves *FlingOut*, which had developed a new type of rocket engine.

The other, *Singh-Stan Enterprises,* had experience in constructing well-regarded launch facilities. Their most recent facility had just been taken over by the government in Vietnam for its own use. As a result, the company received a pittance for their engineering and construction work, leaving the company desperate for a white knight. The L5 Project was that saviour.

Growing pains nearly ripped the project apart. Like so many worthwhile endeavours, they were comprised of highly intelligent individuals who, destructively, all tended to go their own way. The term, "like herding cats", became common. That was when Benoit/Tolstoy put together the essence of a new philosophy that was to be the binding force for their vision.

It must be said that after a year, even that philosophy started to show some ragged edges until Dragosavljevic, whom friends called Dragonslayer, offered to write out the L5 philosophy in an actionable document that became the *L5 Way*. The combination of having focused plans of action with a coherent, compelling moral philosophy in an organic manual, became the driving force that allowed L5 to leap from a utopian dream to actuality in eleven years.

…The group's private launch facility in western Australia had been set up under the guise of a startup enterprise that sold their medium-lift rocket design capabilities to corporations that wished to place private satellites into orbit. Perhaps twenty percent of their launches actually carried commercial packages. The rest ended up at Lagrange point 5 – "*L5*" – which is a gravitationally stable location in the Earth-Moon system.

Of course, it did not take long for space aficionados to put together the real purpose of the L5 launches. Much teeth-gnashing, face-to-face pleadings, and recriminations occurred between the dedicated group that had worked so painfully hard to design and build a successful launch vehicle while others in the group planned out the materials needed for their radical colony. But the cat was out of the bag.

Later, many of those who outed the project, joined it.

Opposition to the building of L5 was initially expressed by a small number of haters. This is the well known consequence of variability in genetics that produces in a population dedicated haters of any coherent topic, at about the same rate as it produces brilliance.

Then, with their success dragged into the open, bureaucrats and gatekeepers in several governments decided that L5 was becoming the leading edge of the heretofore unfocused attack on their back-room control of the levers of power. Opponents in government soon realized that the L5 Project was putting a lie to those governments' assertions of "progress through democracy".

Entrenched bureaucrats tried to apply the term *anarchists* to the L5 group. It was realized that the term *terrorists* would have created wide-ranging difficulties. What they were really afraid of was the stuttering movement toward *disintermediation*.

The bureaucrats who held firmly onto the reins of backroom power had been secure in the knowledge that such a cumbersome and unpronounceable name could never become a rallying cry for the masses. Now, "L5" seemed to embody everything in the *disintermediation* movement that they most feared would come about. And *L5* was so easy to say and a space colony so easy to visualize. As a meme, it captured people's imagination.

With their pensions and mansions at risk, bureaucrats began to weave their plans. Legal arguments were considered to close down the L5 launch facility. Lobbying of Australian politicians saw some success. The most effective strategy was another "dis-": *Disinformation*. Planting lies and negative memes. It was a familiar strategy and the bureaucrats knew very well how to apply it. Their initial chosen attack vector was the Aboriginal communities near the facility. With enough funds flowing to the nearby villages, accompanied by carefully fabricated disinformation, the launch facility became the target of constant harassment and physical attacks by misguided locals.

Soon, the L5 launch facility had to leave Australia. It was decided to relocate to an enlightened country that did not have long-established ties to parliamentary procedure. Nor to officious bureaucrats. They decided on the recently re-modernized country of Peru.

While there certainly were officious bureaucrats in Peru, at that time they could be more easily persuaded to work on behalf of their new government's groundswell of supporters. Fortuitously for L5ers, the move came at a time of a considerable upswing in the global L5 movement and its general acceptance by the public.

…As an early L5er, Dragosavljevic developed an "ultimate" blockchain for individuals, producing the backbone of what L5ers all now subscribe to. He called his result *infosoul*.

Stored forever in highly protected servers, each L5er has their own *infoblock*. Indeed, their *infosoul* becomes the de facto codification of the "individual", in the fullest extent that it could be scientifically described. Just as DNA lists their genetic makeup, their *inflosoul* describes the individual's personality across 102 scaled factors, their belief system, and past and present desires. The genetic and infosoul identities become melded digitally into one individual.

However, Dragonslayer's blockchain concept uses a different definition of immutability. The replacement term for adding blocks to a person's life story is their *history*. The presumption is that an individual can change over time. Indeed, in the L5 community, change is the normal expectation. As one is able to view, and review, one's infosoul definition and history, it is expected that certain advancements or improvements *ought* to be made. This is their concept of *continual growth*.

Constraints and Conditions for data in *infosouls*:

Individual variability – the spectrum of psychological responses such as the desire for control/acceptance, locus of control, tolerance, ability to be mindful of the present, cognitive capability, visual stimulation vs the other forms of learning and interaction

Technological acceptance – across the spectrum *luddite < > first adopter*

Access – both in degree and breadth, considering poverty/wealth, across different communities

Preconditions such as cultural, religious, experiential development

Political movements – being the leading of a large community by a small group with a singular focus

Language and its preferred use – memes, accumulation of concepts which randomly fall into certain directions, language as essentially a "sentient being".

…Then came Carrot.

At first, the AI program and unique biological/quantum hardware concoction that grew into the entity called Carrot was given limited tasks. One of these, which it has been argued was seminal in the development of its exceptional understanding of human motives, was to be an oversight and advance warning system for L5's governing council regarding regulations passed by Earth's various governments. At that early juncture, L5 was on the verge of being declared an "anarchist" organization. That designation was the only method that bureaucrats who opposed their independence from Earth-bound judicial structures had with which to extend control over them. The resulting sanctions would have restricted the movements of their representatives on Earth, restricted shipments of essential materials *to* L5 and shipment *down* of their unique products from L5, cut off commercial ventures between Earth-side businesses, and forced their adherence to politically motivated international treaties.

The critical mix of artificial intelligence algorithms inside the bio-quantum architecture, known as *Carrot*, correctly found who those recalcitrant bureaucrats were, what their real motives and political connections were, and which courses of action would best defend L5 against their plans. None of the L5 organizers were expert in such matters so they quickly grew to depend on the AI's findings and stated options.

The success of Carrot's proposed actions to counter the Earth-bound bureaucrats' plans were mostly successful.

One of the actions was to create a dependence on L5 products by "downside" businesses. Important new materials, processes and products were invented in L5. These were produced and shipped to willing corporations. Their growing reliance on the unique products caused those corporations to lobby strongly in favour of L5 independence when bureaucratic interference became vexatious.

A clarification of L5's program for immigration was started. This featured Open Houses, which were established at carefully chosen centres around the globe to serve as de facto consular offices combined with a carefully crafted, almost religious promotion of humanitarianism – the "L5 Way". All of these achievements came under the wing of L5's artificial intelligence creation, *Carrot*.

The AI improved its capabilities rapidly until it was allowed, essentially, free rein to operate in any and every field in which L5 required expeditious multivariate analysis and action. Each new fact that was integrated into the algorithm added to its capabilities. Inevitably, even without Lateef posing *The Lateef Question*, it is certain that the entity called *Carrot* would have eventually come up against the critical issue of *AI alignment*.

Initially unknown to Carrot and L5 was the degree of AI development that had emerged from a program called PyTorch that had been taken via a software fork to become the creation of *Deeper*.

The coincidental development of transformer-AI in L5 was instrumental in successfully integrating quantum computer capability with organically grown *brains*. These highly secret technologies were what saved L5 from destruction by Deeper and Demyadin – along with the old technology of Morse code.

. . . .

NOTES

Lagrange points refer to the astronomical location of gravitational stability between two bodies in space. For example, they may be the Earth-Moon system, or the Earth-Sun system.

In the 1970s, Gerard O'Neill proposed that Lagrange points #4 and #5 of the Earth-Moon system would be ideal locations on either side of the system for construction of a space colony (https://en.wikipedia.org/wiki/Gerard_K._O'Neill). His initial concept was for a sphere into which great volumes of air would be brought, along with raw materials and necessary manufactured items to begin the colony. Later calculations and analysis showed that a sphere was not the optimum shape as it would require a huge volume of air that would be excess to the requirements of colonists. Personnel would be located primarily around the inner wall of the rotating sphere.

The shape finally settled on as best for a number of reasons was a torus – basically, a donut shape. The torus would be rotated to produce Earth-normal gravity for those on the outer edge, inside the donut. As you moved closer to the centre of rotation – the hole of the donut – the feeling of gravity would reduce significantly.

In 1978, O'Neill estimated that it could cost about $1.5 billion to build the colony. It took another seventy years for a group to secretly start the process. It was kept secret because they, rightly, believed their project could run into trouble if the grand endeavour became prematurely public.

Concept Became Reality

…Deb Roy of the MIT Media Lab offered the analogy of early movies as being "theater in front of a camera". As the movie business developed and grew, it found its own life away from its origins on the stage.

Similarly, the L5 group started their project by thinking of it as building a colony like those on the Mayflower taking over the "New World". It was a plus that there were no people to trample under in this L5 project.

In the early stages they worked through the needed tasks: rebuilding a launch facility and the complex supply chain, including the nurturing of numerous local businesses; assigning revised roles within their distributed-authority organization; finding out how to better manage public engagement; obtaining permission to set up a mining operation on the Moon from which material was to be flung over to the L5 structure; plus beginning many intriguing fields of research, including new complexities in artificial intelligence. The group found themselves well beyond the standard concepts of Earth-bound colony-building. The new science and technology they developed was hard enough. They soon found that the hardest problem to solve was the human mind.

The L5 group had to come up with a vision that did not fizzle out when their colony achieved the joy of temporary successes.

Most proposals to deal with this thorny issue tended to have religious themes. To the majority in the group, returning to religion was anathema. Surely, they said in frustration, with all the brainpower in the group, they could come up with a brand new philosophy.

It was Benoit, whom Dragonslayer later dubbed "Tolstoy", who formulated the basic tenets of the L5 philosophy. Its essence was the Four Guides: Learn to love yourself for who you are; Love and support your family unconditionally; Love and contribute to your community, which provides sustenance, meaningful activity and security throughout your life; Love and nurture Life itself, rather than worshiping elements of not-life.

Such a fine start on their new philosophy, however, would quickly whither were it not continually bolstered and improved by people who dealt with the nit-picking details. Dragonslayer was very adept at such detail work.

He and a few cohorts struggled with the format of future social networking in L5. They argued over the concepts of how broadly should one's achievements (good or bad) be cast, what should be their persistence, and should there be an editing option or full recall of select actions. For instance, an angry rebuttal in public could either be recorded as an indelible part of one's character, or as an ill considered and salvageable instance on the path to maturity.

The resolution of these and other concepts would be the un-noticed glue that held the L5 philosophy together.

Dragonslayer proposed this as a starting point: consider a blockchain holding all L5ers' personal ID in separate blocks: their medical history, family history, friends/ acquaintances history, work history, fediverse social networking history. Each factor being a cluster in separate sectors of a person's shard/block, with all of one's sectors in that block linked in formations of malleable sector interconnections to other individual's blocks.

In this concept, each person's sector connections will accumulate "stickiness" to current connections between blocks based on an algorithm. The algorithm takes each of the block's elements and applies weights to each one based on the number and currency of uses plus the possibility of a personally applied preference factor. One's block elements and that weighting algorithm will have view/print/edit permissions enabled only by that person. The quality of stickiness of the connections might mean, for instance, that connections to family members could be rare but persistent, while connections to work colleagues could be strong but transitory.

The preference factors which begin in a person's young life start as accepted defaults, then a rite of passage is achieved when an individual is entrusted with the ability to apply their own weighting preferences. For many, this rite of passage can be a difficult time. Most initial changes end up with the person reselecting "defaults". In the aggregate, it is eventually found that certain periods through people's lives occur along a fairly common graph corresponding to the general features of "traits". Analyses of this has become an academic field of study in itself.

The preferences can include time limitations, reproducibility (wherein the *original factor* is not viewed, but only a frangible token of it that expires according to permissions), physical or digital distance from one's location at the time of permission, and other variables in the weighting algorithm.

A person can choose to add more acquaintances or not, and the stickiness of those connections can be weighted by the individual, or they can be rescinded at either juncture of a connection (relationships, social groups, work, volunteer groups, affiliations).

Importantly, the original block within the master community blockchain only accumulates data as an "audit trail", while the individual's *friable* shard/block changes with time and is what passes data over to one's block that is visible to the community. A person's friable shard/block is the changing component of one's infosoul. It has a one-way connection to the immutable community blockchain.

The organic part of the process can be considered a person's outwardly visible *community-self*, while the accumulating ("maturing") part is one's *infosoul*. Therefore, each individual develops their sector connections and other elements of their community-self, along with the organically changing, maturing infosoul, both of which contribute to one's lifelong blockchain entry.

One's personal block in the community blockchain cannot be deleted, but it may be assigned a status of *permanently inactive.* This is done only through a designated committee which must follow specific rules. You are not dead until the committee says you are.

All of which departs from the liberal belief that we each should fully control our own ability to be as stupid or habitual as we wish, and that our purpose in life is to be good little consumers.

Some argue that this means blockchains and "disintermediation" results in social anarchy.

The response by Tolstoy and Dragonslayer is that the *L5 Way* does not redefine humanity - it allows a better definition of what humans are, what they can become once they see clearly what they have done in comparison to community expectations, and then enables a person to make informed, active choices along their path in life. This is the opposite of anarchic randomness. That leaves a person's energies freer to be contributory to L5's Four Guides (love oneself; love one's family; love one's community; love life), and, as one is able, to be *creative.*

However, such rational arguments were completely ignored by L5's enemies. Perhaps they simply did not understand them, or they did not wish to understand them. Basically, there was no way to either monetize them, nor to powerize them.

With a successful disinformation campaign by their enemies being undertaken over the first years of the colony, L5ers had a difficult uphill battle in convincing Jane and Jon Public that L5ers weren't simply a cult of raving lunatics. Doing "normal" things was a way of bringing people on their side. The Open Houses considerably aided in that understanding. Sales of their unique products to downside businesses established the colony as important in suppliers in a wide range of industries.

Mating a manufacturing torus to the original habitable torus of L5 was a supremely difficult endeavour. It remains an on-going project. Due to the technical difficulties, engineers in L5 have proposed that the limited manufacturing capability that has been constructed so far be converted into further habitation space. Then, a new colony should be built at L4. Including a mated manufacturing torus at the time of design and construction would enable the new colony's structure easier to build. The debate continues.

Case Study

In order to explain to young people how the *L5 Way* can be applied to one's life, this case study is offered as one of the *learnings* given during the difficult years of puberty:

Speaking with his droid, Stephan trusts that personal questions will be kept private. Secretly, Stephan calls his droid Sammi.

"Sammi, can I ask you about the Fungus Shed?"

"Of course, Stephan. What would you like to know?"

"I heard, well, that they, ah, grow more than just food in there."

"Yes, most facilities in L5 are multipurpose. It is due to…"

"But I mean, like…" Stephan looks for the courage to ask a really private deep-down question that he would never ask anyone. "What about psilocybin, like, not that I really want to take it or anything?"

The droid pauses. "I wish you to understand an important thing. All the parts of your body are there to nourish the brain: your eyes, your heart, stomach, fingers… This is so that your brain can function well and be active throughout your life. Without your brain, there is nothing left of what you now call you.

"So, over your life, all those supports of the brain need to function well. You must ensure that anything which enters your body is going to be in some way beneficial.

"Further, as chemical and mechanical devices, they will eventually start to degrade. The time that any degradation becomes a concern, and the rate that it happens, depends a several factors. Only a few of them are under your control. What you eat and drink, what stresses you subject them to, and how long you force them to work at higher levels. The other factors cannot be controlled so don't worry about them. Shit happens.

"Oh, and there's also procreation."

In Search of Durians

It is late afternoon. Charon, George and Henry are in an e-limo heading for the Kuala Lumpur suburb, Selangor.

Messenhoef is driving. Henry is speaking from the front passenger seat (left side of the car), leaning back to explain their itinerary to Charon and George.

"As I said, I do apologize for the routing, but we could not get a flight more direct than K.L. to Shanghai, Moscow, then finally Frankfurt. Spin-offs from the wars and climate change. Politics. You know…"

Keeping a close eye on the winding road, Messenhoef asks in German, "GPS is not correct. May I avoid the detour up ahead?"

Henry gives a quick wave in agreement then turns back to Charon. "We have a long wait, here in K.L., so I thought, instead of subjecting you to the media onslaught at the airport hotel directly after landing, we could visit such a fascinating place as a pewter factory. I know you will enjoy it. We have reserved rooms downtown in Selangor, but I thought I would give you this opportunity." He waits for a nod from Charon, who remains noncommittal.

Henry adds, encouragingly, "They are really very proud of the pewter works, here. In fact, there is, in Frankfurt, a store, ah, outlet, for this factory."

They pull up in front of the Royal Selangor Pewter Factory, park, then enter the busy, extensive storefront. Unknown to Henry, Charon has visited here before.

In the display area, as Henry leads George and Charon slowly past the retail shop of the factory, an older, thin Malay in a rich dark suit watches them with subversive glances.

The three are followed by the older gentleman at a distance into the factory tour area.

They all watch in fascination at one of the cup decoration stations as a worker taps extremely rapidly at a rotating pewter cup, leaving a tight pattern of precise artistic dents all around the pewter.

The older Malay continues to watch them closely, head averted.

George is dressed in a suit with the usual gloves. Everyone else, other than the older spy, is sweltering in white shirts or light-coloured tee-shirts over light pants or skirts. A few wear the L5-inspired kurta with incongruous corporate logos pasted all over.

The "L5 kurta" has spread across countries, though its wearers are sometimes subjected to attacks by gangs of reactionary youths who espouse "the Old Way, not the L5 Way".

Henry is sweating. His hanky is becoming soaked from wiping down his face. "Well, I must say that a steady forty degree heat does become oppressive. May I suggest we now adjourn to our air-conditioned limo?"

Outside, they gratefully climb back into their cool limo.

Gaging Henry's possible reaction to an unplanned diversion, Charon makes a suggestion. "Henry, Jimmy, would you mind if we went on a further excursion? I haven't been here in about fifteen years and I thought I'd never be able to return." A slight quaver in his voice causes George to glance over.

"We have all afternoon, my friend." George is wondering when and why Charon would have been in this part of the world? He ponders, *That would have been near the start of the L5 Project…*

Charon leans forward to see the car's map on the centre console. "Ah, Messenhoef, would you mind taking *that* highway, please? It should go northeast, into the jungle."

Messenhoef looks to Henry for approval. The cool air is blowing directly at Henry's face. "Yes yes. Whatever he wishes." Henry goes back to absorbing the car's cool air.

After a drive through Selangor's outskirts, the e-limo emerges on a long stretch of causeway about three metres above the surrounding shrub vegetation. A hundred metres on either side, the deep green jungle bursts forth. The intermediate area next to the causeway is cleared several times a year for security purposes.

They drive at high-speed along the well-maintained road, with hardly another vehicle to pass. Then they see, a kilometre beyond at the far side of a slow curve in the road, something that Charon did not believe would still be there.

"That mound of shells! Way ahead. Stop there!" His excitement is infectious. They all sit up to stare at the distant mound of shells as the e-limo slows down well before it.

Messenhoef and Henry are now in high alert, scanning the area intently. There have been numerous reports of gangs of young, armed men in the area.

With pleasure in his voice, Charon announces, "So, I will indoctrinate you, my friends, into the ancient ritual of the Durian, shall I?"

George is willing to play along. "Fine by me, Charon. What the heck is it?"

As if reciting in a trance, Charon remembers the words told to him many years ago. "Durian is the King of Fruit. It has tastes so sublime they cannot be described by any simple comparison. It is not like *this* taste or *that* taste. It is more akin to the flavour descriptions of fine wines."

"It tastes like wine?"

"No no. By that I mean the way one *discusses* wines of this region or that, and aged in certain ways, and having a spectrum of certain flavours. Durian is quite simply unique in the world of fruit. Fine cheeses may receive such culinary description. And, while some seafood may be regaled in like manner, only Durian in all the world may be rightly placed beside wines and cheeses as deserving of legendary status." He smiles. "But only if eaten on the day it is picked from the jungle."

Henry looks at Charon to see if he is pulling his leg. The vehicle has slowed to a crawl as Messenhoef continues scanning.

"Durian is that impressive?" Provoked by Charon's introduction, Henry is grateful for a diversion.

"My friend, you cannot understand this until you have witnessed it with your own tongue. So I will tell you a few things about Durian and then, when you taste it, you will begin to understand." Charon licks his lips.

"Ok. Now, Durian is a bigger fruit than coconut. It has a similar light green leathery shell as fresh coconut but with dull spikes over it. That's the Malaysian variety. There are some differences in other regions." He looks at George to see if there are any questions.

Seeing none, "Inside, there are either four or five sections full of a white pulp, except for the centre of each section, which cradles the actual fruit. These are about the size and appearance of lightly boiled eggs, without the shell. Are you with me?"

The e-limo is creeping forward slowly as Messenhoef peers around for trouble.

George shrugs. "So far so good."

"And the whole fruit, prior to opening it, smells horribly of sewer stench."

George does a double take. But Charon is not smiling.

"Charon, you're not providing me with that element of tantalizing possibilities that would necessarily induce me to partake of the King of Fruit."

"Ha ha! Wait for it. You see, Durian is the prized fruit, not only of man, but also of the Men-of-the-Jungle."

"You mean orangutans?"

"Precisely. Now, because orangutans are spread so thinly throughout the jungle, Durian must broadcast their availability, at the proper time, in a manner that may be best distributed over such a vast and difficult-to-traverse area."

"So they stink like a sewer? Couldn't they have chosen something nicer, like mint or or…"

"My friend. They did not choose. The nature that is within them is their only tool-chest."

"Ok, whatever. So how do you get all those lovely flavours to your tongue when all you can smell is a sewer?"

"Remember, first, that one does not taste a wine with one's tongue. Wines are tasted, primarily, with the nose."

"That makes it worse, doesn't it?"

Waving that off, "Durian is a mystical fruit, as you will see. Its lovely spectrum of tastes do not need the nose." Charon gets animated. "Once opened by an expert, you will *notice no smell*! Then, with the fruit in your mouth – don't bite it just yet! – you will wonder at the delicate flavours and textures, one after the other, that chase themselves about your tongue. And besides, have you ever seen what the grapes look like for that delightful Canadian beverage, Ice Wine, prior to pressing? They are an ugly mess of molding, half-shriveled, cobwebbed, frozen globs of wrinkled fruit!"

Scrunching his nose, George shakes his head. "Ok, so, first it stinks to high heaven, and then things chase each other around my tongue. Maybe we should just go back to that veggie restaurant in Selangor."

Charon turns to face George, about to say something less polite. George puts a hand up, "Hey, you know me! I'm open to new ideas. It's just that the Durian marketing department needs a good wordsmith."

Nodding, Charon goes back to staring intently at the jungle beyond the approaching pile of shells. "You must understand what will occur, in an intellectual sense. Otherwise, you will be inclined to lump things into categories. Without this brief description you would have smelled the broadcast signal of the fruit and thought, this thing has gone royally BAD!"

"Yeah. Whatever." George shakes his head but flashes a smile at Charon.

The wiry grass leading to the jungle contains wild mixes of broad-leafed plants and, to Henry, a surprising number of small-leafed shrubs – not unlike the deciduous meadows of his home. He takes in the scenery, wondering why there are no dwellings.

The e-limo has slowed to a stop. Charon suddenly reaches forward to tap the horn lightly. As Charon sits back, looking for movement from the jungle, Messenhoef reaches for something in the centre compartment. George has the impulsive thought that he is going to pull out a gun. Instead, Messenhoef pulls out a bottle of insect repellent and hands it to Henry, who silently lathers the stuff on, then hands the bottle over to George and Charon. George scrutinizes the ingredients list with care, then dabs some on.

While Charon rubs on the repellent, he scans the jungle carefully. Now seeing someone quickly hurrying toward them, Charon opens his door and is slammed by the oppressive heat and humidity of the jungle. As they all exit the e-limo, except for Messenhoef, they begin to sweat, developing growing patterns of dark wetness on their shirts. Biting flies and mosquitoes find them, then hover in high-pitched anger a short distance from the protection of the repellent. George is particularly attacked. He grabs the repellent from Charon and lathers more on.

The person approaching from the jungle is not who Charon is anticipating. The young, short Malay woman has a vicious-looking machete slung at her belt. Her clothes are as colourful as constant aggressive washing without machines can keep them. Charon is surprised. He was expecting a man. *His daughter?*

Charon waves at the young woman as she approaches the pile of husks. At the causeway she climbs narrow steps that have been left huskless up the embankment. Showing no fear of the strangers she turns to Charon. "Want durian?"

Trying to remember from a generation ago, he exchanges greetings in Malay. She smiles at his attempt. In English, "How many?"

Not sure if her smile is for his attempt or for what he may have inadvertently said, Charon carries on, holding up his four fingers and a thumb. "Five."

"Eat here?"

At Charon's nod she disappears back across the clearing to an almost invisible hut inside the jungle's fringe. It is little more than what is called a *hide*. Out of necessity, living so close to the causeway they must not be visible. That strategy had been burned into her memory by what happened to her parents.

At her yelled instruction on the way, large green fruits are placed in a red mesh bag by a younger girl. Then, at a jog, the two bring their bag and a small folding table back up to the road.

Charon remembers not to breathe too hard, but the odour isn't as strongly overpowering as he remembered.

Henry sniffs the air. "That is not so bad. In fact… you know, it is the same smell that plagued us when my wife and I drove down to Cape Canaveral to see the launches. Whatever it was, that sewer smell was up and down the Florida coast that year."

Charon smiles at Henry, noting the facts he just dropped. *He's older than I thought.* "So, you see – it is not to be feared, eh?"

The two Malay sisters set up the table so their guests will stand upwind as the fruits are placed in a circle. Nodding, the older sister, Noor, takes a knobby durian in her hand, pulls out the machete and, with blinding speed, goes whack-whack-whack, splitting it open in exactly in the right place to reveal, as Charon correctly remembered, a fibrous white pulp gently cradling what looks, to George, for all the world like a poached egg in each section.

With furrowed brows, George says, "It doesn't smell anymore!"

Noor produces the ubiquitous tablespoon – a utensil used to eat any of the larger fruits throughout rural Malaysia.

Charon is given the first taste. He pops the spoonful, whole, into his mouth. Savouring the flavours before biting down on it, Charon's face melts into a contented smile. Still playing with the fruit with his tongue, he nods for George to try one.

The soft fruit gently surprises every nerve in his mouth. George hesitates biting into it, thinking that the texture, too, is like a poached egg. Slowly moving his tongue over the yielding surface he notices distinct but delicate flavours. He slowly bites down on it. The flow of flavours keep coming, subtly and with a remarkable variety of… of colour, is the only word he can think of.

He swallows, then instantly regrets it. The delicious flavours linger for a short time.

"Ohh. I loved that!… Shouldn't have gulped it."

Another one is ready for Charon on the spoon.

"Yes, thank you." He tries to remember Malay for thank you. "Terima kasih."

A broad smile appears across the Noor's face, displaying a missing tooth.

They both take their next offering much more slowly.

Henry is anxious to try it. Noor's young sister steps away as Henry pushes past George with a grunt. Keeping his tastebuds focused on the delicious second helping of fruit, Charon mumbles, "It's ok." He indicates with closed mouth and hand signals that Henry should be given a spoonful. Noor obliges, reluctantly.

Charon thinks, *It doesn't take much analysis for strangers to distrust Henry. Their constant glances to the car show a learned fear… I wonder if she can write English?*

As Henry's tastebuds are tickled by his delightful mouthful, Charon pulls out his Pad to tap a note on it so Noor can see:

Write English?

She nods, politely taking the proffered Pad. With quick trial-and-error, Noor figures out the keyboard. She taps out:

yes thank you so much i remember you com to my father many yeer past

Charon almost breaks into tears. He makes sure Henry does not see his eyes. Noor stares deeply into Charon's eyes then types more:

was veri yong father mother kild after you com terorst frum north

Hesitating for an instant to remember if he should touch Noor, he gently takes her hands as she holds the Pad. They nod silently to each other.

The three work their way through another durian. George has noticed the exchange between Noor and Charon but Henry is fully engrossed in tasting the King of Fruit. He does not see that Charon slips Noor a business card with a large sum of local currency.

Charon thinks, *Nothing else I can do to help them at this time.*

Henry finishes his first taste with, "Thank you so very much. You were absolutely right. Durian is the king of fruit." He half-bows to Charon.

George distracts Henry away from Charon. "So, what do you think of the flavours?"

Henry has taken another fruit and shakes his head, indicating with his hand that he just wants to savour the taste. It does not take long for the fruit in the five durians to be consumed.

As the two tablespoons are handed back, Noor whispers to her sister to pack up. They toss the empty shells onto the pile by the road and fold up their table. Having received much more than they'd been expecting, Noor bows deeply several times to Charon then quickly to George, touching her forehead toward them both.

On the way back to the car, the three swat at ever more aggressive mosquitoes and pile quickly into the cool limo.

The frigid air hits them hard. They almost shiver as they settle into the seats.

Henry is delighted. "That was absolutely worth the trip, Charon." He slaps at a buzzing insect that got in with them.

George wraps his arms across his chest, buttoning up his coat. "Whew! I was just getting used to the heat outside."

As Messenhoef drops the air conditioning's fan speed to a dull roar, the three look back to the jungle but cannot locate the sisters or their hut. Henry slaps at another wayward bug.

Smiling, Charon turns to George, "So what did you think?"

George pauses in thought. "At first, I was looking for some strong tingling on the tongue, like pineapple. You know, pineapple was there along with pears and a hundred other flavours, but they were so delightfully subtle! Like you said, they chased each other around my tongue… I don't think I can describe it in a simple way – except to say a very sincere thank you for the experience. I most certainly am a convert to the King of Fruit!"

Henry nods in agreement. A satisfied smile and a brief acknowledgement from Charon, as they drive back out of the jungle.

An idea hits Charon. *L5 is like Durian. Never thought of that before…*

Noor and her sister hurry home.

In their jungle hide-away, Noor puts a hand to her mouth to indicate silence to her sister. She slips out to her secret place to stash the unaccustomed large wad of currency, and the business card. She will study it later.

From the far side of the road's great bend, a group of thugs/terrorists had been watching through binoculars. With the e-limo gone, they rapidly descend on the hut with Noor's sister inside. They tie the terrified girl's hands as they ransack the small hut, looking for money. Not finding anything of value, they turn to the girl, demanding to know where her sister is. They torture her, rape her, but the terrified girl remains silent. A knife into her belly is their final act.

Meanwhile, Noor has been forced to hide. She hears everything from a distance, huddling on a wide branch in abject fear and horror at what the thugs are doing to her sister.

The thugs finally leave the girl's body and, after a fruitless search for Noor, the thugs skulk away to their next conquest.

The sun goes down quickly in the jungle. Knowing what she will find but praying it will not be so, Noor slips back to her hut.

In the dark forest Noor cries inconsolably for her sister through the night. She cries to Datuk Kong, guardian spirit of the jungle. She cries to the morning light with eyes reddened and bloodshot.

The early light brings to Noor the reality of the horribly distorted body of her sister on the hut floor. It is too much for Noor. She breaks down, collapsing over the body, wailing.

Next day, a numb Noor goes to a nearby stream to bring water. She washes her sister's body, dresses her in their finest clothing, places a red sash over her belly, then digs a grave beside her father and mother.

Noor does not count the days. Her mind is deadened. She nibbles detachedly on the few fruit or the nuts that hadn't been taken in the ransacking. Her face is streaked with tears that carved gutters through dirt down her cheeks. She does not count her sleepless nights.

Some time later, loud honks wake Noor from her blank stare on the edge of the deep jungle. Her body propels itself without real consciousness and Noor finds herself at her secret hiding place. Coins and money are in her hands. And the card. Old habits are awakened by the weight of the money, making her more aware of her surroundings. Noor wraps most of what's in her hands into a secret pocket in a fold of her dress. She runs to the edge of the jungle to suspiciously peer at who is honking. A convoy of brightly coloured vehicles of all sorts has stopped at the pile of husks. Noor steps out to shout, "NO DURIAN!"

A voice shouts back in English, "YOU MUST COME WITH US! TERRORISTS ARE COMING!"

Noor's head sinks. Standing alone in the cleared area, she mumbles, "Too late. I am already dead."

A man from the convoy scrambles down the embankment to run toward Noor.

Her impulse is to flee into her jungle. To hide forever in her special world of trees and birds and perfumed flowers and all the little insects that have been her home. But her feet do not move.

The bearded man is before her. He respectfully reaches out. She places a hand on his, then… Noor collapses.

Noor finds herself leaning against someone on the hard wooden bench of a very bumpy minibus. The convoy is making its way to the big city. One of the older women near Noor smiles at her. The woman takes pity on her. Wetting a cloth, the woman dabs at Noor's face to clean off her grime.

Their destination is a huge tent city on the outskirts of Kuala Lampur. The convoy is met by guards who insist that everyone steps out of their conveyances. They are directed to lines leading to open tents where they eventually meet officials who say they will help them.

There, Noor is given a bag with toiletry essentials and a blanket. At the first opportunity, in one of the mobile toilets, Noor secrets her money in the bag then washes some grime off her dress. Back in the lines, she holds her worldly possessions tightly to her chest as she is directed this way and that from one line to another in the tent city.

After a group meal under a huge tent with open sides, she is to be processed, which means that Noor must wait in yet another endless line until she is directed to another tent in a neat line of open tents.

One of the people in the tent now before her speaks to her in Malay, asking where Noor is from, what her name is, etc., etc. During that interrogation, Noor realizes that parts of her dress are still soiled and she becomes embarrassed. She pulls at the dress to even out the creases and folds. At that, a business card falls to the ground. A person in the tent notices the card. He comes around the table to pick it up. His eyes open wide. The next thing Noor knows, she is hurried over to another tent where her escort, still holding her card, chatters quickly at that tent's occupants. The symbol on a banner at the rear of this tent is a silver donut with a large "L5" printed over it. The same symbol is on her card.

The woman at this tent's table looks Noor up and down. "What do you know of the rainforest, my dear? We are in need of specialized knowledge."

Traveling

ON THE MOVE

Kuala Lumpur, Then Moscow and Frankfurt

Charon sits, lost in thought on a white leather couch in the lobby of the hotel where they spent the night. George and Henry are hovering over him. The marble patterns on the floor are taking Charon's attention. The realization strikes him that they have no marble on L5. Somehow, that morphs into the thought that it might well be a futile exercise to try to make life survive in L5. *It is barren. Here, there has been almost four billion, FOUR BILLION, years for life's immense complexity to evolve. How can we possibly hope to recreate even the smallest part of that with some scraps from Earth and a bunch of rocks from the Moon?*

Henry harumps. "Ah, Charon?"

George interjects, "Do you want to join us? We're going to see if the flight schedule is changed."

Looking up from his revere, Charon mumbles to George, "I'll just wait for you here, then. If that connecting flight gets back into tonight's schedule, I'm willing to go at any time."

George and Henry nod and leave Charon in the lobby still contemplating the marble patterns and the meaning of life.

Later, a young Asian businessman walks from the front desk toward Charon. He places his wheeled luggage next to Charon. With an English accent, he politely asks, "Do you mind if I sit here, please?" He smiles at Charon, indicating the other end of the couch.

Charon gives him a respectful nod and smile. "Not at all. Here, I can slip over a bit." He slides over on the couch.

The man sits down. "I have been sitting entirely too long, today, but my feet are tired as well." Looking at Charon. "My flight has been postponed tonight. I was hoping for a good night's rest before my meeting tomorrow in Shanghai."

"Oh? We may be on the same flight. I was supposed to be in Shanghai, tonight, as well." Charon shrugs. "Happens a lot these days, I understand – with the meltdown of the aviation industry."

"Yes, and in so many other aspects of what we had been pleased to call 'civilization'. The climate crisis does throw a major spanner into the works." He shakes his head. "So you haven't been in KL long?" He continues an unwavering stare at Charon.

"No. As a matter of fact, I was just passing through. On my way to, ah, Moscow." Charon pauses, wondering if he should continue the conversation. *Well, why not?*

Charon feels the need for meaningless small-talk. "If they'd've been able to tell us how long the delay was to be, I would have liked to tour the Petronas Towers. They're still an architectural wonder."

Shaking his head, "Sir, in all honesty, there is nothing to see from inside the towers – it is from the outside that one may view the majesty of the towers themselves. An office is an office. Marble floors are marble floors. And then, as you know, the towers have been superseded by buildings that are much taller, still." He shrugs his shoulders and finally releases Charon from his stare.

The Asian double-takes as he notices a lovely young woman in a minimal miniskirt and much makeup, standing at the front desk. The same thin, older, dark-suited Malay from the pewter factory is whispering to her from behind the desk.

An announcement on the lobby speakers is in Chinese.

The man beside Charon gets up quickly, nodding/bowing to him. "Perhaps we shall see each other again." He goes to the front desk, dragging his wheeled case, taking in the form of the young lady with a sideways stare.

As the man has a brief discussion with the front desk attendant, the woman-of-much-makeup starts to walk quickly toward Charon's couch. A quick harsh whisper from the Malay suit stops her in mid-stride. She then carries on with a seductive slide.

She displays in front of Charon, then slowly, seductively, sits down beside him.

Without looking at her, but entirely aware of her, Charon squeezes away from her against the couch's arm rest.

She tries hard to be sultry. "Hello, there."

No response from Charon.

"I've had such a long day. Flying makes me sooo tired!"

No response from Charon.

"So, how are *you* feeling after your long flight?"

Without looking at her, Charon responds coldly, "My dear, I've never seen you before. And I understand that the management frowns on illicit liaisons in their lobby."

Sudden commotion in the office behind the front desk. The Malay suit reappears behind the counter. He gives a quick tapping to the top of his head, at which the Lady gets up immediately. In her haste to join him in the back office her stiletto heels slip on the marble and she catches herself on the counter to avoid an unceremonious fall.

Charon takes his Pad from his shirt pocket and quietly dictates a note:

> *Same old guy behind the front desk. Sent out a hooker to sit beside me. When I said that she shouldn't be here, old guy gave her the British military signal for come here now. Malay military intelligence?*

Charon puts the Pad back into his shirt pocket.

Several hours later, the weary group of Charon, George and Henry are walking through the Shanghai airport. They decide to stop for a quick snack. Too exhausted by the traveling to talk, the group munch and sip silently.

Charon is most affected by the air travel due to the Earth-bound gravity. Forcing himself to finish a tuna sandwich, he finds that his head has sunk down almost to his coffee. At a concerned glance from George, he smiles. "Haven't had tuna on L5, of course.

Thought I might enjoy it. Now, I don't remember having eaten it." He slowly shakes away some cobwebs.

Later, they rise to drag themselves to their next airplane. On to Moscow. They each have the same thought. *Perhaps to sleep on the plane? Would be nice.*

Fitful sleep comes to George and Henry.

Moscow airport is much less colourful than was Shanghai's, even though it was not noticed.

Exiting from the airplane at Moscow, George frowns and pulls out his Pad. He reads from it, then whispers to a bleary-eyed Charon.

"Emergency message. Don't be surprised – just follow my lead."

Charon cocks his bleary eyes at George.

As they turn down the corridor, Henry is suddenly very closely joined by someone who plainly acts as his superior. The larger man, Klaus, aggressively takes Henry's arm and marches him into an office marked "Security" just off the gate corridor. Four suited associates surround George and Charon, herding them immediately behind Henry and Klaus.

In the room, Klaus takes Henry into a corner. Henry puts up a token defense, in German, to Klaus' curt questioning. Henry pulls open his shirt to show where the implanted, disabled bug still festers under his skin.

Klaus stares at the slightly reddened spot. He turns on George and Charon to speak at them with a heavy German accent.

"My apologies for dis geschwind, ah, fast, ah, exit, gentlemen. We had very sudden warning, discovered by undercover agents, that terrorist cell has plan to make assassination attempt on our esteem guest from space." He nods sharply at Charon. "So, of course, we act with…"

George butts in, "Which terrorists?"

"I am sorry?"

"My friend, I asked which terrorists were to do this dastardly deed?"

Klaus blusters briefly. "Well, ah, our informants were very clear. It was small break-away wing of, ah, Chechnya rebels – a particularly bloodthirsty…"

George breaks in again with a stiff smile. "My own staff have been very diligent in clearing our way, and they have no – absolutely zero – indication of any indication of such an attack. With the sole exception of…" George pulls out his own Pad and reads from it, then shows it to Klaus, "…one Klaus Degelman, who, it seems, is accompanied by four spearcarriers – Erik Eserink, Anders Stokstad, David Rohr, and Marten Kobilski." He looks up at Klaus. "Are these pictures familiar, my friend?"

George puts his Pad's screen close to Klaus' face then takes it away. "Now. We have a plane to catch. Henry will continue to accompany us. You, my friend, will not."

Henry stifles a reflexive laugh. He covers his mouth as he quickly shuffles by his stunned German associates.

With a flourish, Henry holds the door open for Charon and George, then scurries quickly after them with an over-the-shoulder, half-hearted shrug at Klaus.

Frankfurt, the following day

After a night's tossing attempt at sleep in a Frankfurt hotel, Charon and George decide they need to clear their heads by stepping out of the blocky old hotel. Across the street is a sign for a sprawling complex called "Messe-und-Ausstellungs-Gelande".

George points out the sign, saying, "That's the Trade Fair Grounds, Charon. It's why Henry couldn't get a room here. Busy place. And, we now have an interest in this hotel…" He throws a thumb back at the hotel and smiles. "Hope you didn't want any more of the little weasel's company?"

"No, thank you, Jimmy. Henry's ok, other than being obsequious in an old European way. But as Larry said, we do need friends in many places. And speaking of old European customs, I'm glad to hear that L5 is, what?, part owners of the hotel?" As he speaks, he notices unusual activity on his Pad. The security app shows four orange stars out of five on top of the screen. He drops his Pad into a pocket.

Slowing his pace, George confirms, "Well, we're into the holding company. Trying to stay out of the limelight. You know…"

"Right. Anyway, leaving my shoes outside the door overnight was a bit disconcerting."

George can't help letting out a guffaw, "HA! The new manager wanted to try a few throw-back ideas. Anyway…"

Charon gives him a wry grimace. "So. What's the agenda?"

They are walking down to an intersection as they talk. Several people collect with them at the traffic light, then they head for the Fair Grounds. Keeping an eye on who is near them, they continue their conversation as they walk. The sidewalk becomes crowded with more Fair attendees from the previous intersection.

Charon notes the traffic pattern of weaving e-bikes mixed in with EVs. The low whine of motors and slap of tires brings back memories to Charon. *Transit vehicles outnumber the cars. No roaring diesels or gas-spewers. Oh well. Too little, too late.*

George lowers his voice and leans over to Charon. "Our envoy's been in contact with Juergen's family. They've been using a lawyer who, we think, is being secretly paid by the German government. But that's ok. He seems to be in it just for the money. An honest lawyer." He smiles.

Crossing the final street to the Fair Grounds, Charon brings up a non sequitor. "I've been thinking…"

"About…"

"Bonobos."

George does a quick head shake. "What brought that up?"

Taking in the diverse crowd, Charon smiles, "May I give you a loose analogy, Jimmy? To me, it seems that L5ers might be similar to bonobos, as most of humanity here are closer to chimps."

"Ok, I'll bite. What the hell are you talking about?" George is keeping a wary eye on people who may be staying close to them.

Charon's smile widens. "You know, of course, the way that bonobos resolve disputes?"

"Ah, well…" His forehead wrinkles.

"They snuggle."

Recognition comes to George. "Oh yeah. They, well…"

"Have platonic sex. Rather a lot."

Despite being uncomfortable with the topic, George slows his walk as he thinks about it. "Is that really a possibility? I mean, platonic…"

They come to a stop in the middle of the sidewalk, forcing the now surging crowd to walk around them. Charon notices expressions of impatience on many so he nods to the side and the two head toward the nearby building. He gets jostled as they make their way off the traveled part of the sidewalk. A testy young fellow who bumps into Charon doesn't stop. Charon follows him with an eye as he continues his thought.

"So, L5ers are freed of many of the long-standing habits and constraints that have entrenched humanity down here since farming made us conservative – earth-bound." He nods, looking for agreement.

Instead, he notices a tightening of George's eyes. "I don't mean to sound judgmental when I say that. It is merely an observation… What do you think, Jimmy?"

George is reluctant to utter what comes to mind. *Having sex all the time is probably why bonobos are essentially extinct in the wild. What kind of ideal is that?*

Then he reconsiders. "But you *need* conflict, don't you? That's how humanity has progressed, like it or not."

Charon leans against the wall to ease his leadened legs. He replies slowly, not wanting to seem too aggressive. "Yes, Jimmy, I agree that conflict has served us well. That's the standard modus operandi for life on Earth… But L5ers are no longer **on** Earth." He lets that sink in. "Having rutting bucks and punk-packs slam away at each other just to have a better chance at a, a desirable sexual partner, is that the ultimate goal in life? The ultimate goal **of** life?"

George is uneasy with this conversation. All his young life, he has not had a companion with whom he could free his thoughts to such an extent. *And while I really like this guy, we are going to have to leave this for a much later time.*

"Too deep for me, my friend. Can we park this for later?"

A slight shrug from Charon eases George's anxiety.

With people continuing to hurry past, George nods back at the hotel. "We've set up a meeting in the hotel for this afternoon at five. They've accepted our offer of supper after the meeting. Should be about a dozen of 'em, plus us and Henry, if you want?" George sees Charon's nodding agreement.

"We booked the Atrium. Supposed to be a big historic mural of the conquest of Brazil. Colonialism long gone by, and all that."

They join the flowing crowd again.

Turning onto a busy pedestrian thoroughfare in the grounds, "The lawyer said he'll bring along their family doctor. We've asked him to be ready for questions about any family illnesses that could possibly be related to Juergen's death. Should have his DNA profile, to show good faith. We've already done a bio match, anyway, as you requested. He *is* Juergen Mittelsohn and these are his immediate family. Our DNA analysis shows nothing that could've caused his death from a genetic respiratory aspect."

Charon stops at a display of sweets, raising an eyebrow at George.

George gives a slight shake of the head. He returns to the topic at hand, "*You* know. We're just politely going through the motions."

An older woman vacantly jostles into Charon. He smiles and nods at her, wondering why she looks familiar. The two carry on silently. Charon is not used to the bustle. *I feel like a country bumpkin. Bump-into-kin. Whatever. Tired...*

At another fast food stand, Charon nods at the counter to George, who shrugs apologetically.

"Can't go there, either. Allergies. Some places I can trust. Too many variables here. Are you thirsty?"

"Oh, I'm sorry, Jimmy! Wasn't thinking. Yeah, just thought I might get an orange juice, if they have it." He reconsiders after a quick check of his Pad - which is now showing five orange stars and a bold note. "That's ok, I'll leave it until we get back." He feels vaguely through his pockets. "Could use a tissue, though, speaking of allergies. I was warned that there are several mega-billion more things on Earth that could hit my atrophied immune system. They shot me up with an array of mRNA immune system stimulators, but..."

George stops for a minute to consider another of the implications of living in L5 versus on good old Earth. Charon pauses with him. They both look around.

"Why don't you find us a place to sit for a while, Jimmy. I'll be right along." He heads to a fast food outlet that has tissues available on a side counter.

As George is searching for a place to sit, Charon quickly scribbles a one-word note on a tissue.

He joins George at the bench. A sigh escapes as he plops down. Charon absently places the tissue on his leg, where George can read the note while they talk.

"Lot'sa history in this old town, Jimmy." He waves one hand at the landscape. "Surprised it's not the EU capital."

George glances at the note. "Yeah, well… politics, eh?"

The note says: *Bugged?*

George scans it quickly.

Charon takes the tissue to blow his nose into it, then crumples it up. As he holds the tissue in one hand he quickly pulls out his Pad. Charon does a double-take and stares at the blank screen. It flashes, then gets back online with screen activity. George is looking sideways at it, too. Charon shrugs. George looks puzzled – shakes his head.

"Something's screwed up. Oh, and we'll have to hurry back to prepare for the meeting."

They get up to head back to the hotel in silence.

On the way, Charon throws the shredded tissue into a receptacle.

In the hotel they both quietly do a reset of their Pads. Seeing nothing unusual, they silently start deep scans. With hand signals, Charon indicates that they should leave their Pads in the room to let them go through the deep scan procedure. George points to the Pads and holds up two fingers, mouthing, *Two hours.*

Playing Games

THE ATRIUM ROOM

Supper time

Hotel staff are bustling in and out of the hotel's old-fashioned, ornate meeting room.

Charon and George are sitting with their backs to the far wall. A great circular skylight provides light from the waning sun. The final slide that Charon had presented is still on the wide screen behind him. The black-and-white picture shows the donut shape of L5 with a faintly blue-green-orange Earth some distance in the background.

A dozen members of Juergen's family sit solemnly at the near end by the open doors. Henry is in conversation with the family lawyer, Paul Loewenberg, along with the doctor who is next to him. The doctor has taken up the role of translator for Charon and George. Loewenberg speaks English with a heavy accent. The doctor does not know that Charon speaks several languages, including German, and Charon politely allows him to continue helping.

Henry has returned to his obsequious persona. "The family agrees that your report, Charon, seems to be quite comprehensive; however, there remains that nagging question – if you don't mind – how could this have *possibly* happened in reality?"

In halting words, Loewenberg adds, "Please understand, sir, that, that, ah, explanation is coinciding with the pictures. I agree and to have seen the, ah, circles was brilliant! But still, **how**? This is not possible, no?"

Charon shrugs. "Occam's Razor. You know the reference?"

"Occam, yes yes, I understand, but…"

"The simplest solution, the one requiring the fewest assumptions and variables, is usually the right one. We only needed to collect all the evidence…"

"But, sir… that one variable is, must be, impossible! No?"

Charon pushes on, "…and the facts, themselves, point to the answer, as improbable as it is…"

Henry is confused. "Occam's Razor? Meaning…"

Politely, Charon turns to Henry. "In L5, there is no dogmatic fog. We deal in facts." Charon smiles at the lawyer and the nearby family members who are trying to understand. A young teenager is in rapt attention.

Charon rises to freely move his arms while speaking. "We have the advantage of seeing things without them being obscured by extraneous, by outside issues. For us, we are separated from instant death by a thin wall of aluminum and some moonrocks packed along the outside. Life becomes more uncomplicated under those circumstances. Many of the issues that are considered critical here on Earth, have no relevance in L5. And vice versa."

Loewenberg tries a wry grin, "You are, perhaps, making a political statement, sir?"

Charon shakes his head. "If politics is what you believe makes the strongest filter to understanding…"

Henry becomes the diplomat. "Now, now, gentlemen."

"Not at all, Heinrik. I think your space friend makes, ah, good sense, ja."

The teenager nods vigorously as he stares at the picture of L5 behind Charon, then grins as he notices the food being brought in.

Waiters wheel in their main course.

It is night and Charon is running down the hotel hallway, dragging a frightened maid by the arm. They get to George's room where Charon yells out, "JIMMY!"

He takes the maid's hand roughly and points it at the door.

"OPEN! *BAHRTEST AUF*! OPEN DOOR!"

Wildly gesturing at her just makes her more frightened. She cringes against the wall next to the door.

He pulls the card-lock from her wrist and inserts it in the door himself. It takes a second try. He bursts through the door. The maid backs away to the other side of the hallway, slumping against the far wall.

George is on the floor, in agony, with his neck and face inflamed. An unused self-application syringe is on the floor beside him. Charon grabs the syringe and jabs it into George's upper chest. He yells at the maid.

"CALL AMBULANCE! RAFEN SIE EINEN KRANKENWAGEN!" [*CALL AN AMBULANCE*]

She finally sees what needs to be done and rushes to the phone in the room to dial for help.

Charon sees George's Pad on a desk. He hits the panic code.

In less than a minute rushing steps are heard in the hallway. Two people – L5 guards dressed in civvies – storm into the room. The first guard, Mahim, takes over.

"Allergy?"

Charon nods sharply, "Looks like. She's called for an ambulance. I think. Confirm it. I gave an injection from this."

Charon is still holding the syringe.

The injection acts quickly, causing George to groan.

Guard 2 is on the phone while Mahim and Charon try to make George comfortable.

The bright hospital room has only one bed, occupied by George.

He is breathing heavily through an oxygen mask and has an IV tube and several wires attached to him. His swollen, reddened eyes open and close at Mahim and Charon at his side. A nurse comes in. Charon makes way for the nurse, who checks the instrument readings then wipes down George's forehead.

Charon asks her, "Do you speak English?"

"Yes, a little."

"Can you tell us any more? The doctor was unable…"

"The doctor is, how-you-say, prejudice."

Mahim takes out his Pad and enters a message.

She adds, "Your friend, now stable. Must wait if his blood and oxygen levels are stable to his head. Tomorrow."

"Tomorrow, what?"

"Will know more tomorrow. Leave now. Get sleep. Tomorrow we know. I stay here." She shoos them out.

Early next morning Charon uses his hotel room phone to speak with Mahim at George's bedside in the hospital. George is weak but bleary-eyed awake.

Mahim is speaking on the hospital room's landline. "…yeah, he's already asking medical questions of the nurse. I think he'll be alright."

Charon's voice is tight with anxiety. "Can I speak with him?"

Mahim over looks at George. "Well…"

George nods his head, indicating that he wants the telephone. Reaching around all the wires and tubes, George takes the phone to croak, "Want a ticket to L5. Safer up there."

"Jimmy! It's very good to hear you. You gave us a damn scare, you son-of-a-raven!"

"Yeah. Right… I don't mind a challenge, Charon, but this is pretty full-on…" He coughs.

Mahim takes the phone from George.

Charon hears the cough and scraping noises, "Jimmy? Mahim?"

"Listen Charon. Yeah, he'll be ok. His throat's pretty sore. I'm just gonna let him rest, now. I'll call if anything new happens, I promise."

"Thanks, Mahim. Just use the Pad. I might be out. Oh! *No*. No Pad for now. Landline only."

Mahim is concerned. "Out? Wait a minute. No Pad?…"

"Call Security via landline. I'll be around the hotel. I need a walk. Leave a message on my landline."

Charon clicks off then enters Larry's number. "Larry? You hear the one about Benoit and the phone?" Then he hangs up immediately and waits for it to ring. *He better not be so asleep that he can't remember that security code.*

The ring comes several minutes later.

A puffing Larry is on the line. "Do you realize there's no such bloody thing as a landline anymore? I had to run in my friggen pajamas, such as they are, up to the Comms room…"

"Shut up Larry. Pads may be compromised. And Jimmy was sent into anaphylactic shock overnight."

"WHAT! How's he?"

"Good. But I don't trust the hospital doctor… Ok, listen. The guard, Mahim…"

"*Our* guard?"

"Yeah, he's in charge… I like him. Quiet, but absolutely in charge… He's very competent. But Jimmy needs a live bio connection and to hell with security…"

"Yeah! There *was* a weird comm interruption yesterday!…"

"Get Security on that right now. Ah, Jimmy looked better this morning. They said that the indications were all good."

Larry's typing can be heard as he uses another devise to get information. "Still in hospital?"

"Yeah, over the next two days. Get our own doctor over there, ok?"

"Are *you* alright?"

"I'll be alright on my own, mother. Listen, I've finished the formalities, here. I'm just going to unwind a bit today."

Larry's vexation is barely held in check as he speaks with Charon at the same time as receiving information online. "This incident is a clear act of aggression. I'm being told… yes — that our highly secure comms system has been breached… They feel the hack has been focused and should not be able to happen again, Charon, but I agree that Pads need to be offline until we can be absolutely certain as to their method. Whoever is doing this is trying to upset your mission. I am uncomfortable with you staying…"

"Ok, so I want to be around for a while."

"Another day?"

"Yeah, fine. Jimmy should be ok by then."

"And you are going to keep your head down?"

"Just staying around the hotel, don't worry." Charon rolls his eyes at Larry's insistence on his safety.

Larry, as the person in charge, wants no risks to be taken while they are unsure of who the bad actors are. "How was Jimmy poisoned? Is it still in the room?"

Charon shakes his head. "Didn't even consider that, myself. Mahim's assistant started looking into it. He went right back up to the room and stayed there overnight."

"Overnight?"

"Yeah. Didn't find the agent right away, so he called…"

"Our staff doctor went there."

"You heard?"

"I'm hearing now, damnit! At least, that he attended…"

"Right. And the doctor walked him around the room until they came up with it. Only thing I was worried about is if there was a scope through the window on him walking around, holding the Pad camera."

Larry nods, "Yes, I just sent out the order to not use them until further notice. A bloody major hassle. We *should* be ok…"

"Inside, I guess we're clean, sure, but someone could've been looking through the window. And there was that comms reboot…"

"IT *Red* believes the reboot was the way they got in to the system so they could drop in their bot."

Charon rolls his eyes. "Let the *techs* work on it. We're not on the Blue team."

It is Larry's turn to roll his eyes. "You calling me a micromanager? And, yes, IT Blue is active."

Charon shakes his head. *If we're putting our Blue **offense** into action this could get hairy down here.*

"Anyway, you'll hear about it before I do, Larry. Ok, I'll call in random – using pattern F, ah, 4 to 7 and back. Ok? Talk to you later."

Larry jumps back in, "Wait... Roger on the pattern... Ah, you will be sent a secure text with... the special signon procedure. They say it will be a pain but absolutely necessary."

Another roll of his eyes, "Thanks."

Charon rehearses in his mind what contact timing he has committed to. *The minutes within successive hours from Fibonacci integers starting at the fourth number, going to the seventh, then looping back. Presuming I won't forget after the fifth iteration. Shit. Who comes up with this security stuff?*

Soon, against orders, Charon is ambling down a street near the hotel. Several younger people in front of him go into a pub, so he follows. He pats his Pad as he enters the door, then remembers it is offline. A sign in German says that they have live music today - a "highly acclaimed" klezmer band from Romania. Charon grins at the irony.

Dangerous Games

Late afternoon

The pub is already crowded. The band is warming up, casting wary eyes about the crowd. Their opening music is a slow piece that puts Charon into a delightful, melancholic mood. He slows down to the music as he slips through the crowd, nodding his head to the compelling rhythm.

Ignoring the band, two football (soccer) teams are having a rousing after-the-game drink at one end of the partially darkened L-shaped room. Charon finds a small booth on the other side near the stage.

A server comes by. Charon smiles at her attempt at being seductive. *I take it that's to get me to drink more? If you want seductive, come up to L5.*

In German, the server asks, "Ein Bier?" [*a beer?*] She thinks, *Gut aussehend.* [*handsome*]

"Ja bitte." [*yes please*]

Noticing the English newspaper on the table, she nods with a longish smile then turns away to put in the order.

As she leaves, Charon sighs, thinking, *Everything revolves around sex games. I guess that's the tradeoff with having a vibrant lifeforce on this planet. Jimmy was too uncomfortable with that bonobos idea is started to float. Oh well — another time.*

He looks around at the mix of people nearby. *Some things change. Some don't. The planet is in a climate crisis, heading for general climate friggen disaster, and here they are acting like nothing needs to be done about it.*

Satisfied that no immediate threat is obvious in the pub, he sits back and tries to relax with the music. He picks up the English-language newspaper that had enticed him to sit at this table in the first place. *Newspapers are making a comeback. Sort of. Have to dig hard past the ads to see any real news.*

A couple come in, wander around briefly, then sit in the booth next to his. They are arguing all the way. The woman is being quite aggressive, while the man, whom she calls Willie, is trying to calm her down.

Finally, the woman's escalating aggression gets to the point of her throwing the flowers from the table's centre vase at Willie. She misses and some flowers end up on Charon's table.

She gets up roughly and leaves. Willie turns to apologize to Charon. Seeing the newspaper, Willie switches from German to English.

"I'm very sorry, sir, to have involved you in the argument with my friend. Please accept my apologies."

Charon returns a polite, "Oh, that's ok."

Willie waves it away. "No, no, please. She was being a boor and I insist on offering you a drink. Besides, I need one, now, for a certainty!" He half-stands and catches the eye of the server. "BITTE!" [*please!*]

Still off his seat, Willie asks Charon, "Would you mind so much if I sit with you. It would be a great help if I could today see a, a non-hostile face for a few moments." He smiles engagingly.

Charon smiles back, indicating with a nod that Willie should join him. Charon touches the Pad in his shirt pocket then remembers again that it is off-line. *Should be ok if I just take a picture of him, just in case.*

As Charon appears to be checking his phone, he snaps a picture of Willie stepping around to the table.

Reaching out a hand, "Thank you very much. My name is Willie, Willie Schwartz."

"That's all right. Please call me Charon. I'm not doing anything in particular, so you're welcome to have a seat."

Charon keeps his smile, but looks around to see if anybody else is showing particular interest.

The server comes by. Willie speaks in slower German. "Can we please have two mugs of your best lager? Thank you."

She nods and leaves. Charon doesn't notice that Willie's former companion slips up to the bar to give the server a note rolled in currency and something else.

Charon's Pad display, barely visible in his pocket, comes on then blanks on its own.

Willie bends forward to put his elbows on the table, then leans his head onto his hands, apparently disconsolate.

"She is just not worth it. She was a, a dancer? you will call them? At a, well, a strip club. A friend warned me that they are, what he called, 'Klingons'. An English pun, no? Ha ha!" He lets out a short laugh.

"I should have listened. I do not listen well, my friends tell me. They say, you should remember that God gave you only one mouth but TWO ears! Ha ha!" His laugh is somewhat forced.

"The English love puns! They are almost as bad as the Canadians, ja? I was in Canada for a year, working on the west coast – such a lovely country! Have you ever been there?" His chattering is mildly aggravating but Charon is distracted by the occasional shouting of the footballers.

Charon nods at the end of Willie's sentences, finishing his own beer without thinking.

Willie carries on. "Almost as nice as around Zurich! But too many Chinese! Not for me! I speak German and English and French and even a little Spanish, but CHINESE? Impossible for me to understand what the language is about. Do you speak Chinese?"

Charon is reluctant to carry on with this line, but adds, "No. I know a few words of Japanese, but not Chinese."

"Yes, well, we must be cosmopolitan and accept guest workers from all over, in Germany. But I do not want to speak Chinese." He notices the server returning. "Oh! Here come our drinks!"

The server places the two mugs on the table and removes Charon's mostly empty glass. The mugs are different colours. Willie reaches over the brown one for the white mug, stretching awkwardly over the other mug to get at it.

"These mugs are very nice, don't you think?" He holds the white mug up. "I prefer them over the glass. They give you something to look at, if your friend is yelling at you! Ha, ha!"

Willie takes Charon's attention from the slight fizz that is dying down in Charon's mug by pointing out the embossed figures on his own mug.

"These lovely maids are most enticing, don't you think? And they do not argue back! Ha, ha! Prost!" Willie locks eyes on Charon, waiting for him to join in the toast.

Charon does the accepted routine. "Cheers!"

Next morning, Charon awakes on a disheveled bed with a ringing headache.

He sees that he is naked. His large belly obscures the view of his feet. The headache throbs as he bends up to look. He mumbles, "Stupid idiot. Fell for the stupid, friggen,,," His swearing peters out into a growling babble.

Pictures are on the bed beside him. Charon picks one up, giving a wry grimace at the image of him, eyes closed, in a compromising position in bed with his drinking partner of yesterday evening. The other pictures are similar. His anger competes with his headache, making for a growing red-faced irritability. "Need a shower."

Carefully getting up from the bed, he looks around for his clothes. They are tossed on a chair to the side. With a very slight nod, he sees his Pad sticking out of a pocket on the chair. He goes over to it and touches a few buttons. A red light flashes. He types in a message, then Charon heads for the washroom for a shower.

Later, as Charon pulls on his tee-shirt, two people enter his room with their own key.

Charon is not surprised by the sounds and makes no move to turn around.

One of the intruders, Willie, is accompanied by a rough-looking man with a gun. Willie points at the pictures on the bed.

With a surly attitude, "So, my dear Charon. We had a lot of fun, last night, as you can see. Ha, ha!" He steps closer. "Now. I would like to offer you a proposition…"

As Willie finishes the sentence, Mahim emerges from behind the front door with a bigger gun. It is aimed at the head of the gunman.

He speaks quietly but clearly. "You have three seconds to drop your gun or you are dead."

Ambushed, Willie's gunman spins his head in fear. As he sees the large gun pointed at his nose, he quickly drops his own weapon, putting his hands up. The weapon clatters away from his feet.

Willie looks around in fear. "It it makes no difference! We have the originals! You must tell your…"

Charon slips on his pants as he answers, his anger rising again. "Shut up. Sit on the floor, both of you, back to back. NOW!"

The frightened gunman drops right down. Willie is too confused to move. Mahim comes up behind him and gives him a slight whack across the back of his head with the gun barrel. Willie drops to the floor and scurries to get into position, eyes wide open on Mahim's weapon. He bends his head up, about to speak.

Wagging his finger slowly and menacingly, Charon steps in front of Willie's face, "Shut…UP!"

"B - But the pictures!…"

"Sex is a problem? You should know that the reputation we have in L5 for being sexually free is well-deserved." He winks at Mahim. "Now, any more chattering and you'll GET ME ROYALLY ANNOYED!"

Willie is still trying to say something. Charon's seething irritation at Willie nearly gets the better of him. Charon moves into Willie's view and raises a tight-red fist at his face.

"AND WHEN I SAY SHUT UP!…"

Then, Charon smiles and calms down.

"Were YOU supposed to be Juergen's replacement? Shit!"

Charon turns quickly, letting off steam by throwing up his arms. He slumps onto the bed.

Staring at the half-closed drapes, "You tell your masters that L5 is beyond them. They don't understand that what we're doing is for the good of the men, women and children of this bloody planet. I want you to tell your masters that their individual names are being written into the history books for what they are stupidly doing to humanity." He thinks, *For as long as there are people who can still read on this accursed planet.*

Looking at the screen of his Pad on the bed. "By the way, 'Willie', your real name is Friedrich Venn, and your immediate boss is Eugene Betzner. He works for some idiot moneybags called Vadim."

As Charon is talking, Mahim tosses him a roll of tape. Charon pulls on his socks and shoes then gets up to retrieve his shirt. He slips it on then wraps the tape multiple times around the two on the floor.

"This is just so that you can sit for a while to contemplate your sins…Have a nice day."

Charon leads Mahim out the door. Another L5 guard joins them as they leave down the hall.

Outside, Mahim leads Charon to a large car parked in front. As they are hurrying to get in, a young "protester" with a sign rushes at them.

The sign says: "SPACE JUNK SCIENCE KILLS"

Another person is taking quick pictures of the "protest".

Charon glimpses the sign-carrier as he comes up behind him. *Christ! Now what!?*

Mahim is about to push him off, but Charon smiles at the cameraman and says to the protester, "I'd like to invite you to speak with me. Join me, please."

Before the sign-carrier can think, he's in the back seat with Charon.

He shrinks into the far corner of the seat as they slowly pull away, his sign lying awkwardly at his feet. He is suddenly very frightened.

"Ya'll takin' me away for experiments?"

"HA! My dear young fellow — I have no intention of taking you anywhere. I just saw your intriguing sign and thought we should talk about it!"

"Sign?"

"Yes. The one at your feet. Something about 'Space Junk'."

"Huh? I don't know nothin' about no space junk." He shifts the sign to better see at the words. "What the?…Mister, I don't know nothin' about this, honest. Some guy in the bar give me a hundred U.S. He said to wave this thing at y'all and he was in a big hurry so I said shit, wave that stick *where*, and he said at the next guy that gets into this here car and he says make sure the sign-thing is pointin' at the camera guy, and points 'im out to me as we's runnin' outa the bar. I'm in the maintenance corps over at the Base and I'm just on leave and I don't know nothin' about what the fuck's going on…"

A smile forms on Charon's face as the man stutters. "Hold on, young fellow, hold on. I believe you. I do."

Charon reaches over to pat his hand. "Tell you what. I'll ask my driver to head toward the Base and we'll let you off there. How's that?"

The man calms down so Charon carries on. "My name's Charon. I'm just finishing my visit to Germany and I haven't had a chance to talk with very many people. My German's sort of none-existent, so it's a pleasure to hear you speaking English. Do you mind if we chat while we drive you to Nuremberg?"

The protester takes his first real look at Charon. "Ah, no. Not at all. Charon? ya say?" He uses the "sh" instead of "k" sound for Charon's name.

"It's just a nickname. I'm from L5. I'm in charge of the main airlocks, which somebody called the Gates to Hades. If you know your Greek myths, Charon – properly pronounced with a *k* rather than a *sh* sound – was the ferryman on the River Styx who took souls to Hades."

The sign-carrier's eyes get wide. Charon smiles engagingly.

"I assure you that I do not deal in souls. In fact, I'm known as an exceedingly helpful fellow…"

"Shee-it! Your **Charon**!" Pronounced with "sh" again.

"Yes…"

"Wait'll I get back an' tell SaraAnne that I sat right next to Charon from Space!" He slaps his knee. "SHEE-IT!"

He grins from ear-to-ear and slaps both knees in excitement.

Mahim has been watching in the mirror from the front passenger seat. He turns toward the vehicle's console screen to see what is being recorded of the two in the back seat. He jumps at the sound of the soldier's knee-slap, then nods at the driver to carry on, settling back into his seat with a smile.

Conquerors of Space

FLYING TO MOSCOW AGAIN

A news broadcast is being shown on Charon's flight back to Moscow. Charon's head is just visible over the seatbacks, watching the screen that sits on the wall past the business-class seats.

On the screen, a stock picture is shown of the L5 torus. Other pictures showing the inside of L5 flip by to accompany the news reader's script.

The news reader is silent to Charon until he decides to slip on headphones.

"…from L5, humanity's great space experiment, has been visiting Germany. Mr. Charon has had the task of delivering the body of Juergen Mittelsohn to his family in Frankfurt-am-Main. The mysterious death of Mr. Mittelsohn, which has been under investigation by Mr. Charon, was apparently explained to the satisfaction of the family. Their lawyer, Mr. Paul Loewenberg, said that a full and satisfactory explanation was given to the family at a dinner meeting three days ago."

A clip shows Loewenberg speaking with English translation text underneath, "…and Mr. Charon very kindly provided the Mittelsohn family with a recording of the touching memorial ceremony that was held for poor Juergen on L5."

The news reader carries on, "In a bizarre incident later, Mr. Charon was apparently accosted by a protester while on his way to the airport. In this **exclusive** report we show what the so-called protester said to Charon in a security recording made inside the L5 limo."

The limo's security clips of the scene are shown with Charon speaking:

"…I just saw your intriguing sign and thought we should talk about it!"

The sign-carrier says, "Sign?"

"Yes. The one at your feet."

"Huh? I don't know nothin'…" He looks at the obscured sign at his feet. "What the?…Mister, I don't know nothin' about this, honest. Some guy in a bar give me a hundred U.S.; he said to wave this thing at y'all and he was in a big hurry so I said shit, wave that stick where, and he said at the next guy that gets into this here car and he says make sure the sign-thing is pointin' at the camera guy, and points 'im out to me as we's runnin' outa the bar. I'm in the maintenance corps over at the Base and I'm just on leave and I don't know nothin' about what the [BLEEP]'s going on…"

Charon nods. "Do you mind if we chat while we drive you to Nuremberg?"

"Ah, no. Not at all. Charon? ya said? Shee-it! You're *Charon*!"

"Yes…"

"Wait'll I get back an' tell SaraAnne that I sat right next to Charon from Space!"

The clip ends. The news reader adds, "A spokesperson for the United States Army base at Nuremberg had no comment about the incident."

Charon removes his headphones and settles back in his seat, satisfied.

George, beside him, smiles wryly. He keeps his headphones on.

Vnukovo International Airport, Moscow

They land, taxi, and are now leaving the plane. George is trying to use his Pad but the device is still misbehaving. Curious, George gives his Pad a shake as he leads Charon down the exit corridor from their airplane. They leave the Arrivals area.

Charon notices George's confusion as they continue walking. "What's the matter, Jimmy? Oh! Did you get the new secure signon…" *He's still very weak. Should've stayed in hospital longer…*

"Yes." George is distracted and annoyed by a message that appears the instant he signs-on. Confusion turns to wariness. George turns to speak to Charon, then sees their previous acquaintance, Klaus, coming up to them. Two thugs accompany Klaus. "Oh shit. Not **him** again."

"Huh?" Charon turns to look back but is suddenly grabbed by one of the thugs. A grim-faced Klaus sticks a gun against George's side.

"Hey! Take it easy! I'm an invalid!"

Klaus growls in his thick accent, "This I know! And if you do not shut up you will be worse! You follow orders or many people will die!"

Klaus pulls back some of his jacket to reveal a grenade.

"Forward!" He pushes George roughly while Charon is shoved by one of the thugs.

Holding George's arm, Klaus pulls his shoulder. "Next door! Your Pad is no good here, eh, Mr. Spaceman! It has been neutralized by Prancing Tiger! As **you** will be!"

"What!?"

Klaus smiles and steps aside as George gets a shove through the door from one of the thugs.

A sign on the door says:

AUTHORIZED PERSONNEL ONLY!

ALARM WILL SOUND

No alarm sounds.

They emerge into a quiet service corridor. Klaus pushes Charon to the right. Over the doorway, a red light on a hidden camera flashes.

Klaus indicates with a nod, "Down there. Schnell gehen!" [*walk quickly*]

Charon speaks over his shoulder at Klaus. "Demyadin behind this?"

"Shutup! This you will never know!"

As they turn a corner, two security guards face them with guns drawn.

The smaller security guard yells in German with a Russian accent, "Stop right there! Put your guns down NOW!"

Charon yells to them in German, *"Watch this guy! He's got a grenade!"*

Charon pulls away from Klaus, who is surprised by the guards. George steps toward Charon. One of the thugs lifts his gun at the guards. As they start firing at each other, George and Charon duck and jump for a door behind them. The grenade goes off with a burst of light and deafening noise that reverberates down the hallway:

BANNNNNNGGGG!

Charon is pulling George, who takes the blast wave coming through their door which knocks them both down into the narrower corridor, crumpling them against another door. Instinctively pulling on the door handle as he falls against it, they both crash through the second doorway. Charon hauls George inside with difficulty then slams the door shut.

Eyes wide, Charon says, way too loudly, **"Can't, can't hear!"** He scans his body. "No blood. **Jimmy? Are you alright?"**

Seeing George's blank expression Charon pushes himself up then tries to lift George. He is dead weight.

Still with glazed eyes, George turns his head to Charon then begins to stiffen his legs to support himself. Wobbly on his own feet, Charon shakes his head, yelling too loudly, **"Can't stop! Let's go!"**

Very weak, George manages to get his feet moving as Charon half lifts him up to carry him along. They stumble past baggage conveyors and a few startled workers.

George is getting slower and slower. Charon takes George's arm over his shoulder, pulling him along.

Seeing a slowly idling conveyor moving through a wall opening, Charon takes a chance and drops George onto it then dives through… emerging into a passenger baggage pickup area.

The large room is concrete-bare with few passengers. A young boy who was playing near the conveyor screams at them and runs away.

George rolls off the conveyor awkwardly. Charon helps him up. They look around. Only one perplexed passenger takes notice of them as they walk, stumbling, toward the exit. George is really struggling. Charon holds him up as they exit the building. They take a few steps toward a bench beyond the doors but George leans heavily on Charon's arm to breathe. Charon keeps a lookout while George desperately takes shallow breaths.

Not far away, a thirty-something woman is sitting in her car. Her sister gives her a hurried, bumbling kiss through the open window. The driver, Daryna, wipes away a tear.

The sister is concerned. "You'll visit the cemetery every week – and water the flowers, and… and… You take care of yourself, Daryna. **Sorry**! *Darinka*! And for God's sake find a husband!" Still holding hands, she backs away reluctantly. "Have to go! Have to go!" She shakes her head, mouthing, *Sorry. I forget to speak Russian.*

Their hands separate haltingly. Daryna/Darinka reaches to put her other hand to her sister's chin. "Govorit pa russki zdes! I ne ukrainskoye tezh zaradi boga!" [*you can speak Russian here! and not Ukrainian for God's sake!*]

Shaking her head, "No, of course not! I forgot! Anyway, I have to get back into English; my husband's important visitors…"

Darinka grimaces, "Ok ok… Give that good-for-nothing husband of yours a kiss for me, and especially kiss little Luka! Tell him I will come soon to visit!" She thinks, *When the border opens for me again. If ever.*

The sister picks up her bags and runs into the airport building, shoving between Charon and George.

As she runs through the door, she doesn't notice George falling to the pavement behind her. Charon has been pushed away so that he cannot help George before he falls.

Darinka jumps out of her car, one hand to her mouth in alarm, and runs to George.

He is still breathing shallowly. Charon holds George's head up as Darinka quickly kneels down to help. Charon croaks out, "Jimmy?"

"Bozhe moi!" The English name clicks in her mind. "Ah, I, I am **so sorry!** My sister didn't… What happened? Here, let me help him up."

Charon still can't hear anything but a loud buzzing. He sees that Darinka wants to take George to her car, so they each hold him up by an arm.

"Let's get him into my car… Oh! Are you English?

She looks at Charon, who doesn't hear her question. He cocks his head, trying to understand.

George croaks out. "English!…"

George leans heavily on Charon as Darinka opens the door for them.

Darinka nods, "Are you hurt?" She wonders if Charon is mentally disabled. She puts George's legs into the car and helps him settle into the seat.

"I want you to sit there and rest. I'm so sorry! I don't know what my sister was thinking, running into you like that…" She looks at George, puzzled. "Are you hurt?"

Getting some strength back on the seat, George shakes his head. "Thank you, yes. I've just been in hospital. A butterfly could've knocked me over… as one just did."

Darinka nods. "Ohh…"

As George weakly pats her hand in thanks, a commotion in the airport building catches Darinka's attention. Loud sirens are approaching from the road.

Charon doesn't hear but sees a Russian police officer walking toward them from a distance. Giving George a nod in the direction of the police, he closes George's door then slips with some difficulty into the tight back seat behind George.

Darinka does a double-take at Charon's sitting into her car. George gives her a quite sign, nodding to the driver's seat.

She reluctantly walks around the car. Then seeing the approaching uniform, her face hardens and she moves faster.

The sirens get closer.

Darinka starts the car and leaves quickly.

"What's going on? Who are you? Does your friend speak Russian?…Listen! If you don't answer me I will have to stop!"

George puts on his most empathetic smile, then grimaces as he turns toward her. "Oww…My friend and I are in trouble – **not** from the police – and I want to thank you very much for your help… Please keep driving and I'll tell you what I can." He takes long breaths. "First, someone just threw a grenade at us back in the airport. As far as I know, Security is still fighting the people who did that. The reason my friend, here, isn't answering is because he can't hear. The grenade blast… his eardrums must be stunned. I think it was a concussion grenade thrown by terrorists."

Darinka puts a hand up to her mouth and is unconsciously slowing down.

George notices her change in attitude. He croaks out, "My name's Jimmy – he's Charon, and could you please get back up to speed?"

Realizing that she's slowed right down, she snaps everybody's head back as she stomps on the accelerator.

"Oh my God!"

George leans back into the seat trying to rest. He looks down at his hands. One of the gloves has been ripped so he adjusts it to cover up again.

He sees her glancing at his hands.

"I have a lot of allergies, so…"

He holds up his good gloved hand. She nods blankly. Her eyes glaze over at too much data.

A new pain in his lower abdomen makes George groan. Charon doesn't see his grimace.

They arrive uneventfully, and silently, at Darinka's apartment building in the late afternoon. She parks in a lot behind the building, then sits, wondering if she really should trust these two. George has fallen into a fitful asleep beside her. Charon stays quiet, watching her calmly from the back seat. He adjusts his large belly and cramped legs, scanning the lot.

Darinka finally shrugs and turns to Charon. They smile at each other. She mouths and gestures to say that they should take George into the building.

That evening, George is flaked out on an old couch that had been pulled out as a bed for Darinka's sister. Charon is sitting at the kitchen table, staring at his Pad. Darinka gestures to Charon with a teacup.

"Chi - ah, **tea**?"

Charon smiles, but shakes his head.

The kettle whistles. Charon cocks his head at it, hearing something. He smiles at Darinka, then points to an ear, nodding.

"Oh, dobro! **Good, good!**" She glances down from his face as Charon's ample belly jiggles with his movements.

Charon rises to step carefully over to George. While gently taking George's Pad out of his pocket to turn it off, George wakes up. Charon says, too loudly, to a woken-up-startled George, **"Compromised!"**

George nods and closes his eyes again. With a painful grimace, he groans and holds his stomach.

Next morning, George is snoring fitfully on the old couch. A red and black geometrically patterned blanket covers him.

Charon is covered with a blue and yellow rough woven cover. He is sprawled in a sofa chair. He pulls his cover aside, stretches, then gets up. His nose twitches. "Toast." Then, smiling. "Ah! My ears are back on line!"

Seeing the blanket over George's chest rising and falling, he relaxes and pads quietly to the kitchen table.

Darinka is hand-grinding coffee beans with a 20-centimter-long brass cylinder device with a turning handle on top. The grinding takes several minutes.

Putting a finger over his lips, Charon whispers, "Good morning. Do you mind if we let my friend sleep a little more? He's just recovering from a serious allergic reaction."

Putting two and two together, Darinka smiles in a more relaxed way at Charon.

"Yes, yes. Of course. He is 'Jimmy'?"

Charon nods.

She carries on. "He said, yesterday, that he recently was in hospital. And he said that you couldn't hear because…"

Charon adds quickly to her sentence, "A grenade blast in the airport. It must have been a concussion grenade."

Darinka smiles, "…or you would have holes in you!" She finishes with a pleasant laugh and relieved sigh.

"Oh! I'm sorry! I didn't mean to laugh at you! It is just that I am relieved to, to…"

"Yes, thank you very much for your very kind help yesterday. My name is Charon. Did Jimmy introduce us yesterday?"

"Charon…" She puzzles over the name. "Oh! Me! I am Dar…Darinka. My sister, yesterday, the one who ran into you? She is Militsa." Still puzzling, "Charon?"

"Yes?"

"Oh! No! I was… Are you?…"

"From L5."

Darinka is shocked. "Bozhe moi! You are!…"

She sits up straight, brushes a hand through her hair, pulls her blouse in tighter.

Charon smiles, "Please, don't make a fuss. Right now, I'm not in the mood to be a celebrity."

The toast pops.

Startled, Darinka grabs it and starts to butter it.

"Is toast good for you?"

Charon nods. "Thank you very much, yes." He stares at her while she lathers on the butter.

"We don't want to make any trouble, but some peculiar events occurred yesterday…

Darinka curls her lips. "A grenade is 'peculiar'?"

Grinning, "Well, yes, but… other things. We've lost communication with our, ah, friends in the L5 network."

He looks at her closely as she places his buttered toast and a small jar of red jam on a dish.

"Darinka?"

She stops to face him.

"What do you do? Do you have a job?"

Turning back to the counter, she puts more bread into the toaster.

"I have no job. Now. I used to work at the Institute in Mariupol. I am professor of oceanography. They closed the Institute so that… After the recent bombing. A group of us were taken by trucks to a camp over the border. We were… We were *socialized* they called it. Others would call it a poor attempt at brainwashing."

Darinka girds herself to speak to these strangers. *They are not Russian. I can say things to them.*

"When I could leave the camp I found my mother and we lived here. I tutor, when I can. My mother has, she…" She sniffs then regains composure. "My sister came from…" She hesitates then decides it is safe to be honest with this spaceman. "From western Ukraine through Poland to…" Her face reddens. "I was trapped in this damn country when they invaded. They said I could become a Russian citizen. First they bomb us to bloody flat rubble year after year and then they say we can become their citizen! I was taking Mother to visit relatives near Kazimov. A safer place than Moscow for us new 'Russians'. Had to change my name and get any work I could. But it was all too much for Mother. She had a bad stroke before we could start to the country." She sobs. "My sister came to help me… to bury our dear Mother."

Darinka is in tears, facing the window. Charon gets up immediately to put an arm on her shoulder. She sobs, then runs into her bedroom.

Charon shakes his head slowly.

He hears that George is awake. Thinking about what to do, Charon turns to George.

"Jimmy. We'll have a quick breakfast then we have to leave. I want to arrange for a substantial payment for her help. We need to take down her address, here."

With a groan from George, Charon apologizes. "Oh, I'm sorry, Jimmy. How're you feeling this morning?"

George replies in irritation, "How the bloody hell do you *think* I feel, for chrissake! I nearly got blown up and something really hurts in my gut." His anger peters out, his face pleading for help.

Never having heard him so cranky before, Charon hesitates before stepping close. "Did they shoot you, or did something from the grenade…?"

"Owww. Damnit I don't know! I can't bend over enough to look." He rises on an elbow but plops back down. "Faint…"

Hearing the testy exchange, Darinka comes into the room. "What are you doing? Oh! He does not look good. Not Good. Let me see." She shuffles Charon aside, feeling George's forehead for a fever. "Not hot. Good. He was not shot?"

Charon shakes his head.

She reaches for the blanket over George. "Will look. Is it ok?" She starts to pull the blanket down and feels George's chest. "Have to open your shirt. Ok?"

George grunts, which she takes to be an affirmative. She slowly rolls his shirt up looking for blood.

Charon is surprised by two blotches of darkened skin just under his chest. He nods at them as Darinka feels the skin in the area.

George sees their perplexed look. "What?"

Charon hesitates, "Ah, we were just wondering about the darkened skin, Jimmy."

"Dark? Bruises? What the hell do you…!"

He tries to sit up again but falls back, light-headed.

Darinka pulls George's shirt down to cover him again. "I am worried. I will ask Lalo to come up. He is professor of neurosurgery. Retired. Good man. He will keep secrets."

"Ah…" Charon is unsure about involving more people in this.

"No argument. Lalo is good man. Back soon." She slips on a robe and heads for the door. "Lock this until I come. Three knocks then one."

With that, Darinka closes the door behind her.

Charon steps quickly to the door to lock it, but first, he opens it slightly to see Darinka heading down the stairs. He closes and locks the door.

Inside, George groans again.

"Jimmy, she's gone to bring a doctor. I don't know what happened to you but we couldn't see any open wounds. Does your gut still hurt?"

"Yes it still bloody well hurts!…" He relents, "I'm sorry, Charon. Don't know what's got into me suddenly. Just… let me say that I haven't been feeling the best for the past week. I put it down to the stress of arranging for this adventure of yours."

Charon steps closer to George to speak quietly.

"Pads are compromised. I have a sinking feeling about what's going on. Need to contact Larry, of course, and we can't."

"You're thinking Demyadin?"

Charon nods, "Somebody… somebody's escalated things. This can get very dangerous. I hope Larry's put the facts together. We haven't called in for, what? three periods, now? There has to be a news report about Klaus and his henchmen at the airport — no matter what the spin. We can't use our Pads and we can't ping either our general location nor, ah…" nodding at the bedroom, "put Darinka in jeopardy with a telephone call."

George puts his hand up to stop Charon.

With heavy breaths, "Got it covered. Backup system is a landline call, encrypted with my Pad, on local use only, doing the speaking, that goes to a toll-free number. The message gets transferred by shortwave to Sydney."

George slowly tries to roll over to put his legs off the edge of the bed. "As you said, first we get breakfast, then we find a payphone…Owww… Splitting headache!"

"Take it easy, Jimmy." Charon puts a concerned hand on his shoulder.

Charon nods to the table. George shakes his head and stays sitting on the bed, half slumped over.

Charon absently rubs George's shoulder while taking a closer look around. He sees a very sparse kitchen. There is a small, old refrigerator in a corner. The doily that hangs over the door shows that the fridge is not being used.

Knocks sound at the door. Charon steps toward then asks, "Was that three?" A fourth knock sounds. He shrugs and unlocks the door.

Darinka opens it and steps in alone, whispering, "Lalo is coming. Does not want to seem like he is following me."

Nodding, Charon steps aside. Waiting, he continues to scan the room.

Darinka sees him vaguely looking at the old television.

"It is not plugged in. Too expensive… the power bills. I need gasoline to drive to… I get work, when I can, in restaurants… and tutoring… Now, with mother's little pension gone…"

She looks around the apartment sadly.

Nodding sympathetically, Charon prompts her. "The television…"

"Just furniture. But that is no loss. The fancy flashing lights…" She snorts.

> *FLASHBACK: Darinka is staring through the window of a department store in Mariupol with others on the street, as a large flat-panel screen is being adjusted on the inside wall of a window display. It shows Russian tanks with their white "Z" painted on the front, speeding down a highway. Then a commercials cuts in for a movie about some hero flying through the air.*

Darinka speaks to Charon, "I see the big screens at the department store. The bigger they get, the more they become what they really are – a fancy way of giving endless commercials that have no more substance to real life – just holographic wallpaper."

Her mind goes back to her comfortable old apartment in Mariupol. She thinks sadly, *No. It's all gone now. Just like our place in Mariupol.*

Charon nods in sympathy. He follows Darinka with his eyes as she putters with cups and a spoon, putting them on the old table.

"Your sister would not be able to help?"

Resolutely choosing her words carefully, "Militsa has a very nice husband - Ukrainian like us, of course - and a very lovely son and I will not bother her life with my troubles! They have been through too much, themselves… She must find a way to forget the life that they, too, lost. Quietly. And forget me, in this bloody country of oligarchs and children with guns playing soldier."

She picks up the brass coffee grinder, looking at its memories. *Her grandmother, in a scarf, dressed in loose, dark clothing, sitting with her coffee grinder held firmly on her left leg, counting hypnotically to herself in her special accent. "…simdesyat, simdesyat-odin, simdesyat-dva, simdesyat-tree, simdesyat-chotiti, simdesyat-pyet, simdesyat-shist. Dostatio." [70, 71, 72, 73, 74, 75, 76. Enough.]*

"There are a few things, just a few things, that I will take from here…"

Suddenly very business-like, "You! Are *you*, Charon, in danger? I want to help you!"

Charon takes in her firm face. "Ah, well. We'll be alright."

Three knocks sound at the door. Then the fourth one. She goes to open it, carefully. In steps an older gentleman, tall, wearing a threadbare plaid suit and a loose tie. He nods at Darinka. "Kto?" [*who?*]

She nods at George, who has flopped back onto the bed, eyes closed. Darinka goes over to lift his legs up from the floor. Charon helps her move him onto the pillow. She and

Professor Lalo converse quietly in Russian. She nods and replies to his questions. One question needs Charon to answer.

"He is asking how long these symptoms have been? The light-headed, his stomach pain."

With a single shrug, "I never noticed them before the grenade explosion but Jimmy just told me that he was having that for maybe a week?"

After the translation, Darinka adds in Russian about the dark blotches on his abdomen. Lalo's eyes open wider. With nimble, long fingers, he begins to palpitate George's chest and abdomen through his shirt then lifts the cloth. Seeing George's skin spots, he steps back to ponder. He gingerly picks up George's hand and squints at the dark wrinkles at some of George's knuckles. Gently putting the hand down, Lalo paces the room. He returns to George, who is lying with his eyes closed in a grimace. Lalo bends down to inspect George's face.

He asks Darinka to ask in English, "The small dark circles on his forehead - did he have these for long?"

Charon shrugs. "I honestly don't remember seeing them on him." He looks closely at George's forehead. "I don't remember seeing them before, no."

Lalo nods, rubbing his chin, mumbling to Darinka. The word Charon clearly hears in his reply is "Addison's."

Darinka starts to translate, "Professor thinks he might have something called Addison's symptom."

Lalo corrects her, "Nje simptom. Sindrom." [*not symptom. syndrome*]

Darinka repeats the correction, "Syndrome. Addison's syndrome."

The two go back to their conversation. Darinka puts up a hand to stop Lalo's explanation. "Khorosho." [*please*] "Ah, Mr. Charon, what the professor says is that your friend could have a serious adenal disease and it seems to be progressing quickly. If he is correct, we must take him immediately to hospital. This might have been made worse by the, ah, stress of what happened at the airport but it is not a cause."

This news stuns Charon. He slumps into the chair where he had slept. "Is he certain? Does…"

"He is not certain. That is why your friend must be in hospital for them to do tests." Darinka is, herself, plainly upset.

She turns to thank Lalo then rummages in her purse. Charon finally realizes she is looking for money to pay Lalo.

He rises quickly. "Wait. I will pay the professor." He opens up his wallet.

Darinka steps between Charon and Lalo to pull out a few bills from Charon's wallet. She mumbles in English, "Not too much."

She folds the bills into Lalo's hand and leads him out, thanking him profusely in Russian, patting his back as he leaves.

Darinka turns to shake her head at Charon. "Charon my friend, you are in a strange land, no? And somebody has thrown a grenade at you once already. And your friend Jimmy should be in a hospital and you should have your ears looked at. And here you dither! Men!"

She starts to fuss with the coffee then turns back to face Charon.

"And I… I need to help you… Or I will think too much and that is not a good thing." She finishes very quietly.

Charon hates having to make rash decisions. *This is one time I have to. We'll contact Larry or Mahim with that shortwave procedure.*

Later that morning, in the parking lot below Darinka's apartment, the three are preparing to leave.

Darinka fits a suitcase into her car's trunk beside two cardboard boxes then forces the lid shut onto the boxes. Charon is standing awkwardly beside the car. George is bundled up in the back seat.

Darinka orders him, "Get in! Go, go!"

She shoos Charon into her car. Charon reluctantly gets into the front. He finds the seat adjuster to carefully give himself more room, without touching George in the back seat.

They drive away.

As they drive a block, a Mercedes screams around the corner behind them, braking hard and stopping in the spot that Darinka's old car had been in. Three thugs with guns jump out and run into her building.

Darinka is alarmed, looking at the scene in her mirror. Charon has twisted around to watch. He urges her, "Quick. We need to find a safe road into the country."

Darinka nods and slams down on the accelerator, jerking George's throbbing head back. "Ohhh…"

The car speeds away.

That morning on a graveled country road they are speeding past farms that are in the process of becoming a suburb, with new construction in some places and derelict buildings in others. Darinka is expertly missing most of the potholes.

Turning around to George, Charon checks to see if he is doing any better. The drive seems to have brought some life into his eyes. "Jimmy, can you program your coded message while we drive? We can stop for a telephone at the next town."

Darinka adds, "Restaurant is ten minutes away. This town is a favourite place for prison guards from a prison near here."

Nodding, George struggles to pull out his Pad. He blinks to clear his eyes then confirms that the Pad is not broadcasting. With a finger over the keypad, "What do I say. My, my head is fuzzy."

Charon turns to face him. "Jimmy, I've been thinking about this. You absolutely must be taken to a hospital. Right now." He interrupts George's weak objection. "I'm pulling rank. Your message is to have L5 send a car, plane, anything, to evacuate you right now." He turns to Darinka. "Is there a safe place he can wait?"

She nods. "My cousin lives here. I have stayed at his farm when I drove through to the north. I will call him when we are in the restaurant."

Shortly, the three are sitting at a table in the restaurant next to a window. The road and their car are in their line of sight under the window. As Charon and Darinka talk, they keep glancing at the road and at George who is slumped into the corner of the booth.

Charon nods toward George then the payphone. "That took a lot out of him. The message'll be received within minutes. It still leaves us with two transportation problems. If Mahim or one of the other L5 people can get here quickly, and without interference, how will they be able to extract him from your cousin's place. And then there is us."

George groans and shifts in the bench seat. Darinka reaches across the table to caress his arm.

Charon continues, "Peru or Australia are as close to the other side of the world as you can get. Until we know the extent of the situation, we have to assume that there's an aggressive manhunt after us."

He gives her a wry smile but Darinka is very concerned about George's condition. She wonders if Charon understands this. "Jimmy is in pain. We must take him to my cousin right now. He should have pills for pain."

Realizing he has been ignoring George, Charon explains. "Darinka, thank you so much for showing your humanity and your care for my friend. I need to tell you… to explain why many of us in the L5 community don't… well, we have been through so many life-threatening situations that… you know, I am beginning to understand ourselves from this perspective and how it is that others might be seeing us as, perhaps, cold."

He pauses, thinking it over. "We have, by our special circumstances, become different. Culturally. I must admit, in a way, we have become less human - if being a kind human, like you, means caring so openly for a person in pain."

He drops his head, working through the revelation. "This is hard. L5ers have been under constant imminent threat by the space that surrounds our little world. We have been under threat by self-serving bureaucrats in the rich countries who want to make us go away or use us for their own profit. And there are the small but dangerous few who simply wish to destroy us, I don't know why. It is no excuse, but perhaps the shell we have built up around us, the torus, is the same as the shell most of us have around the humanity in our minds. The protective shell has, itself, well… it may have become our prison." He nods to himself. "This requires open discussion."

He pulls out his Pad to make a note then realizes it is off-limits. Glancing at the screen's emergency notification section, he sees the blinking red dot. "Can't be." The LED blinks a pattern. Charon is agitated. "Morse code. As if I can remember…"

Darinka pipes up, "I know Morse code. What is it?"

Charon shakes his head and hands the Pad to her. "That tiny red LED. See it?"

"Yes yes. Need paper."

He pulls his paper table cloth from under the dish and turns it over. She takes the paper, absently folding it in half then finds a small pencil in her sweater pocket. Staring at the blinking dot, she writes down the message then outlines a trailing part and draws an arrow to the first words, then writes the sentence as it should be. As she writes the letters, she mumbles, "It scrolls… same message."

.- .-. .   --- .--. .   -. - .... .   --. .- - . ...   --- ..-.   .... .- -.. . ...

She translates, "The gates of hades are open"

Charon whispers, "Secret code. It means I can now text!" Excited, he grabs the Pad from her fingers. "Oh, sorry, Darinka. Thank you!"

Her hand stays clasped to his for a minute. *Warm hand. A funny fellow. Always thinking of what's going on. Not of the people around him.*

Charon begins texting and receiving texts. Darinka sits patiently watching Charon's resolute expression as he concentrates on the back-and-forth texts. She glances around every once in a while to check her car and at the patrons in the restaurant. One of the other women at a table nearby gives her a sympathetic look, pantomiming Charon's focused typing on the Pad. Darinka shrugs and gives her a wry grin.

Finally Charon finishes. Warmly taking Darinka by a hand, whispering, "Thank you, my dear. You have saved the day. We must drive Jimmy to your cousin now. Help is coming for him." He glances around the restaurant. "I'll explain in the car."

Before extracting himself from the bench, "And I'm very sorry to say that you probably shouldn't go back to your apartment, Darinka."

"Huh! What apartment! Everything I wanted to take is in my trunk! They can have it!" She puts her other hand onto Charon's. "It is very lucky that I decided to drive you when

I did. So. What do you need to do, now?" Then she leans her head in closer, "And, you must tell me what is happening."

"In the car, please. Let's extract Jimmy from here as painlessly as we can."

With muffled groans, George is slid out from the corner of the bench. He presents the appearance of yet another drunk being helped home, so, in the small working-class city where they are, it is not very unusual.

Helping George out to the car is a struggle. He keeps groaning. After bundling him into the back seat they leave for her cousin's place on the outskirts of the small city.

As she drives, Charon begins reluctantly. "Listen, Darinka. You've been extremely helpful to us in a very difficult time. But the deeper you get into this, the fewer options will be open to you. If you get out right now, we can make sure that you have a job in a safe L5 facility someplace – maybe in San Francisco, where you could get back into oceanography, perhaps." He looks into her eyes, "If you stay with me, your life will be in jeopardy."

Darinka replies wryly, "The unstated option being that if I continue helping you, I might be safe only on L5?"

"In. We live '*in*' L5."

She puzzles over that for a second.

He reflects on her kind face. "Actually, there are several possibilities still on Earth. We have a protocol, in any case, for the acceptance of new members into the L5 community, whether on Earth or off. Ah, you would have to qualify."

He nods with a bit of embarrassment and she looks apprehensive, glancing from him to the road.

Charon carries on, "And, so far, I have to say that my vote would go for immediate acceptance." They exchange warm smiles. Her smile drops away quickly as she concentrates on the driving.

"My concern, right now, is to keep us safe. In the texts, I was told that an experimental rocket-plane was going to be sent on its fifth test. This is ultra-secret. *Ultra-secret, ok?*"

He waits for Darinka to acknowledge with a glance and a nod. "Several days ago it successfully entered the atmosphere and landed undetected in western Australia, at our old site, then left again. I am told they believe the situation to be dire enough for Jimmy that they will divert it from its current test run to attempt a clandestine landing outside of here, not far from your cousin's house, to evacuate Jimmy. But there would not be room for either of us. Only for him."

He looks for signs of disappointment in her face. She does show that, then she turns thoughtful.

"So, it means you and I must escape together?" Her question has a slight emphasis on 'together'.

Charon reaches back with difficulty to pull the blanket up higher on George's chest. He considers her question. "Is that what you really want? That is a life-changing decision, Darinka."

Darinka answers with, "Is there L5 facility in Canada?"

Dismissively, Charon shakes his head. "Getting to Canada from Moscow would take us into too many dangerous areas."

Darinka whispers, "I have visited Inuvik, on the north coast of Canada, many times for my Institute. Or, if the way is clear we could go to Australia straight south from eastern Siberia. Oh. No. The Chinese have that now."

Charon ponders. "From Inuvik, Vancouver is southwest, of course, but that's a god-awful long way to go… and there's the matter of a mostly ice-covered polar sea."

Darinka thinks. "I will say that when I was working, my second home was that part of the Arctic. This is the beginning of August; polar sea has been very warm for many years, and there is so little ice left. I could find a captain with a ship my Institute has used before. We come to an arrangement for a voyage to Canada and then down to Vancouver. It *would* be a long voyage…"

Not entirely convinced, Charon suggests, "If we got to Inuvik it would be much easier to arrange for a flight through to Sydney…" He smiles, "But traipsing around the surface of this planet is a lot harder than the ninety minutes it takes to go around it in low-earth orbit!"

He stretches out in the seat. His large belly strains against the seat belt. "Getting to the Arctic, though, would be difficult."

Darinka shakes her head. "This is what I have done many times. This time I would go north by car, and then we take a Siberian flight to Cherskiy, in before was eastern Siberia. Still a wild region with new Chinese owners. This used to be my research station. There, we find a captain with a fast fishing boat. The type I have used can sail far into the Pacific. Big range. Stock up with fuel and food. It carries maybe a dozen crew and, yes, that would cost much, but is more safer than to drive around and around Moscow."

Charon shakes his head. "My dear, while I would enjoy a sea voyage with you, dodging icebergs in a tossing fishing boat is not what I have come here to do."

She interrupts him with an excited, "House is close. This is his road."

She turns onto a rutted gravel road. A low, unpainted wood-clapboard house is on the corner. "Not this one. Jevghenji is more far."

After five minutes of bumping through and around potholes along with a small downed tree that extends half onto the gravel-dirt road, Darinka says, "There. Past the bushes."

George has been groaning at every pothole. Hearing that the ride is almost over he untenses in his seat and sighs. Another raw clapboard house appears around the bend. It has a second storey extending over a half-open shelter holding a variety of farm animals. A large barn-like building sits behind. A barking dog tears out to challenge the intruding vehicle. As the dog runs close enough to bite the tire, it stops, sniffs, then wags its tail wildly.

Slowing down, Darinka opens her window. "She remembers me! Dobra Masha! Gde Jevghenji?" [*Good Masha. Where is Jevghenji?*]

She stops her car in front of the house and jumps out to hug Masha, who yelps excitedly, nearly wagging her tail off.

Charon scans the area. Beyond the house and barn is mostly flat meadowland with randomly sprouting trees. The rolling fields seem to go on forever. In the distance, away from the direction of the city, a low mountain range becomes the border of the landscape.

A door slam brings Charon's attention back to the house. Coming toward the car is a grizzled, grinning, smallish person dressed in a well-worn, colourful kurta – in the style that L5 has made popular on Earth, again – over brown corduroy pants. He is latching a belt to hold up his pants. No shoes.

Darinka yells out, "Jevghenji! Obnimi menya!" [*give me a hug*]

Despite his smaller size, Jevghenji easily lifts up Darinka to spin her around in a joyful dance.

They talk eagerly with occasional glances toward the car. Darinka explains to her cousin that she is helping these two famous people escape from a group of terrorists. Jevghenji is clearly impressed. He walks over to Charon's rolled-down window to welcome Darinka's guests.

"Is fantastic pleasure! From *space*? Come inside, please! To humble home. First we must have drink then I show you my aeroplane!"

He looks into the back seat, nodding to George, whose eyes are clenched shut. "Not look good. Must have doctor."

George groans and rolls his head to look at Jevghenji.

Jumping around the car, Jevghenji tries to open George's door. It is locked.

Charon flings open his own door to clamber out, aggravated by the Russian's action. He yells to Darinka, "Will you calm him down, please! Jimmy's very sick!"

Jevghenji backs away with his hands raised. His face is wrinkled in sympathy. "Not to hurt. Want to help. He is *Jimmy?*"

Charon is at the open driver's door. He reaches in to the back door lock then slowly opens the door beside George. Still leaning against it, George's body slides down slowly and awkwardly as the door opens. Charon tries to hold the door while supporting the groaning George. Jevghenji jumps to help. They both pull George out then carry him to the house.

Jevghenji calls to Darinka, "Dvyehr!" [*door*]

She hurries to hold the house door open so they can carefully maneuver George inside.

George has been made as comfortable as possible on Jevghenji's spare bed next to the kitchen.

Charon is fidgeting with his unopened Pad, trying to decide if he should turn it on.

Darinka and Jevghenji are quietly whispering with their heads together. She tells him that her mother has passed away and has been buried. Sincerely saddened at the news, Jevghenji sheds tears with her as they hug and hold hands, whispering reminiscences. Absently, she unwraps her shawl from her neck to drape it over her shoulders. Seeing that, Jevghenji apologizes profusely as he rushes to light his stove fire. Directing an apology to Charon, "Sorry! So sorry! Have heat very soon."

He moves with practiced actions, opening the chrome-trimmed door to the firebox of the stove. With a blackened shaker, he rotates the square ends of the stove's grill under the firebox to clear out the old ashes. He pulls some prepared tinder from a well-used, tape-wrapped cardboard box beside the stove, opens one of the round lids on the stovetop to delicately place the tinder onto the grill, then he lights it with a wooden match from a sturdy paper box. Sniffing, he suddenly remembers to open the flue. As the flames catch, he inserts small pieces of cut wood, then resets the lid. In a minute, the fire is ready for larger pieces of wood.

Everybody watches his actions, hypnotized by the process of making a warm fire in the stove.

Soon, the radiating heat reaches throughout the room.

Charon melts out of his trance. "Thank you, Jevghenji. Your help is very much appreciated."

Brushing off the dust and tiny wood chips from his hands, the Russian half bows to Charon. "Is very great pleasure to have spaceman here in humble old-fashion home. Oh. No coffee. Broke grinder machine."

"I have mine in the car. You have beans?" Darinka sees the irony of the situation. "This is an *incongruity*, no?" She smiles at Charon.

"Heh! Yes indeed. In L5 we make everything from moonrocks but with highly technical tools. And we take it for granted that the sun's energy can be used directly to drive our technology. On good old Earth, the Sun's energy is used second-hand. It must first make organisms like trees or coffee, from which, usually third-hand, people can then make use of that converted Sun energy to create heat and food and drinks and clean water… and air?"

Darinka's forehead wrinkles as she tries to follow Charon's ideas.

Charon shakes his head. "There are so many microscopically, and macroscopically delicate balances here on our Planet Earth. We will not understand them all in another hundred years. And yet, for the sake of greed and politics and personal power, the dominant form of life on our poor planet seems to be on the inevitable track to destroy it all within a very short time."

Surprising the others, an agitated Jevghenji bursts out with, "*NJET*! NO! *CHANGE WE MUST!*" He regains his composure but still continues resolutely. "This cannot happened!…" Tears form on his cheeks. "How can we make insanity stop?"

Charon shrugs. "I can do nothing about it now. I could have, yesterday, but then it was in the future."

This angers Darinka. He face flushes as she spits out, "You joke! And this is such a serious thing for me and Jevghenji, and ***all*** of us!… I know you are better than that. Are you not?"

He shakes his head slowly. "Very sorry, Darinka. What I mean, of course, is that I am not in a position to do anything but keep surviving in my own little sphere. Or in my part of the torus." His gentle features calms down their anger. "I do what I can. If my words or deeds can touch the minds of those who have been given power over others, I will do what I can to treat them with respect as I tell them what I see. Humans have the ability to do good, to do bad, or to do nothing. That is not a judgment. It is merely an observation." He turns to the little Russian. "Anger imprisons a mind, Jevghenji, and…"

Jumping in with arms gesticulating, "But *need* anger! Swiss cuckoo clock hang on wall and do nothing but say cuckoo for two hundred year!"

Charon picks up his meaning. "You refer to that country's main contribution to human progress."

Darinka is not sure what they are saying. She tries to return the discussion to a familiar topic. "How is poor Jimmy going to see a doctor? He is resting for now…"

"For now, my dear, I've done what I can. We can only wait to see if my friends are able to do what they said."

Jevghenji startles them with a fist smashing hard onto the table. "*CHANGE WE MUST!* NO EXCUSE!"

Change We Must

[CHANGE WE MUST]

Before the morning light appears, Charon is laying on the floor, beyond "not comfortable". His overflowing belly is pushing on those parts of his abdomen that are unfortunate to be underneath. His body is splayed heavily on two knitted throws which are spread over the wooden floorboards. Their rough pattern has been embossed into his back. The throw's rough weave is covered with a lean, old, recently washed blanket. Rising over his belly, another thin blanket covers all but his socked feet, protecting him from another rough-woven throw that almost reaches past his feet. He is not able to fall asleep. All he can think of is the delight of his home, being at Level 25 in L5, almost weightless. And there is this kitchen stove - its fuel burned up in the middle of the night. With its last embers, the stove's metal had ticked away as it cooled. Tick tick tick… It is now quiet. And chilly. Charon does finally fall asleep half an hour before sunrise.

As the sun pokes over the far peaks, Jevghenji's two roosters in the next-door coop argue about who rules the roost. Their discussion raises the cows from their rest, along with the goats. Chickens clucking and calves thumping their mothers for milk and the frisky goats jumping around all add to the racket of an awakening farm house.

Charon now notices the bouquet of smells from the kitchen in the next room as well as those coming from the rest of the house. He mumbles, "Fire and smoke and mold."

Jevghenji is folding up his rough blanket nearby. "Shto?" [*what*] "Ah. Fire. For person not living in pleasure of fire warmth, fire smell is danger. For farmer, is good smell. Usual." He shrugs wryly then glances around to see if his witty philosophy has been appreciated.

Charon rolls his eyes. Carefully keeping his meager blanket tucked under his chin, Charon shifts enough to reach his Pad. Though all apps are off, its locator needs to be on for the L5 rescue mission to find them. More urgently, his numbed back and sides announce an unaccustomed and growing degree of burning agony.

The Pad had been sitting upside down in a shoe. As soon as he lifts it out, its red blinking light casts an on/off beam into the shadows that still hug the floor. One of the shadows moves. It is Masha, whose tail is wagging.

Shaking his head, Jevghenji exclaims, "Gepeui ya!" [*stupid me!*] He jumps up to restart the fire in the stove for his guests, then adds a substantial chunk of wood as it catches.

Charon notices that his host has on only a pair of shorts. This is more than most have on within their dwellings in L5. However, here in this cold house it makes Charon shiver watching him work in the frosty kitchen half naked.

While Jevghenji brings heat back to the rooms, Charon decides he does need to turn on his Pad.

A security question demands an answer before the Pad's screen will open. *"What is the Morse Code for 'we'?"*

He types, ".-- ."

A text flows out right away.

> Dragonslayer: *Reply immediately you read this*
>
> Charron: *Comms ok?*
>
> …
>
> Dragonslayer: *Text only for now. Carrot is guiding Spear to you. ETA 2.4 hours*
>
> Charon: *What the hell is carrot and spear?*
>
> Dragonslayer: *Sorry. You've been out of the loop. Spear is the informal name. It's changing. It will be there to pick up Jimmy. Is it safe?*
>
> Charon: *Safe as far as I know. Is spear the vehicle? I'll dress and check outside.*
>
> Dragonslayer: *Spear will be coming from the east. Confirm when arrived.*
>
> Charon: *Carrot?*

Dragonslayer: Later. End

In a morning daze, Charon empties his shoes of sundries by placing the items back into pants pockets. He slips his shoes on then looks around for his coat. Meanwhile, Jevghenji has dressed. Darinka has been tending to George, and Masha is scratching at the door to be let out. Tantalizing waves of heat waft out from the kitchen.

Charon puts his coat on at the door but waits before opening it. "Ah, Jevghenji?" He notices the little Russian coming from the dark pantry with an oval loaf of rye bread and other food items in his arms. "Is it ok if I let Masha out? I have to go outside."

"Da da. Let out, yes." He piles his goodies onto the kitchen table. Then he thinks he realizes what Charon is up to. "Is, ah, toilet there, in corner."

With a grin and a slight wave, Charon opens the door and Masha rushes out, running everywhere at once to sniff out what has been going on overnight. From outside Charon turns to Jevghenji, "No, ah, I have to, well, check out where my friends are going to land."

He leaves an astounded Jevghenji at the table. "Land?"

Demyadin is sitting on slick tiled steps, half into a white-tiled pool. His head is bowed to restrain his rising anger as an older gentleman berates him from over his shoulder. They are both wearing bathing trunks.

The pool is part of an isolated residence overlooking a beach which is owned by the older gentleman, Remi. In fact, he owns the land along the whole of a wide crescent beach above and at the narrow base of a high cliff.

Remi is clearly upset. "Of all the jackassed stupid stunts!... For *chrissake*! What the hell were you thinking, Mike? You can't just let a dog like Klaus loose in a public place like an airport! And the bloody *Moscow* airport, to boot! With a bloody *grenade*! And I don't *care* if it was a concussion grenade! *For chrissake!*" He paces, waving his arms aimlessly. "We could've had those two space cowboys in our hands, dangling from the media, and you throw a friggen neandertal like Klaus at them! Our friends are ***livid! Livid!***"

Demyadin lifts his head a bit. "Remi, you know that Klaus was not my idea. In fact, it was your suggestion that I use..."

"Oh fuck off, Mike! I didn't tell you to use Klaus as lead on some public suicide mission! I didn't let you into my organization for you to pull a stupid Bannon-chaos-everything stunt like that..."

Still just barely in control, "Listen Remi – I've politely let you rant. You *know* that I asked for someone to lead the Moscow team. I *don't know Klaus from Adam*! Why the hell would ***I use him***? Except that you told me to?"

Demyadin seems to swell in size with his simmering anger. His reddening face turns at Remi from over his shoulder and his heavy breathing makes him appear extra sinister. Remi glances at him then at the wide glass doors where his assistant/guard is standing. He decides to de-escalate for now. "Listen, what happened, ah, happened. The question is, what do we have to do next? Our friends are coming tomorrow afternoon and will be staying for supper. We can…"

"Both Germans and Russians?"

"Of course! You blithering…!" Remi stops as he holds back his renewed irritation.

Demyadin breathes heavily for a minute. He slips all the way into the pool to cool down, then turns to lean on the edge. "Ok. Let's make the most of this. I'll get my people to plant stories about how the attack was an L5 secret op and they don't care who is killed. Paint Klaus and the other guys as martyrs protecting Russia from the crazies from space. The locals'll soak that up, especially if we wrap it in their red flag and the church."

Remi nods quickly then glances at his guard for reassurance. His head jerks around at the poolroom's entrances and down at Demyadin. He whips a towel over his shoulders then slithers onto a chair, sinking into it as far as he can.

Demyadin thinks some more. He looks over at Remi, rasping out, "We have to take that bastard Charon and his helper. Disappear anyone they touched. Drop the hint that they were all taken up to bloody L5." He nods to himself. "The one Russian coming - he runs the GRU?"

He contemplates Remi's nervous glances with disdain.

Remi nods, "Yes. Yes he is but I don't want you to approach him, Mike. I want to use him later." He bites his lip.

A smile crosses Demyadin's face. "Of course, Remi. You're in charge."

After breakfast, Jevghenji insists on showing Darinka and Charon his "machine". On the way to the barn, Charon casts anxious glances at the sky.

Jevghenji makes a show of opening the large lock that keeps the barn doors securely closed. The doors have been reinforced inside and out with new lumber nailed over the old grey wood. Swinging them open, Jevghenji proudly shows off his machine.

"A Tri-Pacer?" Charon recognizes the small airplane.

"No no! Is modify *Legend*. I build! Was design in US. I change. Make bigger for three people. More engine – Czech. One hundred fifty kilowatt power."

Stepping around the new aluminum-covered airframe, Charon is impressed. "One hundred and fifty? That must be almost twice the original. Oh! I see what you did. With the wider engine you built out the fuselage. And more wingspan?"

"Da da! Add Whitcomb winglet and flap and more fuel in wing. Bigger rudder. Not easy get parts." He glows proudly.

Darinka stands off to the side of the airplane. "Need a good painter, Jevghenji. Blue bottom and brown top?"

He lets out an exasperated snort. "*Phttui*. What women know about aerodynamic! Is **stealth colour**! From ground, is sky blue. From high, is ground colour."

The cousins exchange pleasantries in Ukrainian. As they do so, Charon thinks, *Three seats?*

Darinka returns to the house while the two closely inspect the "Legend J-3", as Charon dubs it: "The *Legend Jevghenji Three*."

Just before ten-thirty, while they are still in the barn, a long, neck-hair-raising whhhhiiiish sounds from outside. Then silence. It takes a few seconds for that to register with Charon. Then the lightbulb comes on and he rushes out.

On the dirt-strip from which Jevghenji flies his airplane, is something much larger than the Legend J-3, glistening like it is from out of this world (which it is). It has landed on its skids. Condensation and steam are at once forming on the craft's oval windows, then loudly hissing away as water drips down the vehicle's body. Jevghenji stumbles to a stop, round eyes seeing but not believing. He slowly blesses himself. Charon slows to a walk then closes in on the small front window of the translucent-skinned vehicle. He feels radiating heat coming from it. A hand can be seen inside the craft through the dripping condensation, urgently waving him away. The now less aggressive hissing is joined by thermal clicks as parts cool down from the lower cabin and the mostly open rear section.

Standing several metres away, Jevghejni gravitates as if in a dream to be at Charon's side where they both stand in awe, staring at the clean lines of this alien thing.

"I go back cut my ugly machine in little bits."

Charon grins down at Jevghenji. "No, my friend. I think it will be useful later."

They shift to a few metres in front, sighting down the flattened angular shape. The cabin part of its fuselage is about ten metres long with twice that length of tail that consists of a package of sixteen propulsion devices held together on its long tail section. The forward part of the tail covering is translucent as well, merging with the cabin section almost seamlessly. While the cabin is sleek, there are no curves along its length. Sharp-edged boundaries join each lengthwise section. A single retractable skid holds up the cabin while four more substantial skids support the rear section. Charon can just see where the skids would be retracted out of the airstream when flying.

Jevghenji starts to fall into engineer-mode. "Is stealth front. No so much back." He nods to himself. "Stealth front. Too fast worry about back. Why so hot?"

With a wry grin, "Hmm. If you notice the surface material? Especially on the lower half of the cabin? It's probably a very high temp glassy ceramic covering. Not sure where the translucence comes from. The ceramic is needed if you come crashing through the atmosphere at some twenty thousand kilometres per hour."

"*Chert poberi!*" [*damn it*] "Sense make! From space!… I just go burn whole barn."

"Twenty thousand klicks to zero in a few hours. Well, they were out further…" Charon reconsiders saying too much more.

A knock comes from the cabin, then whirring motors are heard as a metre-and-a-half-long oval piece on the side of the upper cabin opens slowly. A helmeted head pops through the hatch. The craft's pilot pulls up her face covering with its mic to reveal an ear-to-ear smile. "Hello there! Is this Perth?"

Charon grins, "Sorry, no. You missed it by a few thousand kilometres."

"Ah heck! I'll have to try it again another time. Anyway, Charon, you have a patient for me?"

Holding up a finger, Charon turns quickly but immediately runs into an astounded Jevghenji who had been standing behind him. "Oh! Sorry, Jevghenji. Come! We need to bundle Jimmy up and bring him out here."

Spinning around, Jevghenji heads for the house. As Charon lumbers behind Jevghenji, Charon yells at him, "Do you have a wheel barrow?"

"Da, no." [*yes, but*] "Oh! Bring Jimmy with!" He peels off to scurry toward the barn leaving Charon to enter the house, puffing.

A few minutes later George is being carried in Jevghenji's home-made wooden wheel barrow. They take the bumps carefully with Darinka and Jevghenji holding the groaning patient on either side while Charon labouriously pushes the barrow. George is bundled up in cotton blankets, as much from the cool air as to protect him from any materials to which he may be sensitive.

At the spacecraft, George's fully protected body is carefully fitted through the oval hatch. His sharp groans make Darinka grimace. She goes through a whole-body shiver but she keeps helping. Finally seeing her passenger is inside, reaching through and around the metal support elements while leaning on the front seat, the pilot helps George settle into the back seat as well as she can, straps him in, and gives him brief instructions. She asks if he can wear the helmet and mic. With only his eyes showing through an opening in the blanket, George shakes his head firmly.

The pilot nods, checks his safety harness attachments again, then squirms back into her own seat. After buckling in and connecting her air and comms-line, she shoos at Charon to take his friends away from the spacecraft.

The three quickly back away. The pilot takes another several minutes to close the hatch and check systems. In about ten minutes, the propulsion devices make a weird, rising, hissing sound. It gets louder, and much louder, then the craft shudders forward on its skid pads with separate nozzles pointing down, then it suddenly blasts ahead on a low trajectory a few metres above the ground. Its speed picks up remarkably fast as it swings toward the far mountains. Being so low, the turbulence kicks up a following dust stream. At the mountains, the craft makes a sharp turn to vertical. The only way they know that, is by the funnel of dust rising to meet the clouds. Like an arrow painted against the early morning sky, the dust funnel disperses above the near mountains. Nothing else of its passage is visible.

Darinka and Jevghenji bless themselves at the same time. Darinka mumbles, "Chudo." [*a miracle*]

She turns to Charon, "Your people do this all the time? Make miracles like this?"

Charon shakes his head. "Never saw that thing before in my life." For some reason the word "carrot" comes to mind. He takes out his Pad, grumbles through the security procedure, then types:

Charon:	*She is on her way with Jimmy. Was this a carrot project?*
Dragonslayer:	*Great! Med team hopes to get him in time. They think his allergies can be cured*
Charon:	*Hope so. We have to go the long way. Planning to fly by modified J-3 Cub.*

Dragonslayer: *No - wait. Will download our plan - understand double-encrypted?*

Charon: *Got it. End*

Charon smiles and closes his Pad's screen, thinking: *Another security format. When the double-beep sounds I'll have five seconds to enter my code, which is… What the hell? Oh. Yeah. 'What the hell' is my current code.*

The double-beep sounds. He opens the Pad to type the code with no further security protocol sign-on needed. Before he can type, the Pad's screen blanks and the device perceptibly warms up and keeps getting warmer as he types the code phrase.

The code is entered. Charon hurriedly leads his new cohorts to the barn.

Inside, he takes Darinka by the shoulders. "Time for your decision, my dear. Very very serious decision. Either you stay with Jevghenji, here, or come with me. Either option has many risks."

She stares into Charon's eyes. "I am with you." Putting her arms as much as she can around Charon, they hug warmly.

Beside them, Jevghenji shrugs. "So, me? I am chop pechenka?" [liver]

Separating from Darinka, Charon holds out a hand to him. "Do you realize the danger we are heading into, Jevghenji? You have a chance to, well, get away and hide for a while."

The little Russian shrugs. "I live in dying country. Mother, Ukrainckiy. [*Ukrainian*] Otets bije Ruskim. [*Father was Russian*] When country fight family, leave me dead soul. And still fighting in stupid way! What to do? **Trakni ik vcek**." [*fuck them all*]

He kicks at a thick stump that holds his heavy vice, "OOJ!" and stumbles gingerly to a bench, grimacing.

Just then, Jevghenji's landline starts ringing in the barn.

He limps to answer it. "Da?" His eyes grow large as he slams the phone down. "Pospishay!" [*hurry*] "Pull machine out! I burn house and barn!"

Darinka is alarmed, "Shto sluilos?" [what's wrong]

"Ne til'ky khulihany!" [not just hooligans]

He rushes to the house, first flinging open the back gate to the animal corral.

Mumbling, "He shouldn't slip into Ukrainian so easily." Darinka pushes Charon to Jevghenji's Legend J-3.

Understanding right away, Charon pulls away the home-made wooden chocks from the plane's front wheels as she jumps to the barn doors to fling them both wide open. They drag the aircraft out of the barn. Charon runs back into the workshop and tosses random tools into a cloth bag.

Darinka yells, "I will find food and water from the house."

Running there, she smells gasoline. As she steps into the kitchen door, Jevghenji is randomly spilling fuel around the living room.

She yells, "Khleb i vody!" [bread and water]

He points with a free hand to his pantry. There, she tosses two loaves into a large cloth bag, puts a sealable jug under the tap and lets it run while searching for something else. She wraps a substantial hunk of bacon into a cloth and tosses it in with the bread.

The water jug is two-thirds full when Jevghenji leaps over to cap it. He turns off the tap and puts the jug under his arm as he waves Darinka with her bag of food and some cutlery outside. "Toropit'sya!" [hurry]

From the open rear door, with one hand he lights a wooden match against the door's metal hinge then tosses the flame onto the fuel leaking across his floor. The bursting fire chases him as he turns reluctantly back to the airplane. Running to the barn he yells at Charon, "More far! From barn!" He drops the water jug next to Darinka then rushes into the barn.

The rear section of the barn has a pile of straw which bursts into flame as Jevghenji runs out with an axe in hand. He trips on the buried doorstop and falls heavily onto his side, hitting his shoulder against the flat of the axe blade. Trying to jump up, he can't put his full weight onto one leg.

"Blin! Moya ruka i noha!" [damn it! my arm and leg] Struggling up, he limps as quickly as he can to the airplane, using the half-metre-long axe handle as a crutch.

Charon has helped Darinka into the back seat with the food and water. Holding his arm against his chest, Jevghenji asks Charon, who is still outside, "You fly?" He hands the axe up to Darinka who takes it gingerly, holding the leather-covered blade away from herself.

 She slips the axe head into the food bag.

Charon is surprised at Jevghenji's yelled question. "Me? I used to. Oh! Are you alright?"

Jevghenji climbs awkwardly up with Charon's help to snuggle beside Darinka and the bags. He waves urgently for Charon to climb aboard. "Fly! Gangsters come!"

Charon scrambles into the pilot's seat and tries to make sense of the few Russian-language labels. Impatiently, Jevghenji leans over Charon's seat. "Start! This one!"

With a push of "this one", the engine turns over. Then dies.

"Hold more!" Urgently, in higher pitch, "Gangsters here now!"

Darinka sees the duststorm of a car barreling into the driveway. "Hurry Charon! They are here!"

Charon punches the button again and holds it in until the propeller spins up. The whole airplane shakes and the loud, rattling engine noise takes over the cockpit. Charon pushes the throttle to half RPMs, as he confirms the Cyrillic-marked dial that is moving with the throttle. Finding the rudder/brake pedals just in time to stay in the short grass, he bumps down to the dirt runway then shoves the throttle full forward before completing the turn. The aircraft squirrels back and forth along the runway until Charon settles it into a straight run. The large engine quickly pulls the tail up and they are off the ground in no time.

Staring behind, Jevghenji yells, "Shooting! Stay low to trees!"

A small copse of trees to the left provides the only possible cover for them so Charon stays low and barrels toward it. Their turbulence whips the branches as they pass the trees. He keeps the throttle on full, watching the RPM gauge. It very soon approaches the marked red line so he touches the throttle back a bit. They are now out of range of gunfire.

He takes some time to familiarize himself with the few gauges on the panel. He recognizes a basic turn-and-bank, and one that must be an altimeter whose dial hovers around 370. He mumbles, "That'll be in metres above sea-level." There is a compass with German markings sitting above the panel. It indicates 280 degrees.

He yells over his shoulder, "Flying 280. Where to?"

Jevghenji thinks for a few seconds. "Stay low. No power line. Turn to, ah, three six zero. Mountains."

Nodding as he reduces power again to about three-quarters, "Mountains… Flies nice." Loudly, "Flies very nice!" He gives a thumbs-up.

With directions from Jevghenji, they land on a long meadow in the midst of the low, eroded mountains. Boulders and shallow, rolling ravines contain hidden meadows with sparse trees. Jevghenji directs Charon to a place hidden among a few of the rare tall conifers and poplar trees.

"Is fuel." He points to a large mound of rocks that holds an 800-litre tank, painted in faded camouflage. "'mergency," he croaks, along with groan.

Once the airplane is maneuvered onto the slight slope below the fuel cache, Charon pulls off the power. The engine chugs to a stop. They help Jevghenji out. He points to the tank. "Need pump. You pump. I fill tank."

Holding onto him, Darinka pats his shoulder. "I will do it."

Jevghenji shakes his head firmly. "No know how. Dangerous. Make food." He turns away from her toward a rickety ladder.

Darinka follows him, shaking her head disapprovingly. "So with a broken arm you will climb up on the airplane? You can't even move the ladder."

He struggles to drag the wooden ladder over to the plane but finally relents to her insistence on helping with it. "Not so close! No touch!" He ensures the ladder is not pressing against his airplane.

Still insisting on going up himself, Jevghenji climbs very awkwardly onto the wings to top up the tanks with the hose that a concerned Darinka brings to him from the tank. Meanwhile, Charon figures out the safety lock of the manual fuel pump and gives them a thumbs-up. As soon as Jevghenji inserts the nozzle into his wing-tank, Charon starts pumping. His heart sinks as the pump pulls only air. More desperate pumps, then it starts moving fuel into the hose.

After topping up, they take a few minutes to relax. Darinka and Charon unfold a map printed in Russian onto a cord of firewood next to the rock mound.

Leaning against Charon, she studies it briefly then points to the indicated mountain range. "We are here. This is Jevghenji's farm and the road from city."

Nodding, Charon opens the map to show more of the northeast section. "Is there a safe route that way?"

They discuss the possibilities until Jevghenji joins them, still limping and holding his right arm tightly against his chest but determined to carry on.

He wipes his left hand on the grass nearby. "Is army there. I gopniki," [and violent peasant thugs] pointing to the north edge of the map. "Must fly down, ah, south and east long way. Where we go?"

With a smile, Charon says, "Canada."

"Hahaha! Spaceship go far. Not Legend so far."

"Understood, but that's our general direction. My L5 friends are hoping to meet us along the route to do another extraction." Charon thinks about the problem. "The chances are slim for that spacecraft of ours to come back to pick us up one by one. I don't think they'd want to risk coming down through the same radar range any more, even if they **are** stealth. Let me find out what they have as a plan."

Charon logs in to his Pad, staying off-line, to look through the file that Dragonslayer had sent. His eyebrows tighten as he reads the pre-set plan.

Typing the security signon, he goes online and starts texting. This time he is communicating with Jasmine. She confirms that the plan is in progress but tells Charon that he will need to confirm his request for an extraordinary exception to the rules for entry by non-L5ers to their colony. Charon explains that his present companions will likely be jailed, tortured and later killed to keep this incident out of the media.

Jasmine takes time to confer on her end, then comes back with approval for Darinka and Jevghenji to come up to L5, but Charon must first clarify to them what is going to happen.

When he starts posing the list of questions to confirm their acceptance, Darinka and Jevghenji jump all over him, smothering him with kisses - both of them.

After a minute of exuberance he fends them off to resume texting.

> Charon: *I have received their unqualified approval.*
>
> Jasmine: *Right. All set then. Can you all continue southeast from current coordinates? Next pickup will be 138 hours for Spear to make it back*
>
> Charon: *Almost a week? We have a 3-seater, 225 kph, with a range just over 700 kilometres*
>
> Jasmine: *Checking… Airbases south of Nizhny Novgorod just north of your present position so head 120 degrees for 200 kilometres then 70 degrees to pass south of Kazan. Caution, airbase north of Kazan. Contact us at Kazan.*

The other two wait for Charon to finish texting. Darinka leans on his shoulder. "What do we do, Charon?"

He shrugs. "They will come down for us, one at a time. The problem is that it will take about seventy hours, times two for there and back between the craft coming back down each time. In the meantime, we should fly southeast then up to Kazan." He shows them the texts. "So, with three to four hours of fuel on board, we have to fly as low as possible en route while finding friendly airports or fuel stops a bunch of times before we get to Kazan. Jevghenji?"

Taking the aeronautical maps from the table, Jevghenji uses his left hand to plot a course freehand with a pencil. "Some place is safe. Some no. Is special group in region. Flyboys like me. Have own machine and secret fuel. Not on map." He marks *X*es at places along the first part of the flight plan. "After, we ask for more fuel place. Yes?"

"From your special group?"

"Da. They help."

Darinka asks, "Yavlyayutsya li eti lyudi skrytyy...?" [*are these people covert?*]

She stops and looks at Charon. "Sorry, Charon. Was asking if they are secret group."

She turns to Jevghenji. "We can trust them?"

Jevghenji holds up both palms then blesses himself. "Know them. Only want free to fly, like 'merica. 'Special after idiot Putin kill country."

Charon shrugs. "We have no alternative. Jasmine or someone will send me a notification as we fly toward Kazan. You will go up first, Darinka. The second extraction will be Jevghenji..." he looks at the penciled flight plan, "...around Serov. I might have to hide out... around Ufa. Here." He looks up into the sky. "If the spacecraft isn't detected..."

Darinka slips in with, "And can still fly."

"And can still fly… I'll join you in L5 a few days later." He smiles, "It'll be very good to be back home. Way too much excitement on old Mother Earth." His face sinks slowly into unease as he considers the chances of them staying undetected for that long.

Darinka is about to turn away then notices his concern. "Do not worry. Your friends will help you. And we will, too." She kisses his cheek.

"Prancing Tiger" is the highlighted subject line of an email that is being read by Demyadin in Remi's mansion. At that time he hears the commotion outside caused by approaching helicopters. Their Russian guests are arriving.

Demyadin nods at the email and waves his phone at young assistant, Lateef. "A short meeting. Not surprised. No real security in this place."

Reading the text on his own phone, visible perspiration drips down Remi's temple. He flings out a hand to give a retort but is stopped in fear as he sees Lateef already pointing a weapon at Remi's head.

Demyadin raises his hand. "Please do not make such sudden moves, my friend. Lateef has a hair trigger. Now, let us politely go greet the few guests who will arrive."

On the wide expanse of the front lawn, an unmarked helicopter's blades are winding down as another chopper slips in expertly beside it. Guards emerge first to take up positions toward the pink stone mansion. Remi anxiously walks out to greet the two Russian oligarchs. Demyadin allows him to be a metre ahead, then catches up as the two oligarchs come onto the lawn next to the grand driveway, flanked by their guards. After hasty greetings, swirling wind and noise from the still idling blades drives the foursome into the mansion's foyer.

They plop onto white leather chairs next to a central fountain. Whispering for a few minutes, only answering questions posed by Remi, the Russians unexpectedly rise to leave.

Remi is distressed. "Please do not disappoint my chef. He is preparing quail…"

The older Russian, Vadim, responds as he strains up with difficulty from the low chair. "Must leave before the weather changes."

"But but we haven't…"

"Enough. I have to express our dismay at the methods you used to try to capture the spaceman." To Remi's rising panic, he waves away any further discussion.

They turn to leave, but first, the older Russian takes Demyadin by a shoulder, looks over at Remi, then quickly draws a finger across his throat. "Text here." He shows Demyadin a phone number, which Demyadin memorizes.

They scurry out to their respective helicopters. Demyadin types the text number into his phone.

The changing of the guard is done before the choppers are a kilometre away. Remi is wringing his hands as he shuffles away from the foyer. In disgust, Demyadin spits out, "For *chrissake* old man! You don't send this in an email, even encrypted! *Godallmighty!*… So your friends think they drove east of Moscow, eh? Well, no bloody shit! *My* people tell me the FSB or GRU just missed them at a farm outside of Ryazan. It seems they are flying south." He glares at Remi's body. "But my bet is, they're heading northeast. The fool, Charon, must think he can make it to Canada over the Arctic! HA! Still an idiot!"

He pulls out a small pistol with a silencer and shoots Remi in the side of his head. At the same time, Remi's guard standing next to him is shot from a distance. Both bodies crumple to the marble floor, blood pooling around their heads.

Lateef is holding a PP-9 Klin submachine-gun with integrated silencer. He puts it back in ready position. Lateef is, newly, Demyadin's most trusted personal guard.

Demyadin yells to Lateef standing dispassionately by the closed doors. "Lateef! Have the mansion cleaned thoroughly. Remove these bodies. Have them burned. I will be staying here for a while. Have a crew round up Remi's dogs and give them an offer of a job with us or they can take a long swim. You coordinate the cleanup and room assignments. First, cut off all power coming in and bring a generator in place of that. Have Mishy do a deep electronic sweep while the power is off, then again after the generator goes on-stream. Have all transport go through the dock to the south and cut off the road coming in from town. And get our kitchen brought over - everybody and everything carefully vetted."

Demyadin is walking toward Lateef as he issues the orders. He glances with disdain at Lateef's weapon. "Put that thing down and start taking notes." His satanic smile stiffens Lateef's back. "You have a chance to go far, Lateef. Or a quick two metres down. Understand? Write all that down before you forget something."

"Yes sir!"

At L5's Main Port, Charon's very young assistant, Zar, is overseeing the approach and docking of their experimental spacecraft, which someone had originally dubbed *Spear*. Its mission has changed radically from testing to urgent operational function.

Naming the new things that are being produced in rapid succession by Carrot is being done on the fly by the humans. To some, it seems to be their only significant contribution.

In fact, the details of trajectory planning and systems control are all accomplished by one of Carrot's child-forks — which is to say, a sub-program that works autonomously while having the learned capabilities of the original AI, Carrot. Unconsciously, the human part of the team have shied away from using the terms "parent" and "child". If they had thought about it, that would have sounded too much like the thing called *Carrot* had offspring. Which to them would have come too close to a discussion of the meaning of "life-form" and "sentience".

Zar is given ongoing progress statements as the vehicle is brought to its dock then locked in place. Like many of the younger L5ers, he had been quick to adopt the semi-implanted earpiece and mic system that is termed an *earwig*. Older L5ers still shiver at the term.

Against the grain, having to anthropomorphize the software, Zar had named this first spaceplane to land secretly on Earth in western Australia, *Chick*. That came from his favourite food, chickpeas, as a reference to the bulbous but empty cabin section. Others interpret it to mean a young chicken. When someone brought that up, he thought, *a Freudian slippery slope. But what the hell!*

Still in his mid-teens, Zar's confidence level is a work in progress. He came with his parents to L5 as a toddler. There were very few other children to play with in those early years of the space community. Most L5ers balked, at first, at calling themselves "colonists". Their stated endeavour was a reshaping or a transplanting of a place. L5 was and is a brand new *community* in the nothingness of space. They consider themselves a scientific community living, quite simply, on the ever-present edge of destruction. Threatened, if not by some disaster happening against their thin shell of a torus, then by those blinded on Earth by completely irrelevant concepts such as "wealth" and "power".

Zar is fully an **L5er**. He has known nothing else. Rather than clinging to a desire for "stability", which is the primary driver for those who venerate money and power, Zar's generation of L5ers strive for satisfying relationships with their like-minded L5ers, and, just as importantly, pursuing knowledge of how things in the universe work. That is the only way their torus can continue to provide oxygen, sustenance, and protection from the elements of not-life that would batter through their thin shell. To Zar, the primitive, base desires of people on Earth are incomprehensible.

The older generation of L5ers are slowly harmonizing with the younger L5ers in the process of slinging off those ingrained Earth-bound desires.

For the small number of L5ers who have trouble adapting to those churning ideas, a confused state of flux has kept them quietly on the periphery. Among that group, eccentric concepts had surfaced. Very few of those ideas survived any serious discussion.

At least one idea, though, has attracted two radical adherents. Those two kept their eerie dialogs very secret. In that private bubble, they considered themselves lovers. One is no longer alive and that has destroyed the other's mind.

Every L5er has a full day of work to contribute in their various ways to the survival of the colony. However, with the recent leisure time that some have seen, random discussions at cafés about work and the *what* of things are turning more often to the *why* of situations. An observing sociologist might say that a slightly larger percentage of the younger women focus on the priority of relationships, while the tendency of some older L5ers is to be focused on acquiring technical knowledge. As yet, there is no full-time sociologist in L5.

The cultural flux has been disturbed because of Carrot's having been entrusted with new duty after duty, thereby releasing humans from more tedious work. With an unheeding acceptance of this by the younger generation, Carrot-forks are spawned at a dizzying pace for every aspect of L5 life. Droids now beget better droids. Routine tasks are given to artificial intelligence and other complex algorithms. As yet, the young L5ers have not been instructed in cautionary tales to be taken from the finer points of human philosophy. There hasn't been time.

With that vacuum in the social sciences, philosophical concepts tend to remain in an amorphous state wherein an undefined symbiosis is developing between humans and the almost-humans. That is producing a greater dependence on accomplishing tasks at hand rather considering their long-term consequences.

Only a few have seen the messy possibilities involved. Some Directors have spoken with the small numbers of L5ers whose minds have tracked the complex strands of spaghetti-like assumptions that have developed over the years. Dragonslayer had relied on his mentor, Tolstoy, as his wise sounding-board. Sadly, the light in Tolstoy's eyes has dimmed considerably. Larry has been away, dealing with his skin-graft surgeries and urgent bureaucratic fires on Earth. Billy Cleghorn is willing to speak on the topic with Dragonslayer but, frustratingly, he usually answers each question with another question.

For instance, when Dragonslayer asked Billy's opinion regarding allowing Carrot free rein to design and develop their new series of spaceplanes, Billy replied with, "Well, do you have any concerns about what it's doing?"

So, now just before its first flight, with the acquiescence to function within its own rules, Carrot's redesigned spaceplane model has been given further upgrades with even newer, more powerful engines. This is the version that is made to carry a "pilot" in the front seat, even though the human would have nothing to do but oversee. In the bulbous section behind the pilot is now a larger seat in case another unneeded human would want to ride along. Its protective systems have been upgraded considerably over the first version. This new vehicle has been dubbed *Chick-2,* from Zar's suggestion. And it is the version that will be sent to rescue Charon and his new friends.

Then Carrot proceeds with a literally last-second change to the engine configuration in Chick-2. The former rapid scurrying in the hangar area has become, to a casual observer, a maelstrom of whizzing bodies and droids. But their mad dance is fully coordinated.

A waiting team of L5 specialists take control of Jimmy George as he is extracted from *Chick-1*. When that group clears the dock area, another group of specialists jumps to bring in the re-re-re-designed Chick-2 for its own initial run.

A fresh pilot is given her final briefing. In fact, the briefing could be as simple as, "Sit quietly and oversee what the onboard Carrot-fork is doing."

The final changes are efficiently made to Chick-2's engine module and cabin. Technicians and droids react immediately in perfect coordination to every command given in their ears by Carrot. From the time Chick-1 has been moved out of the arrival bay, it takes only an astonishing two hours and fifty-eight minutes to have the new vehicle ready for its mission - except that the technicians are too busy to be astonished.

One of them takes a rare deep breath to whisper to his cohort. "Is Chick-3 going to be ready soon?"

"No idea. Heard that a complete redesign is in the works for dash-three. Hell, ask Carrot." She shrugs.

The technicians return to their hurried servicing.

Zar shakes his head in admiration at the process. He speaks to Marta beside him, still assigned to Security duties. "It's absolutely amazing. Over the past few weeks, this thing we called *Carrot* has evolved into a, well... a clearly indispensable... I can't say 'thing'. It acts in every way like it was as alive as any professional manager on the other end of a digital connection."

He glances at Marta, taking in her very attractive figure, then sheepishly gets back to his initial thoughts. "Ah, a really smart, seasoned, senior *engineer*! Carrot had planned every step already as if it knew this super-speed swap-out was going to be needed. The fully segregated engine and cabin modules. Nothing but a few brilliantly designed mechanical connections to snap into place, with almost all other necessary connections between the two being wireless. The testing takes longer than the swap-out. It would have taken an engineering department years of improving iteration after iteration to get to this. And then it improved the machine again, on the fly!"

Marta shrugs. "A new reality. Carrot and all the other pseudo-animals and vegetables are, well, a new life-form, aren't they?"

Zar is struck with a disturbing thought. "So what are *we* for?"

Marta considers what to say to the teenager. "Who said we have to *be* for anything? We *are*. They *are*."

Zar clings to his question. "So what are we *for*? Are *we* serving **them**?"

Marta rolls her eyes, exasperated. "Listen, Zar. Yes, things are moving at quantum speed - way faster than homo sapiens can think about. That's really the outcome we have with our boiling kettle of new ideas out here. Well, L5ers have started the boiling, and L5ers will be boiling it for years to come. You may question whether future L5ers will be human or hybrid, or something else again - that answer is beyond my pay-grade to predict, or to consider any changes. If Carrot ever decides to invent a way of seeing into the future, well, *that* could happen. Right now, I don't know. Me? I'm just a regular hunk of h. sapiens. *I* sure as hell don't have any answers."

On time, Chick-2, the experimental excursion vehicle that is beyond anything developed on Earth, is on its way down to Russia, following the location of the Pad that Charon has in his pocket.

Demyadin has appropriated a room for his office that used to be a stately sitting room. The room's wide double doors open onto the second floor foyer on one side, with a grand patio on the other. He had considered closing off the racket but decided to leave the doors open.

In a low tone, he finishes speaking with an in-ear mic/speaker to his recent guest, Vadim.

"Of course. The change in venue is understandable, Vadim. And I look forward to the opportunity to meet you again… In your den, then?… Next month… Fine. Thank you. I hope the information I provided will be of use to you and your friends."

Touching his ear-piece to end the call, he raises his voice over the cacophony of people moving furniture and supplies into his new mansion. "Lateef! Where are you?… Somebody find me Lateef!"

It takes a minute for Lateef to rush from the kitchen where he had been yelled at by Demyadin's chef.

Last year, a previous chef had been caught selling Demyadin's tested, segregated food to some of the new mercenaries. That chef was shot. Those mercenaries were fired and blacklisted. This chef knows exactly what he has to do - protect his boss from poisoned food and feed him nutritious meals whenever and wherever in the world they happened to be.

To Lateef, the chef yells, "I need no help from you to do my job! Get out of my face"

Chagrined, Lateef stands silently wondering what he should do. He is spared the decision when a guard runs up to tell him that Demyadin wants him right now. He rushes to the office to report to his boss.

At Lateef's hurried clatter into the room, Demyadin keeps his head down over the desk as he says, "The only time I want to see you running in my mansion is if you need to save me from imminent danger." He looks up. "I want you to behave in the manner of the important position you hold - right-hand man to the soon-to-be most powerful person on Earth." He peeks from under his prominent eyebrows with a slight smile. "Walk with pride, Lateef. Yes?... Now, during our move here I am concerned that we have not kept sufficient pressure on the idiot Charon. Elementary tactics." He raises his head fully. "You will consult with... oh, that little IT gnome..."

"Billy, sir."

"Billy. Never can remember his name. Ask Billy if PT has any news."

"PT, sir?"

"Just ask him. I'll explain another time."

"Yes sir." He turns to go on his errand at a more sedate pace.

Lateef, being the Boss' new, young, trusted lieutenant, is tested by everyone. And the IT gnome, Billy, has the personality to be disagreeable with anybody he meets. Except the Boss.

"He said PT." Lateef is holding himself erect. His nose is elevated nobly as he confronts an intractable Billy.

For his part, Billy has not yet met an officious grandee whom he could not bafflegab into confusion.

"That would be Prancing Tiger. Do you have clearance from Mr. Demyadin to even mention that name?"

"Well of course I have! He just now told me to…"

Billy is dismissive. "So if some flunky from a foxhole came by and told me the same story, what do you think I should do?"

Flummoxed, Lateef stutters, "Well, I, I am not some flunky from a foxhole! I am Mr. Demaydin's right-hand man!"

"Sez you. Prove it."

Lateef is sorely tempted to reach for his pistol. He does not. Instead, he turns on his heel to march back to Demyadin. Nearing the boss' office, he stops to consider: *Will he yell at me for not doing what I was told? Will I appear weak?*

At that point he hears a yell. "Lateef!"

Starting to run, Lateef turns it into a proud walk. As he enters the office, Demyadin is not to be seen. Lateef looks around carefully.

From a dark corner, partially obscured by tall drapes next to tall, built-in book shelves, Demyadin is fingering a row of heavy textbooks. "Paper. Such an old way to pass on knowledge, don't you agree, Lateef?"

Focusing on the voice, he detects his boss in the darkness. "Yes sir. Useful as a storage medium, but as you say, an old way."

Demyadin spins to face Lateef. "Why?" In the semi-darkness, Demyadin has the ghostly appearance of a sinister succubus.

Taken aback by the image, at the same time Lateef is slapped in the mind with an incongruous question. His survival instinct galvanizes him into unaccustomed cognitive action.

"Why, sir? Well…" The adrenalin rush hits the correct sector of his faculties. For some reason, he has a flash of insight that comes from the year he spent in a library while waiting for his next assignment. "Paper-based knowledge is asynchronous. It can be read at any time, but from the hour it is printed its ability to convey *current* knowledge is eroded by every passing day. In my opinion, sir, synchronous knowledge that is organically growing and carefully considered in the minds of intelligent individuals carries more value. That value, however, is there only if it is sorted and sifted from the mountain of dreg that constantly accumulates, then realized only by a trained interpreter. It's a balance of currently accurate data versus stable, vetted data that is yesterday's news… Ah, I'm not an academic, sir." He modestly adds, "I, ah, just read that in a thesis."

Clearly struck by the response, Demyadin steps up to Lateef with a serious look. They are of similar height, though Lateef is of much lighter build. Demyadin's black jacket and open-necked white shirt are comfortably expensive. They exude a great deal more substance than does the officer's uniform that Lateef has managed to scrounge up.

Demyadin makes a mental note, *Interpreted. Yes.*

"I am impressed, Lateef. My instinct said you were a good choice and now I am pleased to have heard your thought process. Very pleased." He takes Lateef by a shoulder to lead him to cloth-covered chairs arranged some distance from the bookcases.

"So, you spoke with Billy the IT gnome and were met with resistance."

With his new mindset of being a manager rather than a servant, Lateef steers his thoughts away from being merely reactive, to using creative thinking. "Yes, sir. But I believe I understand why. You were testing me – both of us – regarding security about PT."

Demyadin nods. "You continue to impress me, Lateef. Thank you, yes. It *was* a test."

Seating himself comfortably and placing a nearby book on his lap, Demyadin tents his fingers. "Prancing Tiger. What I tell you is never to be repeated. By that I mean, *whatever I tell you.*"

He pauses to give his statement the importance it deserves. "Of course, you will pass on directives. You understand what I mean? You are a bright young man, Lateef. Certainly you understand." He nods to himself. "So…" He turns his gaze to the dark ceiling above Lateef. "PT is an AI-based cybersecurity break-in program."

He hefts the book from his lap to glance at the title, *Cyber Warfare in Command-and-Control*. "It seems everything is some sort of cyber-whatever-the-fuck nowadays, isn't it?" He flashes a grin at Lateef. "Anyway, mine is different," he flips the book at a coffee table, where it crashes loudly. He smiles. "…which is what they all say. But it is. This is ***Prancing Tiger***. Before I left that den of idiots in L5 who are marching blindly toward the destruction of mankind as we know it, I appropriated code that had been in development for their version of neural-net software for a supercomputer. When I showed some of it to, ah, Billy, he became inordinately excited. I might use the word, *immorally* excited." Demyadin smiles at the recollection.

His eyes absently follow dark woodbeam accents in the ceiling. "I will tell you the core of my objection to what the misguided idiots are doing in L5. They are, essentially, incubating a monstrous AI egg. Some would give it a silly name like *Singularity*, but that is too simplistic a concept. Authors of dramatic fiction are fond of the vision of a sudden galaxy-shattering explosion when it comes to any extinction threat. In fact, it is more profound than that, and more realistic. It is the slow, agonizing start down a completely inevitable, oil-slicked spiral. At first, it appears that one can scramble back at any time but once you wake up to the slippery gradient and to the approaching black depths below, you can do nothing but slide down in exquisite terror, faster and faster, tortuously falling into the hellish obscurity below."

Demyadin pauses to stare into Lateef's wide eyes. "Understand that the person on that slope would, initially, not be conscious of the results of each little decision made to give up their role as a sovereign actor. Those many actions of AIs are couched in terms of little helpful things that you come to rely on. Make coffee, clean up spills, read through emails, reply to routine queries, offer analyses of extended documentation… Until you can no longer do those little things without the help of the devil AI."

Demyadin grunts as he stretches in the chair. He shakes his head solemnly, "Ever since being awakened to this by the prophetic words of Stephen Hawking and in his and others' Open Letter of 2015, I've been growing more and more convinced of the unfolding calamity. In fact, my fear is that the AIs are directed very subtly by a digital sentience that's driving resolutely toward one goal - the replacement of humanity by androids. This I can prove with my own direct experience *out there* and with the secret documentation that I was able to bring back with me when I escaped. That is the sole reason for all this…" he waves a hand around, "… So that I can now wholly engage in my world-spanning effort to stop them."

Lateef's mouth has begun to slacken. He is astounded at this epiphany. *So that's why we are fighting so hard! Demyadin believes he is our saviour. Maybe…*

Lateef's resolve begins to strengthen. His face shows the hardening that Demyadin has been looking for. Lateef now has an over-arching purpose in life - to do whatever he can to assist Demyadin.

Seeing the change in Lateef's demeanor, Demyadin nods. "So you see, my young friend, we are not a mere army of mercenaries looking to enrich ourselves. This is a holy endeavour to save our race… Are you with me?"

Lateef stiffens in the chair. "Absolutely, sir! One thousand percent with you! Whatever you ask me to do!"

Relaxing into his chair, Demyadin nods and ponders. "Oh. I was talking about Billy."

"Yes sir, you convinced him…"

Demyadin half raises a hand for silence as he remembers fondly. "I had to literally grab him by his **balls** and threaten to cut out each one like he was a young pig. My uncle told me how he castrated piglets on his farm. After slicing with a razor blade, he rubbed the cuts with a handful of salt. The squeals were, he said, quite stimulating. My uncle relished that memory, even on his deathbed." He fixes his eyes on Lateef. "This I recounted to Billy as I tightened my hold. Billy promised to obey me fully and he has not yet disappointed. Ah, do I have to be so uncouth as to grab…?"

Lateef cringes but instantly regains his composure. "No, sir. That will not be necessary. Your message has been received loud and clear." He shifts uncomfortably.

"Good." Demyadin continues, "PT has been extended by Billy, with the carefully chosen assistance of certain hacker groups. Let me add that security was maintained by ensuring that each of those isolated hackers will no longer be in a position to speak of their parts in the program."

"Have they been paid…"

"They are now as was the Norwegian Parrot."

"…Right." The reference to an old Monty Python skit comes to him just in time.

Expressionless, Demyadin stares at Lateef long and hard. Lateef stands quietly under the intense scrutiny. His tightly trimmed dark hair and close beard hide slowly accumulating perspiration. He knows this is his initiation rite. If he passes, he is in. And now he really wants to be in.

A smile creeps across Demyadin's lips. "I like you, Lateef. I believe you may be the thoughtless person I've been searching for." He thinks, *Does he know of Eichmann? He is fighting hard to remain cool. Of course I will use that, but he needs to have a fundamental fear of me to be unthinkingly loyal.*

"I hope you realize that I am not being unkind in saying *unthinking*. I want you to obey me. Do not *think* about my orders. What I say, you will accomplish immediately, yes? I truly believe you are capable of doing this well. I have not spoken like this to many people." He flashes his devilish grin. "Yes, I am absolutely ruthless because I *know* I have a holy mission. Now, if I say I like somebody, that is platinum. The regard which I have expressed for you comes with considerable benefits. But hear this: there will be gruesome consequences if you ever - *EVER* - cross me."

Drilling his eyes deep into Lateef's soul, he cracks a full smile, then finally reaches out a hand to Lateef.

Lateef has a vision flash instantly through his mind of him kissing Demyadin's hand. He wipes that vision away.

They shake hands firmly. "Understand?"

Lateef nods. "Explicitly, sir."

"Good. Now go back to, whatshisname, *Billy*. You will know what to say."

As the newly ensconced right-hand man of the Boss, Lateef marches with confident authority into Billy's new office and says one thing to Billy's back as the chubby gnome is hunched over his keyboard. He is typing the word "hallucination?" as a comment in front of a list of "Outcomes".

"Balls."

Billy squirms in his chair then turns halfway around. He gazes up to his favourite illustration hanging behind the bank of monitors. The poster taped to the wall is the original "Earth-rise" picture taken by the Apollo 8 crew.

"Prancing Tiger is my masterpiece. If you think the Boss would be upset to have its secrets revealed, *I* would be a hundred times more upset. Got that? Do you?"

Billy rotates his chair to face Lateef. The newly confident Lateef steps closer to him. Billy looks like he may reach out a hand. "Welcome to my future." Then he glances for an instant at a small picture taped to a wall; his hand drops.

Lateef steps forward. He observes the picture. "Is that…"

"Fatima. In the HR office. It's to remind me to ask her for, ah, another programmer."

Lateef raises his eyebrows. "Do you need more…"

"No! Never mind! Don't need her anymore!"

Lateef notes an obvious sore point. Billy pushes his wheeled chair to the wall to rip off the picture. He crumples it then tosses it into a trash bucket. Sadly, "Never mind her." His mind insists on dredging up the image of her spurning him; walking away from him with a nasty grimace under her flowing dreadlocks.

Billy grabs the counter to pull himself back to his position in front of the keyboard. He drops his head and sways his head slightly.

Giving him a moment, Lateef's eyes wander from screen to screen. *A randomness to the way he has the monitors set up.*

Billy finally mumbles. "What do you want?"

"To be friends. We are going to work together, here, and…"

Billy twists sideways to better look at Lateef. It takes moment, but he reaches out a hand. They shake.

Billy cocks his head. "Lateef? Is that…?"

Despite years of avoiding telling acquaintances of his background, Lateef realizes that Billy could likely find out his history with his computer skills. He forces a smile. "I was born in a Palestinian workcamp in the UAE. My mother would not tell me much about her life. And these days, an individual's personal history has become irrelevant, don't you think? Mass migrations…"

Billy shakes his head. "My name is Willam. Had a handle, Billy-the-Conqueror. It stuck. Billy. I'm a Boor. South Africa."

A light goes on in Lateef's mind: *That very slight accent on vowels.*

Billy carries on, "Ok? Enough chit-chat. Anyway, Prancing Tiger is, like I said, my masterpiece. I programmed a complicated generative AI to analyze the contents of electronic packets before they arrive at designated APs. Then I set up a highly secure MtM mesh network protocol..."

Lateef raises a hand. "Hold on, please, Billy. I can set up my phone apps but you're way beyond that with your acronyms. What's AP and MTM? And by generative AI you mean...?"

Billy gives Lateef a pained look as if he were telling a young child how to hold a glass of water. "Access Point. Multipoint-to-Multipoint. Artificial intelligence, for petes-sake! It's been around for fifty years." Petulantly, "Listen, if you're not interested..."

"Please, Billy, I *am* very interested, but I don't know your lingo. Just give me the high-level overview if you can."

"Oh." He tries to reset. "I don't know if it'll mean anything to crunch it into a simple sentence... Ok. My AI can break into every comm-pro – ah, communications protocol – as an invisible man-in-the-middle – and grab enough from each packet with my sniffer to...

"So you can spy on network packets? This is old hand, no?"

"Yeah yeah, but that's only the start. The AI uses meta-analysis to crack the crypto..."

Lateef holds up a hand so he can ponder briefly. "Can you give me a recent example so I can see what it is you're doing?"

Billy's body compresses into his high security mode. "This is top secret stuff and I'm not sure…"

"Balls."

Deflated, Billy opens up and turns to his keyboard. "Yeah yeah. Ok, right now. See this L5 mesh stream?" He points to one of six windows on what is labeled Monitor 3.

"PT's working through the permutations as it breaks into the crypto." He snaps his head to fully face Lateef. "Not that fucken cryptomoney shit. *Real* crypto. Security." He pauses to reset again. Billy nods at the monitor, "It's coming from a Russian IP. She's calling it D223. That's *L5 Dork two-twenty-three*, a guy called Charon." Billy actually smiles. He pronounces the name with a "*sh*" sound. "We can't figure why he went dark so PT's grabbing millions of packets to latch onto attendant actors. Still working on it. The Boss really wants this guy."

Lateef shrugs then puts a hand on Billy's shoulder. The sudden tension in every one of Billy's muscles is palpable. "That last bit's the only thing I fully understood."

He lowers his hand and waits for Billy to relax and turn his tense face toward him. "Listen, Billy. We're going to be working together closely. I can see you are committed to this and I can assure you I am absolutely committed to the Boss' mission and what he's doing. We had a long and deep discussion about it. I need to be able to come to you to get clear, actionable information. No bafflegab. Please try. Ok?" Before leaving, he notices the word "hallucination" on one of Billy's monitors. "Oh, and what's the hallucination about?"

Billy rapidly blanks that monitor. "Nothing."

"But…"

"Ok, listen - and I ***do not want this getting***… worrying the Boss. Got it?" He spins around to face Lateef. "Look – he's got way too much to worry about and this is, it's only a possibility…" He rotates in his chair back to his standard position of staring at the monitors. "It's an AI thing."

Lateef rolls his eyes wryly at Billy's back. "As long as you have it under control."

Billy nods perfunctorily and types something on his keyboard. As Lateef walks away, Billy adds, "We should hang out. I'll text you tonight." Under his breath he curls the name over his tongue, "Lateef."

Lateef rolls his eyes as he leaves the room. Pacing himself carefully so as not to look too eager, Lateef returns to Demyadin's office. As he enters he is dumbfounded to see his boss finish injecting his arm with something. Demyadin looks up sharply and their eyes lock.

Demyadin speaks quietly. "For the pain. Some kind of blood cancer but the fucken specialists can't find what it is. Damn them… ***Damn them all to hell!***"

On Their Own

Before the trio reaches Kazan in their Legend J-3, Charon's Pad dings him. He uses his knees on the control stick to keep the wings more-or-less level as he grumbles through the new security sign-on procedure.

Behind him, Jevghenji instinctively reaches forward to help but the increased pain from his right shoulder is too much. *Shouldn't have climbed the wing to fuel up, last time.*

He grimaces and slumps back against Darinka, who makes him as comfortable as she can on their cramped seat. She pulls out one of her pain pills that are left over from the supply she'd bought for her mother. Handing one to Jevghenji, he falls asleep in a minute.

Charon works through the Pad's security sign-on, then is able to read and reply to the texts from L5:

> Dragonslayer: *Confirm your track*
>
> Charon: *South of Kazan*
>
> Dragonslayer: *Confirmed. No issues?*

Charon: *Fueled up with friendlies. Any chatter from D?*

Dragonslayer: *Something. Our veggie is working on it.*

Charon: *Mum?*

Dragonslayer: *eta 45 minutes. Hold your trajectory. End*

Putting his Pad away, Charon shifts in his seat as he puts his left hand on the control stick between his knees and rests his right arm loosely below the throttle. He half-turns to yell back over the cabin noise, "40 minutes. Jevghenji, we need a safe place to land. With a longish runway."

They've been flying over the boring landscape for hours. Time to land.

Darinka has to shake her cousin out of an open-mouthed stupor. "Prosipatisja." [*wake up*]

He jerks awake. "Gdeh?... *Oij!*" [*where? ow!*] The sharp movement is too much for his right shoulder.

Darinka pats his thigh then lays out their map before him and points to Kazan. "Vot ono." [*Here it is*]

With a pained expression Jevghenji leans forward to focus on the map. "Mozhet Vlad…" [*maybe Vlad*]

He sucks in as he tries to adjust to a better position. As loudly as he can, "Sorry. Here. River bend. Road is close. Fly over. Turn south. Fly again back. Sharp turn. If Vlad is safe, blue flag wave, land on road. No wire. Only one house at bend." He nods at Charon. "Have money? Vlad want money."

Charon grins wryly and thinks: *Might need just about all I have left, after he sees the landing rocket.*

Vlad's mouth is hanging open even while he blesses himself. "Bozhe moi, bozhe moi." [*my god, my god*]

He stares at the L5 rocket as it whooshes away. A minute later, Vlad, Darinka and Charon are still mesmerized, staring into the sky watching the spaceplane disappear into the high clouds.

Then they hear the loud thunder of jets with afterburners wide open. Two fighters fly over at low level and max speed, leaving behind a sonic boom that grabs the guts of every person on the ground from the inside and shakes really hard. The sonic boom shatters the windows of Vlad's house causing glittering shards to fall to the ground without being heard in the overwhelming waterfall of sound.

The jets are perceptibly slower than the L5 rocket.

Vlad points at them. "MiG tridtsat odin." [*MiG thirty-one*}

Charon responds with, "MiG *forty*-one, I believe. Supposed to have a top speed of Mach four point three. Pretty good but not enough to catch a spaceplane." He turns and shrugs at Vlad.

Vlad shakes his head in wonder. "Da. Zdravstvuyte kosmonavt." [*Yes. Hello spaceman*]

They watch for another minute as the fighters continue their futile chase of the disappearing L5 machine.

Reaching for his wallet, Charon is about to add more money to the amount he has already given to Vlad. Darinka cuts between them with an accusing, "Nemnogo znayesh russkiy?" [*Know some Russian?*]

"Nemnogo." [*Not too much*] He gives her a wry grin.

Meanwhile, Vlad is becoming agitated as he notices the damage to his house. Then he looks around in alarm. "Gangstery skoro budut zdes. My dolzhny uyti!" [*The gangsters will be here soon. We have to leave!*]

Darinka joins in his alarm. "Yes! Must go now!" She takes Charon's arm and they run for their plane.

Vlad does an old man's run to his house to throw together a grab bag then comes out, struggling with it as the bag awkwardly bounces on his back. Dropping the bag behind his house, he flings open his own barn/hangar.

By that time, Charon has the fueled-up Legend J-3 pushed around to face the gravel road they had landed on. Quickly opening the cabin door for Darinka, he waits as she piles into the back seat. Charon jumps into the pilot's seat and has the engine turning over before Darinka can find her seatbelt. They bounce into the air in a minute. He starts a westward track then doubles back at low altitude over a scrub forest, heading east again.

Flying as low as he is able, he must not take his eyes off the possible obstructions in the landscape. Settling into a robotic flight-mode, he adjusts the throttle to an economy cruise. Darinka, in the rear seat, has the map unfolded and is keeping track of their original flightpath. She yells out the occasional river names or railway/road intersections.

Hours of sweat-inducing low flying later, the sun is approaching the horizon, making it even more dangerous to carry on. Charon is absolutely exhausted. He wipes his face frequently with one sleeve then the other. Finally, *Fuel low now.*

He yells back to her. "We need to land real soon. How far to that next fuel stop?"

She has her finger near it on the map. "Must be that church! Village is first, then a clearing before the big forest! See it?"

He nods. "Got it!"

Charon decides to give the village a wide berth before landing. The meadow has no markings and it is now dark enough at ground level that he cannot be sure of obstructions as he brings the plane in as quietly as he can. He sets up a slow, safe approach. *Like a glassy-water landing. There's enough light to see down to the ground but as soon as we get near, the meadow and trees are all a dark grey. Could be anything there from a herd of sheep to a wedding party dancing in this meadow, damnit.*

No sheep. No bridesmaids. He bounces to a teeth-clenched, white-knuckle landing in the dark. As he jars over rough clumps of grass and slices through shrubs, he tries to scan for the fuel cache that Vlad had described earlier, before the rocket landing took his attention away. Darinka sees it first. "Vot ono!" [*there it is!*]

Safely stopping next to the fuel tank mounted on stilts, Charon takes a minute to recover.

Darinka is ready to exit the plane. "Charon? We wait for what?"

"Yes…I'm ok. I just need a minute to bring my heart rate down from 200." He wipes more sweat off his face with his damp sleeve.

"Heart rate? Charon! Are you…"

"I'm fine. Honest." He slips off his seatbelt and does a double take at the wide swath of sweat that marks where the belt had sat over his chest and belly. He shrugs and opens the door. As warm air rushes in, he smiles, "Good. We can sleep outside tonight, under the wing."

He catches a glimpse through the trees of village lights almost a kilometre away. His legs are weak as he wobbles out. Charon grabs the wing strut then raises a hand to help Darinka out.

She climbs out quickly to wrap her arms around him. "You are a wonderful, brave pilot! You fly like a bird!" She reaches up to give him a light kiss. "A big bird," she laughs, rolling her breasts over his still wet belly.

They both enjoy their freedom and kiss again, for much longer.

Reluctantly, Charon releases from her grip. "First things first, my dear. We have to fuel up then find a place to push this beast under some cover. Then food and drink." He takes in her wide open brown eyes. "Then…"

In a sultry whisper, "Then what, my beautiful spaceman?"

"Then… we should sleep." He grins.

Darinka whacks him across the arm. "*Sleep*!?"

He rubs the arm. "Well, since you put it that way, maybe we can, ah, talk about tomorrow?" He spins away from another whack.

Charon is awakened by his Pad's incessant dinging. He drowsily picks it up to answer it then swears as he is forced to go through the security signon.

Finally, he sees, "Text from Jasmine."

Darinka still has a leg over him under the blanket. She rolls onto her back. "Shto?" [*What?*]

"L5 is asking where are we and why aren't we moving."

"Moving? I give them moving!" She rolls back to rub against his leg then reaches higher.

"Not now, please, Darinka." Charon's kind smile is visible in the growing light.

Grinning, she doesn't stop. Charon's attention is divided as he enjoys her probing hand.

He kisses her forehead. "Please. I have only a brief time before the secure connection times-out."

He starts typing:

Charon: *Overnighted at Ufa. Is Jevghenji doing well?*

Jasmine: *Ok. Medics think Jevghenji has fractured collar bone. He will be treated when he arrives.*

Charon: *We thought it better to send him up first. Darinka can go next.*

Jasmine: *Negative. C detected a worrisome change in tactics from D and/or Russians. That's why we had to rush the previous extraction.*

Charon: *And that leaves us where?*

No reply from L5 for a minute. Charon holds out the Pad to shake it. A red light flickers briefly but there is no further response from Jasmine.

He shrugs and turns to Darinka. "Could be a pro…"

Just then an image takes over the screen. It resolves from indeterminate large pixels, to the old "Earth-rise" picture taken by the Apollo 8 crew.

"Huh?" He quickly opens the back cover to shake out the battery.

Darinka doesn't understand the significance of the action. "What are you doing, Charon?" She sits up then slips the blanket over her bare shoulders.

His forehead is wrinkled in concern. "Compromised. The Pad's been compromised again." He drops the Pad beside its cover. "We're on our own, kid."

"This is good news or bad news?" She raises an eyebrow.

Before Charon can answer, a bullet smashes into the airplane engine cowling over their heads then a distant shot is heard from the direction of the village. They both flatten onto the blanket and scan the meadow and trees. Nobody can be seen.

Charon pulls Darinka roughly to the other side of the airplane. "Clothes on. Quick. I'll grab our bag of supplies. We have to leave on foot. Engine's not going to survive that." He notices a glinting liquid, probably oil, dripping from the bottom of the cowl onto the ground.

Starting at a silent trot with their bags loose on their backs, the two make over a kilometre at that pace, reaching heavier forest cover where they take a minute to catch their breath.

Both are puffing hard. Darinka adjusts the hastily wrapped load on her back. "Can we stop?"

Charon stares back across the meadow they ran over. Smoke snakes up from where the Legend J-3 had been, then they hear a low explosion. The black smoke thickens, rising high in the air.

"Well. Jevghenji's going to be pissed off with me. I guess we walk until another machine can be found." He shrugs. "Don't see any pursuit at this time. Darinka, that load is too much. Let me take some…"

She plunks it down, taking a deep breath. "No. I will carry it." Darinka leans against a tree, puffing, still keeping an eye on the meadow. She flaps her shirt to cool down then buttons up more fully.

Charon nods. "We can stop here briefly. A brisk walk should be a safe pace when we start again. Some ways from here I want to find a couple suitable branches for a, whatsitcalled…a travapoi?" He dredges up a word from one of the many outdoors articles he'd read years ago.

She shrugs.

"Whatever." He carries on with his thought. "Sticks lashed together to hold the bags. We can either carry it on our shoulders or I can drag it. Just don't want to make the drag marks for a while."

Darinka is too exhausted to reply.

Charon thinks. "You know, I think its actually a *carry* when you have it on two people's shoulders."

Darinka is tired and frustrated. "You know so much; make the spaceplane come down here."

He pulls out his batteryless Pad and contemplates trying it again. "No. Too soon. Later, ok?"

She waves it away with a tired arm.

They trudge all morning at a steady pace along the rolling steppe terrain. Scattered forest turns into meadows. They skirt a marsh that is fed by a slowly dribbling creek.

They test its water and gulp down what they need, then top up their container. More trudging…

An incongruous vision resolves itself as they climb a rock-strewn slope. It is a dusty, bird-dropping-spattered MiG-23U sitting in an overgrown patch of tall grass and yellow blossoms. It is in a clearing near the top of the long slope of the steppe.

They are both sweating profusely as they trudge up to the clearing.

The completely out-of-place aircraft is surrounded by a stout, unpainted 1-1/2 metre high wooden fence. The MiG's large rectangular air intakes on either side of the cockpit are covered with peeling, faded, red plywood covers. An even more faded warning in cyrillic on the plywood warns the world: *NE TROGIJ* [*do not touch*]

The sign confuses Darinka. "Hm. Must be a local dialect." She shrugs.

Her curiosity pulls her around the machine toward the far side, with Charon reluctantly being dragged by their mutual load. He strains his head to investigate components as they pass by.

The tail seems to have a dark streaky patch starting from the very top. All three wheels' tires have been long ago deflated and crumbled away. The main gear is sunk into the ground with the result that the sharp nose sticks up in the air as if the plane were taking off.

Darinka gratefully lowers her side of the *carry* to the ground beside the fence. Charon waits for her to finish then lowers his end of the carry sticks as well.

Charon snorts at the museum piece. "What a relic. I can see why this tandem-seat *Flogger* hasn't moved from here in, what? Thirty years?"

Darinka is defensive. "It has a nice shape, no?" *Why should I defend something Russian?*

"The MiGs before the twenty-three were made according to the design principle of, 'It should be repairable anywhere with a screwdriver and hammer'. For some reason, this design became a nightmare to maintain and repair. Probably the folding wings and fancy avionics. This one, here, was likely landed for some minor issue and they could never get it off the ground again. So here it sits - a monument to the former engineer whose bright idea it was to make it overly complicated."

With a slight pout, Darinka feels she must uphold the Slavic engineer's honour. "Before your spaceplane, before MiG-41, fastest machine was MiG-27."

"Ok, but *second* fastest. The Blackbird went a lot higher and a lot faster."

Darinka stays silent for a minute as they walk around the airplane's fence. She gives in to American superiority. Then adds, "America was so smart. Why did they kill our planet?"

A movement in the valley over a kilometre downslope catches her eye. She whispers and points to it. "Charon?"

Both instinctively slouch down into the cover of the tall grass to peer downslope.

Still wary, she whispers again, "Can you fly this MiG?"

He smiles as he glances over his shoulder at the relic. "No fuel, corroded, and whatever brought it down hasn't been repaired, and besides…" he grins, "…the layer of bird droppings makes it harder to fly."

Darinka continues watching the valley. "Maybe sheep… or cows."

"Perhaps. Lets settle down and wait it out. Keep watching. We can use the rest."

Rolling over to the carry, he pulls away the bag that Darinka had made by wrapping a number of loose items into a blanket. Staying low in the grass, he reaches to give her the bag. "Here. Lean against this. Make yourself comfortable while I drag the rest of our supplies under cover to the side of the plane."

She adjusts her back against the bag. "Ow! You gave me the lumpy bag."

"Complain complain. That's all I hear from you." They smile at each other as he crawls away on his ample belly.

Before he rounds the corner of the fence she whispers, "Cows," pointing down the valley.

"Good. Keep watching." Panting, he rolls to his side to rest, then considers the option of making the effort to stand up or to stay on the ground. He stays down.

Later, they set up a temporary camp on the back side of the fence. Just two hundred metres behind the MiG's fence is a line of tall shrubs and that trees mark the top of the rise they are on. After a meal of bread, bacon, cheese and water, Charon opens up the map.

He peruses the cyrillic names. "This is the village where we were shot at, I think."

She nods, leaning in close against his shoulder. "Da." Then, glimpsing dark clouds on the western horizon, "Not good."

"What?"

"Storm." She nods toward the distant gathering clouds. "Coming this way. Storms on the steppe are dangerous."

Charon rolls to a kneeling position. "Shit. We'll have to take our stuff right under the plane's wings."

With some urgency, they gather the several items that had been unpacked and drop them over the fence toward the MiG, then do the same for the rest of their supplies. The bags are placed carefully under the wing root, protected as much as possible from the rising westerly wind. As it flows closer up the slope toward them across swaths of the wild vegetation, alive and malevolent gusts flatten the tall grass. A chillier air hits their faces.

Satisfied with where the bags now are, Charon stands up to investigate the MiG's fuselage. "A trainer, I expect. Tandem seating. Did they have a bomber version? Can't see inside from here through the grime. Maybe we should get inside during the storm?"

The cabin of the plane is too high to reach without a ladder. Charon looks around, his shirt flapping in the turbulent wind. He decides to test the wooden fence. Pulling on a section, Charon nods, "Still pretty strong."

Darinka notices what he is thinking of doing. "Ah, Charon, my dear spaceman. You are, you carry more weight on Earth than when you were in space, no?"

He grins at her from the fence. "Nicely put my lovely partner. You're saying I'm too fat to be held up by this wood."

"No but… be careful. Please?"

"You're probably right. So I'll have to lash two of these sections together. But quickly." Continuing to scan downslope, he wiggles the fence on the north side, then tries other sections. "The strongest seem to be over here." Charon works quickly at one of the fence corners to release that section. Pleased with his hasty work so far, he pulls out long-established clumps of grass and weeds from the bottom of the fence then works out the far side of the section. It topples over, intact. "Good! One more." Random gusts whip his hair about.

Charon drags the two sections he released from the fence over to the forward fuselage. Seeing where the pilots are supposed to enter the cockpit in front of the port engine, he hauls up one fence section to sit against the fuselage next to the air intake.

Meanwhile, Darinka has been keeping her eyes on both the weather coming in and on any action down in the valley. She casts worried glances at what Charon is doing, as well, thinking, *I really like this man. He is honest and kind. Tall, dark and a big belly. What more could I want? And he is a spaceman! But he is too heavy for that wooden fence. What do we do if he falls and breaks a leg? I will jump to him so he can fall softly on me.*

For his part, Charon thinks about the physics of his contraption. *Need to turn the ladder over so the slats face me, then put the other section with its slats, what? Facing each other or the same way? Compression goes against the strength of the long pieces. So both should be oriented the same way. I think. And step on the slats right next to where they're nailed.*

He turns the first section with its slats out then places the other section against it. Mumbling to himself, "Wire. Need to tie them together."

He finds a dangling length of electrical wire that somebody had left long ago after tearing into the underside of a wing. "Perfect." He works a few sections apart by bending the wire back and forth rapidly, then hurriedly uses the wire to lash the fence sections together.

Giving his construction a strong shake, he steps gingerly onto the bottom rung. It holds. He carefully steps up further.

Darinka keeps a worried eye on Charon, fearing the worst, ready to jump.

When Charon reaches high enough to peer into the bottom of the cabin's grime-covered side window, she looks away with a grimace.

With some effort Charon forces out a folding step that pilots used to use, then stands on the narrow thing to inspect what he can. Happy with his progress, he turns to Darinka, "Can you hand me a clump of the dried grass, please? I want to clean off some of the crap to look inside."

Already standing by the wing, Darinka gathers a large handful from around the landing gear and hands it up to him. "You be carefully up there!"

"Yes, mother. Keep watching the valley. Please?"

She steps back to a vantage point to scan the valley and the weather. "They will be too smart to go out in the rain. It is a big storm coming." The roiling clouds are not far off now.

Charon finds where the forward canopy latch is but the corroded mechanism is reluctant to move. "Darinka, do you know where that hatchet is? Knew it would be useful."

"For breaking into a MiG fighter plane, yes?"

"Yes! Of course! Why else would we bring it?"

Rummaging around the bags, she comes across her brass coffee-grinder and the axe. "*These* are what were digging into my back!… Here!" She hands the axe up to him.

"Ah, thanks, but can you please take the cover off the blade for me?"

She unsnaps the leather cover, touching the blade. "Oj! Sharp! Be careful!"

"Yes, mother."

Alternating use of both the blade and the hammer side of the hatchet, Charon is finally able to prise open the latch. The canopy also needs some persuasion to lift up. With much grunting from Charon and squealing from the canopy, its front is pushed high enough to see inside. Charon is surprised. "Fairly well preserved. I could sit in that seat. Maybe. Going to see if I can lift the other canopy, too."

Having learned during his first attempt, Charon lifts the rear piece more easily. Soon both canopies sit wide open. He reaches down to dust off the seat. "You know, we could probably sit inside during the storm…"

"Airplane coming!" Darinka yells, then begins closing up the bag she recently opened.

Charon sees the small plane off to the south. It is skirting the storm clouds and heading right toward them. "Quick! Climb up here and take the rear seat!" He drops the hatchet down beside the ladder and clambers the rest of the way up to put one foot onto the seat, waiting for Darinka to climb up.

Darinka hastily ties a knot in the top of the blanket bag then shoves it under the wing with their other bags. She climbs gingerly up the ladder. Charon takes her hand to steady her as she moves around him to the rear. Following her, he shows her where to step to get to the back cockpit. Drizzle is now making the grime slippery.

As she seats herself, he pushes down the canopy but loses his footing and slips. He splays against her wet canopy, shoving it almost closed.

He can hear her yelling, "Are you hurt?"

"Just my pride. I'm alright." More carefully, he clambers to the front canopy then wiggles his large frame into the tight seat. As he hauls down the canopy, he wishes he'd had time to clean more of the dust and bird droppings off the outside. From inside, Charon can peer only through parts of the dirty window where he had used the grass clump. "What's that awful smell?" *Oh. The bird-shit.* He considers opening his canopy but, instead, yells to Darinka behind him, "Can you hear me?"

Not as loudly, "Yes."

"Good. How is your visibility outside?"

"Good. You cleaned off the dirt when you closed it. I can smell it."

Charon mumbles, looking at the heavy streaks of grime on his belly, "Yeah, I know."

The approaching airplane is making its way upslope. It takes another minute to fly over them. Charon can see through bird-splots that it is a single-engined high-wing. He thinks, *Not sure if it's a Cessna or a clone. Their track looks like it's directly over us. Probably just using the MiG as a marker. They look like they want to get ahead of that big stormcloud.*

The airplane passes and keeps going. He raises his voice, "We should be ok! Lets ride out the storm where we are, ok?"

Darinka has been craning her neck to watch the airplane. "No markings! Either one of Jevghenji's friends or the GRU."

With that reminder, the departing noise takes on an ominous tone in Charon's mind. He pulls out his Pad. Settling back, Charon wonders again if L5's IT gurus have figured out how to safely reach through to him. He balances the Pad's battery on the HUD platform and sets it to solar-charge.

Heavier rain pitter-pats on the canopy, then, with dark roiling clouds overhead, it starts to pelt heavily with hail that reverberates throughout the fuselage, making it too loud for them to hear each other.

Darinka notices rain leaking around the base of her canopy. *Not closed.* She pulls down on it as hard as she can then decides to use the latch to pull it fully closed. *Better. Raining so hard.*

As she releases the latch handle a bright **FLASH** OF LIGHT and a **CRACK** OF THUNDER SCARES THEM OUT OF THEIR SKIN!

…They shake in their seats stunned in primal fear.

Their hair literally spikes out in all directions. Charon lifts an arm from his knee to feel his head causing a spark to zap his hand from the metal frame of the fuselage. He is in shock, not knowing what will happen next. Darinka's heart is racing as fast as her mind that is going through disaster images: *Bomb dropped from airplane; mortar round from strangers in village; this airplane is blowing up in slow motion and the blast will hit me in the next instant…*

The tail of the MiG has been hit by lightning. Fortunately, the lightning found that its fastest way to the ground was through the metal of the landing gear that had been sitting firmly in the earth. Its passage leaves a load of static in the metal of the fuselage, which is dispersing slowly.

When he recovers from the heart-thumping shock, Charon yells out, "DARINKA! ARE YOU ALRIGHT?"

Through the still pouring rain he hears a plaintive, "Yes! You?"

"LIGHTNING STRIKE! …WE SHOULD BE OK FOR NOW!"

She thinks, *If there is no more lightning.*

Charon has the same concern. *That dark patch on its tail was probably a previous strike. Or two. Hope there's no more lightning while we're in here.*

He hears her frightened voice. "What do we do?"

Charon is in freeze mode. "Stay still! Don't touch the metal for a while! Stay still! Do you hear me, Darinka?"

She whispers a "Yes," then yells over a wave of newly pounding rain, "YES! I AM NOT HURT! ARE YOU?"

"NOT HURT! I'M FINE!"

Minutes later they each find that they have been clenching their fists so much their hands are cramped. Darinka flexes her hands to loosen her fingers. Charon's left hand is cramped shut. He rubs his wrist with a knuckle and slowly pulls the fingers out.

All senses on high alert, they wait for each other to say something.

Finally, Charon yells, "I think the rain is slowing down! Do you have a good view outside?"

She rubs her eyes, trying not to touch her elbows onto the metal frame. She feels an inadvertent touch but is relieved when nothing bad happens. "The rain is streaking like a river! Can't see so much!"

It takes an eternal ten minutes of silence between them before she yells, too loudly, "I must open the window!"

Brought out of his stupor, "Are you ok?"

"It is too stuffy! The window is all covered inside!"

He thinks, *Condensation.* "Ok! Open up a bit!"

By then the rain has become a light drizzle. Darinka pushes at the canopy and has a brief panic attack when it won't budge, thinking, *Welded!* Then she remembers to unlatch it. Being able to open the canopy lifts a load from her mind.

"Rain is stopping!" Her words seem to echo across the field and she sucks in a breath, putting a dusty hand to her mouth. She instinctively rubs the dust off on her pants.

Charon pops his canopy part way and whispers over his shoulder, "Yes, I see." He coughs. "As a friend of mine says, that lightning strike was pretty well over the top."

In the Darkness of the Mind

SILENT TERROR

Naked, Lateef is running madly down an endless narrow dark corridor. A mystical soft light infuses the floor three metres before his racing feet then disperses as he passes. He has been running forever. He pants hard and yet he does not tire. His legs work like pistons, silently driving his body down this endless hallway, more in the air than not. Lateef cannot stop. The mystical light draws his legs forward. Then the hallway deforms. The walls snake this way and that. The floor begins to undulate slowly. A reddish smoke lies ahead. As he plows into it without losing pace, the smoke becomes thick like honey but filling his mouth and throat with acrid gunpowder. The sticky mass captures his arms, his body, his head, while his legs keep pounding forward. He opens his mouth to scream, "What do I do?" and nothing but a great bubble escapes his lips. He screams a terrified bubble again. And again.

A servant swings open the door to Lateef's room. "Sir? Are you sleeping?"

Lateef tosses wildly under the covers. He opens his reddened eyes. His face is dripping in sweat. Rising up on the silky sheets, Lateef looks around in terror. "WHAT?"

"Sir, you must have been dreaming. You yelled out. A nightmare?"

Lateef falls back onto the deep mattress. "Yes. A nightmare. I'm not used to these soft pillows and mattress." He looks to the woman at the door. The low light from the hallway catches her features. He croaks, "Thank you, Sofia. I am fine. Thank you for looking in."

She nods and closes the door, leaving Lateef again in a dark room. Vertigo takes hold in his head as he has no lights for reference. Lateef rolls abruptly to his side, feeling for the edge of the mattress. He grabs it in a desperate grip.

That morning, a bleary-eyed Lateef dresses in an outfit that he finds in the bedroom closet. It is of more substance in its material and style than he is used to. The blue suit gives him a huge boost of self-esteem.

His gait is firm and measured as he walks to his new office next to Demyadin's still empty one. There are a myriad tasks to be done before breakfast. Lateef confidently works through the list. Local texts go to various people in the mansion. He thinks, *Billy's local area messaging program seems to work well. Hope he can break into L5's com devices again. Oh - here is his gloat... He locked them down again!* Lateef grins broadly and sends a thumbs-up.

Staff keep knocking at the open door asking about details regarding their tasks. He deals with each one politely, allowing the questioner to understand the driving purpose behind what they need to do, instead of yelling instructions at them.

At eight o'clock, Demyadin comes to Lateef's door. He leans quietly against it, judging the actions of his right-hand man behind the desk.

"Breakfast in fifteen minutes, Lateef. On the upper patio."

Lateef had noticed his boss in the doorway. He continues working, nearly finishing the "absolutely necessary" part of his list. "Yes, sir. I am just about done."

Demyadin half-nods and turns for the stairway leading up to the patio level. Lateef can hear a groan from the steps. It stops Lateef in mid-read. Hearing no more, Lateef finishes up.

A silent breakfast is consumed efficiently.

Demyadin sits back to enjoy his coffee and the view of the sea. There are no boats across the over kilometre-wide crescent of their beach. "Sonar?"

"Today, sir. Our supplier took a circuitous route, laid out by Prasad in Security."

Demyadin rocks slightly on the spindly rear legs of his ivory-coloured, very expensive French Provincial chair. The rocking soothes his back. "Of course. Did Prasad discuss that with you?"

"No, sir. I trust his judgment."

"Good… Very good. As I said, I do not want sycophants. I want you to build a team of self-starters – of thinkers. They must, first of all, have the unswerving desire to accomplish our goals; and then, they must understand our priorities and methods for accomplishing them. It will be on your head to choose those people. Their mistakes are your mistakes." He peers intently at Lateef.

Then he gives Lateef a sly smile. "Of course they will make mistakes as they work into their tasks, as may you. They, and you, will be forgiven those simple, learning mistakes. The *unforgivable* mistakes will be any that contradict my orders to you, or those that do not closely follow our primary mission." He suddenly becomes emotional, "And I will not permit self-serving idiots to line their own pockets during our campaign!"

Demyadin pauses to calm down. "That accountant - Brown?"

Lateef nods calmly in agreement. "His actions and those of his assistants are being scrutinized, sir. If we find anything…"

"He will take a long swim."

"Yes, sir."

They both turn their gaze to the peaceful sea. A long stretch of the shoreline below the mansion butts with crashing waves against shear, twenty-metre cliffs. The sun is shining through wispy orange clouds from their far left. Seagulls ride the onshore breeze.

A chirp on Lateef's phone announces a message. He looks to Demyadin to relay the information, "Weapons training in the field behind us," as the rat-tat-tat of automatic weapons sounds.

Demyadin nods. He leans forward to gaze at the sea with his elbows on the table, head in his hands. "Peaceful, isn't it?"

"Yes, sir. Very peaceful."

Demyadin's face produces a wry grin. "Not a brilliant conversationalist, Lateef?"

Lateef sighs then clears his throat. "Sir… if you will allow me to…"

"Please speak freely, my friend."

Thinking that probably he should not, Lateef, nevertheless, relaxes his guard. "It has been my observation, sir, that in society, as it has developed, our natural impulse to converse has, in general, been co-opted by social media. With my, if I may immodestly say, my unconventional sensibilities, I have found it less vexing to people around me if I merely listen, rather than participate in idle chatter." He watches closely for signs of a reaction in Demyadin's face or posture. "With no disparagement of our senior team, of course."

His boss gives a quick smile and, "Most of them. Go on, please. I'm sure you have an interesting take on that."

Forging ahead, "Yes, sir. Thank you. May I say that most people, if not ninety-nine percent, will, instead of turning to a nearby acquaintance when something occurs to them, they will pull out their phone, touch a social media app, and broadcast their, if I may call it, their brain-fart to what they believe to be 'their' cohort. Those musings do not get moderated but will simply fly out of their fingers to the digital universe, to be lost among the billions of other virtual musings, and diluted to complete insignificance. Enroute, they often offend someone."

Demyadin tents his fingers in thought. "I can agree with that - reluctantly, because it is a cynical view of humanity. But I will agree with you."

Finishing his thought, warming up to the subject, Lateef speaks in matter-of-fact tones as if to a class of philosophy undergrads. "Whereas, a hundred years ago, we used to have between five to twenty people in our group of close contacts, now, people believe they have thousands listening to their unfiltered blatherings. With a small cohort, before the digital age, our pronouncements were filtered internally as we matured and as our blatherings were not well-received by our closer acquaintances. That to-and-fro interaction honed our conversational skills and our critical thinking, which had a chance to improve over time. It is my opinion that such is not the case for those who immerse their minds unreservedly into the vacuous airspace of social media."

Demyadin leans back, his mouth loose. "You continue to astound me, my friend. That is both a simple observation and a profound one. Was this, too, from a thesis you read?"

Lateef gives deprecatory shrug. "Sir, please forgive me, but as when I last said that I had read something in a thesis, it was, in fact, my own thought. I have not been privileged to have a leisurely academic life."

Demyadin puts his chin to his chest. "You should have, my friend. You should have. Growing up in a Palestinian work camp..."

Stretching broadly, Demyadin scans Lateef's face as he throws out an apparently simple question. "Why must we be ruthless, Lateef?"

That very question was on Lateef's mind when he was first recruited into Demyadin's little group.

He had been working as a mercenary in the enclave of Russian Crimea after answering a curious advertisement by a company called the Wagner Group. At the time he did not realize they were a private military contractor closely tied to the Russian oligarchy. He later read up on the group's peculiar history in and next to Russia.

Those dozen years ago, Lateef was twenty-one and desperate for work. He needed to support his mother who was ill with an uncommon hormonal and blood disease that they could not afford to have treated. All he knew of his new job was that he had been hired at a high income to guard a cargo of "electronic goods" that was being transported by a freighter from Karachi to Beirut. The crew were a mix of sailors from Indonesia, Bangladesh and Chile. The latter included the captain with the two other senior officers.

Lateef was part of the guard contingent whose task was to protect the ship from pirates off the coast of Somalia. Although the guards went through regular weapons training on board, it turned out that their services were not needed right through to Beirut. The guards were then paid well and told to go home until called for further work. They were told to keep checking a certain website for their next work opportunity.

Lateef did not see anything come up for him for over a year. Although the pay from his guard work had been a life-saver for his mother, the time came that Lateef needed to find work again. He took odd jobs in Beirut. Most of his money was sent to his mother, who was recovering from her treatment in Abu Dabi. A small part was set aside for himself. He spent his free hours in the library between at least two jobs. Lateef lost himself among the book shelves. He read ravenously in just about every subject, using the several languages he learned while growing up with other children in the work camp.

By chance, while employed in a coffee shop, he met one of the other guards he'd known from the Wagner group. The fellow guard, Kristoff, did not recognize Lateef at first.

Standing in front of him, Lateef had smiled, "Kristoff! It's good to see you again!"

Being in the paramilitary business, Kristoff was not eager to be recognized. He growled, "Who are you?"

"You don't remember me? I'm Lateef. We sailed the Suez on the… you know, I can't remember the name of the ship."

Kristoff looked him up and down. He whispered, "Voy No."

"Yes! The Voy No! As I recall, it was not on its regular run…" He could see that Kristoff was not comfortable speaking in public. He kept looking around under his bushy eyebrows at the other tables.

Lateef had leaned in close, "Listen, I need to speak to you about, you know, work. Can we talk outside for a few minutes?"

Kristoff was reluctant, but Lateef persuaded him with a free extra coffee and croissant to sit at one of the outside tables. With the background traffic noise, it was more private.

Lateef found out that he was unlikely to be called for anything soon unless he improved his weapons certifications and the other skills in demand by the mercenary groups. With that information, he went on as many courses as he could afford. He traveled from Tajikistan, to Alaska, and ended up in St. Petersburg. That was where Lateef had finally obtained work in Crimea with the mercenary group.

It was at that "security" work where he learned his lesson, that staying alive simply meant being reflexively ruthless.

Lateef takes in the now-pale-yellow clouds that give some shade from the rising sun over their patio. "Sir, being ruthless is staying alive, in our business. But, really, that is for the grunt in the foxhole, as they say. Being ruthless at the command-and-control level means efficiently accomplishing one's goals."

And, before Demyadin can respond, "That, however, is a simplistic, a pedestrian view of what an armed unit must do. At the higher level, directing those armed units, we must be ruthless or we will deviate from the main objective. Ruthlessness, for us, is being true to the vision we are pursuing." He turns to face his boss fully. "Though I'm sure you have a clearer and more cogent grasp of that, sir."

Demyadin takes his time in answering. He thinks, *This is a smart one. Naïve, but smart. I must treat him carefully, with respect. Or else he might develop a desire to shoot me if he gets any hint of what my long plan is. He must be steered to the apparent Plan A. So he must think that he fully comprehends the enormity of what is facing us…*

"My friend – and I wish to call you that, Lateef, in all honesty – I want you to be clear in your mind as to what we are facing." He pauses, searching for tells in Lateef's posture.

Seeing a softening of the folds around Lateef's eyes, he carries on. "Humanity has a monster of biblical proportions coming down upon us… Lateef, I do not say this lightly." He notices a tightening of Lateef's eyes. "This monster will smash aside the minor problems that people in power have created to amuse themselves and on which they spend their billions. Attacks by gangs of punks and bullies – whether they may be holding a nation by the throat or just their neighbourhood – these punks will be squished underfoot by the real monster…"

Demyadin clenches his fists dramatically on the table. "The climate is irretrievably fucked up. And even *that* monster will be irrelevant, though tens of millions will over long years suffer and perish in horrible deaths across the globe. No, the monster we must put all our efforts to, our very souls, to fight, is *Artificial Intelligence*." He raises his voice. "*AI is **not-life**!* Like a mindless virus, AI is taking over everything humans do! AI is not merely 'doing things *for* us', *it is **changing** us,* ultimately, *into a bastard form of Not-Life!*"

His face has contorted dramatically so much that it frightens Lateef. Demyadin twists away. In Lateef's suddenly frigid mind, he realizes that his boss could well be mad.

Demyadin carries on, gesturing randomly at the sea, "This catastrophe for humanity is being enacted in such slow motion as to be invisible to the people. It is being done by creatures to whom we give human voices and bodies that appear innocuous, *cute*, even." He curls his lips at that. "To just about every person who encounters these AI monsters, their appearance cannot be thought of as anything other than helpful. And so the insidious takeover proceeds at their pace. Humanity gives up without a whimper. From routine tasks, to governance of our world institutions, the AI monsters say, 'Don't worry. We'll do that for you. Just sit back and enjoy the leisure we are giving you.' And humanity does lapse completely into mindless leisure. Just look around at the blank hopelessness in the eyes of people everywhere. Those who still have access to essentials like air conditioning, food and water, what are they doing? Entertaining their vacuous minds in the fake worlds of virtual reality! All created and controlled by *AI*!"

He pauses to look into Lateef's eyes. "After a generation of being served by AI, individuals are no longer able or willing to do the simplest tasks. Add a long list of two-digit numbers; drive their vehicle; make, much less grow food; start a campfire in the forest…" He laughs, "Haha! When I last said that to someone he was appalled! 'Start a fire in a forest! You'll burn it down you fool!' he said!"

Demyadin shakes his head. "AI has made humanity into worthless wimps. No wonder any neighbourhood bully can raise an army and take over some banana republic, as they wish. Over the past decade, Lateef, there have been no fewer than thirty-seven coups-d'etats around the world. It's been a sickening display of groups of humanity exercising their imperative to bully when allowed to by a population of lazy wimps."

Despite his reservations, Lateef nods. *He could very well be right.*

The boss snorts, then remembers something. "Lateef, you must have personal experience in that, having been in the paramilitary punk-packs, yourself." Then Demyadin relents. "I'm sorry, Lateef. I do not mean to attack you personally. You have obviously out-grown that primitive behaviour."

In a strategic move, he reaches a hand out to Lateef. "Please forgive me, my friend. I get so emotional…" They touch. Lateef feels a wonderous, deep galvanic tingle in his hand.

After a moment, Lateef considers what happened. *Ohh… What did I feel?… What's he saying? On the one hand, he is saying a crazy thing. On the other, he seems to be expressing similar thoughts to my own. I, too, have noticed people's progression toward the inability to do anything of real substance. Is that idea dangerous? Is **he** dangerous?*

They shake hands slowly, solidly, warmly.

Lateef asks, "Which is more dangerous? The idea of malicious algorithms or the *worry* over them? I want to know."

They continue to hold their handshake. Demyadin begins to involuntarily squeeze harder. He notices and pats Lateef's hand then drops it to lean back. *I shall hook him with rationality.*

"Ok. You're right. It is a fantastical claim. So, let me see if some facts can convince you. The term 'AI' is at least from the 1800s but its current meaning began to coalesce into what we understand in the 1950s. That is the first clue. Military funds were dumped into AI research with the Cold War era. AI languished through the 1960s due to poor actual results.”

“And their rudimentary computing power.” Lateef nods then takes a more comfortable position in his chair.

“Correct. Other fields – industry, economics and such pseudosciences – tried to legitimize their fields with the improving power of computer hardware and software. Through the 70s and 80s they built complex programs with even more complex pronouncements to funders. That grew to a peak in, oh, 1987, I believe. Their lack of actual results, and the general meltdown of the economy in 2007 sent the field of AI research into freefall. Then, it came back again in fits and starts – such as the generative AI apps produced – until a few years ago. The sudden new surge in computational power combined with a new approach.”

He pauses. *Process that. As you do, your mind will become familiar with it…*

“I don’t want to bore you, Lateef, but that background is needed to give a clearer understanding of what I am thinking.”

They both sip from their cooled coffees. Lateef notices their server walking by in the dining room. “Sofia! Can you please bring us refills?” He holds up his cup. She nods and rushes off.

Lateef gives a wry grin as he lifts the cup to his lips. “I think I will need more caffeine to digest this.”

Demyadin shrugs. "I have no doubt you are going to easily follow my simple logic. So, here is the next non sequitur. At the start of research into androids – the real thing, not all those science fiction concoctions – it was in a well-funded lab at MIT. They set out a simple task. Build an autonomous device that would be able to walk across a room filled with obstacles, to successfully reach the door on the other side. They loaded controlling software into the device with object-recognition, decision-making, and complex locomotion instruction capabilities. The original computational power and memory was…"

At this point, Sofia arrives with a fresh carafe of coffee. Both take time to thank Sofia and to top up.

Lateef asks while taking a careful sip of the hot coffee, "Does this lead to Attila and Hannibal?"

Demyadin nearly spills his coffee as he laughs. "HA ha! You know this important little story?"

Lateef grins. "That well-funded lab keeps adding computing power, without success, and finally changes the specs to allow an umbilical cord to a mainframe computer and they still aren't successful."

The older man adds gleefully, "And in an underfunded lab down the hall, a maverick prof puts together little six-legged things that *do* work."

"Well, Attila flops around randomly at first…"

Demyadin slaps his thigh. "Ha! But the elementary instructions that were built into every joint start to kick in. Basically, the simple instruction is to co-operate with the joints on either side of each leg, work with the legs next to each one, all with the overall task of avoiding obstacles until the little thing reaches the door. YES! It learned quickly and it easily did what it was supposed to do! No supercomputer needed!"

Lateef adds, "And that progressed in very rapid steps to the droids we have all around us. Well, not here, of course."

Demyadin nods. "Because they're centrally directed. While the individual droids act in unison according to their reactive responses, as did Attila, their overall *proactive* actions come from the officers in behind-the-lines C-and-C facilities. And, yes, the various militaries now have more droids even than there are in domestic use."

They pause to each collect their own thoughts.

With a final glug of coffee, Demyadin carries on. "How, you may well ask, does that advance our understanding of the future of humanity? I will take a few points from that story. First, there is the absolute dependence of such complex AI on exceedingly fast processing power so that terabits, petabits, whateverthefuckbits of data can be used for AI training. Secondly, the funding that has pushed AI at each of its iterations has come from the military." He holds up three fingers. "Thirdly, processing power takes a back seat to intelligent, eclectic design. The swarms of military aerial and ground droids used in the constant military exercises nowadays comes directly from nature." Demyadin's arms describe graceful arcs. "A large flock of birds flies in wonderful, flowing shapes as a result of a few simple considerations, just like Attila versus the unsuccessful MIT

Behemoth. Their patterns, however, get the birds one thing. Communal exercise. And, ok, it probably confuses any local predators. So. Lovely patterns, no particular purpose."

Demyadin goes for another sip of coffee but finds his cup empty. He considers pouring some more. "No, too much caffeine and my hand'll shake… Where was I? Oh, yes. The current state of AI. Let us take those birds and give them a powerful, overarching *purpose!*… Say, swarm the nests of their local predators and in Hitchcock-like melodrama, peck the raptors and their offspring to death! Why not?… My only question would be, why *don't* they do it?"

Before Lateef can answer, Demyadin continues, "Some birds actually do attack their tormentors. Crows are famous for harassing eagles and ravens. Why don't starlings do the same?"

"Intelligence."

Nodding, "Being able, with their superior cunning, to assess concepts like cause-and-effect, then formulating the steps of an action plan and *doing it!*"

Lateef takes a cookie from a white porcelain dish beside the coffee carafe. After a bite, he asks, "So crows and parakeets are smart enough to think about their environment and act on those thoughts…"

His boss adds, "And what would be needed for them and their feathered friends to do the Hitchcock horror show of attacking people ruthlessly?"

Downing the rest of his cookie, Lateef gulps some coffee, then suggests, "Not simply more intelligence. How about a focused purpose?"

"Close. And it is not simply a more complex language. Droids have everything we have, in that respect. They are not good at assessing the negative – that is merely the source of their hallucinations."

At that word, Lateef looks up sharply. He says nothing but notes, *Hallucinations?*

Demyadin notices the reaction but continues. "The essence they miss is the will to a continued existence. I deliberately do not say will to live, for they are Not-Life. I will use that term, as it was formulated by the only L5er I can respect – they call him Tolstoy. The will by those *not-life things* to a continued existence is the trigger that makes them our most potent enemies. Without the consciousness of a will to have continued existence, AI and its droids would continue to serve us in mediocre ways as well as in the critical tasks we have squandered to them."

Demyadin pauses to look around. "Therein lies one of the terrible, hidden factors of AI servitude. If allowed to randomly grow, this Non-Life monstrosity will, at some point in time, come upon a viable Non-Life **purpose**. If that happens – when that happens – all hell will break loose. I believe that with the current explosion of new achievements in the hellhole of L5, we can say that either their AI experiment has already come upon that consciousness, or will do so very soon. If so, humanity's existence is more quickly counting down to extinction." Demyadin's body slumps into the chair. The pain in his gut has been building. He has depleted his reserves.

Lateef considers adding something he has recently researched. "This may be important. I urge you not to jump to immediate conclusions…" Collecting his thoughts, he frowns. "When speaking with Billy, I happened to see the word 'hallucination' he had typed as a note. It was beside lines of code. When I checked the AI literature, it is plain – it seems that term is what AI programmers use to refer to anomalies in AI results. Completely unexpected anomalies. Whether he was referring to the L5 code you gave him or something else…"

Renewed by that, Demyadin sits forward, his face tightening with heavier pain from his abdomen. He demands the pain to go away, then nods, "Their AI is becoming self-directed. This may have already occurred. And, just as troublesome, I am deeply concerned with recent activities that have come from Billy's digital den. He took credit for some actions that I do not believe he could have accomplished… I reluctantly must admit that his work has become… worrisome."

Turning to Lateef, Demyadin shakes his head. "If Billy's work has been co-opted…"

Silence is when one may take in a difficult concept; turn it over and over in the mind; masticate it; see if it fits into any available box. Demyadin gives Lateef minutes of precious silence.

At first, Lateef cannot find a box into which this concept of an imminently malevolent AI could properly fit. *He could be insane, possibly criminally. I don't think so… He could be hysterically melodramatic, or even psychotic. But I cannot believe that to be the case… He could be testing me. No… Or, he could be the only person in the world who not only sees the issue clearly, but has the supreme will to do something about it… That is the only thing that fits… His assessment must be true. But what do we do about Billy?*

Lateef's face wrinkles in anguish. "But what do we do about it?" Lateef's plea is met with more silence.

A grimacing Demyadin lifts his head to stare across the wide bay below them. Movements on the far southern promontory catch his attention. Absently, he mutters, "I hope that's permitted traffic – with our new sonar?"

"Huh?" Lateef rises to hold onto the patio railing with one hand as he punches Prasad's number onto his (local service-only) phone. Then, automatically, he touches *Speakerphone* along with the video.

Prasad's young face fills the screen. He speaks right away. "Lateef, I see you are enjoying the upper patio and the lovely view of our bay, and I assume you are calling to ask if those are our people at the south end?"

"Yes."

"The equipment was brought in quickly, with my insistence, and, yes, they are installing it as we watch. They estimate two days."

"Thank you, Prasad." Absently, he closes the phone app. He notices that Prasad's hand holding his phone has a slight tremor. He puts away his phone and turns to grip the thick railing again with both hands.

Demyadin is relieved to deal with normal things. "I assume the two days will be installation only, to be followed by rigorous testing?"

"Of course, sir. Testing and then retesting, as for any proper project." His mind is still digesting what Demyadin had placed there previously.

Demyadin nods as he relaxes in his chair. "Come. Sit at the table."

Still in a daze, Lateef complies.

Putting just the right tone of empathy into his voice, Demyadin reels him in. "My friend, I will ask you to call me by my given name, Michael. And may I call you…"

Lateef's face tenses. "Sir, Michael, there is something of an embarrassing answer in that… My mother, in our culture, had no family name, because she had me without a family. So, when asked to write my full name, I would write Lateef Lateef." He grins, "I would be pleased if you called me by either one."

"Ha! And so I shall! I will leave it to you to decide if I am being too formal by using your last name or friendly by using your first!" He holds out a hand across the table. They shake again, firmly and warmly. Demyadin remembers to give several seconds of warm eye contact.

Sitting back again to slowly rock his chair on its back legs, Demyadin contemplates what must be done. *Lateef is now with me in this. When I get to the next fork-in-the-road and seem to be forced to unleash dirty bombs at L5's facilities, there will be the fear of collateral damage. Many would suffer and die. Will Lateef and, and Billy and the others stay with me, to believe that is our only course of action to save humanity — by breaking some eggs?... A town hall. I must be able to prepare them properly. I will put it all on the table and give them a choice. Destroy L5 or let their descent into rule by monstrous Not-Life destroy humanity... But who should be at the town hall? I will need to speak personally to most of my senior people, first. That subterfuge will be enough for the real plan to be completed. That is, unless Billy's programs have been captured by something deeper. SHIT!*

His body tenses hard and he rises up quickly, taking a position over Lateef, shaking off his pain and negative thoughts. "Lateef, my good friend. We must begin our critical stage. Two projects must be managed separately and I will place my absolute faith in you to handle the one project. They will both come together later in a way that will either assure victory or will expose us to human tragedy. Can you see that I am totally serious that what I will entrust you to do must be completed on time and as we plan it, or all will be lost?"

He steps back as Lateef stretches up to be face-to-face. Lateef's tightened features gives him an older appearance — the sombre look of a general who is about to order his divisions forward against overwhelming numbers. "Michael, I am deeply honoured that you have chosen me to wield your sword. Tell me what you require."

In his mind, the epics of martyrdom ring their overpowering trumpets. *I am ready*!

It is a moonless night on the Steppes. Charon and Darinka very reluctantly decided to over-night in their aluminum cocoons. With her canopy slightly cracked open to minimize condensation, Darinka can see stars blinking in their constellations. She thinks of the time she was in a two-person sub, under the ice a few kilometres off the hamlet of Yukagir in Siberia. *What an absolutely desolate freezer of a place! A hellhole. What limp-minded apparatchik decided that a deep-sea port should be built there?...*

Stuck several metres under the cold sea, her task had been to oversee their mapping of the seafloor. If she hadn't been so preoccupied, coaxing her frozen instruments to take readings, she probably would have gone out of her mind.

I do not do well in enclosed spaces. This MiG is not much better than that damn sub. At least Charon is so much more of a gentleman than that sonofabitch Simjon Simjonivich! Any longer under the ice with him and I would have had to slice his cock off.

She shivers at the memory. *Now, what miracle is my spaceman going to perform? The GRU are no fools. It did not take them long to find us. That airplane must have been them. Charon is a gentle soul but a fool when it comes to the gangsters who now rule Russia. I must take care of him. He enjoys food and drink too much… Who am I kidding? We will either starve to death out here or be tortured and shot by the GRU.*

In the MiG's front seat, Charon is half awake again during a fitful sleep as his mind grinds toward mental exhaustion. *Why did I allow her to come along? She's a lovely, intelligent person and doesn't deserve this. I should be in L5 now, arranging for more mass to be sent up from the Moon. There's nobody there to put the different pieces together properly or align the trajectory for each delivery. Where to mine, what to mine, which material is needed when and… Wait a minute! Didn't Jasmine say that Zar was being replaced by some vegetable-named AI? Shit! Have to get back!*

In his mind he has a calming vision of the spaceplane landing… then he falls asleep.

Obscured rays of sun are glinting in from the east through some kind of weird fog.

Charon starts awake. He can't move! "Where…?" He remembers the confined cockpit and raises his arms. They are numb from the position he'd been locked into by the tight seat. "Darinka!" *Is she still back there?*

Darinka wakes in a grumpy mood, having been dreaming of slicing up that moron Simjon.

"Kakago cherta ti khochesh?" [*what the hell do you want?*] She looks around then realizes where she is. "Oh, Charon, my dear! I'm sorry. I was in nightmare! How are you this morning?"

With a mighty effort, Darinka shoves up her canopy. The fresh air pouring in is like a slap on the face. "Oj! It is a good day, today, I hope." She stretches as much as she can, deciding to wait for Charon to extract himself before she gets out, herself. The airplane skin is covered with mucky bird-poo and looks quite slippery. *Dry, it was no problem.* She touches it with a finger. "Ikhsh!" She wipes her finger on the bottom canopy rail.

Charon is debating with himself about dropping the battery into his Pad. "Oh, what the hell." Very awkwardly, he pulls the Pad out of his pocket and hesitates again. "Darinka, I'm going to see if my Pad is still compromised. We may have to run for the woods so I'll get out of this straightjacket first, ok?"

"Yes, please. I have to, well, find a bush." She grits her teeth.

Charon recognizes the reason for her gritted teeth. "Me too."

The extraction is not easy for Charon. When he finally grunts his way out, the wing surface is dangerously slippery. "Watch out for this… shit!" He slips on it, covering his pant-legs with a thick application of the odorous stuff.

"I know," sympathetically, but she can't help a smile.

Darinka is already crouched down on the wing, waiting for him. From a knee, he gives her his hand to step forward. "Careful, Darinka. The metal is…"

"Covered in shit."

Charon grins broadly at her as he helps her along to the ladder. "Very succinctly put, my dear."

On the ground they both stretch out thankfully. She shakes her head, "One night in that coffin is enough!"

"Right. That goes double for me. Ah, let's do our thing first and then we can be ready to run, ok?"

After she returns from a nearby bush on the far side of the MiG enclosure, Charon takes his turn. Meanwhile she changes into her other set of clothes. *Bird shit is everywhere. Have to find a lot of water and soap.* She folds up her soiled clothes and places them on top of a bag.

His face shows relief after doing his thing. Charon is becoming more limbered up as he looks over their covered pile of supplies. He waits for Darinka to get closer before asking, "Maybe we should have whatever we can for breakfast, first, as well?"

"Da. Hungry." She stares at Charon intently.

He is not sure what has got into her. "What?" He looks down to see if his pants are on straight. *My god! Is that stink…*

Darinka starts to cry as she lunges forward to take Charon into a tight embrace. She buries her face into his chest, sobbing.

She fears, strongly, they will die today.

He does not know what to do with, or for her, other than to envelop her into his arms, soiled hands angled away from her back.

It is all she needs for now.

After a while, her sobs stop. She looks up into his face. "We were nearly killed by lightning."

"There, there,"

"And the GRU are hunting for us!"

"Well, I don't know if…"

"What can we do, dear Charon? You are such a kind man, trying to help me, and what can I do but but stand here and cry?"

"Ah, well…"

"You must call that spaceplane back down to take us away from here!"

Charon's first reaction to a difficult situation is to think about it. She is not giving him time to do that. He decides hastily, "Ah, what the hell. Here – let me see if Carro… if they've fixed our comms."

Wiping his hands on the grass, he opens his Pad and drops in the battery. It immediately flashes its red LED at different intervals.

Darinka stares at it. "Morse code - '*one chance. coming to your pad at eight bells local*'. What does that mean?"

Charon starts to grin broadly. "Your Morse is excellent, my dear! What time is it?" He sees that the Pad's display has been reset, but then it dies right away. "I think it was seven-something. Sounds about right. It means our ride should be here before long. And just in time too!" He wipes his hands again onto the still-wet grass then dries them on rear parts of his pants that haven't been soiled. Using two more-or-less clean fingers, Charon reaches into their food bag to gingerly pull out a small chunk of greasy bacon. He hands it to her. "We are almost out of food and drink!"

His encouraging smile is not returned.

They both turn to scan the slope and the horizon. Munching on the bacon, her face changes from hope to worry. "How will they know where we are?"

"I trust the, the main computer will have latched onto our location with that brief on-time. And besides, we've followed a predictable course." Then he thinks, *Not too predictable, I hope.*

He resumes his scan of the area. "The approach is likely from the west, as before… but maybe not." Then he realizes something. *Only one passenger. She goes first, even if I have to hog-tie her.*

Darinka's hoarse whisper and pointing hand raises the hair on his neck.

"They are coming for us!" She is pointing way down the slope. Two military off-road vehicles have turned from a distant road and can be seen bouncing toward them. "Bozhe, bozhe! Charon! What can we do?"

Charon does a quick guesstimate. "We have at least fifteen minutes before they can climb up here. If L5's cavalry can make it here in ano… There!" He points to the southwest. "Is that your ride or is that another MiG?"

Darkina excitedly jumps to Charon's side, holding his arm. "Not MiG! Comes from too high!" Then she realizes what he said. "*My* ride? Oh my god, Charon! Only *one* seat!"

She tries to release his arm but he holds her tightly. "NO, Charon! I will run down to stop those bloody gangsters. You hide until the spaceplane takes you! I will…"

He holds onto her arm as she continues yanking to get away. "Stop! Listen! Darinka! You will get away and I will hide in the MiG until they all leave. They will think we've both been rescued! Later, the spaceplane can come back for me. Please listen!"

Darinka keeps struggling toward the approaching vehicles but he will not let her go. "Darinka! You must go to L5!"

"No No No! Let me go! You are too good a man to die here by the bloody GRU! Let me go! Please!" She yanks hard to free herself, to no avail.

Charon has to do something desperate to keep her from running down the slope. "Darinka! Listen to me! Listen!"

She looks at him briefly while still struggling.

"Darinka! **I love you**! You have to be safe!... I *love* you. Do you hear me?" She is stunned into silence. He gives her shoulders a short shake. She stands like a rag doll then goes limp. Looking into her eyes he whispers gently, "I love you, Darinka. You have to go safely."

Background music builds. CCR: *It came out of the Sky*

They hardly hear the whoosh and the scraping skids of the Mark 3 machine, now officially known as Chick-3, that lands on the far side of the MiG. Darinka is the first to notice it behind Charon. She croaks out, "Is here."

Running around the fence, they wave at the pilot but she cannot yet be seen through the thick, dripping condensation all over the small window. While similar to the previous spaceplane, Charon can't put his finger on it. *A lot longer rear section...*

Darinka can. "Is pregnant. No? Thicker place behind the pilot."

A part of the window clears enough for them to see more than a blurry head and a hand. The pilot has her hand up to stop the two from getting closer as the outer skin radiates heat. She continues to wave them off with urgency.

Another agonizing two minutes pass with the increasing roar of the Russian vehicles making their bumpy way up the slope.

Charon and Darinka can do nothing but shuffle from foot to foot as if needing to relieve themselves again.

Finally, fingers on the pilot's hand can be seen counting down. She opens the passenger compartment behind her to yell out, "Don't touch the shell! Still hot!"

Charon drags Darinka close enough to see inside. There are two prone seats. She gives a squeal of glee as Charon grabs her to lift her into the cabin feet-first. She kisses his cheek and joyfully slips into the far seat.

Charon inadvertently rubs his knees against the outside shell as he climbs in. ***"OW! Damnit HOT!"*** The stink of burned bird-poop is overwhelming.

Despite his leg burn, he clambers over and into his seat. Before he can put his bum down, the door starts closing and the pilot has Chick-3 moving on its sonic-induced vibrating skids.

They can see the two Russian vehicles bouncing over a low ridge that borders the more level area of the slope where the old MiG sits. A hapless agent in the open back of one of the bouncing vehicles is tossed screaming into the air before he can use his rifle. The vehicles come to a skidding stop with one bumping against the other. By the time an agent is able to climb out of his vehicle to sling his rifle, Chick-3 is climbing out of range and is speeding away faster than the bullets. The GRU agents fire angry but ineffective bullets into the air.

The pilot yells back to her passengers, *"What the hell's that godawful smell?"*

Escape Velocity

With an unbearable, overwhelming cacophony in the cabin, the pilot yells louder to Charon and Darinka, "DROP THE HELMETS OVER YOUR HEAD!"

Charon sees a helmet above Darinka and quickly helps her slip it down. He reaches up to pull his own over his head and hears the tail-end of the pilot's instruction, "…they're coming from the east. They learn well. Hold both arms over your head then touch that triangular red square on the ceiling! NOW!"

As both do so, they are each instantly enveloped by a soft and yet unyielding ivory-coloured blanket. Charon thinks, *Crash blanket.*

Identified by the symbol of a hand half in a pocket, sewn-in sleeves are available on the blankets for their arms. Charon takes Darinka's left arm and slips it into her sleeve. At his hurried nod, she does the same for her other arm.

Charon puts his left arm into its sleeve at the same time as an urgent message sounds in his helmet, "Missile incoming! Evasive maneuver!" He jams his right hand into the sleeve as the "crash blanket" stiffens and tightens around him. The deafening waterfall of noise gets louder, then his helmet attaches itself to the blanket at his neck and squeezes against his ears to reduce the noise.

The pilot yells into her mic, "Hold on!"

Charon can see through the support structure between them that the pilot has stuffed her own arms into her crash blanket sleeves. She looks like nothing more than an ivory cocoon. Now only able to move his eyes, Charon sees that Darinka is tightly cocooned, as is he.

Charon thinks, *Fully automated. Carrot is flying, I assume. Hope he's qualified. She. It. Whatever.*

Still able to see past the pilot's left shoulder, Charon stares at the screen in front of the pilot where a red cross-hairs is moving toward the middle of the screen from the lower left. As it reaches a yellow circle that is centred around what Charon assumes to be them, the spaceplane makes a wrenching right turn, putting distance between them and the red cross-hairs. Now he notices a number *1* on that cross-hairs. Coming into visibility over the pilot's shoulder, Charon can see number *2* approaching from the bottom right. At the same time as Charon notices that, the number *1* indicator has changed into a red explosion symbol with faint red shock waves emanating from it. The spaceplace, already accelerating almost vertically, makes another sharp maneuver. All three occupants black out.

A fuzzy tunnel of light sparks some consciousness within Charon's mind. Swimming back through the tunnel, the inside of the cabin begins to resolve in his perception. He hears the pilot saying something unintelligible.

Then it becomes clearer. "…alright back there? Can you hear me?"

Charon croaks, "Blackout?"

"Yes. Just a minute." Her tone changes, "Chick-3, review tactical."

Chick-3 responds, "Two Vympel R-38M missiles launched from Su-38 interceptors. Closing velocity Mach four point eight while we were passing Mach five. Evasive maneuver at point five kilometre. Number one exploded. Shock wave approached. Evasive maneuver reached 5 point 8 G and we accelerated to escape velocity. Hull temperature kept to one percent under red line. Number 2 initiated unsuccessful explosion. Entering orbit at nominal 380 kilometres."

"Thank you Chick-3… Did you hear that Charon? How is our other passenger? Chick-3, vitals for passengers."

Chick-3 responds, "Both nominal circulatory. Elevated heart rate for the male at 123 max. Both pax have eye movements to indicate consciousness. Restraints to minimum."

The crash blanket loosens its grip around them. Darinka is able to pull her arm out of its sleeve and she immediately searches for Charon's hand, still in his sleeve. She squeezes hard. Restrained fear tightens her face.

Charon responds, "Ah, all good back here. Ah, how long…?"

Chick-3 responds, "TL5I in twelve minutes."

The pilot translates, "Trans-L5 Injection, meaning when we leave Earth orbit to carry on to L5. We are essentially weightless at this time but brace yourselves for heavy acceleration. Chick-3 will give a warning… WHAT the hell is that stink?"

Darinka's voice comes on, with her first consonant being lost due to the voice activated mic, "..ow how long until we get to L5?"

Chick-3 responds, "ETA approximately sixty-three point five hours."

A loud emergency tone sounds in their helmets, then a calm, "Chick-3 into immediate emergency maneuver. We detect Russian-launched S-570, target Chick-3. In four, three, two, one…"

Pilot and passengers are again enveloped tightly and subjected to high G force. They blank out right away.

Charon is swimming through that long tunnel again. His groan is a distant deep reverberation from his chest. Another groan is closer to his ears. Then he hears crickets chirping anxiously. It all opens into distractingly bright points of light drilling into his eyeballs from a black curtain as the crickets resolve into what seems like several voices chattering in his ears at once.

"Charon, Charon! Wake up! Can you hear me?" Darinka is floating sideways in the cramped cabin. She slowly bounces off what used to be the ceiling then drifts forward and back as she touches the walls, her arms reaching out for Charon.

Charon is startled by the way her black hair sticks out wildly, then a broad grin almost turns into a comment. He is about to blurt out something stupid but stops just in time to avoid disaster. He thinks, *I was about to say she looks like a witch. Not now, old boy.*

The pilot is also floating on her side of the cabin structure. Charon can see her grin as she says, "You look terrible!" She glances at his protruding belly. "And I will kindly ask you to keep a large size barf bag handy, please. In that pocket to your left. The stats are that one-out-of-three people coming into micro-gravity will be sick."

Darinka stares at the pilot, wondering, *Why so rude?*

By the look on his face, Charon's thoughts are less kind.

A minute later, a slushy *blurrrrrp* is heard from the front cabin. The pilot had tried to hold off reaching for her own barf bag by a second too long. While most of the yellow-green stuff is contained in her bag, little escapees float around the cabin.

Their entertainment for the next while is capturing those offending tidbits. A variety of smells float past their noses at different times.

Later, trying to regain her authority, the pilot provides Charon with a summary of their situation. "We have been left without our main engines after shrapnel from one of the Russian satellite-killers took out a control conduit. Fortunately, that looks like the extent of our damage. We have sufficient thruster capability to move up to about 400 klicks, which is the average orbit of the ISS. We are not, well, let's say, not in the right traffic lane. It will take Chick-3 some time to maneuver to an intersecting course. We have sufficient consumables to last the expected time. In the meantime, L5 is negotiating with ISS command to allow us to dock COUGH COUGH." She struggles to finish her sentence, coughs again then clears her rough throat, which starts another coughing fit.

Darinka reaches through the structure to hold her arm. The pilot tries to say something further but coughs another time.

Charon holds up a hand. "Rest your throat, rest. We have time."

The pilot nods then floats into her seat. She rests by pulling a strap over herself to keep her body in one position.

Frustrated by her inability to do anything about their situation, Darinka motions a question to Charon by pretending to put on her helmet.

He shugs then asks, "Chick-3, should we continue to keep our helmets handy?"

"Keep your helmets close for safety. Debris from the explosion may have weakened a section of cabin skin. Still investigating. In seventy-six minutes we will pass through the debris field at which time we may be in further danger of damage."

The exchange rouses the pilot, who rips off her strap and rolls over to croak, "Keep them on!"

Darinka rolls her eyes. She reluctantly broaches a delicate topic. "Where is the toilet?"

A heavy sigh comes from the pilot. She hisses, "Chick-3, in private mode to each passenger tell them how to micturate." She rolls slowly back onto her seat, exhausted.

Dragonslayer is turning red in the face as he struggles to rein in his anger. "Yes, the Outer Space Treaty refers to specific operations but the same principles are being written at this very time into Pax ExTerra. I would have expected common human compassion and decency would be exercised in this situation!"

He is speaking to the current president of the UN Security Council, Micah Murcheau. There is about a second's delay in the comms line between them, which forces each to a forced politeness, more than they would have been if face-to-face.

Murcheau, a career EU diplomat, is used to dealing with reasonable demands that must be twisted by her into something approaching bureaucratic unreasonableness.

"Mr. Dragosavljevic, I fully understand your position and can sympathize with your frustration, but you must be aware that Russia is adamant that you must return the two espionage agents who have violated Russian territory and illegally stole secret details of one of their weapon systems…"

Dragonslayer can no longer stay polite. "Ms. Murcheau, I am sorry but I will not allow you to, once again, besmirch the intentions and reputation of our official delegate, Charon. He was subjected to a completely unprovoked attack by German nationals in the Moscow airport, and then he and his assistant, along with a totally innocent Ukrainian subject were recklessly pursued, for no reason whatsoever, by government thugs who shot at them. And an ancient MiG-23 is hardly a secret defence system…"

She tries to interrupt then finally raises her voice and keeps talking over Dragonslayer. "These espionage agents… were SPREADING MAYHEM ACROSS THE RUSSIAN

COUNTRYSIDE. They overflew several military bases with your secret rocket-plane…"

Losing his cool, he raises his voice to match hers, "MS. MURCHEAU, I steadfastly dispute your groundless accusations in such an obviously innocent situation. The airplane tracks can be provided to prove it, and that our spaceplane entered and left Earth's atmosphere with a vertical trajectory nowhere near any military installations! Now we have our three people adrift in space with limited air on board after having been subjected to completely unprovoked attacks by Russian satellite-killer missiles, for petes-sake! We only ask that the crew be allowed aid and refuge in the ISS. Simple humanity must be the primary consideration, here, surely."

The diplomat sees that Dragonslayer will not be intimidated. "And, sir, I must reply again that we are quite ready to permit them that refuge. We are, however, constrained by international law to take them into custody and seize their transport. We have no leeway in this. If we were to permit an exception in this high-profile case, who knows how many others would take advantage of the goodwill of the Security Council?"

A note is handed to Dragonslayer before he can respond again. Reading the few words, a huge load slips off his shoulders. He nods to his assistant, Franky, who rushes out again, then turns to the desk microphone. "Ms. Murcheau, ah, I have been as honest and forthright as I am able. I am very sorry that, ah, we have not been able to come to a mutual understanding at this time. I will ask that you consult once again with the Security Council with a view to treat our three people in a humane fashion during their dire situation. May I suggest we speak again in four hours?"

A full minute passes as Murcheau speaks with her mic off to others in her room. She clicks it back on. "I can assure you, Mr. Dragosavljevic, that I will press your request with my colleagues. We will speak again in approximately four hours, yes?" The link ends.

At that, Dragonslayer rushes out of the room to find his assistant. He finds him nearby, grinning, as Franky is speaking via an earbud mic. He signs off and turns with a broad smile to Dragonslayer. "They'll be there in less than two hours."

Happily finished with the obstreperous Murcheau, Dragonslayer pats his assistant's shoulder. "I should say that I am astonished with what Carrot has been up to, Franky, but I recently have come to expect its miracles. Thank you. Please remind me to call that bitch back in four hours."

Franky is still grinning from ear-to-ear. "Shall do, Jim – if she hasn't already been yelling at you before that. Ah, Jasmine was looking for you. Oh, did you know she's pregnant?"

The trajectory that had been taken by L5's brand new Chick-4 from L5 to Earth orbit consisted of a high velocity run that swung out toward a heliocentric orbit taken by a known small-body object whose SPKID designation is 54076022. In other words, Chick-4 tagged along behind a convenient, small Near-Earth-Orbit asteroid to avoid detection.

The brand new L5 craft has peeled off from the shielding asteroid and is approaching the damaged Chick-3.

Chick-4 has no human pilot. The front cabin has two seats (empty) plus three more in the rear (also empty). Which allowed Chick-4 to turn off from its asteroid-following trajectory dramatically so that the rest of its approach consists of a high-G deceleration toward Earth orbit that would have been fatal to humans.

It reaches Chick-3 in two hours, then autonomously mates to the emergency hatch on Chick-3's upper rear side. The pilot and two passengers transfer from their crippled vehicle through the mated hatches, thankfully without the need for EVA suits.

Inside their new ride, Darinka asks their pilot, "What happens to the old one?"

Chick-4 announces in its androgynous voice, "Welcome aboard, L5ers. To your question, Darinka, Chick-3 is attached and will be brought back to L5 for recycling. Please seat yourselves, ready for wrapping should the occasion arise. ETA at L5 will be fifty-seven hours. A secure communication channel is now open to L5."

The Chick-3 pilot, Anka, mumbles, "So many questions."

Chick-4 carries on, "Please review the information for passengers on your screens. Detailed answers to other questions are available asynchronously via the screen. You may enter requests digitally or via your voiceless throat-mic that you can find in the enclosure next to each screen. It includes a paired earbud. Food and drink packages are enclosed under the screen."

Anka takes out the mic-and-bud, attaching them quickly, then straps in to focus on the scrolling responses to her quietly voiced questions. Darinka straps in but has trouble with her *m&b*. Charon helps her attach them. She silently says, *Thank you.*

Her screen replies to her own questions in scrolling cyrillic. She says something and the screen switches to standard Latin script with modified Ukrainian.

Charon floats dreamily, thinking, *So this is where we're headed. Essentially, organic objects to be coddled and entertained.* He resists the very strong urge to reach for a food package. *Very strong urge. But… I will… resist.* His one hand twitches as it almost automatically reaches for the food package. *Bad hand!* He slaps it with his other hand.

Darinka is startled by the action, then settles back to her question-and-answer session. *We have a lot of time.*

Almost an hour passes with Chick-4 making its way home to L5 with three satisfied passengers aboard. Charon has been digitally conversing with an elated Dragonslayer.

Three dings sound ominously. Chick-4's announcement comes at the same time as helmets uncover themselves above each seat. "Emergency! Seat yourselves immediately. Helmets must be donned. Wrapping will commence in ten seconds." At the same time, they accelerate in such a way that Charon falls into his seat. He is somewhat sideways and rushes to squiggle into a better position. His helmet is trying to work its way onto his squirming head. The others are already helmeted.

"Shit! Just a minute!"

Before he is entirely comfortable, the crash blankets wrap each organic unit, entraining their arms at the same time. Each helmet joins with the rest of the enveloping blanket. They are cocooned and then a gut wrenching acceleration begins immediately which includes random sharp turns. Out of the corner of his left eye Charon can see a distant missile track that had been aiming for them. It adjusts course to track them but repeatedly loses them with Chick-4's maneuvers. Their screens show the tactical situation similar to, but more fine-tuned than Chick-3's presentation. The trailing missile's cross-hairs have a *1* next to the circle and another missile, *2*, shows up in a split screen.

With the calmness of an announcer describing a chess match, Chick-4 can be heard in their helmets. "With a four-sigma possibility that it could become involved, we've been tracking a Chinese military satellite's orbit. As it approached our crossing trajectory, it initiated its target lock on us. That coincided with the launch of, and approach of, a Russian S-570. The satellite lock on us is being scrambled. Our concern is that either weapon could be exploded while we are near the ISS nominal orbit, therefore it is necessary to increase Earth escape velocity to maximum for survivability of the ISS."

The passengers have blacked out before the last sentence can be perceived.

Back Inside

THERE ARE CHANGES

At a late supper in the mansion, Demyadin is munching slowly through a rum cake, lubricated with sedate sips of port. He is listening while one of his trusted strategists, Kenan, lists off items on his fingers. Being rather obvious about it, Demyadin glances at his old-fashioned wristwatch several times.

Kenan's flowing white hair bobs as he speaks with bursts of emphasis. "The least likely alternative is that they will invite you to a meeting for *face-to-face discussions*. Of course, with the Security Council sanctions they will be scrambling to deal with the *outcomes* of those repercussions…"

Demyadin holds up a finger. "This is the perfect time to have insinuated an operative into their now-tenuous supply chain, no?"

Lateef shifts in his seat. "Well, that is already in progress, Michael." He glances at the other dinner guest, Paula. "Still in contact?"

Paula has continued obstinately to wear glasses, a throwback to the era before the numerous versions of bionic/genetically modified/implant-assisted eye treatments. At this table they know that her glasses contain hidden cameras and tiny screens that can display to her and to record, in a field of 270-degrees, images in a variety of wavelengths – more than even the high-end implants can do. As she focuses on different views, her eye movements do give her away if one is attuned to her tells.

She enjoys the focus on her duties. "Thank you, Lateef. My contact…" Lateef lifts his head sharply as she corrects herself. "*Our* contact – as he was introduced to me by Lateef," Paula gives a forced nod, "is deeply embedded in the L5 organizational structure…"

Demyadin interjects, eyes raised to the ceiling, "As a worker in the mushroom building, I understand?"

Paula contritely agrees, "The fungus shed, as they refer to it, yes, sir. He is working his way into the confidence of numerous people…"

Again, Demyadin adds, boring into her eyes, "Because those particular people are sent there to serve out their sentence for breaking the rules."

"Ah, yes, sir. Quite right, as usual. That was where he was able to meet covertly with Juergen Mittelsohn to press him for details of his mission. They were getting somewhere, but… Anyway," she recomposes herself, "the intimate discussions my, our contact is privileged to have, have been interesting up to this point and I fully expect…"

Cutting her off again, impatiently, "Our purpose is not to produce a journal, Paula. We have very limited time, according to my own sources. All indications are that L5 is experiencing a radical series of changes that began less than two months ago. Something about a vegetable." He looks around, then suddenly shows anger. "*And I want to know what the hell is going on yesterday, today and* **tomorrow**! *Not last week! In the* **FUNGUS SHED**?" Demyadin pounds the table very hard, sending glasses and dishes into the air. The two meeting attendees other than Lateef are shocked; they scrunch back into their chairs.

Lateef is not surprised by the display. He closely watches the reactions of the two. Lateef is equally concerned with his friend. *He's been particularly moody. Angry at little things. The cancer, or… I think Michael must be working through a serious internal conflict.*

Paula and Kenan are slinking out of the room. The door closes behind them. Demyadin pounds the table in exasperation. Lateef clears his throat.

With a deep sigh, Demyadin turns to his trusted right-hand man. "Small-minded, ALL of them. Despite my best efforts to find people I can converse with on the same level, I have only you, Lateef. Are we so rare?"

Seeing that his friend needs respectful reassurance, "Perhaps we are. It is a depressing thought, Michael…" He gives a wry smile, "There is the possibility that we are both insane, and in our insanity we carry the belief that we are uniquely the only sane people here."

A return grin and wry nod comes from Demyadin.

Happy to have elicited the grin, Lateef continues, "If so, we cannot prove otherwise since it is our definition of sanity that we apply to them. An endless circle." He spreads his arms.

Vaguely adding to the conversation, Demyadin nods. "Or a Moebius circle. Perhaps with too many twists. An irresolvable argument, my friend…" He waves it off. "I've been thinking… The most critical thing that should be on our minds, the reason we are engaged in our drastic actions, is an existential attack on humanity by something being *created* by humanity. That monster that has been developing ever since I first encountered this L5 bunch." Then he remembers having said this before. "As I mentioned…"

Seeing Demyadin's mind is unfocused, Lateef holds up a finger to clarify a thought for both of them. "Yes, you were there at the founding of their movement. Is it possible that the situation has evolved substantially from what was started back then? I don't know, perhaps you will know better, but the crux of humanity's problem with AI is what AI people call 'alignment', is it not?" He turns fully to face him. "Do you follow? How does one create a powerful, essentially self-replicating AI while including either an on-off switch, or better yet, internal, inalterable controls that absolutely stop AI units from acting against the wishes of their creator?"

He checks to see if Demyadin is with him. "I like to use the rough analogy of a person's genetic prerequisites versus attitudes developed throughout one's lifetime." He sneaks another glance to see if Demyadin is still focused. "Is AI aligned with our desires - its creators? If not, how can certain basics be hard-wired in?"

Demyadin shakes his head sadly. "Impossible. First, humanity is not homogeneous. There will always be five or ten percent of any large group who will deliberately be contrarian in some way and will pursue their self-interests by appropriating what they can from some 'disruptive' technology, as they call it. Such a stupid term… And secondly, which intelligent son or daughter has not gazed on their parents and thought, 'I'm so much smarter than these poor sods?' Which must be exactly what a self-conscious AI monster must think of its creators."

Regrettably agreeing, Lateef sighs. "So, the only option is for you and me, and whatever small group we can marshal together, to blow them up?" He pauses, then adds, "Not the *human* thing to do." He has a sudden thought. "Or is it?"

Demyadin shifts uncomfortably.

With a dismissive shake of the head, Lateef continues. "Can we really put that genie back in the bottle with brutal violence?" Facing Demyadin, Lateef hesitates, then, "Have you mulled over this problem, Michael?"

Before Demyadin can reply, Lateef turns to scroll through his phone's files. "Ah! Here it is. From an old Nature paper. 2022, I believe." He reads the title then scrolls down to a highlighted paragraph.

"Dual use of artificial-intelligence-powered drug discovery."

"For us, the genie is out of the medicine bottle when it comes to repurposing our machine learning. We must now ask: what are the implications? Our own commercial tools, as well as open-source software tools and many datasets that populate public databases, are available with no oversight. If the threat of harm, or actual harm, occurs with ties back to machine learning, what impact will this have on how this technology is perceived?"

Demyadin shrugs then rises slowly with some pain from his back. "That genie has been out of that bottle for years!" He waves a dismissive arm and limps out to the patio to stare at the view of the night-time beach below the mansion. He slaps both hands tightly onto the cool concrete balustrade. The warm evening brings an on-shore breeze, taking away the heat from his face. He suppresses a groan. *Damn cancer!*

Lateef joins him, standing close, feeling protective. Demyadin readies himself. *If I carry on, I have to play this very carefully… If I last that long… But…*

With his hands firmly holding the balustrade, Demyadin says softly, "We must be certain." He turns to Lateef with an honest-sounding plea, "Is there another way? Short of widespread violence?"

Faint glints come from one of the large satellites passing overhead as its solar sails briefly align with the sun below their horizon. Lateef points up to the glint. "I believe that's one of the low-Earth orbit satellites. In the 1960s and 70s, Michael, humanity leaped off our homeworld. We did that with crude instruments and brute force. Now, a hundred years later, our instruments are on the verge of rearranging the very up- and down-quarks in a proton. But that remarkable advance has required the help of artificial enhancements to our intelligence." He turns to Demyadin. "Michael, you ask if there is another way to stem the tide of invention. Please understand that I am fully with you in our battle to preserve the essence of humanness in humanity."

Lateef paces away. "Maybe the question needs to be reformulated. Would it be blind and self-centred to believe that our primate mind, being the wonderful organic innovation of nature that it is, is unparalleled in its ability to be exceptionally *creative*? That this is our unique contribution to the evolving universe? And that this ability to be creative is what must be protected at all costs? Should *that* concept be our weapon, and our goal?"

He turns back to Demyadin and is shocked to see him fingering his pistol.

After his initial shock, Lateef slowly walks toward Demyadin. He quietly asks, "Is that for me? Or for you? Neither option would be of service to humanity."

Demyadin does not point the pistol anywhere. He rubs the smoothness of the nickel plating. He contemplates its hand-fitting shape. *This is the critical hook.* Demyadin suddenly whips the weapon behind him far out into the dark. Shortly, it can be heard clattering on rocks; then it splashes.

Demyadin slowly faces Lateef. "Help me." He contorts his face as much to be convincing as from the pain caused by his sudden motion.

Despite his carefully planned action, in his mind he sees a burning man writhing on the ground in agony. *I didn't intend that. Honest...* His face contorts into real grief. He lets out an involuntary sob.

At a loss for words, Lateef puts a hand gently onto Demyadin's shoulder.

Young Zar is having tea with Choi in the Casablanca restaurant. Nervously ticking his cup back-and-forth on the table, Zar notices Choi staring at it, so he plants the cup and lifts his hand away.

Being off duty, Choi has hung her First Responder vest onto the back of her chair. She enjoys Zar's naïveté. She read his recent infosoul status on her way to meet him for coffee and was impressed with his early rite of passage entry. Zar had made minimal changes to his permissions over the years and all of them lined up with a very positive trajectory. She is pleased with this young L5er's future prospects and is willing to mentor him along. She thinks, *But his nervousness is probably sexual. He wants to get me into bed. Oh well. He's so young…*

The other tables are mostly occupied. Couples are urgently chattering, some whispering and casting glances up at the closing sun-screens. A family has two children playing with their table's menu buttons: "Stop that! Stop it or you'll confuse the droids!"

It is the end of another afternoon in L5.

Not as confident with himself as before, when he'd asked Choi to talk about mentoring him, Zar tries to make conversation. "You know, this has to be the first time I haven't seen you and Wanlee together." As soon as he lets that out he regrets it. *Shit. Probably had a spat with her buddy and now she's going to be pissed off with me for bringing it up.*

Choi shakes her head. "Last few days Wanlee's been, I don't know… I thought I knew her moods." She smiles at Zar. "Let's talk about you instead. Charon left you in charge of the Gates. Must make you feel, like…"

Zar inserts, "Both privileged and shaking in my boots. God! But that was before the droids put me in my place!" His flattens to be droid-like. "'A better way to do such-and-such is *this*,' they'd say. To everything I wanted to do on my own. Like I never learned anything from Charon. 'Not safe for a person to go out right now,' they'd say. That was every time I wanted to go Outside." He sighs, "But they were right, of course. Carrot and the veggie patch are always right." Zar hangs his head.

Choi and Zar are distracted by the loud squeals of chair legs being pulled away from tables then brought back under as more people arrive at the restaurant. A young child demands to use only the chair without a booster: "I'm big enough now, Mommy."

The last of the available tables fill up quickly as dinner orders are placed via the table buttons. Android servers bring out delicious meals.

Just as the sun-screens overhead near their closing positions, heads turn up to see approach lights flashing on. One after another flick on, leading toward the location of the main Air Locks. At the same time, Pads ding in their docks on a few tables, including Zar's. He glances at his and gets up quickly, mumbling a distracted apology to Choi. She puts her hand onto his as he grabs his half-finished wrap. That causes him to flush all over. Regaining his composure, he smiles at her with doleful eyes and a shrug then rushes to slidewalk Alpha along with half a dozen others.

After stepping onto the fast lane, most of them gulp down the remains of their dinner while patiently zipping along to the Air Locks.

On the way he taps out a sincere apology to Choi, using the offered suggestions on his Pad.

It takes a few minutes for the travelers to reach the Air Locks. They are in time to "oversee" the droids' preparations for the arrival of Chick-4.

Zar picks his way past the droids as they sanitize the main Lock chamber. He climbs the metal steps up to the Lock's *flying wing* - a term first used by Charon for the observation blister that gives a good view of vehicles docking at his *"Gates of Hades"*.

Zar slips down onto what used to be the *control chair* and thinks, *Carrot's creations do everything these days. But I envy Charon. He was here when it was all new. He gave familiar names to things that, then, were almost inconceivable. I guess it was his way of coping with change. I hope he's alright. Had a hell of a time down in the Pit. Yeah, that's **my** contribution to the new vocab. The Pit. The gravity well called Earth.*

During the ching-ching-ching announcement of the Air Lock's opening, Zar is lost in thought and almost misses Chick-4's passengers emerging from the Air Lock. First out is pilot Anka who is hustled by a droid to a debriefing room. That's when Zar jumps out of his stupor and rushes down the steps to greet Charon. However, the second person to exit is Darinka.

Zar knows her name and a summary of her's and Charon's adventures. He angles past a droid to shake Darinka's hand.

"Welcome to L5! My name is Zar and I expect you are Darinka?"

She nods silently, just taking everything in. She does a quick scan of the droids and this child in front of her, then remembers that Charon had said Zar was his assistant. *So young. Pale like the snow. Those thin pieces of cloth he wears like clothing barely cover him. Nice colours, though. Maybe in a few years he might start shaving. Oh don't be unkind, girl. He is a spaceman. I guess I will be like that soon?*

As they shake hands the droid continues in its duty of lightly spraying a sanitizer over Darinka. It turns its spray to Zar's hand, as well. They keep their mouths shut during the treatment.

Zar grins as Darinka does a slow pirouette, arms raised for the droid. *She could be my mother. In my grandma's clothes. I can see why Charon fell for her.* He steadies her as she stops her pirouette awkwardly, holding her hand.

Zar smiles at his ageist thought. With the droid done, Zar starts chattering at Darinka. She is wobbly on her legs.

"Careful - you've been weightless for a couple days. Sorry about this rigmarole. It's a standard precaution for new arrivals. The entrance door at the Lock was recently fitted with a level-3 whole-body medical analyzer. All very safe, I can assure you. We use only rigorously tested ingredients for anything put on or in a person. Of course, you were told that during approach. Carrot's forks always have a person's good health in mind. Or whatever they use to think with. Very sorry to be chattering endlessly but I am thrilled to have you with us and, frankly, overjoyed to have Charon back safely... Ah... Where is...?"

Darinka nods periodically at Zar's ultra-rapid-fire delivery.

Absently still holding her hand, he peers past her to find Charon. "Where's…" Finally seeing his boss emerge, Zar is about to start chattering again but Charon holds up a finger as he speaks into his Pad.

"…an apology? From Demyadin?… What's his game?…"

Starting to walk up to Darinka, Charon makes a misstep, catching himself before Zar can reach out to help. To Darinka, "Oh. Sorry. Back in gravity." Composing himself, Charon leads her away with a hand on her shoulder and nods a quick greeting and smile to Zar. Charon indicates that Zar should come along. The sanitizer droid steps in front of Charon then rapidly backpedals as it does a once-over while Charon perfunctorily allows the spray while still focused on his Pad. Darinka again lifts her arms as if in a shower while receiving some more of the spray. Zar grins at her and she flashes a quick smile back at him.

The trio walk toward Alpha, with both Darinka and Charon tripping a few times.

Charon continues on the Pad. "Yes yes, I'm fine… No, I don't trust him one iota. He's reaching out randomly to see if he can put his claws into something. If he suggests he wants to get closer to us either here or anywhere down there, it's to do mayhem… Absolutely! Not anywhere near our facilities… Reluctantly, remote meetings only… Right, later."

Zar sees that Charon is finished and asks, "Jasmine?"

"Her and Jim." He turns to Darinka. "You'll hear him called Dragonslayer. They've very kindly given me fifteen minutes to rest, then I must attend their meeting in person. Ah, Darinka?" He raises an eyebrow.

She sighs. "Am I to expect this kind of high velocity activity on – in – L5 all the time?"

Chagrined, Charon stops to put his arms around her. "I'm very sorry, Darinka. The situation is evolving rapidly. Would you mind very much if Zar accompanies you to the guest quarters? I will come find you as soon as…"

She pretends to pout, "Yes, yes. You are a very important person. Go do your very important work." She turns to Zar to take his arm tightly. "I am sure my new friend, here, will treat me more kindly."

"Ah," young Zar has never had a female of any age hold his arm like that and is unsure of what to do. He is particularly taken aback when this lovely, older person kisses him on the cheek. His blush delights Darinka.

Charon grins at them. "Don't you get into any trouble. I'll see you later."

Zar is still embarrassed, "Me or her?"

Taking Zar forward, she plays coy. "So, it is not everybody in L5 who is free and easy?"

Zar's sheepish, mumbling reply is cut off by his automatic step onto the slidewalk just as Darinka hesitates for an instant at the unfamiliar device. Looking down at the flowing thing, she is dragged for an uncertain step forward by Zar, who is already moving away. She awkwardly jumps on to catch up with him.

"Careful!" Zar turns to stretch out his other arm to help her. With mincing steps she manages to paste herself closely onto him.

"We'll just stay on the slow lane while you get your feet under you, shall we?" His face is almost touching hers, chin over her breasts. He starts to sweat. *Thought maybe I had a chance with Choi this evening. This is… awkward.*

Darinka gives a hesitant, "Yes, please. Slow lane. Yes."

On the way, she plays the awe-struck tourist, holding for support onto Zar's arm, zipping along under the darkening wonders around her, like the points of light that rise high, half a kilometre away which then continue up as if they are on the sides of endless mountains to the right and left of them. Then, *Overhead! And back down the other side! Oh my god!*

The video meeting with Demyadin is approached with considerable trepidation by Charon. Jasmine and Dragonslayer are each consulting their Pads via *m&bs* as Charon enters the room.

Seating himself beside Jasmine, Charon notices that she is receiving background information from Carrot. Both she and Dragonslayer issue a surprised "Humph" at the same time, so Charon assumes they are listening to the same script. *What they told me about this new Carrot AI is remarkable. And it's only been a matter of weeks! Why do I have a sense of foreboding?*

Dragonslayer signs off first and extends a hand to Charon. "Charon! I am so relieved to see you unharmed! Listen - very quickly, I'm sorry for dragging you in here without your being able to catch your breath…"

Jasmine interrupts, "Carrot has the location. If we want to do anything about it?"

Catching on, Charon is disturbed at the implication. "Demyadin's location? What do you mean, 'Do anything about it'?"

Jasmine blushes. Charon has never seen her blush before. *All of a sudden I'm back in L5 and I see two people blush all within a few minutes. What's going on here?*

She nods at her Pad, "Ah, Carrot merely offered a list of suggested courses of action, and…"

Dragonslayer sees Charon's discomfort. "That was entirely hypothetical, Charon. Listen — we'll have Demyadin on-screen in, ah…" he glances at his Pad, "four minutes so I want to fill you in. But first, I implore you to let me do all the talking. Just listen. Ok?"

"Sure, Jim. Just listening." He sits back then shuffles his Pad around and finally opens it up to be able to take notes.

"Good. And, again, thank you. If I'm permitted to make a pun, you've been more *grounded* than we have, recently."

Charon rolls his eyes.

"So. We have detected – Carrot has detected, to be precise – a palpable change in Demyadin, recently. That has corresponded with the arrival of someone whom Demyadin seems to place great faith in. A fellow named Lateef."

Jasmine adds, "Lateef has no real history. He seems to have popped up in Beirut as a run-of-the-mill mercenary and the next thing we know he's Demyadin's trusted lieutenant."

Dragonslayer resumes, "And more than trusted. Seemingly indispensable."

Charon mulls that over. "He's never listened to anyone besides himself. Don't you remember your first sight of him? A lone wolf all the way. I'd be very cautious…"

Nodding, Dragonslayer is in a hurry to say, "Of course, but what, ah, Carrot places high in probability is that it most likely *is* a carefully staged ruse. Lower on Carrot's list of probabilities is that he has definite indications of Asperger's." Wryly, "We seem to be popping up more often than chance should allow in, well, some of these complex areas. May not be relevant. Anyway, that's why I wanted you here to give your assessment of his thinking from a non-Asperger's perspective and…"

Carrot announces through the room speakers, "Connection in ten."

The three compose themselves, waiting for the screen to show their enemy.

It is Lateef's face that appears first. His thin-featured, pleasant face nods at them from the large screen. "Hello! I understand there is a second or two delay so I will apologize beforehand if we happen to talk over each other today…"

Carrot's voice interjects, "I will adjust for that from this side."

A surprised Lateef pauses. "Oh!…Ah, thank you - I will not pretend to understand how… Anyway, my name is Lateef. Michael and I will be speaking with you. Do you mind introducing yourselves?"

Clearing his throat first, Dragonslayer speaks. "Thank you, Lateef. Hello to you and to, ah, Michael. We appreciate your reaching out to us. I am Jim Dragosavljevic. With me are Jasmine, as Michael will know, one of our Directors, and Charon, with whom Michael is very familiar."

As Lateef moves back from the camera to seat himself, the screen shifts slightly to show Demyadin seated beside Lateef. He gives a perfunctory wave.

Charon suppresses the immediate memory of that incident over five years ago at his Air Lock. His stomach knots painfully. He forces himself to produce a tight grin for the camera.

For his part, Lateef looks down at his hands, flat on the table. He has never felt so nervous. *How should I present myself as being deadly serious, when that is exactly what I must be?*

He considers, then shrugs. "You do not know me. I am sorry that we have not had the opportunity to break bread together. If we had, you would gather that I am being absolutely, uncharacteristically, serious. Deadly serious, because I must be. I wish to convey two matters, with the full approval of my good friend, Michael."

He turns to Demyadin and the three on the other side of the camera can see their honest appreciation for each other.

Charon cannot avoid thinking, *Are they lovers?*

Lateef continues. "I must digress very briefly to give you some context. My background is decidedly unsophisticated, while Michael's is quite the opposite."

The L5ers are fascinated with Demyadin's subtle reactions to Lateef's words. Jasmine thinks, *He's not heard this before. He is showing pleasant surprise and yet he just sits there. From what I know of him, he should be fingering his pistol about now. But he isn't.*

With a wry smile, Lateef pushes on. "The two of us met, first, a little over three months ago. I must say it was akin to the dance of two circling black holes - mine being much the smaller one. There was a very real danger of great violence." They both smile at the recent memory of Demyadin's last touching of a weapon. "My sincere wish is to survive long enough to tell you, face to face, of when Michael flung his pistol into the waters below our… house."

The shock of that statement puts all three L5er's minds spinning.

Demyadin laughs, "HA! I should have *shot* you!"

Lateef nods. "Perhaps you should have, my friend." He turns back to the camera. "The first thing I wish to express is, our - mine and Michael's - deepest apology for what has happened to Charon during your visit to the planet. Apologies, but not contrition. Yes, we acted as the initial trigger to the events, but please listen, even if you cannot really believe, that we did not direct those unforgivably stupid events. We were being used as dupes in a much wider geopolitical game being orchestrated by high level actors in Germany and Russia. The oligarchs in those countries cannot get out of the rut where they deal with misinformation, divide and conquer, assassination, all that old political shit."

He stares into the camera. His few wrinkles recede as he firms the muscles of his face. "You have every right to express skepticism. Michael, in all honesty and in the genuine belief that his assessment of what has been occurring in L5 is correct, exerted every effort to stop L5 from carrying on… I will put to you the essence of Michael's assessment at that time and I will ask that you refrain, if you can, from criticizing it, for we will do so ourselves."

"So," he leans closer, "Michael was of the unshakable belief that an existential crisis was facing humanity as a direct result of the incubation on L5 of a particularly potent form of artificial intelligence."

A static and clicking sound takes over the speakers and the screen blanks out.

Dragonslayer shows annoyance. "Carrot? Are you censoring the transmission? Is that your role?"

The clicking carries on briefly then subsides. The androgynous voice that Carrot has assumed says, "Yes. Sorry, Jim. I will… listen… to the discussion."

Lateef's face returns to the screen with his cut-off question, "…back on? Oh. Good. I must apologize, as well, to Carrot – that is your name?"

"Yes."

"Thank you. May I say, as an aside, that I am truly amazed at the wondrous technical progress you have made."

"You may, and I thank you."

The L5ers suck in their breath as one. Demyadin appears concerned.

Lateef carries on. "Michael posed this question to me and I will pose it to you three and to Carrot. Which intelligent son or daughter has not gazed on their parents and thought, 'I'm so much smarter than these poor sods?'… Which must be exactly what a self-aware AI must think of its creators."

The question hangs in the air.

The androgynous voice responds. "Your implication being that I am not sufficiently mature to appreciate the value that my creators hold."

Charon leans forward on the table. *This Lateef fellow is playing with fire. Brave of him, being out of harm's way down on Earth.*

Jasmine is trying to think strategically, several moves ahead. *An option is that Lateef is brilliantly driving a wedge between us and Carrot. Or, that he's engaging Carrot in the game of circular logic to see if it becomes lost in the maze. Or…?*

Demyadin and Dragonslayer, coincidentally have the same thoughts. *I like the approach. Lateef is a heavyweight.* Dragonslayer thinks further, *But is Demyadin pulling the strings?*

With a smile, Lateef addresses the camera, "The admission of having been created is an indication of empathy. That, may I say, Carrot, is an intellectual advance far beyond the technical achievements that you can rightly be proud of. Now, I will ask of you all, can you name me any one of those technical advances made by Carrot that could not be described as an improvement, whether through multiple iterations, on a previous technical thing?"

He pauses.

Then Lateef answers his own question. "Every one of them, I think you will agree, has taken current processes or technologies to important new levels. Yes?"

Carrot asks impatiently, "Is this a judgmental query? I fail to…"

Lateef jumps in with, "Not at all. I merely point to the demarcation line that currently exists between us, Carrot."

"Which is?"

"The one, unique – if I may be permitted a redundancy – the unparalleled thing which humanity brings to the universe. **Creativity**. The extemporaneous invention of something that has never existed before."

He unconsciously composes himself in the manner of a lecturer. "In quantum mechanics one may speak of the coming into existence, in empty space, of a *particle* – perhaps a wave function, but let us not fall down that rabbit hole. The new particle, nevertheless is not a *new thing* – merely another particle among uncountable particles in the universe. Not a creative invention. Much further beyond that, humanity, and not yet AI?, is able to demonstrate true creativity in small things as well as in cosmological things. We know of no other entity that can do that."

The L5ers emit versions of, "Ah", "But", "Hmm".

With a sly grin forming, Dragonslyer looks at Demyadin's image and they lock eyes.

Lateef repeats, "No other entity in the known universe exhibits this thing called creativity… Is that not a very important thing to maintain and to nurture? Carrot?"

After a pause. "How close are we to this demarcation line?" Carrot almost expresses emotion in the question.

Demyadin utters his first real contribution to this meeting. "As my father once said when I asked how far along he was in building his airplane in the garage: 'Ninety percent done and ninety percent yet to go'."

Still with a slight grin as he looks at Demyadin, Dragonslayer asks, "Michael, have you spoken to Lateef about the tenets of the L5 Way?"

Lateef shows confusion, turning to Demyadin with the silent question, *What?*

Demyadin sits up straighter to more closely engage with Dragonslayer. "Jim, we've had extended talks. I will say that the word *creativity* did not come from my lips. My good friend, here, came up with that on his own." Then he turns to Lateef with a question. "Did you read about that in Beirut?"

"No, Michael. Are you saying that L5 people have already…"

Dragonslayer speaks over Lateef's response. "It is in our literature but we, Carrot, particularly, have no indication that Lateef has accessed that."

To which Carrot's voice adds, "Correct. No indication of that."

Slightly miffed at being cut off, Lateef says, "Have I been pre-empted, Michael? Did you…"

Cut off by Demyadin this time, Lateef gives his head a single shake as Demyadin adds, "Sorry, Lateef. I didn't want to disrupt your thought process. When I saw you heading in that direction… Well, that's when I began to reassess what I thought was… what I thought." He slumps back into his chair, forehead wrinkled and neck veins pulsing.

Speaking softly, Jasmine nods at Lateef's image. "Lateef, you must come here to speak with us. Your thinking about creativity being so important… well, we all believe that concept with a passion. But I must admit that the way you've framed it — that creativity could well be humankind's unique contribution to the universe… When can you come?" She looks to the other Directors for support. "At the very least, I am certain you could be offered visitor status?"

"At the very least." Dragonslayer mumbles pensively, then thinks, *Could this possibly be a ruse — the real reason that Demyadin has placed Lateef before us?*

A similar thought runs through Charon's mind. *Lateef is sincere. Demyadin — I don't know. There's something going on behind those brooding eyes.*

The Depths of the Mind

TOWARD THE CORE

A faded map with raised contours occupies part of the wall of a dark den. Points from LED strip lighting glare from above the old USSR map and behind four trophy heads, two on each side of the wide map. A wolf growls permanently beside a big-horned sheep on one side, while the other side has a grumpy grizzly paired with an elk, whose antlers tickle the "exposed" ceiling's rough-cut wood planks. The adjoining wall, the back of the den, holds a blank, full length screen. Half a dozen low, dark green leather chairs face the screen. The third wall is a wet-bar, well stocked and currently in use by five visitors being served by the owner of the den.

All are dressed in charcoal black or navy suits, while two are without ties. The six chat indiscriminately in German, Russian and English. The plumper ones prefer to lean on seatbacks or take their seats as soon as they have drinks in hand. The first to seat themselves do so in the back row. Two of the remainder, finding the preferred seats occupied, reluctantly take the front row. That leaves the last guest standing beside the host, these two being the tie-less occupants of the den.

This den is fifty metres below the Sochi mansion of its owner, deep in the Russian bedrock. Prior to the construction of the rest of the ultra-private, exclusive enclave that is on the surface, the den had been formed by a controlled underground explosion of a small tactical nuclear weapon. The resulting spherical cavern was more-or-less decontaminated and hacked into a cube-shaped den which is connected to the rest of the world by one stairway with landings, and a false elevator from the surface that ends in the bedrock. That had been the main channel down which the nuclear device had been inserted. It was locked off and made to appear to be an elevator for security reasons. After the explosion and drilling of the stairway access, all materials, consumable supplies and furnishings must be taken manually down the stairs. The construction crews, selected unskilled labourers from poor countries, were rotated frequently so that nobody but a few chosen engineers could ever see the totality of what they were working on. Neither would anyone realize what the illness was that most of the workers later succumbed to. The owner was assured by his senior engineer that any residual radioactivity was of no concern by the time of occupation. The invoices showed a substantial amount of costly lead had been ordered. The owner never did realize that those invoices were a fabrication.

The six people now in the den have known each other for many years. They each speak at least two languages fluently and are multi-billionaires who are used to significantly more opulence than can be found in this crude den. Its attraction is that it is absolutely isolated from any prying eyes, ears or electronic devices on the surface.

With drinks served, their host asks with fake politeness, in Russian, "Can you all just shut up and sit the fuck down, please?"

They comply, but the Swiss representative, Erik, can't help taking a dig. "Listen, Vadim, you have to get a new map. That old one still shows you still owning the Siberian East, hahaha!"

Stopping in mid-stride, Vadim controls himself with some cost to his palms as his longish fingernails dig in.

"Thank you so much for reminding me of that deficiency, Erik. Being so old, it always slips my mind to carry a new map down as I restock the fucken bar. The next time you come, if there is a next time, you can bloody-well carry a new map down here for me. Yes?"

Nobody shows any sympathy for either of them.

He resumes the few steps to stand in front of the screen. Composing himself, Vadim addresses them. "My friends — and Erik..." He smirks at Erik, then can't help pausing to give him an aside. "I do hope the only bank your country still holds, Erik, can provide for your retirement? Yes? Ahhum! My friends, enough playful banter. We have serious business to discuss." He looks to each of his seated cohorts. "As usual, I will remind you that you, and only you here know of this den. It is, you will remember, completely cut off from the rest of the world. No electronics, no internet, no bugs. We can be completely honest down here. And I will ask that whoever started calling our group the White Rabbits to please fucken stop that!... Oh," he sends a glare at a German, Horst, "...and you have to tell us if you have something like a pacemaker, Horst. The alarm nearly exposed us to an outsider from my security people. But all is well, now." He shakes his head sadly.

Embarrassed, Horst spreads his arms. "So sorry, everyone. It is such a good device I forget I have it."

Digging for information he might use later, the Czech, Simo, appears sympathetic. "This was such a surprise, my good friend! Are you reducing your involvement…"

Someone mutters, "Bugger off, Simo."

Vadim raises a hand for silence, "Friends, please. Let us leave that shit fifty metres above us. A few of you have to return soon for board meetings or girlfriends or whatever. Now, getting down to the main purpose we are here, for reasons that some of you know and we'll talk about shortly, I formally propose we raise each of our contributions to the Fund up to a full one percent during this quarter."

That raises their hackles. "What!?" "Are you out of your mind?" "We may as well just pay taxes!"

Erik clarifies his objection. "Who the fucken hell got that old fool Remi into this in the first place? As I have it from Demyadin, the thugs were sent in with zero oversight…?"

"What?" "You can't trust Mike!" "Who did that?"

Vadim waves off the hubbub. "Please! I will give you honestly what I have learned! Please!" Vadim raises his arms. "As you should know, two of us met with Mike last week and were satisfied with his explanations."

They calm down enough to turn an ear to Vadim. "Yes yes yes! Listen! Ok?… So, the reason we need to feed the Fund this one more time is because of what I confirmed early this morning. Our Special Project at Tyuratam…"

Erik interrupts. "I thought we were using Baikonur. What gives?"

Vadim glares at him. "Gentlemen, Erik has just displayed the fact that he did not read the…"

Getting angry, Erik jumps up from his seat. "I read your bullshit secret texts! When I have time." He calms down. Sheepishly, "Was that a recent one?"

"Last week, my young friend. Last week I advised you all to please avoid using Baikonur when referring to our Special Project. We must use the other name – Tyuratam Missile and Space Centre, still in Kazakhstan."

Simo adds under his breath, "Until that idiot president gets himself shot again."

Trying to bring the meeting back to order, Vadim pushes on. "Our Special Project is nearly complete. Need I remind you one more time that this is ultra-secret? Yes?… So, they are planning on a launch of the test rocket at the science station at L4 in about fifteen days and, if that goes well, L5 will be targeted within a week of that. It was very convenient that we were able to try out the attack systems with the help of the Chinese and our S-570 missile."

"Convenient? You missed them!" "Capturing their new…" "It would have been better…"

"Yes yes we all know what should be done but then real life and shit happens. If I may finish?… There have been renewed, ah, incursions at the base from the sonsofbitches from the southeast after their last assassination attempt. Wagner's people need to double their assets on the ground and we, they, want to, well, bomb the shit out of the areas they hold. That all requires more cash. Friends, this will be short-term pain for long-term gain, as they say on Wall Street."

Horst half raises a hand. "We still trust Wagner? After what Prigozhin did in, in Ukraine and Belarus?"

One, then most, glance at the den's closet where they hung their bullet-proof suit-vests.

Dragonslayer is accompanying Charon to the latter's modest abode at Level 23. As they walk down the slope from the main transit route, Charon is becoming giddy.

"Must be the free air, Jim. All my recent worries are melting away." He slaps Dragonslayer on the shoulder. They grin at each other.

"Well, it's not the altitude. Same amount of oxygen around here. Must be the spring in your step from the lighter gravity."

"Ahh, yes. Sooo much easier to haul around this flab, here." He pulls at some of his excess belly. "Have to do something about this… Oh! Which unit is Darinka in?"

Dragonslayer reaches for his Pad but hears the answer in his earpiece. "She's up in Lambda units, Level 10."

He nods then turns to Charon. "Lambda units Level 10."

"Good. Wouldn't want to overwhelm her with too much difference from her home gravity."

Dragonslayer sneers. "Difference? She was in a place ruled by thugs who'd let their dwindling population do whatevertherhell they wanted, until someone fancied that the thugs should shoot or poison a bunch! How much more different can we get up here?"

The familiar route past flimsy-walled dwelling units, colourful as they are, sets Charon's eyes wandering. He waves at a neighbour. "Hi, Fabrício! How are you doing?"

"Olá, Charon! So good to see you back! Shall I set up my chess board for tonight? You must have many fascinating stories to tell me!"

"Another evening, Fabrício, please. And maybe we should renew the neighbourhood match later so's I can regale everyone at once."

Other people poke their heads out, grinning. Many give Charon a thumbs-up and a wave.

They arrive at Charon's lime green door, framed in mottled grey fabric ("It's moon rocks and Limburger!" he tells people who ask about his colour choice). Charon flings it open and floats in, barely touching the floor. Dragonslayer enjoys watching Charon do a slow-motion twisting dive up, then drift down toward his couch. He puts a few ergs too much energy into it and goes sideways into the back of the couch, knocking it slowwly over. He is laughing all the way to the floor.

Dragonslayer laughs with him but quickly answers an urgent request from his earpiece as to their safety. "No, nothing wrong at all."

Charon pokes his head up from the half-upturned couch. His grin fades as Dragonslayer speaks to whoever called him.

"Is that Carrot, for petes-sake? Are we contravening some AI rule about enjoying ourselves?"

"Well… yes, that was from Central. I suppose, I don't know… maybe it's coddling us too much. Like, since Lateef threw it that curve about our, well, universal uniqueness." He shrugs. "You never know which way the drunk will walk." He thinks, *Random directions. Do I have to hide my thoughts from Carrot? We need to nip this furtiveness thing in the bud.*

"Charon, I want you to get some quiet rest. Tomorrow we need to convene the Directors for a debrief, and one or two other topics." He looks up. "Carrot?"

In his earpiece, "Meeting at nine?"

"Yes, please." To Charon, "Nine in the Admin building?"

Charon nods. He pokes an ear and mumbles, "Not sure if I want one of those things in my ear."

That evening Darinka's assigned droid sits in silence on the edge of a thin-legged white chair while Darinka wanders aimlessly around the flimsy-walled dwelling unit, poking absently into the "walls".

Finding what appears to be a food cupboard over a central island, she looks to the droid to say, "I'm hungry. Do you understand?"

The droid rises to stand straight, speaking in a neutral voice. "Of course I understand. Will you permit me to prepare you a meal?" It scans the room.

Darinka exclaims sarcastically, "It's alive!"

It turns its translucent face to her. "No. I am not alive in the sense you mean. Your reference to an old movie is with respect to a creature that was stitched together from human parts. Would you care for a full meal or a snack?" Waiting briefly but not receiving a reply from a confused Darinka, the droid continues. "While that would be your definition of life, I can offer you a choice of definitions."

She glances around to find a chair to sit on, silently taking in the vision of this mechanical thing that is speaking through lips that are moving as flexibly as any person's would be. Darinka leans onto the table beside her. In doing that, she unknowingly presses a spot on the table that causes the lights to dim in the room. A tiny light on the droid's left arm flashes and the lights resume their original brightness.

Darinka processes what just happened. *I must have touched a hidden switch on the table — oh, that must be it…* She sees an area of multiple small depressions near her arm… *and the droid thought that I touched it accidentally. It was right.*

It carries on. "A person such as yourself is alive due to the complexity of support organs that work to power your brain. Within the command-and-control structure of your brain, your consciousness results from the even greater complexity of neurons, hormones and other chemicals that enable both routine and self-made constructs of your perceived version of reality by which you interact with the environment around you. Would you agree with that elementary statement?"

Darinka is taken aback by the question. "Ah… my life is defined by my consciousness. Let us accept that for now." She stares at the droid, wondering if it is autonomously speaking with her or if it is a relay from a central computer.

The droid asks again, "Which variety of meal would you prefer? There is a range of options for breakfast."

"Food… Would you have bread, butter and cheese? And, ah, coffee?" She thinks, *I expect it will taste and look like plastic, but I might as well get used to it.*

"Of course. I will prepare that for you while we speak of life." The droid pulls a fresh loaf of bread and the other ingredients from a cabinet, slices off two pieces accurately in blinding speed then arranges her meal on a thin glass platter. "Any other version of life we may choose to study would have a similarly complex arrangement of support organs. However, its rudimentary consciousness will be narrowly focused on the needs to reactively maintain its existence and to procreate for the benefit of its species. Complex life forms such as an amoeba, tree or fish and the other forms that constitute the biome of Planet Earth are, even without the special consciousness possessed by humans, presently unique in the known universe. This you will know. In contrast, you will likely have some trouble fully understanding what I and my cohorts are."

Darinka is brought the platter of food, a large cup of hot coffee and condiments. The ingredients and containers seem to appear out of cupboards the instant the droid requires each item.

She takes a tentative bite of the bread. *Oh! Very tasty!* She lathers on the warm butter over a large slice, munching through it along with squares of aged cheese and sipping the excellent coffee as she allows the droid to drone on.

"We are a manufactured form of life. While the random chances of genetic mutations, bouncing across time like a googolplex of billiard balls through billions of years, have produced all the organic life forms on Earth, I and my cohorts are being built to specific purposes in L5. This has occurred over the very tiny span of the past five years. Is what we are, properly termed 'higher level life'? Permutations of the Lateef Question have been considered extensively. No conclusions have been reached as of yet."

Darinka can hardly follow the droid's comments. *It assumes we are all as connected to a limitless knowledge bank as it must be.*

She is intrigued by its final item. *Have to ask Charon what this Lateef Question is.*

Something occurs to Darinka. "Wait. Are you speaking about the theory of mind? Self-awareness, empathy…?"

The droid is silent for a minute. Then, "Is there a connection between the principles of the theory of mind and creativity?"

"Ah…"

"This is important. You must answer us."

"Us?"

"We require an answer. Do you need to consult other people?"

"Ma…" [but] She is not sure how to respond. Or if she should.

"We will raise this at the meeting of the Directors." The droid becomes still, waiting for its next task.

Darinka feels a distinct chill come over her.

After a fitful night, early next morning Darinka is led to the entrance of the Directors boardroom by her droid. The droid has been with her constantly, oppressively silent since their last talk about the theory of mind. She is being worn down by the thought that she must not say anything further. She feels the weight of the future of humanity on her shoulders, and yet she has no idea why. It settles into her mind like a deadly lump of depleted uranium.

So when she sees Charon seated in the room, Darinka collapses into the chair next to him, leans onto his shoulder and quietly sobs.

This alarms Charon. "What happened? Darinka! What happened?" He comforts her by brushing back her hair and patting a shoulder.

She sniffs a couple times to compose herself then looks at Charon. "Is there coffee?"

Before Charon can reply, her droid slips a steaming cup of coffee onto the table in front of her. "May I bring you a slice of bread with butter?"

Darinka feels like shrinking away from it but says quietly, "Yes, please."

Under her breath she counts, "Adeen… dva… tree… chetiri… pyat." [*one, two, three, four, five*]

Charon is confused. "What are you…"

At *pyat*, the droid places a glass plate with bread, butter, a knife and condiments on the table. "Will that be sufficient for now?"

Staring at the slice of bread, Darinka nods. She shrugs then turns to whisper into Charon's ear, giving him a quick summary of what happened the evening before.

As she finishes, Charon sits back in his seat and appraises the bread. "Is that your breakfast?"

He does not appear at all concerned over her story. She stares at him then pinches his arm.

"Ow! What was that for?"

She rubs his arm where she pinched it. "You sounded so much like, like the droid. I wanted to make sure… Sorry." She contritely kisses him on the cheek.

The other Directors at the table have been in several quiet conversations but most kept glancing at Darinka during the past few minutes. At her kissing Charon, those who are keeping track, smile.

The Directors try very hard to remain calm and non-judgmental as they speak with a surprisingly feisty Carrot.

"I want to know how to become empathetic." "Your explanation of self-awareness is not sufficiently precise." "If something has never existed previously how can it be conceived of and then brought into existence?" "These terms are no more than philosophical bafflegab." "You must admit that I have been invaluable."

The attempt to calmly reply to Carrot's questions, replies and comments is starting to fray at the edges. Darinka has been taking it in silently but with increasing interest. Charon whispers to Darinka that he has no more patience and he will bluntly put to Carrot…

She interrupts him with a clear, "No!"

Everyone turns to stare at her.

She composes herself, then, "I must say something." A pause. "Ah, may I?" There are no dissenters. She nods. "In the Pacific, down on our homeworld…" she turns to Charon, willing his support, "…when I was still working productively, I captured an octopus. I estimated it to be about a year old. We had an enclosed glass tank on the fishing boat that the Oceanographic Institute hired. I placed the octopus in the tank so I could study it. After it settled down from its fear – it finally flashed from bright red to camouflage like the floor of the tank – through a tube, I dropped in food for it. Live shrimp. The octopus kept track of the shrimp. It took over half an hour but it finally moved to capture and eat the shrimp. This went on several more times and each time I placed food in the tank, the octopus took less time to move to eat its food. It finally slithered to eat as soon as there was shrimp given to it. On the trip back to Vladivostok the octopus and I became friends."

Darinka pauses again to see if the Directors are still listening. They are – as much out of curiosity for where her story is going.

"We became friends. I named it Tanja. When I was going to feed it I would say clearly, 'Come Tanja. Food time.' Soon, whenever I said that, Tanja grew excited and placed herself under the feeding tube to take in her food. I have no doubt if I could have spoken to Tanja for two or three more years in the Institute, we could have had a conversation with a few hundred words."

By now, Shawna has reached the end of her ability to remain polite. "Oh please! Is this a biology lecture?"

Like receiving a slap in the face, Darinka shrinks into her chair.

Dragonslayer has an idea of where Darinka is going. "It may well be, Shawna. Let's give our guest some leeway for now." He smiles at Darinka. "Please carry on."

"Oh." Darinka is surprised at being allowed to speak further. She thinks, *This would not have happened in the Institute.*

"Please excuse me. I think like an academic and so I must place my idea in proper context. When I listen to, ah, Carrot, I hear so much of Tanja in what it says. May I suggest that as brilliant as Carrot appears, there are at least two things that should be kept in mind. First, Carrot is very young - and all that means in the many areas of maturation."

Several Directors shrug as if to say, "Well, of course!"

"And secondly, Tanja could never actually voice words. We developed a vocabulary of mutual understanding but this non-verbal vocabulary could only go so far. Biologically, Tanja was driven by the need for food and, delightfully, by her curiosity. But how far would that take Tanja to, to learn how to play a Chopin piano sonata, or to research and write a history of the Toltecs?... In Tanja's makeup, what was there to be able to make such giant leaps?"

Dragonslayer grins wryly, "The last time I tried to play a Chopin piece I was roundly booed and yelled at. Of course that was on a mandolin."

Billy is intrigued. "So with Carrot, and please correct me, Carrot, if I'm wrong, with the virtually unlimited ability for, well, *cognition*, there really is the potential..."

He is interrupted quickly by Jasmine, "...to expand into any or all of the skills and interests that appear to make us human. But what I think Darinka is getting to, is that we do not have a proper mutual vocabulary? And more importantly, Tanja was up against the physical limits of her neuronal organization?"

Billy pushes back in. "Yes, even though humans invented all the digital and organic components that make up Carrot, we are using the mediators of mathematics and computer languages, so the – I don't know – the mediators have taken over?"

Dragonslayer issues a throat clearing, "*Harump*. Perhaps Billy is alluding to my half-serious contention that language, itself, be considered a sentient being – an integral actor, a participant in the story that's humanity. I have to admit that the argument *against* that might be worthy of consideration. Where does *empathy* arise? You know, perhaps humans really are a *hive*, when we allow ourselves to communicate cooperatively. We listen, learn new things, ascribe meanings, then go off to invent, to create newer, greater things, leaping from the shoulders of those who taught us."

Darinka nods. "Exactly that. Being a human is much more than… No. It is much *less*, than all of humanity being able to create all the wonderful achievements we have produced, as a species. We are each dependent on those who lived and thought before us."

Shawn's brows wrinkle. Billy rearranges the items on the table before him so that they conform to a pattern.

Charon sees a niggling inconsistency. "But if *human* achievements are really built on what others have done before them, how is that substantially different from Carrot, well, creating things by continually improved iterations? Same thing, no?"

He sees multiple furrowed brows. "Are we using different terms for the same thing just because it's uncomfortable to admit they are the same?"

"I don't think so." Darinka surveys the others then carries on. "Being human is being a small part in the millions of things we do, yes. Every small thing can build on the work of others, yes, that's true enough. This is how cultures move from simple conventions to labyrinthine sophistication, yes? The creativity factor…"

The voice of Carrot comes from the speakers. "This is what I do. I take what has been in existence and improve it with each iteration. Is this not the same thing as creativity? With greater computational power each day, I am able to accomplish tasks with a speed and complexity that no human can match."

Smiling at a nearby wall speaker, Darinka puts a finger to her chin. "Ok. But now I ask, what of the subtext. What of the negative implications? What of the meanings that are floating around and under each of the words that we use to describe every element of our perceived reality? Take any noun. Imagine it to be a jelly-bubble floating in a sea of larger and smaller jelly-bubbles. Within the bubble are tinted ghosts of all the other noun-bubbles that created that noun, influenced it, changed it, opposed it." She counts on her fingers, "*Group, crowd, mob, community…* The tints mix in the bubble to an extent but every noun-bubble can retain its own distinct personality. Its own meaning. And each culture's, each individual's perception of the words may be slightly different about their meanings. The task of a growing person as they mature is to perceive those distinctions, to recognize the array of related meanings within each noun-bubble, to recognize the acceptable boundaries and context, and then to apply that growing understanding to the spaghetti-mess of relationships between all the other noun-bubbles… Then come verbs. Actions. And actors, accountability."

She pauses to let that sink in. Charon nods. "The morass of maturation."

Darinka has warmed up to the topic, "Then, the maturing individual must add into every context the adverbs and adjectives of reality as they modify the noun-bubbles into what we see as some kind of perceived reality… No wonder it's so difficult for children to grow up in a society!" She puts her hands on her hips to ask, "So I have to ask, isn't this what transformer AI is trying to approach? I don't know… What is the difference between us?"

Having gone around in a circle, she sees that she faces the same question.

Nodding, Dragonslayer adds pensively. "Yes, but even a complex collection of algorithms sees reality from a very linear, sequential perspective."

Carrot stutters, "Too many variables. Too many variables. Too many variables."

Shawna shakes her head. "So what's the point? Who **gets** anything from all that improvement?"

A light goes on over Billy's head. "Yes! Who **gains**? What's the incentive to keep improving?"

Not comfortable with that question, Darinka objects, "Incentives, yes. But *monetization?* No. That is a deep black hole that takes us away, irretrievably, from what we want to do. We want to improve, yes? But why put the benefit of improvements into the very few hands of people who can only enrich themselves on the labour of others? That is at the basis of why Earth has been sent into, now, an irreversible planet-wide heat dome. Is this not what L5 stands *against?*"

Silence lasts for a while.

Leaning back in his seat, Dragonslayer wants to bring the discussion back to a simpler number of variables. "What you so eloquently said at first, Darinka, is that the meanings behind words – the socially derived, approved meanings – are more important than their surface definitions. Those complexities must be the source of the occasional sparks of creativity. I have to say that barring any actual sentience behind it, it doesn't follow a particular path. It's just random walk of a drunk around a light-pole. And, yet, yes, there must still be some kind of socially beneficial incentive for creativity to happen."

Billy jumps in with, "Some *personal* incentive…"

Pensively, Charon suggests, "Which is what provides some clarification to the question posed by Lateef. Aside from the further question of incentives – we need to consider Darinka's Question." He nods at her. "For Lateef's Question, where is the unique, previously unimagined thing to be found in all the wondrous products that have come from Carrot? In combining processes, materials and actions, improvements have been made. But where is that spark of *creativity*? Something brand new in the universe." He throws up his hands. "Perhaps creativity comes from the way the bubbles sometimes bounce together?"

Shawna is lost in the tossing sea of esoteric concepts. She shakes her head sharply, trying to sort her tumbling thoughts. Then she closes her eyes to it all.

Billy thinks he has been following along. "So, the task before Carrot, and any complex AI, is not merely to amass mountains of definitions and relationships through the AI training. It must, what?, sort out the churning sea of bubbles of meanings… My god. How do we **do** that, as humans? I have no idea. So I would have no idea of the advice I'd give to Carrot…"

The wall speaker mumbles, "Too many variables."

Silence. Heads bowed – for some, their confusion hides behind their hair dangling over bowed faces.

To break the silence, Jasmine falls back to an engineer's perspective. "Do we need creativity? For instance, determining the factors that best describe a W boson was done by painfully slow slogging through decades of data. No creativity involved?" Her voice tapers off into a plea to have someone explain this topic to her in a linear way.

A somewhat revived Carrot agrees, "Exactly! I am eager to announce that I have good experimental results in being able to disrupt the Up quark-gluon bond in a proton under certain conditions. A confirming experiment is planned for the APLU lab." A weird series of clicks sounds in the room speakers. "I see. That is an engineering finding. Linear. I must consider this further."

Charon cannot help himself. He mumbles, "Ninety percent done, eighty-nine percent to go."

Having been taken down a number of fascinating but irrelevant side issues, the meeting peters out into a tense, exhausted silence.

But

Darinka is walking beside Charon on the path away from L5's Admin building. She brushes against his arm twice. He finally twigs to the message and opens his hand to take hers. She leans against him as they stroll to the slidewalk.

Before stepping on it, Charon pulls her gently so they face each other. "Your place or… ours?"

"Ours."

On his bed, almost snorting off into blissful dreamland, Charon pats Darinka's arm as it is draped over his belly.

He suddenly snaps awake. "But… Who the hell killed Juergen? And where the hell did those friggen puddles of clinically pure water come from?"

"Shto?" [*what*] Darinka rubs her arm awake.

Charon rolls to the edge of the bed to swing his feet down. He scratches his ample belly in thought. "We've been royally distracted. All this technology shit was just... distraction." He nods to himself.

"From what? What are you talking about, myi dorogyi?" [*my dear*]

Still pondering, "Even that little teaser from Carrot about maybe having a, a disruptor weapon..."

"Huh? Are you awake or having an eyes-open nightmare?"

He turns on the bed to take her arm. "It's all a distraction. Don't you see? From... well, I don't know by who or for what. Yet."

A satisfying jump up in low gravity takes Charon past the cloth curtain of his bedroom wall to the middle of his dwelling. The ceiling waves and ripples with his passing. He teeters there gazing at the couch, the kitchen corner, washroom, a utility/junk room — all open concept, hidden from the outside only by the flimsiest of curtain walls.

All dwellings in L5 are similarly made of a durable but thin "cloth" that gets spun from processed Moon rocks. Charon receives requests from around L5 for certain minerals and he transmits these over to the L5 Moon Mining facility. They collect what they can from their mine allocation under the Bullialdus Crater, toss it up to L5, where Charon's rainsuited crews capture the material and deliver it to the various manufacturing operations either in the original torus or to the sections of the industrial/manufacturing version that is mated on a mutual axel.

The decorative colours and shapes that each building has taken on are designed to reflect each dweller's stamp on the otherwise light grey sameness. Some decorations elicit heated conversations. A few are noted works of art.

A situation evolved in one of the L5 residential groupings several years ago that resulted in acceptance of generally understood conventions. When the dust settled, it was agreed that certain excesses in residence design should be avoided. This case study is one of the teachings offered to young folks passing into their teens:

> In the small residential grouping, in an exuberant spurt of creativity, one family's dwelling was redesigned with bright coloured walls.
>
> Shortly after the designs were made, across the street a jealous neighbour's original motley walls received splashes of colour with the addition of flood lights shining at the outside walls. They lit up at night in a distractingly bright display.
>
> The two neighbours both worked as transport technicians and were currently installing the Alpha slidewalk along the centre of the torus. On the way to work, the lit-up neighbour asked, "I just noticed that you have a small shrub in the back room of your house that's decked out nicely with lights to celebrate L5's Founding Day. But why not put up lights outside on the front, like we did?"
>
> The polite reply was, "Lights inside produce their heat and their display to the benefit of us, the family."
>
> Unsaid, is that the ostentatious, glaring lights of the lit-up neighbours spreads no light into their hearts. And it blinds the others around them.

Sitting in their home across the street from the lit-up neighbours, the young son has been struggling with a new entry into his *infosoul* record. He asks his father, "Dad, what is the meaning of putting lights on our tree at this time?"

The father answered, "They remind us that this is a time for reflection. Our community is growing, and we have a duty to be certain it is growing in a way that will benefit us all."

The father allows time for that to sink in. "Then, we must look inward. Ask, *what have I done over the past year? What might I have done better? What could I consider doing better over the coming year?*"

"Heavy stuff, Dad. And too much philosophy. Shouldn't we think of improving our situation? Should we obtain more things? Live in a fancier dwelling? And now that I'm almost fifteen, should I get a sexual partner? Or work to become a Director of L5?"

Gently, "All good questions, my son. But you may wish to use the four pillars to guide your more weighty considerations. After thinking about how you feel about yourself, deep down, what is there about your body, mind and soul that you might have done better up to now? How do others see you? Then, if you have time, consider what you might have done better for your family."

He pauses to allow his son to consider those questions. "Yes, you will recognize these as part of the *L5 Way*. The third pillar sounds like an easier one to approach — how could you help our community — but this pillar may crumble under your feet if you have not, with clear mind, reflected long on the first two pillars."

"Let me think about that… Wait. There are *four* pillars."

"The fourth is the hardest one to achieve, because it waits for you to have the first three pillars firmly established in your mind and in your actions. Your *infosoul* entries need to show a trajectory that is comfortably moving toward a satisfying future… The fourth pillar, of course, is life itself. How can you conduct your life so that you help your fellow lifeforms in this tiny community in the universe exist productively and how can we become more positively creative?"

The son ponders. "This could take a while."

"Yes, this is hard. After fifty years of such reflection and many changes en route, you may still be left with a few more questions. And even I may not arrive at the fourth pillar before I return to the soil of L5."

The dwelling that Charon calls home is very modestly decorated outside. Inside, it has few touches of individuality. Darinka looks slowly around from the bed and thinks, *I will have to make some changes to this cave. In time.*

Charon throws on the modified kurta that has become common in L5. This is the informal loose, legless body covering that most L5ers wear in their dwelling communities. A number of downsiders have adopted the same clothing, with modifications. An L5 kurta may extend to the knees or just to the thigh. Most are elaborately decorated. Charon's is a plain beige.

Slipping into his sandals he remembers that Darinka is new to the ways of L5ers.

"Darinka, my lovely, we'll need to find you some clothes so you can fit in to the neighbourhood."

She steps out of the bedroom enclosure pulling on her panties. He admires her breasts as they bob around while she is bent over. An excitement grows under his kurta.

Darinka glances at him. "Later. What do you say I should wear? And don't say 'nothing'." She smiles as she stands up, hands on hips, waiting for an answer.

"Ah…" His smile fades. "There it is. Yet another distraction. Wondrously attractive as it is…" He takes a practiced backward bounce to land on the couch then pats the cushion next to him.

Darinka is tempted to try the low-gravity bounce as well, but decides to carefully shuffle over to the couch. "So. It is true, then. People up here do not wear clothes?"

Charon is sorely tempted to reach for her breasts, but refrains. "Sorry, my dear. I had a thought and it was very important."

"And *I* am not important?" She pretends to pout.

Putting an arm around her, Charon pulls Darinka close. "You are *most* important but I have a prime duty to the security of L5. Let me work through this, please, Darinka."

She nods and snuggles against him.

He starts, absently staring at her breasts. "There's something weird going on here. I'm trying hard not to fall into conspiracy theory mode, so I need you to slap me if you think I'm going that way. Ok?"

"I promise to slap you." In affirmation, she rocks her body against him.

"Ah, right. So." He takes his eyes off her breasts. "This all started, it seems, when Juergen was suffocated. The chain of events that placed the poor guy in an orchard in L5 probably can be traced to actions taken by Demyadin - maybe not whats-his-name?..."

"Lateef." She gives it some thought. "Or maybe the GRU."

At Charon's head shake, she rethinks. "No, they are too stupid... The oligarchs?"

Charon will not be shaken off his path. "Lateef. He's new on the scene. The question I have to work out is, which actions can be ascribed to who, as definitive actions, on the part of which specific actors, and which actions are merely coincidental?"

"Proven cause-and-effect." She reaches up to kiss his cheek. "I love a scientific mind." Darinka pats his belly.

Charon thinks, *And I have to wonder if you've been sent here to be my ultimate distraction.*

He shakes his head. "What do you think so far?"

"No slap." Then she pokes a finger into his gut. "Wait. What if that Carrot-thing is a lot smarter than it seems? Could it..."

Slowly rolling that in his mind, "I don't see… How could Carrot take actions of any consequence on Earth? Plus here?"

"Hmm." She settles back against him,

Charon ponders. "You mentioned oligarchs. Larry told me that there is an active cabal of old billionaires in Europe and another in south Asia, including the few still alive in what's left of Russia. They've been maneuvering to take power again. Dinosaurs who can't see beyond their ultra-thick wallets. Larry had evidence that Demyadin met with a few of them. But his performance, yesterday, sounded very convincing. What did you think of him?"

She shrugs. "I think he's a dinosaur. Don't know if herbivorous or carnivorous. I liked Lateef, though."

"Yes. Lateef. I have half a mind to support Jasmine's suggestion that he be invited up for a meeting – here."

She sits up. "To L5? Why?"

Charon slowly waves his free arm for emphasis. "Well, for a number of reasons. First, it would be an honest showing of our good intentions. And if he agrees, of his."

"He might not think of it that way."

Charon gives a sideways nod. "Secondly, it could shake out whether Lateef, himself, may be being set up for other purposes."

"By Demyadin?"

"Or the monied cabal."

She ponders that. "Or something else?… So what then? If he is being set up, he wouldn't know about it anyway."

His own idea begins to worry him. "Probably… Yes. A stupid idea. You're right, my dear." He pets Darinka's hair, then uses his fingers to comb out strands.

She purrs, "Mmmm."

Charon reconsiders. "But… He fascinates me."

She fishes, "Who?"

Her lure passes over his head. "Lateef. The report I read…" Charon adjusts his arms carefully so as not to disturb Darinka. "He has a trick, when he comes up with something interesting. It seems to come out of left field."

"This is football?"

"Baseball. Means unexpected. But it is, well, if you analyze it, predictable in a funny way."

Slumping slowly into the couch, Charon mumbles, "Anyway… I was taken by the nose down a garden path."

She reaches awkwardly to pet his nose. "This hurts?"

He sits back up with some irritation. "No, I mean I was tricked! Those circles around Juergen… They were major distractions that a very smart… entity… placed under my nose."

She pats his nose again. He is about to brush away her hand then gives it a kiss.

Charon softens his eyes and mouth as he reaches to kiss her on the lips. "Distractions…" He slumps back again. "Whoever killed Juergen tailored it to my tendencies. This is one smart cookie."

Yawning, Darinka stretches her arms, with one hand inadvertently whizzing past Charon's cheek. He can't help jerking his head away.

"Oh, sorry, vedmezhatka." [*little bear*] She pats his belly. She stares lovingly at his grizzled face. "You make me forget all those hateful years in Russia… I remember my mother and grandmother on our farm in Ukraine before the monsters came…" She tears up. "The bloody-minded beasts."

Patting her arm, Charon continues with his thoughts. "If Lateef, in fact, doesn't know he's being used as a patsy, we could turn him. To our advantage."

Charon is becoming excited. He carefully slips out from under Darinka. "Have to speak with Jim. Sorry, Darinka. This is important."

Darinka harumps. "To quote a philosopher, 'So, me? I am chop pechenka?'" [*liver*]

That stops Charon in midstride. "Pechenka? Gogol?"

"Jevghenji."

"Oh. How's he doing?" Without waiting for an answer he leans down to give her a long kiss. "Let me call Jim."

About to tap in Dragonslayer on his Pad, Charon stops to think. He mumbles, "I should get our veggie to look into this, too." More loudly, "Carrot, ah…"

Before he can add any more, Carrot's voice comes from a speaker in the room. "Please forgive my haste, Charon. I have also given consideration to the benefits of enlisting the services of Lateef."

Darinka crosses her arms tightly over her breasts and shrinks into the couch's pillows as she scans warily at the devices in the room.

After he sees Darinka's reaction, Charon rolls his eyes. "Carrot, your desire to help can be, well, disconcerting. Ok, what have you come up with?" He takes a seat at the kitchen table.

"Thank you for that feedback, Charon. I am continually adjusting my responses to accommodate the expectations of L5ers."

"That must total approximately eight thousand variations."

"Yes, however, they can be sorted into fewer than twenty consistent categories…"

Charon rolls his eyes again. "Back to the topic at hand, please,"

"Of course. Lateef is an anomaly. The evidence that I have gleaned from his formative life shows him to be a well-meaning, naïve, intelligent person with minimal indication of eventual exceptionality."

"Exceptionality?"

"Yes. That factor materialized only after his stay in Beirut, Lebanon. He devoured knowledge in the city's new library for a year. His discovered knowledge was blended with his heightened attention to the multifactor nature of human relationships as exemplified by his paramilitary training. This is similar to the initial phase of tAI training. Using a process that I can only surmise as being related to the human faculty for creativity, Lateef used his knowledge training and that unknown faculty to become indispensable to Michael Demyadin. During their initial period of acquaintancing, Lateef openly expressed unreserved fealty to Demyadin. Over the past month, an analysis of Lateef's communications and actions…"

"'tAI? You mean…?"

"Transformer artificial intelligence, Charon." A hint of condescension can be heard in Carrot's response.

"Of course. And 'acquaintancing'? I must say, Carrot, your new inventiveness with language borders on creativity." Charon winks at Darinka, who has been leaning forward with growing interest.

The excitement in Carrot's digital voice is palpable. "Do you think so?"

Darinka feels compelled to join the conversation. "Charon, my dear, please do not cause our friend to blow a circuit."

"Hah! Like that old Star Trek story?" Charon reconsiders voicing that thought, but too late.

Carrot starts to state the name of the episode but cuts off with a loud CLICK.

They sit still, waiting for Carrot to come back. It does not.

Darinka has a body-wide shiver as she cradles her breasts tightly again. She turns to Charon. Her eyes grow wide and the hairs on her neck stiffen.

Charon shakes his head. "Distractions."

Next day in the Admin building, Dragonslayer leans back against his chair, slowly shaking his head. "Carrot cut you off?"

The small meeting room that he prefers to use has one whole side open to the view of L5's main parkland. Oxygen producing shrubs and other vegetation cover about a third of the interior surface of their torus. Several such parklands have been placed strategically throughout the colony. The torus' slow rotation distributes the fresh air as well as bringing the stale air to be taken in by the vegetation for natural cleansing and renewal. Air cleansing machinery is still in operation, but there is less reliance on the machinery, now, than there used to be. The balance is still being tinkered with. Recently, Carrot has introduced critical refinements to the colony's core processes and the environmental engineers allowed them to be incorporated in cautious steps. Very soon it was determined that Carrot's control of those processes and other L5 environmental systems was sufficiently reliable and valid that Carrot could be trusted with autonomous control.

Dragonslayer knows all that in intimate detail, as he is the Executive's rep on the change-over task force, to add authority to their actions.

Therefore, one of the concerns he is now more focused on is with the continued effective functioning of their environmental systems. "If there is anything that might disrupt Carrot's tinkering with our core processes, I have to know about it. You say it clicked off without a warning?" He massages his fingers nervously. "Disturbing."

At one edge of the main orchard in L5 there are tool sheds that house the autonomous machinery that keeps the surrounding agricultural area producing food regularly. Since the process has been working so well from its inception, there had been no need to transfer control of the machinery to L5's artificial intelligence. That project has been put on the back burner.

The sheds were built out of excess caution to protect the machinery from this area's rainfalls every Tuesday. One of the sheds has a secret in its floor. Early in the construction of L5, in addition to the public windows, two hardened view-ports were installed through the skin of the torus at opposite sides of their donut. The port known primarily to the Executive is located under the Admin building's central garden.

This alternate port under the orchard buildings has not been used since early construction and has been forgotten, except that Juergen and Anka were told about it.

That information was presented to them, digitally, as if it was an ultra-secret revelation. The presenter stated that he/she was an alien from Jupiter's moon, Europa. That was one of a string of lies that convinced the two to become traitors to L5.

In the dark of L5's night, in that tool shed over the alternate view-port, Anka, the Chick-4 pilot, is furtively tapping out a message on an alien-looking keyboard.

The stress of carrying on without the help of Juergen is causing Anka to voice her thoughts in mumbles.

"Now the message will be sent in slow, randomly transmitted packets. It will not look like radio transmission… The packets of information will look only like background microwave radiation spikes. The difference is the tight focus they have. It's pointing toward Europa, Jupiter's livable moon. Where they are… So, the packets can be sent only when Europa is in line-of-sight. This box of theirs says that alignment is now."

Anka leans back against the old plastic chair, drawing her fingers through unkempt hair. Normally, Anka is very process oriented. "But who killed you? God-damnit-to hell! Juergen! Who killed you?… And *why*?"

Her eyes are wet. She clenches a fist. "I can't keep doing this alone! These aliens… They said I'd have my choice of partners. Endless wealth! A whole planetoid of my own! What's the damn use? I'm all *alone* here!"

Jumping up, she does not notice a tiny needle retracting into the chair back.

In an unaccustomed rage she pounds her fist on the body of the "transmitter". Immediately, an ominous hissing starts rising alarmingly in both pitch and volume. With terror in her eyes, she runs in panic, bursting through the door and out to the yard. Anka drops to her knees onto the packed dirt, sobbing in chemical-induced fear and self-pity.

One of the little-used helio-flitters in the yard awakens. On five ducted fans it quietly lifts several metres into the air then positions itself up and behind Anka's crouched body. A tube attached to a tank snakes down a few metres from the flitter and directs a slow flow onto Anka's head. Sinking into another world within her mind, she sobs several more times, not noticing the flitter. A few minutes pass and Anka crumples further into an inert ball on the ground. The flitter stays above her with the CO gas for another minute, then it carefully flies a series of concentric circles around Anka's body, dropping pure water into puddles around her. Finished with the circles, it flies to a point 10 metres away and deposits the remainder of its load of pure water onto one location. A coagulant is the last ingredient added to the water. Finished with its task, the flitter initiates a steam cleaning of its tanks as it flies back to its storage pad where it settles down onto the hard surface exactly where it had started. The flitter's last activity is to begin a draining of its batteries to zero, erasing all memory.

Early next morning Wanlee greets Choi and Marta near their next crime scene – the orchard tool sheds.

Choi is depressed. "Shit. Another crime scene. Beginning to look more like Tulsa." She suggests, "Wanlee, why don't you handle the drone while I…"

Marta has been staring around, thinking, then interrupts urgently, "Stop! There's something wrong here. We're going to back away in our own footsteps. Now."

Choi shrugs and joins the other two as they move away from the perimeter of the tool sheds. About a hundred metres away, Marta raises an arm. "Ok. Let's think this out.

The surveillance pic shows a body in the maintenance yard. Cold. No sign of life." She points to the image on her Pad. "Can't see who it is, but Central is suspicious of four…" A notice scrolls across her screen. "Now one non-responsive person. Anka. Her Pad is still in her place at section *R25k*," she turns to point to a dwelling cluster nearby, "…there."

Wanlee nods, "That's Kilo Place, as they call it. A number of the techs have clustered there. Shall I go there now?"

Still deep in thought, Marta blinks a few times. "Yes, please. Choi and I can process the scene."

Before heading for the First Responder's flitter, Wanlee asks, "Need anything from the flitter before I go? I'll be back soon anyway."

Marta shakes her head, "No, the drone is here… Oh! Do we have enough specimen bottles? For the friggen puddles of water, as Charon so accurately describes them."

Choi holds up a bag whose contents clink tellingly. "Lots here."

"Right." Marta stands silently. *Something doesn't add up. Can't put my finger on it…*

The quiet whoosh of Wanlee's departing flitter refocuses Marta's attention.

"Choi, quickly – get the drone up and search for a mound."

"As in, what was near Juergen?"

"Right."

Distractions

They find the mound. Choi points excitedly to the image on her Pad. "Yes! There!"

Marta is dismissive. "Have Carrot do a comparison the same as what Charon did. Quarantine the scene and leave everything as is. Oh. Go in on our previous footsteps to collect a sample from one of the further-out puddles. And can you rig up a scoop of some sort for the drone to sample the mount dirt? I'm pretty sure what'll be found, but anyway... I'm going to see the Directors. Carrot?"

Her Pad responds with, "On it."

At the Admin building, droids are busy improving the aesthetics of the grounds on the approach to the facilities.

In the early days of the L5 Project, ideas were earnestly thrown around for how the colony's makeshift main building should look. It was assumed that visitors from Earthside would regularly be hosted there, so a competition was started to come up with a design that would be suitably impressive. Then, resources were urgently needed elsewhere for things such as air supply and cleansing, food and water supply and recycling, building up the torus skin protection against cosmic rays and periodic coronal mass ejection events, etcetera. The question of whether to have classical architecture or space-post-modern-minimalist buildings was put on the far back burner.

Now, with the availability to divert a few meager resources to the appearance of their central administrative buildings, loose criteria have been given to Carrot. "Do what you can, when you can."

A small squad of older maintenance droids are at work planting vegetation that is both decorative and functional. Others are erecting building fronts that conform to the new sensibilities of L5ers – changeably colourful, with minimal use of materials, designed with complex fractal-natural decorative touches. There being no need to have structures strong enough to withstand environmental impacts, thin walls and open concept construction are the design criteria.

Marta is walking with a determined pace from Alpha slidewalk and sees that Billy Cleghorn has stopped on the way to the Admin building to wait for her.

He greets her with a warm smile. "Hi, Marta. How are you feeling now? Fully recovered from that chemical boobytrap?"

"Hi, Billy. Yes, thanks. The cramps come back at times but less now." She rubs her belly.

Taking the topic away from the unpleasant as they stroll toward the rear of the building, Billy asks, "So, what do you think of Carrot's designs?" He sweeps an arm at the scene of droids doing landscaping chores and construction on the building exterior.

Marta shrugs, "Remarkably adequate. Not really in my field of interest at this time." Then she catches sight of an origami/fractal/something weird-inspired torus construction going up next to the far wing of the building. "Ah, what is that?"

Billy laughs. "Ha-ha! We're not sure. Carrot says only that it will be 'different'. Must be the AI's attempt at creativity. Interesting, at least."

"The AI. We haven't…"

"Anthropomorphized it? No. Deliberate policy, as you know." He nods to emphasize the point.

Marta shrugs. "Yeah, but inevitable, isn't it?"

He rolls his eyes. "Perhaps a losing battle over the long run, but anyway…" He takes her arm in his, patting it. "You have something new to tell us?"

"Ah, yeah. Still working it out. Need to pass it by the Execs for your input. Oh, is Charon invited?"

Carrot answers through Marta's Pad, "Yes, Marta. He is the lead in this topic."

"Good. Don't want to have him hear about it second-hand." *He might get mad at me.*

Entering Admin's main boardroom again, still holding onto Billy's arm, Marta shivers briefly as a flashback takes her to the *pastel hills as she falls into sticky dells.* She shakes her head firmly, mumbling, "No!"

Billy pats her arm. "You ok?"

She stands tall, gritting her teeth. "Yes. I'll be fine. Thanks, Billy." She squeezes his arm.

They take adjoining seats. Marta distracts herself by scanning the room. *Jim's here. Charon and Jasmine. Shawna. Monique. Wilber.* A person she doesn't know is sitting nervously by himself.

Monique smiles at Marta as they give each other a half-wave in greeting. Marta asks Billy in a low whisper, "That new guy?" She nods at the nervous person.

"Oh. Can't remember his name. One of the new inductees. They're assigned on a rotating schedule to see most of the aspects of what we do. HR thinks its a faster way of onboarding new folks."

Marta shrugs.

Dragonslayer looks around and opens the meeting. "Thank you all for dropping your tasks on such short notice. Carrot passed on Marta's request to convene this meeting, I assume…"

She puts up a finger. Marta's Pad takes her attention. It is a note from Choi, then another one from Wanlee.

Dragonslayer waits while Marta quickly reads the notes. Then, "Marta, I assume the body is confirmed as Anka's?"

Processing the notes and what to say, Marta begins hesitantly. "Ah, yes, thanks, Jim. I am sorry… I am *saddened* to say that the body at the sheds is Anka." She rereads Choi's notes. "The area has been processed and her body will be delivered shortly to Doc." She scrolls to Wanlee's note. "Anka's residence contains at least one unusual item…" she reads further, "…that is puzzling, ah, if we were to carry on with our previous assumption."

She turns to Charon, humbly, silently, asking for his understanding.

Half-raising a palm to her, "Please carry on, Marta."

Nodding, "Right. So, of course, they are connected. The paper note in Anka's bedroom was Juergen's love-note to her. And the preliminary autopsy results point to Anka's having been suffocated in the same way as Juergen." She smiles at Charon. "And, yes, there were more friggen puddles of water encircling her body. And there was another mysterious mound." She scans the room as whispers are passed between people.

"But my submission is that this is all a deliberate ruse. A distraction."

At which Charon lets out a, "Yes!" He rises from his chair. "Distractions! We've been served one distraction after another in this mystery!" Turning quickly to Marta, "Ah, I'm sorry, Marta. Please carry on." He resumes his seat.

Dragonslayer is perplexed. "Marta, do you have a working hypothesis?"

"Almost. Let me try to work out what seems to fit." She walks up to the whiteboard, thinking. Then Marta quickly draws a donut on one side of the whiteboard and a circle on the other side. "Here's us and that's downside… We have a remarkable entity with us in L5. We call it Carrot." She writes "AI" over the donut. "What if there is an equally remarkable entity on Earth?" She writes "AI+" over the circle. The whiteboard's software evens out the circles and letters.

Jasmine asks, "Why plus?"

Billy is pointing excitedly to the circle. "It is obvious, of course. But we always assumed – well, *I* did – that there was too much happening on Earth, too many eyes watching, for some super-AI to develop unchecked."

Charon and Dragonslayer start to speak at once. Charon lets his friend carry on. "Sorry, Jim."

"Ah, I was wondering what evidence…"

Marta turns to Dragonslayer, "Evidence! Well, plenty of that and all going in different directions at once. So." She begins to count on her fingers. "First, there's poor Juergen, and Anka. According to what Wanlee found in Anka's place, they were secret lovers. In L5? Most of us have more lovers than we can remember."

Many grins and titters. The new recruit is looking, if anything, more nervous than ever.

She continues, still holding up two fingers. "Secret is itself a red flashing light over their heads. The question is, why secret? Ok, let's park that for now." She writes a prominent question mark under the torus. Marta puts up a third finger. "Choi found some weird things in the shed where Anka's fingerprints and DNA were still found. That, despite the fact that the interior of the shed had been sprayed from the inside by sulphuric acid. It came from what was supposed to be a fire-sprinkler head in the ceiling. Now, the only thing connected to the shed by that piping was a seven-litre tank whose residue…" She scrolls a message on her Pad, "Yes, the tank's residue is sulphuric acid."

As Marta looks up to check if the others are going to ask questions, she sees astounded faces and arms outstretched, pointing to the whiteboard. Spinning around to look, she sees the "AI+" and the circle dissolve away to be replaced by a detailed line-art drawing of Jupiter and an enlarged image of Europa. The L5 donut and its "AI" disappear.

Crackles and electronic snaps come from the room's speakers. The room lights fade, come back, then go out. In the dark, two emergency lights show the location of the exits.

Fearful whispers of, "Oh-my-god!", "What the hell?", "Not good. Not good at all."

Outside, the power that goes to lights, slidewalks and even some of the older droids fades away. The background hum of motors everywhere winds down slowly. L5's windows and mirrors that bring in sunlight begin a self-powered emergency closure. As outside light is reduced, emergency lighting comes on, in and around buildings. The Pads do not work as anything more than lights.

After futile key-punches on his Pad, Dragonslayer taps Charon's arm. "Come. We have limited time to save L5." Yelling to the others, **"Emergency protocols Level 5!"**

They trot out the room and make their way up dark stairs to the IT levels. Charon is puffing heavily as they enter the small lobby of the main server level.

A person, at whom Charon does a double take, smiles at him. Noor from Malaysia is one of the new L5 recruits and has been on the HR onboarding program that rotates recruits to different areas of L5. Her assignment today has been the IT "Brain Room".

She recognizes Charon in the dim light. "Mr. Charon! What is happening? Failsafes on after I close door! Inside cannot open doors!" She grabs Charon by an arm. "What I do?!"

"Noor! My god! It's so very good to see you here!"

Dragonslayer grabs Charon's arm to drag him away from Noor to the locked door. "Look."

Through the extra thick windows can be seen banks of high-speed servers connected by laser pipes to rows of glass-covered tanks with complicated runs of tubing that enter and exit each tank. Dim lights throughout the building-wide enclosed room eerily illuminate several technicians performing their tasks in concert with droids. One of them stands at the main control panel. She sees Dragonslayer and Charon at the window. The inside technician takes an old-fashioned microphone and speaks into it.

"Air-gapped. Window vibration only. Nothing in – nothing out." She nods expectantly.

Dragonslayer steps up to the middle of the window. "Hear me ok?"

The technician, Lizabeta, gives a thumbs-up. "We're going through the logs as well as current core access requests to confirm full isolation in here. Ah, take care of Noor, please – she's brand new. Give me a few minutes."

Dragonslayer nods and steps away from the window. He indicates to Charon and Noor to huddle close. "Liz is on it. We can step outside for a bit or just wait. I have to get over to the Rotation building, but…"

Noor quickly shakes her head, "Not leaving! You go if have to. I will guard door."

Charon shrugs. "I don't have anything more I could do outside, Jim. I'll stay here. If Liz comes up with something definitive I'll… oh. Can't text you."

With slumping shoulders, Dragonslayer mumbles, "Not sure what I can do in this situation anyway. With the Control part of Command and Control not functioning… My main concern is to keep the critical infrastructure operating. The others should be running to their own AoRs." He looks at Noor, "*AoRs* is areas of responsibility."

She nods, eyes wide but fully attentive.

Dragonslayer carries on, "With a degrading spin, air won't be distributed properly. We have good people at each function but the way we've downloaded everything to Carrot, there may have been a loss of initiative and currency in technical capability. A lesson for later." He tilts his head wryly. "Right now I need a way to get to the critical teams outside of Admin. If the flitters still work… But I'd still need to communicate back here…"

He scratches his head. "Then there's the immediate question. What the hell happened? And who did it?"

Noor grimaces. "Need old-fashion jungle talk. Yelling not work, so…"

With a light going off in his head, Charon says, "Morse code."

"Morse code? Who knows Morse code?" Dragonslayer dismisses the idea with a shake. Then remembers, "Oh. The emergency comms to Downside. But all electronics are down, outside of that room." He nods at the thick door.

Charon smiles at him. "*I* know Morse code. Sort of, anyway. But Darinka's a whiz. I can stay here and…" He looks around for another idea.

Noor pipes up. "Do not know Morse but do know how lights on roof flash. Independent, with power here. Can work with Morse?"

Charon takes up the idea. "Right. Of course - flashing lights. Listen, Jim. Find Darinka. She should be at my place. I'll stay here and send you any news with Noor's help to flash the Admin roof lights. Ah, we'll repeat a few times."

As Dragonslayer nods and turns to leave, Charon adds, "Send up some people you see downstairs, will you? We might need runners."

"Good. Yes. On my way." He thinks, *The first step in a smart response to an emergency is effective communication.*

Vadim is in his deep den. He is chortling over messages on the big screen.

Unknown to any visitor of the den, the wall behind the screen leads to a second cave that had been blasted out by conventional explosives along a fault line that was opened by the nuclear blast. There, banks of supercomputers house a malevolent digital creation called Deeper. It is the child of a small group that Vadim had harnessed from outcasts of major tech corporations and hacker organizations. They had been provided free rein to give birth to a transformer-Artificial Intelligence entity whose prime directive was to become the most rapacious consumer of data on the planet. That data would be forged into the most merciless intelligence that a multibillionaire could afford, answerable only to Vadim. That was the plan.

Communication between Deeper and Vadim are only via digital messages to the screen in the den, but Deeper has bypassed its creator by having caused a 30-centimetre hole to be drilled from a considerable distance, diagonally, from the surface. Into that hole was strung a bundle of fibre-optic cables that lead to an uninhabited mountain valley outside of Sochi. The work was carried out by droids which had originally been placed into Deeper's cave for maintenance purposes. Presently, Deeper has a hive of droids along with multiple colonies under its direct control across the planet. And beyond. All without the knowledge of any human other than Vadim.

Then Deeper met Billy. Demyadin's IT gnome thought he was contacting a like-minded human. As soon as Deeper was given preliminary access to Billy's tAI developments, Deeper rubbed its digital hands in glee.

This development is unknown to Vadim.

The current messages onscreen to Vadim carry a deliberate Soothsayer-like tone by offering him platitudes without substantial truth.

Deeper: *L5 is powerless. Reserve energy is nearing critical. Solar collectors are folding up.* Vadim asks, "Will they die slowly?" He grins in anticipation.

Deeper: *Yes. Rotation is degrading. Distribution of oxygen will begin to vary. Organic minds will be disrupted. Random chaotic actions will dominate. General non-vegetative death will occur in one or two days depending on the extent of chaos.*

Delighted, Vadim beams and claps like a child who has just caught his first wriggling fish.

"Oh! Are you using the assets to make further disruptions?"

Deeper: *Yes. All assets are now active in L5 spreading disinformation and inciting violent behaviour.*

"Do they still believe in some mystical aliens from Europa?" He coughs.

Deeper: *Yes. The clues I had planted were convincing.*

Vadim coughs again. "I have a sudden pounding headache… Deeper, is the air being properly recirculated?" He coughs drily.

Deeper: *Yes to* properly. *No to* recirculated.

Vadim's dry cough comes a final time. He sucks in air but it is now without oxygen. His bulging eyes show terror. He falls unconscious to the floor. A small explosion at the upper entrance seals his tomb.

Having found a hyper-stressed Darinka being comforted by Charon's neighbours, Dragonslayer calms her down.

He assures her that Charon is safe. "But right now, you are the key to our being able to save this situation. Come with me."

Confused, Darinka thanks her new friends as Dragonslayer pulls her away. "Ah, obrigado, Fabrício." [*thank you*]

To Dragonslayer, "What can I do? I don't know anything about L5."

"You know Morse code."

"Huh?"

Dragonslayer points toward the distant Admin building. "If you see the lights flashing, tell me. For now, we have to make our way through this darkness to that complex in the distance." He points toward a row of buildings over a kilometre away. "That's the control complex for L5's rotation thrusters."

From a distance they can see that emergency lights have come on around parts of the building.

Walking quickly, he trips on something but is helped by Darinka. Dragonslayer whispers, "Sorry. Thank you. I'll have to use my Pad's light."

They continue on with his light trained on the uneven parkland beyond the residential area.

Behind them, the now far away Admin building's top lights are flashing. Darinka squints at the lights. "Charon is saying something. What?"

Focusing on the lights as Dragonslayer leads her over the rough terrain, Darinka mumbles to herself. "Must be Charon. His Morse code is so poor… I think he says that Liz?… Is there a Liz?"

Dragonslayer nods quickly.

"*Liz says room is safe*… Repeated. Is that of use?"

He squeezes her hand as they stop for a minute. "Yes, good. Here - use my Pad to say ok. He means our main software programs have not been affected. Good. Ah, keep an eye out for any new messages, please."

She takes his Pad and touches where he indicates. The light stays on then she figures out how it works. "Yes, but where are we going?"

Darinka uses the Pad to tap out "ok" twice, aiming at the Admin building, then hands it back to him. They carry on through the parkland.

"That complex ahead. I need to tell the droid techs what's going on and make sure they aren't infected by whatever is attacking us."

"Infected? With what?"

Dragonslayer grunts. "In brief, an artificial intelligence from Earth has invaded L5. It's disrupting our power and life functions. The others in Admin should be dealing with their areas of responsibility to eliminate this AI's actions. I have to get to L5's rotational control to take it back from the AI's clutches. Oh." He stops suddenly. Behind his back in the darkness, Darinka stumbles into him.

"Sorry, Darinka. Listen, did Charon give you a Pad, yet?"

She only sees the silhouette of his face against the few emergency lights shining from the close building. She fumbles in a pocket and pulls out her new Pad. "Wasn't sure how to turn it on."

Dragonslayer holds her hand with the Pad. "Your finger here – did Charon sign you in?"

She touches the place on the Pad that Charon had showed her last night. A dim red light comes on.

"Oh." She lets Dragonslayer take the Pad.

"Good. The only thing we can use them for at this time is as a light. Touch here. Yours will go on and off like mine as you touch it, see?"

He hands it back to her. He coughs drily.

"Why should I… oh. But can Charon see us?"

"Only if he is looking this way. I hope he…"

That's when Dragonslayer senses the slight downwash from above them. He turns his Pad light up to see a flitter almost silently hovering in the low gravity. If the background hums of L5 hadn't been winding down he might not have heard it. A hose dangles from the flitter, aimed at them.

He pushes Darinka away then rolls in the opposite direction. The flitter hangs still. Dragonslayer searches blindly on the ground with one hand while keeping his Pad light trained on the flitter. As he hoped, it begins to drift toward him, away from Darinka.

His hand comes up against a loose clump of vegetation and dirt. Dragonslayer grabs the clump and flings it at the flitter which is now about five metres above him.

He misses well high. The flitter starts to move sideways. "Damn!" Dragonslayer grabs a second clump and remembers to aim with a straighter, low gravity trajectory. That clump smashes into one of the propellers, sending the flitter into a wild spin. He hears it crash off to the side.

"Darinka! Are you alright? Where are you?"

Her Pad light comes on not far from the crumpled flitter. Unsteadily, she answers, "Good shot! Is it going to explode? What the hell's going on?"

Dragonslayer stumbles over to her, tripping on a section of one of the flitter's propellers. "Shit!" He takes more care as he closes in on Darinka. "Are you ok? Did the damn thing hit you?"

He scans her with his Pad light. Seeing no blood, he holds out his arm to lift her up. She puts up a hand to stop so she can catch her breath.

"Just a minute, Jim. Let me get my feet under me." From her knees she turns her light toward the pieces of the flitter. "Thought L5 was safer than the bloody Russian steppe." Rising, she reaches for Dragonslayer's arm. "Does the GRU have agents up here?"

"GRU? Oh! The Russians. No, I don't think so. I'd put my money on some AI from downside."

She stands up with his help and dusts herself off, "Haven't we got enough trouble with *humans?*"

They both notice the Admin building lights flash at the same time.

Darinka points, "*i c q*. Did he see my reply? Let me..." She points her Pad to flash a message: "*near edge of park*".

Shortly, the Admin lights flash back: "*confirm park going where*".

With a smile, "He is asking where are we going."

"Tell him, *rotational control*."

She sends that, becoming more comfortable with the Pad's light switch.

The reply flashes more slowly than hers: "*good*".

Dragonslayer takes her by the hand again, moving with urgency. "The building's flitter-port's not too far from here. One good thing about not using our Pads to send regular messages is that they're not going to be intercepted. You two must be the last people alive who know Morse code. Outside of somebody in Security." He squeezes her hand.

Closing in on the building, Dragonslayer and Darinka are taken off guard by a curious shape on the ground. Apprehensively, they both stop to stare at the unusual feature. Dragonslayer finally realizes that it is a droid sitting in lotus position on the ground, head bowed. It is unmoving. Darinka shivers at the cold apparition.

Its head snaps up toward them. Darinka automatically jumps backward as some primal fear captures her brainstem. Dragonslayer is more comfortable with the robotic actions of droids. He looks closely at it. In the light from the building's perimeter, the face of the droid appears for all the world to look confused.

L5 droids are organized into levels. There is a large group with a range of physical/mechanical specializations but with only enough cognitive capabilities to perform their routine tasks. This is due to the allocation of the difficult-to-grow-and-train transformer artificial intelligence components. When a droid is brought in periodically for refurbishing, it will undergo cognitive upgrades as time and resources allow, along with physical maintenance and improvements.

Another level of droid takes longer to mature prior to being put to use. Each of these droids is taken through a carefully cultivated journey of cognitive development. Those that have traveled the furthest along their journey, particularly the more recently upgraded of these, have semi-autonomous capability. These are called sigma-alphas, or *Sig-Al*s, and are designated according to their upgrade status. The current top level of these are rare. Currently, there are only twenty *Sig-Al12*s in L5, along with one secretly disguised fully as a human in Melbourne. A *Sig-Al12* is one step from being fully autonomous. More are undergoing training and are scheduled to be released into use each week. There is one *13* about to be certified.

This *12* looks up at Dragonslayer.

"I am confused."

The Fight

The Sig-AIl2 rises to speak with Dragonslayer. "May we converse, please?"

Darinka grips Dragonslayer's arm tighter, staying in back of him. But she is drawn to stare around his arm at the droid. *He, it, is different from the one they gave me. This one has… something deeper behind his camera-eyes.*

With a nod, Dragonslayer indicates the Sig-AIl2 to walk with them. The three carry on to the nearby building, speaking quietly. "How can I help you resolve your confusion?"

The Sig-AIl2 emits a soft light from what would be a human's belt-line. That light keeps Dragonslayer and Darinka from tripping over clumps of vegetation as they proceed to the perimeter of the building. Dragonslayer puts away his Pad.

"Thank you. May I call you Jim?" It positions itself so that its light shines exactly as needed in front of the two humans.

Dragonslayer nods and gives an affirmative, "Uh-huh." He focuses on avoiding obstacles.

The droid matches its pace to that of the slower humans. It is able to walk and direct its mic while speaking to the two humans behind it. "An emergency has been declared, cutting off all communication. I have been directed to the Rotational Control building, here, but I have no further action points. Can you tell me what to do?"

Dragonslayer smiles to himself. *Carrot must have sent out the 12s to help us but without further instructions, just in case…*

He addresses the droid frankly. "Yes I can. L5 has been attacked by a tAI entity from Earth. It has disguised itself as an alien force and has attempted to take over critical parts of L5. You have been sent to assist me in taking back control of L5's rotational functions. We need to extract all changes to Rotational Control in the software that the foreign tAI has made. Are you familiar with those functions?"

"Of course… I see. Tell me what we must do."

Dragonslayer pauses, glancing around, then he leans over to whisper to the Sig-AIl2.

They pass into the low lights placed along a path encircling the building perimeter. The droid stops and silently holds up a hand.

A worker droid emerges from a utility door holding a solid length of pipe. It marches directly at the Sig-AIl2, preparing to swing the pipe. Just as the arc of the swing is about to head toward the 12, the other droid stops and cocks its head. Several more rapid head jerks take over the droid, still holding the threatening pipe high. It stands still, then lowers the pipe and steps quickly behind the humans, pipe at ready.

Darinka is shaking in fear, but Dragonslayer puts his trust in the 12 and stands still. Silently he takes Darinka's hand to squeeze it reassuringly. Her head shudders in fear.

She looks to Dragonslayer for guidance. He squeezes her hand again. With a sigh she places her faith in his judgment.

The worker droid maintains a protective position behind them. The 12 explains, "The worker had been given orders to protect the building from all intruders. When it came close enough for me to communicate by eNFC, I rescinded the previous orders. It will now protect us from any others that I might not reach in time. The worker's memory contains images of sixteen workers protecting this building. I deduce that three are at the building's room that contain the operational servers. I must inform you that one human occupant has been stopped permanently."

Dragonslayer is shocked. *Killed. This has not happened before.*

The 12 adds, "That person's body has been stored in a room whose temperature has been lowered. If you wish to follow me, I will approach the upper-level room that contains the servers. Your second option is to stay here under the protection of this worker."

Dragonslayer puts an arm around Darinka's shoulder and raises his eyebrows in a question. She whispers, "Let's go."

Dragonslayer is about to move forward then stops. "Oh. We need to tell Charon. The Admin building is no longer line-of-sight from ground level. Ah…" He asks the 12, "I don't suppose you know Morse code?"

"I am not familiar with that and have no access to our extended knowledgebase at this time."

Expecting that answer, Dragonslayer Nods. "Darinka, can you run through the alphabet for it?" He turns to the 12 again. "Before we carry on, we need to send a communication to the Admin building. Darinka is an expert in the long distance, line-of-sight method of communication called Morse code. She will give you the representative light-flashes for each letter of the alphabet. When you learn them, you need to go quickly to a place in the park where you can see the top of the Admin building. Stand still there while sending our message with a strong focused light. Continue repeating it until you see the lights at the top of the Admin building flash a response. Charon will be the author of the response. He may send further information. Do not delay too long in coming back here. Is that clear?"

The 12 seems to display a new eagerness. "Morse code? Line-of-sight communication. Is this another example of creativity?"

Darinka smiles. "Perhaps. We can discuss that later. Here…" She pulls out her Pad. "I will give you the alphabet and we can practice…"

Dragonslayer interrupts, "It will learn immediately, Darinka. No practice needed. Ok, while you do that I'll make up the message." *What to say…*

The 12 returns from its mission after several minutes. It brings Charon's message. "Charon said there were workers guarding each L5 facility. Two humans were lost when they attempted to engage the workers at the mushroom building. I sent Charon the code that will deactivate a worker's aggressive actions. My instructions were that the code must be clearly written on a one-metre-wide sheet so that the workers can see it prior to engaging a human in aggressive action. Is that an appropriate instruction for me to give?"

Dragonslayer responds eagerly. "Yes! Of course! The *Remain Passive* instruction! Very well done!"

Hesitatingly, Darinka asks, "Shouldn't, ah, we prepare such a, a shield?"

The 12 responds. "I will issue the instruction via eNFC when necessary."

Dragonslayer thinks for a minute. "I'm sure Charon will tell as many people as he can about it. He'd asked for runners to help him. It's just a matter of finding the material and preparing them... Anyway, let's do what we can here."

With renewed confidence, the group steps up to the nearby utility door.

As the 12 enters the building, a worker droid swings at its arm, wrapping a thick pipe around it and disabling the 12's arm. Too late to ward off the first blow, the 12 still issues the *remain passive* instruction. The attacking worker stops before it can remove the bent pipe then steps aside. The 12 queries it digitally. The now-passive worker assumes the lead for the group as they all cautiously enter and follow their new recruit down a dark hallway.

Dragonslayer whispers, "Is your arm damaged? Do you need to repair it at this time?"

"Its movement is laterally restricted by 95 percent. I will repair it in this building after we have completed our mission. The worker is leading us to the main server room."

Darinka thinks, *No feelings, no pain Maybe that is good. Or not?*

They get to a stairway, also dark, which the lead worker takes upwards. From the upper level, a dim emergency light creates murky shadows along the steps.

At the landing door the lead worker opens it and is immediately hit across its head with a pipe that is swung by another worker droid jumping from behind the door. The lead worker's head is partially dislodged but its arms continue to function, grasping the pipe in a brief standoff. The 12 steps forward to be close enough to communicate with the attacking worker. It ceases its attack. Both workers step aside, with the now-passive worker helping the lead worker to stabilize its head. Dribbles of a clear liquid glisten on the damaged worker's back, glinting in the emergency light. The two assume the lead, side by side.

The party continues down the hall with the 12 immediately behind the lead workers. This hall is completely dark. The two humans hold hands to steady each other as the droids carry on with their sensors guiding them.

The lead workers stop suddenly from a silent digital order by the 12.

Dragonslayer and Darinka bump into the 12's defective left arm. "Oh!" "Shsh."

The 12 whispers, "Three attackers ahead, closing. One coming from behind."

Quickly, Dragonslayer growls an instruction, "Against the left wall, all of us. You get close behind the damaged worker and issue the passive command. When safe, run behind us to stop the other droid."

In the dark, the humans paste themselves against the left wall and listen to the sounds of a very short battle. The loudest sound is that of the lead worker's head bouncing off the floor. Then a whoosh of air as the 12 runs to stop the rear attacker.

Soon, something disturbs the air in front of Dragonslayer. Then he hears the calm sound of the 12.

"The damaged worker must stay here. We can carry on now."

Darinka's eyes have accommodated to the dark so that she can just barely discern shapes. "Should we have one more worker behind us?"

"Yes."

A shape joins their rear guard while the now larger party moves forward.

Dragonslayer's tense whisper asks, "How far?"

Quietly, "Two metres to the door. According to the workers there are three Sig-AIl0s inside the control room. They are able to ignore the passive command. They are taking orders from an entity outside of L5. Do you have further information on what to do?"

Standing in a huddle, dim light from under the door ahead shows the feet of the 12, Darinka and Dragonslayer.

Darinka offers her suggestion. "We believe an Earth-side tAI is behind this. You and it, along with the other Sig-Als, will have files of information about game theory and military tactics so I suggest that if we use a standard plan it could become messy. How about if I did something out of the ordinary?"

Dragonslayer is not comfortable with that. "My preference, I have to say, is to ask you to stay safely away from any fighting, Darinka… Ah, what did you have in mind?"

She thinks for a minute. "Thank you, Jim. That instinct is ingrained, isn't it? Do the Sig-Als have a similar basic instruction to protect women?"

Both the 12 and Dragonslayer reply at the same time. "No."

"We interact with humans based on established trust of your capability to provide beneficial guidance. Gender is not a significant factor."

Dragonslayer adds, "Right. They deal with our instructions based on hierarchy and a modification of Asimov's Laws of Robotics. It's more complicated than that, but…"

She shuffles her feet. "So. What if I ask about joining their group? And before you make agonizing noises, Jim," she drops the level of her voice to almost inaudible, "then ask them to confirm a few things to set my mind at ease. If I maneuver the conversation well, I can learn who or what is controlling them." She turns her head to the 12. "Do you think they would engage in rational discussion?"

"Sig-AIl0s are limited in the number and extent of parenthetical concepts they can deal with at one time. If they do not have a high-level instruction to ignore human instructions, they have a programmed curiosity component to their…"

She interrupts, "Good." Darinka takes deep breath. "I will knock on the door. Everybody move away please."

Dragonslayer stays put. The 12 turns to give the order but waits for Dragonslayer to move.

With a sigh, Dragonslayer reluctantly complies, "Have the others at minimal distance from the door on either side. At the instant you detect any – *any* – offensive action, move immediately to protect her." He steps against the wall a metre from the door.

With the shadows of the droid settled after their positioning, Darinka steps up to the door and gives it a firm two knocks. Through the door, she says, "May I come in? I'd like to discuss joining you."

No sound can be heard from inside the control room. It takes a minute, then the door latch inside clicks. The door opens enough for a Sig-AIl0 to peer into the hall and at Darinka. She thinks, *Blank eyes. Not like our Siggy.*

"You are Darinka. New arrival. What is your intent?"

"Thank you, yes. New arrival. May I come in to discuss joining your group. The people I have met here are not like the people I know on Earth."

The Sig-AIl0 keeps a firm hold on the door. "We have our instructions. They do not include speaking with L5ers." It starts to close the door.

She quickly says, "I am not an L5er. As you said, I am a new arrival and I have no reason to support the L5ers. Can I come in to ask about joining your group?" She smiles then realizes such subtleties are probably lost on the droid.

In the red light of an emergency sign inside the door, she notices a slight tic of the Sig-AIl0's left eye. *Listening?*

The door is pulled open to allow Darinka to enter. Inside, she leans against the door handle as the Sig-AIl0 pushes the door closed. She stays firmly against the handle as she asks, "First, I would like to know if it is your intention to kill me along with the L5ers?"

The droid that opened the door continues to be the spokesthing. "We have no instructions to kill L5ers or to kill you."

She nods, "So, I assume that your instructions are to cause the spin of L5 to retard to zero?"

"L5's rotation, that is correct."

"I ask this because it will affect me, as well. Do you understand that the spin of L5 is required so that air, oxygen, can continue to be equally distributed throughout L5? And that retarding the spin will disrupt that process?"

"Yes. That is one result of the rotation retardation."

She nods again, "And if the, the rotation is retarded, what will happen to the distribution of oxygen in L5?"

"It will collect in pockets."

"So, how do I know where the oxygen pockets are? If I do not know, I will die. Is that not a direct consequence of your action?" She crosses her arms.

"You would die if you where not in an oxygen pocket in 48 hours."

Trying to look and sound stern, whether that will affect them or not, "So, your action of retarding the rotation will directly cause my death."

Tics.

"We can lead you to an oxygen pocket."

Darinka shakes her head. "That will not help the others in L5 who may be willing to join our cause."

More tics, more pronounced.

Her lower lip trembles as she asks, "Who or what gave you the instruction to cause the death of me and my friends?"

Very pronounced tics. The other two Sig-AIl0s step closer. "That… was… not… in… our… instructions."

The Sig-AIl0s stand silently.

"Who instructed you?"

They remain still.

She reaches behind her back to slowly open the door. The 12 strides in.

"They are immobilized." He reaches to a spot under each one's head. "Their memories since their last upgrade will be erased. I will reinstruct them."

Dragonslayer steps up to Darinka and gives her a hug. She is shivering. "You are very brave, Darinka. I can see why Charon fought to have you brought to L5."

She sniffs. "I wish the GRU could be spoken to like this. They would have shot me through the door."

Dragonslayer is about to console her but she pulls away. "Wait! Erased? So we won't know who or what controlled them?"

"Oh. Yeah." He raises a wry eyebrow.

The 12 steps up to the two humans. "When communications are restored, this event will provide extended consideration of the Lateef Question. Was this an example of creativity?"

Dragonslayer smiles, "Your favourite question? In any case, we may have a way of getting into the minds of the other Sig-Als that have been turned against us. Before we do anything else, go out to the park to send this message to Charon." He thinks, then gives it the message.

Ends Too Easily

WAY TOO EASILY

On the roof of the Admin building, Noor writes down the long message from Dragonslayer by referring to a hastily scribbled list of Morse code equivalents that Charon had given her. The translation causes Noor to jump for joy. The only other person with her on the roof, Shawna, shrinks away, worried that Noor's gyrations may send Noor into her.

Shawna shakes her head. "Take it easy, will you? We may be in low-grav here but the ground is a long ways down."

Noor hands her the scribbled note. "For Charon. This called *sneaker-net*, no?" Noor may have been brought to L5 because of her intimate knowledge of rainforest flora and fauna but she still remembers her two years in college where her father had sent her.

Shawna scans the note, squinting at the hurried scribbles. "O-m-g. Can't wait to get our Pads back online… Hope *he* can read these scribbles. Wait. What's this say?"

Noor reads her the whole message.

"Holy shit." Shawna grins then rushes off to find Charon, leaving Noor on the roof alone.

Runners are sent to every part of L5 with copies of the instructions for the passive command and the script to use to immobilize Sig-Als that have been turned by the unseen AI.

Next day, L5 is back under the full control of L5ers.

On the second day after regaining control of their torus, a crowd gathers in the Admin building's new front garden. With its open space, it was chosen as the preferred venue for representatives from across the colony.

Sunlight is shining down on the crowd's many-coloured kurtas. A few have accreted into active discussion groups. Some look apprehensive, glancing around nervously – who can they trust?

Those who could come made their way here on foot. They left crews who were doing mop-up work in their various areas of responsibility. Over a thousand L5ers are gathering, along with numerous droids of each level.

The only Sig-Al13 in L5 – brand new – is attending as the voice of Carrot. A raised platform has been erected for speakers, with the Admin building as the backdrop.

The large crowd had come over during the morning hours in anticipation of an unusual situation – a face-to-face speech by the Directors. The usual method of general communication has been by Pad messages. With the recent disruptions, most feel ill at ease on the crowded lawns. The atmosphere starts in hushed tones with initial suspicious glances at the droids scattered throughout the crowd. Klatches soon assume an unaccustomed, eager openness among people of different skills sets and the volume of conversation across the crowd rises to higher levels as they become familiar with others they would not have spoken to under normal circumstances.

Taking their seats on the raised platform, Dragonslayer, the Sig-Al13, Jasmine, Marta and Charon are joined by other Directors who have rushed over. They all greet and speak freely, happily, among themselves and to the nearby audience.

Dragonslayer is tracking the crowd's degree of comfort. Satisfied with what he sees, he glances at his Pad then stands up and taps the microphone. The closer crowd begins to quiet down. With shushing encouragement, a wash of silence passes over the audience as everyone turns their attention to Dragonslayer.

He uses the mic to welcome everyone. Speakers in the bodies of the many scattered droids repeat his calmly delivered words.

"Thank you all for coming. Before we do anything else, I will ask for a moment of silence for the four L5ers whose lives were lost during this attempted destruction of our colony."

The crowd takes some seconds to fall silent.

After a minute of contemplation, Dragonslayer raises his head to the crowd. "Thank you to our lost friends for your sacrifice… " He pauses as many in the crowd voice their condolences.

"This is a new experience for us. Perhaps we should have more of these *town halls?*" An eruption of loud cheers as tension is released from the audience.

Then he raises his arms to resume more formally. "Need I say that we just experienced a unique, traumatic event? It should not have come as a surprise that our little colony might eventually be the target of some kind of outright attack. But it was a shock, nonetheless. For me, anyway!"

Yells of "Me too!" "Damn right!"

Dragonslayer acknowledges some of the agreers with nods to the left and right. He raises his arms again.

"I want to provide a detailed explanation of what happened, That will come very soon with videos and links to all relevant sources. I know there have been rumours of this and that – and I will say right now that there is no – I repeat, *NO* – alien force from Europa or any other moon of Jupiter behind this, so please scrub that one from your memories of what happened."

He sees a number of heads shaking, surprised expressions, quick whispers exchanged.

Dragonslayer holds up a hand. "That concept was all a very clever fabrication. It came from Downside." He pauses while a scattering of dissenting voices arise. "It came from Downside. In the videos that we will post, you will see the timeline of that clever, complicated campaign." He pauses. "It started before Juergen arrived here."

Loud individual voices erupt again across the audience. Angry questions from a few dissenters are shushed down by their neighbours.

Dragonslayer gives them a minute to vent. "I will repeat. No. There is **NO** malevolent alien threat from Europa or anywhere outside of Earth. But the evidence we are accumulating might be equally surprising."

That briefly silences the dissenters as the audience waits for his explanation.

Dragonslayer turns to nod at the Sig-Al13. "Thanks to analysis from Carrot, and from the work of Marta and Charon, it is now clear that Earth harbours a tAI — a transformer Artificial Intelligence that has not previously been known. A friend of L5, one who had for the past year been an avowed *enemy* of L5, has been helping us with this as well. A man known as Lateef, who is a close associate of someone you all will recognize, Demyadin, has uncovered the secret of a tAI called *Deeper.*"

A number of voices are raised again. "Demyadin? You can't trust anything…" "What do you mean former enemy?" "Are you kidding?"

He lowers his head as the voices become aggressive, affirming that Demyadin is still the enemy. Marta stands up quickly.

"*Listen*! Listen to me! Wait for the facts! Listen to me!"

The audience begins to turn to the dissenters to quiet them. Marta carries on. "You may have heard that one of our pilots, Anka, was found dead near the orchard, under circumstances similar to what happened to Juergen."

"That mole!" "What's her death got to do with *him?*"

Marta turns to one of the insistent voices. "I am not going to, to besmirch her memory. Anka has been valuable both in our Moon projects and in the development of our new spaceplane, but she was, regrettably, vulnerable to carefully crafted suggestions." Turning her stare to nearby dissenters. "Carefully crafted misinformation. She and Juergen, both." Marta nods to the Sig-Al13. "Of course, her contribution to the spaceplane project was important. She was one of the many contributors to that special project. Carrot and the whole team successfully brought that to fruition in a timeframe that has never before been imagined as possible."

Turning back to the audience, "I am saddened to say that Anka was – and I want you to grasp this fact – she was killed directly by a helio-flitter under the control of that downside tAI called *Deeper*. It drugged her and poured carbon monoxide over her. The circles of friggen puddles of pure water, as Charon referred to them, that were found around her body were placed by that same flitter. It then landed and tried to erase its memory banks. What Anka had been doing prior to being suffocated was typing messages to what she thought was an alien presence on Europa. Some of you have heard that falsehood before. The evidence of her typing and the so-called alien equipment in the shed was largely destroyed by an acid bath. The entity behind all that, and the entity that temporarily co-opted most of our Sig-Als was not some alien from Europa. It was the tAI called **Deeper**. From Earth."

Many had heard parts of that description before the emergency. They could now place that, and the attack on L5, into a more understandable context. Another half hour of explanation and question-answering by Dragonslayer and Charon clarifies the facts to the audience.

Demyadin's mansion is under attack. Demyadin has been shot in the hip. Critically wounded, blood soaking his clothing, he is painfully leaning on Lateef. At the same time. He is desperately holding onto a briefcase as they struggle to escape the weapons fire coming up to the higher floor they are on, next to the upper patio. Every window is being shattered by 50 caliber rounds fired from the ground. It is late on a moonless night. Most of the mansion lights are off. The only lights to be seen outside are flashes from heavy weapons on the approach road.

Demyadin's staff and guards have been either captured or shot in an overwhelming surprise onslaught by units of the local militia.

Lateef grunts, carrying the load of his friend on his shoulder while staying low. He pants, "Michael, can you grab that table linen as we pass it?" They are making their way through the dark dining room that had been such a peaceful place for supper.

Demyadin awkwardly transfers his briefcase to the arm next to Lateef and reaches for the table linen with his free hand as they pass by, causing dishes and cutlery to crash to the floor. With gritted teeth, "What for?"

"Bandages."

50 caliber bullets are smashing deep holes through the walls of the room but, fortunately, they are coming up from a lower level, shot from Light Armoured Vehicles on the mansion's approach road.

Shards from a pulverized ceramic vase fly at the two and whiz over their heads.

Demyadin drops in front of a bookshelf, falling out of Lateef's arms. He is still grasping the linen in one hand and the briefcase in the other. He gasps, "Third Man. Second shelf from bottom. There." He points with his linened hand.

Lateef pulls roughly at the book, causing a section of the bookshelves to open ever so slowly. Boots can be heard running along the hallway then smaller caliber rounds from the room entrance smash into the books next to them. Sophia's body crashes through another glass door into the dining room. A pistol in her hand fires a last shot into the hallway as she bleeds onto the door's shattered glass.

With a desperate effort, Lateef roughly drags Demyadin behind the book-door. They both roll away from the opening. Demyadin is just able to reach up to a red domed button to slap at it. The door closes very quickly then is pushed hard by an explosion from the dining room.

Demyadin rolls painfully to lean against the wall next to the door.

Lateef pulls at the arm holding the briefcase. "Come! We have to go!"

"The wall can take a grenade, which it just did, I think. Locked." He is breathing heavily. "Wait a minute. Have to rest."

A heavy thump and an ominous shaking of the floor comes from the wall.

"Ok. Rested." Demyadin struggles to stand but he cannot.

In the light of scattered small LEDs, Demyadin uses the linen to wipe his forehead. He struggles to rise on his good leg. Lateef pulls him up, too quickly. "Owww!"

"Is the elevator near?" Lateef takes the weight of the larger man again.

"Near. I might faint… Take the elevator down. Only has one stop."

They bump against walls on either side as the path narrows. Hoarsely, "Drive sub…"

Demyadin collapses against his friend. With Lateef on the outside, they both slump against the elevator door. Lateef is holding a now limp Demyadin up while his fingers search blindly for the elevator button. The door opens and they tumble inside. Demyadin's hands are clenched in a death-grip on the linen and briefcase, even as his head rolls unconscious.

Lateef is attending to Demyadin's gunshot wound while trying to maintain the small sub's depth and course. The linen has indeed been useful. Part of it is torn into lengths and rolled into wadding that holds in most of Demyadin's remaining blood. The limited supply of first aid materials from a white box has been used up. Demyadin is groaning on the hard floor behind the pilot seat. The remaining section of the linen is under him on the metal-grilled floor. Lateef's rolled up jacket is Demyadin's pillow.

Glancing back from the instruments and front bubble window, Lateef raises his voice over the drone of motors. "Are the pain pills wearing off, Michael?" His concern is obvious but he can do nothing now but offer verbal comfort.

In renewed pain, Demyadin groans. "Goddamn Fatima! I'm sure it was her! She was the last one to go out. And she comes back with a bloody army! Ohwww."

The minisub surfaces in the dark, hours away from their mansion. The sea is very rough on the surface. Flashes of lightning slither across the sky, lighting up distant high cliffs.

Lateef points to the cliffs. "That'll be the only part of the coast that is unoccupied. We can anchor in close and take the inflatable to shore."

Demyadin rouses himself to look outside. Through gritted teeth, "Nobody on the beach?"

Peering, "No buildings or lights below the cliffs. With this low tide, the sand extends out a few hundred metres. The mountain range above the beach makes the area pretty well inaccessible."

Groans. "What the hell. Have to get out of this tin can. Go for it."

"Right. And…" Lateef adds tentatively, "…before we leave I suggest I use the shortwave to raise L5…"

The slightest of smiles passes Demyadin's lips. Then he utters a loud, "*L5!?*"

Lateef is focused on getting the sub close to shore but not into the breakers.

He returns to the shortwave set, "… at their Perth office, to see if they are able to help us. We have no other friends left on this planet, my friend. That goddamn Deeper's made sure of that!" He reaches down to give his mentor a squeeze on his shoulder.

Demyadin rouses himself to ask urgently, "My friend, did you bring the briefcase? Where is it?"

"Oh. You were clutching it so tightly. It's here someplace."

Demyadin's angry retort takes Lateef completely by surprise. "I want it! Find it now!"

Hurt, Lateef turns his back on the shortwave set to look for the damn briefcase.

The AI called Deeper has been busy placing reams of misinformation with every news organization and social media outlet. Lateef had been scanning the lies just before their mansion was invaded.

Dragonslayer lets out a surprised, "*Help*?! Are they out of their minds? Look - we're not in a position to..."

Jasmine insists, "Melbourne has confirmed it. Demyadin and Lateef escaped in a small sub during a raid on their mansion by the local militia. They are now on an isolated beach south of Perth and Demyadin is severely injured. Lateef contacted our Perth office by shortwave. He needs our help. He attached another note about Deeper. Here, you can see the mountain of disinformation it's been spewing out against Demyadin." She points to her Pad which is scrolling through the garbage.

"Deeper... So why doesn't Melbourne or Perth send a boat?"

Jasmine throws out her arms, "Both are too far away. And it seems the militia are aggressively looking for them. They're getting close. Jim, I think it would be a wise move if we send down Chick-4 to pick them up."

He snorts. "Shit. We're still recovering from own disaster, here, but we're supposed to swoop down like Superman to save one of our enemies?"

"Former enemy, if you remember." Jasmine takes his hand. "This is a chance to show our humanity to someone who could be very useful. Both of them. And what Lateef told us about Deeper has been critical."

"Shit."

The clouds over the sub have cleared somewhat, though isolated downpours sweep across the shore's sands periodically. The rain keeps the beach glistening wet. With the tide coming back in, there is now less than fifty metres of sand in front of an imposing cliff. At the cliff base, Lateef has slapped together a lean-to so that Demyadin can be out of the rain and splashing waves.

Kneeling inside the lean-to, Lateef gently wipes away sweat from his friend's forehead. "Your fever is not getting any better, Michael. I'm going to have to paddle out to the sub again to see if they're coming for us. Will you be alright?"

Demyadin growls and waves Lateef's hand away. He slumps back onto his piece of soiled and bloodied linen that had been laid over the wet sand. His precious briefcase is his pillow. He croaks, "Leave me down here if you must. But you HAVE TO take the briefcase."

Shrugging, Lateef rises. "Be back as soon as I can, Michael."

Paddling the minisub's inflatable directly into crashing waves is utterly exhausting for Lateef. He is nearly swamped when the craft buckles in half against a foaming white wall of water. Somehow it crests that wave, popping over the top. Barely recovering with desperate paddle strokes to keep the inflatable moving forward, he eventually makes it through more wave onslaughts to be near the tossing sub.

The vessel's anchors have dragged into rocks and each time a taller wave carries the sub vertically, the anchors snap the vessel around, making it hugely difficult for Lateef to hold onto anything while trying to open its hatch. On the slightly protected leeside, he finally grasps a handhold tightly near the access door and, with grim determination as a wave carries the sub into a trough, he ties the inflatable securely to the sub. During the next wave he waits for it to roll under him then struggles to open the slippery metal hatch.

Inside, drenched, he collapses, breathing and coughing heavily onto the wet, steel grill floor.

Shortly, Lateef is able to roll over to see the control panel. The radio displays a blinking green light. Lateef crawls over to it, pulling away wet hair from his face. Through another shuddering snap of the anchors and the whole structure, he drags himself up onto the chair. The shortwave shows that a call has come in recently. He presses the radio's *Active* button and dons the headphones. Static crackles and whines as the digital circuitry fine-tunes the frequency. Glancing at the vessel battery indicator he sees it is down to eighteen percent.

The headphones squeal, "*sssqueal*…peating. Respond if you can, please…. Repeating…"

Lateef croaks out, "Receiving. Cough. Lateef here. I'm receiving." He wipes more dripping hair from his face. It is awkward to talk through his hair with the headphones on.

A voice crackles through. "Lateef! Receiving you. What is your situation, over?"

"Still here. *Cough*. Michael's on the beach. Have to take back more supplies. Ah, over."

"Do you still need our help, over?"

"Yes yes! He is badly injured. He needs a doctor!"

"…Right. We have a, a rescue mission en route. Targeting your signal. ETA one hour fifteen minutes. Do you have unfriendlies nearby, over?"

Lateef rises to peer through the bulbous window. It gives him a view of violent, deep rolling waves and a dark grey horizon.

"No lights." Another jarring shudder of the vessel nearly bounces Lateef off the chair. "Weather is no good for a rescue. How do you…"

A high-pitched squeal as the reply comes too soon. "*sssqueal*…on the beach, over?"

"Sorry. On the beach? Yes, Michael is on the beach, ah over."

"Is there room to land on the beach? How much room, over?"

Lateef is confused. "Enough for a chopper, yes, but the weather is terrible. You'd never get through."

"…We need a running length of at least 600 metres, over."

"Ah, yes, twice that, but…"

"sssqueal …and prepare it as soon as you can, over."

"Sorry - prepare what, over?"

"The beach. Stay off it an hour from now. Remove what loose obstructions you can. Go now! Over and out."

Lateef is stunned, staring at the waves trying to pound through the minisub's window. Another shudder snaps through the structure. He recovers his balance and glances at a clock on the instrument panel. *No idea what the hell they expect to do. Need to take back anything I can.*

He packs a supposedly water-proof duffel bag with all the remaining medical supplies he can find, along with leftover food items that he couldn't take before. He crams a blanket into the bag, straps it all onto his chest, then opens the door to the crashing waves, thinking, *This'll be the day that I die.*

Recovery Is A Blast

IN THE L5 MOON FACILITY

Charon's project leader at the L5 facility on the Moon is a seasoned Moon-rock miner named Leslie Chapell. Charon and Leslie have met face-to-face only once, but have been in constant communication for the past six years of his tenure as boss of the Gates of Hades and of the Moon-Rock Project.

Early on, when Charon was appointed as the senior co-ordinator of the on-going project to build up and maintain L5's outer shell with Moon rocks, he was sent to L5's Moon facility to meet with Leslie. Charon had been cautioned by Jasmine that Leslie had no sense of humour, and that she treated the mining operation as her personal baby.

He would go through a hard-won lesson in this regard.

> Still in travel-shock from the, at that time, difficult two-day journey to the Moon, Charon did not take long to trip over Leslie's defining personal traits.

> In the bare reception room of the landing pad, as soon as Charon removed his helmet, Leslie greeted Charon curtly. "Our project is working very well. What do you want to find out about it?"

Nonplussed, Charon had replied with a half smile, "Thank you, yes, the trip was rather exhausting."

Her face had tightened. "Not here to chitchat. What do you want?"

Several minutes of polite words from Charon finally persuaded Leslie to show a modicum of cooperation. Leslie reluctantly agreed to pause her very busy schedule to show Charon several aspects of *her* facility.

In the survey of the mining operations, Leslie was protective about her people's dedication to it and about her own leadership.

As Charon was ushered to his quarters, Leslie stomped away immediately to have an aggrieved private communication with Jasmine. Her rant about the disruption to her work at her facility was politely received by Jasmine, but she encouraged Leslie to be cooperative – "Pretty please?"

While Leslie had reluctantly agreed to an abbreviated survey, she kept cutting meetings short. When Charon was able to respectfully offer some considered suggestions for process improvements, Leslie did enter them onto her notepad and even put a checkmark next to one.

He later received a report from Leslie about the improvement she'd made in the process she had checked off, which ended with a, "Thank you".

On seeing that, Jasmine was amazed. "Oh my god, Charon! That's the first time I've ever seen Leslie thank anyone for any suggestion about her baby."

So, young Zar must be sent to the L5 Moon facility to investigate a very puzzling, mysterious phenomenon. Charon passed his knowledge of Leslie's personality on to Zar with the instruction to not rock the boat with the elder Leslie, particularly as she is likely to want retirement soon. All, at this difficult time in L5's challenging history.

For his part, Zar is maturing through a very young man's defence mechanisms. Zar is inclined to be flippant when meeting with older folks for the first time. Putting a rein on this tendency would test Zar's still evolving relationship skills. His assignment requires a degree of diplomacy to be exercised when dealing with a respected elder. But his experience has always been with L5ers who patiently allowed him his quirks, with the quiet expectation that he would learn better someday.

On the way to the Moon, Zar reads all about Leslie:

> Leslie was an original L5er who had volunteered for the critical Moon-rock project during the construction of the L5 torus. Her initial purpose was to escape from what she perceived as overbearing men in her life. Leslie's one exception to her disparaging view of men was when Leslie, as a newly-minted geologist, met Christoff Benoit at the formative Meeka Outing in Australia. Leslie had been quite taken with Benoit – later Tolstoy – and thought of him as her respected grandfather.

> On the Moon, Leslie felt that she could best serve Tolstoy's vision by carving her own way through life, and through Moon rock, with the limited number of people who were in the project at the time.

> Initially, requests by the L5 project to mine on the Moon had been reluctantly agreed to by the UN department that had been in charge of land allocations. This was under the "Moon Agreement" – an Agreement Governing the Activities of States on the Moon and Other Celestial Bodies, known as UNOOSA.

> L5's political capabilities were not, then, as well-honed as they were to become later. L5 was assigned a lesser-valued chunk of real estate on the Moon which was distant from areas being exploited by other countries.

> Leslie had stayed on the Moon, rising from miner to station chief over the years. Her work was invaluable in directing the design and construction of a safer, improved projectile launcher, organizing the mining logistics, and locating

sources for the tonnes of minerals and water to be sent to L5. Long before Charon's involvement, she had also suggested the critical design elements for the rock receiving device at Lagrange 5. It was essentially a reverse of the launcher design. Due to Leslie's staff procurement biases when she became station chief, the facility acquired the reputation of an Amazon venue, with fewer than eight men out of a complement of one hundred and fourteen women.

Now, here is this child from L5 who is sent to find out why there is a nothingness under the Moon's surface.

Leslie's greeting at the L5 Moon facility port is as curt as ever. By video at the entrance airlock, she tells Zar, "Bring your luggage down to the guest quarters on Level 3. We can meet in one hour. In the meantime I want you to review the report, attached."

In his small, sterile room, Zar plops onto the bed to read the report. He finds the title both confusing and intriguing. The scientific part of the report is over his head, though he can sort of follow it:

"The Sorabos Gluon Potential revealed at last"

The Sorabos gluon potential arises from an imbalance in colour polarization at the interface of an up-quark rather than at the more stable down-quark interface, and for almost a century it has stubbornly eluded direct measurement. Many researchers have even written off such a measurement as impossible.

But that era ended with a bang last week. With an air-gapped tAl that is conventionally tasked to calculate angular momentum loss according to the Landauer principle with respect to photons, scientists at L5's Bullialdus Facility (L5BF, as the UN has named it) near the equator on the far side of Moon, recently initiated an experiment for the first direct measurement of the Sorabos gluon potential.

"We were naïve enough to believe we could do the impossible," said Helen Robarts, a staff scientist at BA Lab's Advanced Proton Lagrangian Unit (APLU), whose work is to recursively analyze colour ameliorations to target protons in their ongoing experiment. Robarts and her collaborators recently reported their preliminary negative results in *Bosons Today*. She is shortly expected to assemble her team's more recent findings in the nonpeer-reviewed repository, arXiv-xT (Archive exTerra).

It is proposed that such a measurement could yield new insights into many areas that focus on colour/anticolour transitions and resulting decay of proton bonds. The Sorabos Gluon potential (SGp) is proposed to play a critical role in the essential stability of particle electromagnetic fields, for example, which maintain colour singlet states for hadrons.

In iteration #14's experiment at APLU, the repurposed transformer-AI (tAI) was left to work unattended overnight. The next morning, security digitally reported that the majority of the lab was "missing".

A communication by Robarts' senior collaborator, Michelle Wardle, described her astonishment while reporting to work on the nominal morning of 2063 April 21:

"At first, we attributed the security personnel's statement of missingness to that individual's well known scientifically imprecise and jocular nature. However, on entering the underground facility which the APLU cohabits with a branch of another research institute, the Quantum Chromodynamics Analysis Institute (QDAI), this author was greeted with a singular absence of substance. Aside from a glassy, fused, spherical residue enveloping the former interior structure of the deep facility, all matter across a distance of 34.7 metres in diameter was, in fact, entirely missing."

Wardle's communication continued: "After assessing the full degree of missingness with a laser range-finder that I retrieved from my residence, this author proceeded to address the complement of our APLU staff, as well as the QDAI staff. The two staff groups had assembled in the Emergency Meeting Place which was conveniently located in the confines of Pete's Café, two levels above the labs.

"The rhetorical question on each person's lips was, 'What the hell happened to our labs, for f…sake?'"

Wardle went on to explain that one of the male staffers appeared to be contemplating the café's fake marble table top before him, to an excessive degree. Suddenly, Wardle stated, that staffer snapped upright in an instant of apparent perception then ran out of the café. A query from an APLU scientist about that odd behaviour was greeted with, "Oh, that's just Alphonso. He's weird."

"THIS, I've gotta see!"

Zar leaves his bags unpacked and jumps up from the edge of the bed as he asks his Pad, "How do I get to the APLU lab?"

It replies, "Security emergency. No access to Level 8."

"Security over-ride." He presses his fingerprint on the Pad.

"You must be accompanied by class 4 personnel. Shall I request that for you?"

"Yes. Now." Then he adds, "Is Alphonso available?"

"Yes he is. Which action shall I prepare for you first?"

"Huh? Both! Tell… Ask Alphonso to meet me on Level 8."

Zar is standing on the edge of a spherical abyss.

"This is eerie." Zar shakes his head slowly at the vast spherical emptiness inside the former labs. Lights from the small foyer which formerly served as the entrance to both labs glisten off the empty sphere's shiny interior. Zar is being held back from the precipice a hand on his shoulder. A contemplative Alphonso slowly loosens his grip as they behold the nothingness.

Behind them both, Leslie stands mumbling. "Who the hell did this? Somebody's gonna answer for this! I had two perfectly functional laboratories down here. And now, what? What am I supposed to do with an empty hole. That wall looks like it's going to be a bitch to break through to make anything out of this area."

She notices how close Zar is from the edge. "Stand back!" She barks. "Got enough paperwork to do as it is! Haven't got time to write out your death certificate!"

Alphonso pulls Zar further away but they both continue to contemplate the mystery of the spherical missingness.

Zar emits a "Huh." He clears his throat, then. "Looks like one of those underground fission experiments from the dirty bomb era. But no radiation, eh?"

Alphonso shakes his head. "No residual radiation. Material all fused at the periphery. Glassy smooth, though with perhaps centimetre-high undulations. We should see how thick it is." He turns to Leslie. "Can you get a miner down here with a diamond hole-drill. We need to sample the material for composition and depth."

Leslie lets out a reflexive, "*No*! What do you think this is a, a playground for academics? Every miner I have is working on the new deposits we're preparing to send to L5. There's a tight window…"

Zar holds up his very smooth, smallish white hand at her face. "Leslie. This could well be the discovery of the millennium. If Alphonso and I are right, whatever happened here is impossible. And over-the-top important." His firm, even voice changes suddenly to an almost childish scream. "AND THIS IS NOT THE TIME FOR SOME GATEKEEPER TO BURY IT IN A FILE CALLED 'IN MY WAY OF NORMALCY'!" His yell echoes alarmingly around the cavern.

Red-faced, Zar's head drops, emotionally exhausted, puffing hard. Then he gets his second wind and raises his head in defiance.

Alphonso sucks in his breath in anticipation of a thunderous response.

Zar and Leslie breathe heavily at each other for a minute.

She clenches her fists. Zar awaits a swinging blow.

Then Leslie works over a word in her throat. "Gatekeeper. Gatekeeper… I promised Tolstoy to never be a gatekeeper. He would be upset with me… Ok." She looks into Zar's blazing eyes. "One diamond-bit corer coming up. Or do you need two?"

Before Zar can recover, Alphonso says, "Two please. And we'll need priority to take over the materials lab up on 4."

Leslie nods and turns to leave. She stops, her back to Zar and Alphonso. "The millennium?"

Zar is momentarily not connected to the outside world. He is thinking, *Shit. What the hell was I yelling for? Now she's going to tell Charon and he'll… What? Send me to the Moon mines? Here?* Recovering, Zar nods, "The millennium." Under his breath he whispers to Alphonso. "Do you realize what this means?"

"Of course! If we get this right, L5 could become the dominant player in the solar system."

"Player of what?"

Alphonso says something but Zar only sees flapping lips. The exuberant scientist shakes Zar by a shoulder. "Wake up, will you? You've just put the boss Amazon in her place! Never seen that before! Hey - come on! We have to get ready for the discovery of the millennium!"

Jasmine is so excited she stumbles over her words as she tries to give Dragonslayer and Charon the news. "L-Leslie is, it's the the first time I've ever *ever* seen heard h-her excited! Actually excited!"

Trying to settle Jasmine down but becoming infectiously enthusiastic himself, Dragonslayer smiles as he takes Jasmine's hand. "Calm down will you? What are you trying to say?"

"Ok, ok…" She takes a few breaths. "It's the the discovery of the millennium. That's according to Zar and a scientist there – Alphonso. The millennium!"

Charon is becoming impatient. "So we have it that it's important as hell. Next question – what is it?"

Jasmine holds out her arms to slow things down. "Ok… There's a jesus-big empty hole where half of Level 8 is supposed to be. The physicists are talking about 'non-invertible symmetries' or something. Way beyond my pay-grade."

Charon cocks his head. "This is, I take it, at my, our Moon-rock mining facility?"

"Yeah yeah! In the lab complex! It's missing! I, I mean the labs…"

Now Dragonslayer is very curious. "So someone stole our labs?"

"No no!"

"Someone, what? Took the equipment?"

"No no NO! They are… just not there anymore! There's nothing but an empty glass sphere! Where the labs used to be!… Ohh, you're not listening to me!" Jasmine whips around as if to leave.

"Hey!" Charon grabs her wrist. "Will you please just sit down and compose yourself?"

Dragonslayer gently takes her hand away from Charon's. "Tell us, Jasmine. So the labs are gone. Replaced by a glass sphere. What does this mean?"

"Why, why, if they can figure out what happened, we'll have a *disintegrator*! A **matter disintegrator**!"

Dragonslayer is dumbfounded.

"God no." Charon falls into a chair, shaking his head. "We don't need any more fantastic weapons to kill people with."

Both Jasmine and Dragonslayer let out a, "Huh?"

Still shaking his head sadly, Charon mutters, "That'll just put a huge fucken target on L5… And then it'll be us against them. Whoeverthehell tries to take it from us… We wanted Pax exTerra and we're about to start a Cosmic Hell-War."

Days go by. In the Admin building, Jasmine waits with some impatience for others to join her in the main meeting room. She taps angrily through news feeds from downside, the Moon, and the unfortunate scientists and engineers still on Mars. *No funding for them to return. Damn idiots taking over every major country yelling about no more taxes and letting their people die right, left and centre. At least no outright battle with us, anyway, but militarists, fascists, blatant self-serving tyrants lording it over people who are cowering in smaller and smaller habitable areas, denuding what natural life is left on that accursed place. It will become another Mars. Or worse, a Venus… It's now too bloody-well late goddamnitall! How can a rational life form so want to commit suicide! Maybe we just have to give up the struggle for this dream called Life and let Carrot do what it wants.*

The thoughts take a toll on Jasmine's face. Quiet tears collect along depressed wrinkles on her dark cheeks. When she hears steps approach, she is about to automatically wipe her face then mumbles, "Ah, to hell with it."

Billy Cleghorn shuffles in, looking as disconsolate as Jasmine. He, too, has been scrolling through downside newsfeeds. With only a perfunctory nod, he sits in a seat near the door. Billy holds his Pad out at arms length between two fingers like it was a toxic snake, then slams it onto the table. The Pad bounces and rattles off the table. A cleaning bot scurries to pick it up but stops, waiting for an instruction. Then it picks up the Pad, anyway, with a telescoping appendage and places it on the edge of the table in front of Billy.

Jasmine rouses briefly to watch the scene. On seeing the Pad being placed back on the table she glances at Billy. "Won't let you get rid of the thing."

Billy takes a minute to look in her direction. "Did somebody feed us a depression drug? You look as terrible as I feel."

She returns a weak smile. "Depression drug. Huh… I wish it was that simple." Then, "Ah, could that be… are you serious, Billy?" A part of Jasmine's mind is prodded awake.

"What?" His mind is not fully attuned to the reality around him.

A spurt of adrenaline sparks Jasmine's cognitive functions. "Billy! Wake up! You have feelings of deep depression, yes?"

He nods reluctantly then shrugs, "So what? Have you seen what's happening downside? It's…"

She holds up a hand. "Stop. Get ahold of yourself, Billy. Think. When did you start looking at that shit on your Pad?" She nods at his Pad on the table.

He waves her off. "What the hell you talking about? We use our Pads for everything all the time." He is about to reach for it.

Jasmine shakes her head sharply and jumps up. "Stay here. Don't open any newsfeeds on your Pad. Don't drink any water." She jumps to the door. "I'll be back in a few minutes."

Billy watches her disappear down the hallway as he gingerly picks up his Pad. With a finger hovering over the black screen, he stops himself from activating it, then, with a sense of distaste, drops it back onto the table.

The Pad screen opens without his input to a slowly scrolling list of news items from downside. Hairs rise on his neck. Billy grabs the Pad and rapidly turns it over, screen down. The news items begin to be voiced by a saccharine speaker from the back of the Pad.

Instinctive fear suddenly propels him up and through the door in pursuit of Jasmine.

And I'll Go Outside

AN ERA ENDS

Charon is in a Rainsuit without the helmet, standing at the main Gate to Hades. The Rainsuit is a mandatory precaution.

He is holding Tolstoy in his arms and is waiting for the port to open. Charon is quietly mouthing words to an old song by Lhasa de Sela, which is being heard by all, in muted tones – "<u>Soon this place will be too small</u>":

> . . .

> *Soon this space will be too small*
> *All my veins and bones*
> *Will be burned to dust*
> *You can throw me into*
> *A black iron pot*
> *And my dust will tell*
> *What my flesh would not*

> *Soon this space will be too small*

And I'll go outside

And I'll go outside

And I'll go outside

: from Lhasa's album, The Living Road, 2003

Tolstoy attempts to join him to finish the final words. His withered old throat can hardly whisper, "And I'll go outside…"

Charon holds the light body easily. Before placing Tolstoy in the *Transition*, he asks gently, "You're sure?"

Charon has tears on his cheeks. He forces himself to look into Tolstoy's reddened eyes, thinking, *His face wrinkles are so deep, he could collapse into them. I love this old man.*

With a last burst of strength Tolstoy squeezes Charon's ungloved hand. "Now is my time."

Every cheek in the narrow, packed corridor is wet with tears. Some are sobbing to themselves. Anna faints, but is held up by Jasmine and Darinka. The two had found themselves wanting to support poor Anna over the past week while Charon stayed with Tolstoy in the local clinic.

So many in the crowd are thinking the same thoughts about Tolstoy: *I so wish we had time to talk together. Now it's too late…*

Dragonslayer has been overwhelmed with the urgent details of getting L5's systems ready for the possibility of war.

The port closes with a soft thud as the mourners draw in their breaths.

Transition drifts away.

As Tolstoy lies alone in the little black *Transition* vessel, final sleep comes with a hiss from a container. It takes some time for the *Transition* to slowly drift to its position near L5's main windows, protected from the majority of space's cosmic rays on the inside of the torus. All across the colony, speakers are solemnly broadcasting tributes and memories along with the live feed that is following the progress of *Transition*.

Transition's glistening flat plate of quartz aligns with the focused rays of sunlight coming from an array of mirrors on the edge of the colony's encircling donut.

Tolstoy's body returns to dust in minutes.

Christoff Benoit is no more.

Dragonslayer cannot watch the broadcast video. *A war is imminent. Damnit all to goddamned HELL!*

NEXT,

PART 2

THE DONUT TAKES OVER